CROSSROAD

CROSSROAD

A Novel

W. H. Cameron

CROOKED
LANE

NEW YORK

Published in the United States by Crooked Lane Books, an imprint of The Quick Brown Fox & Company LLC.

Crooked Lane Books and its logo are trademarks of The Quick Brown Fox & Company LLC.

Library of Congress Catalog-in-Publication data available upon request.

ISBN (hardcover): 978-1-64385-280-5
ISBN (ebook): 978-1-64385-281-2

Cover design by Melanie Sun
Book design by Jennifer Canzone

Printed in the United States.

www.crookedlanebooks.com

Crooked Lane Books
34 West 27th St., 10th Floor
New York, NY 10001

First Edition: December 2019

10 9 8 7 6 5 4 3 2 1

To Jill
I couldn't have done it without you.

PART ONE

Wreckage

Remember me as you pass by
As you are now so once was I
As I am now so you must be
Prepare for death and follow me
                    —Traditional epitaph

ONE

Over the Crest

For the second time in as many weeks, I cross the spine of Shatter Hill at midnight and spot fire at the crossroad below.

The Stiff shudders to a stop. From the ridge, the Oregon high desert stretches out before me. The moon hangs low over my right shoulder—the broad splash of the Milky Way and the sulfurous glow of the town of Samuelton on the horizon are both brighter. I'd like to believe I'm the only girl for miles.

"Kill the headlights, Mellie."

A knot forms in my gut.

Kill the lights . . . shift into neutral . . . let gravity drop me into the heart of outrage.

Cold air pours through the window and raises gooseflesh on my neck. I don't need this. I don't want this. I've got an empty cot in the back of the Stiff, the fusty brown Transit van that serves as first call vehicle for Bouton Funerary Service. Waiting at Crestview Assisted Living is Edna Crandall, who passed away two hours ago after a long fight with cancer. According to her funeral planning work-sheet, Edna is survived by four children, eleven grandchildren, and a Pomeranian named Mickey.

"You got this, Melisende," I mutter to myself.

The fire is an orange point of light a half mile away. Bonfire—high school kids at the crossroad. Supposedly to summon the Shatter Hill Spirit, Barlow County's answer to the ghost of Bloody Mary.

But a séance can turn into a party in the time between everyone spilling out of their cars and someone lighting the fire.

My last midnight at the crossroad, two weeks back, it was a mud-caked SUV and an electric-yellow pickup. I'd have kept driving if one of the partiers hadn't thrown a beer bottle as I rolled up to the intersection. It banged off my front bumper, then shattered on the road. Through my open window, the stench of beer-vomit and burning sage watered my eyes.

I'd heard the shrill squeak of the pickup's springs. But it was the boys laughing themselves stupid, as one of their number screwed a girl in the bed of the pickup, that planted my foot on the brake. I didn't know their names, but I recognized faces from Barlow Consolidated High School. Before any of them realized I'd jumped out of the Stiff, I was grabbing the boy in the pickup by the tail of his shirt.

I've moved a lot of bodies in the fifteen months I'd worked for Bouton Funerary, but this was the first to fight back. I wasn't having it. I yanked him off the tailgate and let him drop, dick down, in the dirt. The others jumped back as he rolled and tried to untangle his jeans from around his ankles. He looked like an animal.

The girl sat up and blinked as if she was coming out of a trance. In the stark firelight, her fawn-colored skin looked blotchy and bruised, her expression desolate.

"Landry?" Her voice was a squeak. "What were—?"

He answered with a harsh laugh. "You know you wanted it."

For a long, anguished moment, the only sound was the crackle of the fire. Then, in the distance, a coyote barked.

The girl screamed.

The other boys scattered like cockroaches, tripping and dropping beer bottles as I pulled the girl out of the truck bed. The SUV's tires threw gravel and then tore off down Route 55.

Which left the animal on the ground. I put myself between him and the girl, one hand out to steady her. He managed to get his pants up over his ass and scrambled to his feet, his fists balling and his knuckles popping.

"What you lookin' at, bitch?"

That's when I recognized him. Landry MacElroy, All-State linebacker, which made the girl Paulette Soucie. I remembered their picture on the *Samuelton Ledger* homepage last fall, juniors in the Homecoming court—him sandy-haired and whey-faced, with a big-toothed grin; her with dark, intelligent eyes almost hidden by bangs. Eight or nine years ago, she could have been me.

Landry was a head taller and at least fifty pounds heavier, but he seemed to be weighing his options. Maybe he wasn't used to someone standing up to him. Or maybe he recognized my unruly, mouse-brown hair and the "Got Formaldehyde?" shirt peeking out of my jacket. Wouldn't be the first guy who didn't like the idea of being touched by a woman who handles the dead.

I dropped my chin like I was about to charge.

"Don't need this shit." With a roll of his head, he backed away, then threw himself into the pickup and tore off. Drunk as he had to be, I could only hope he killed himself before he killed anyone else.

I drove Paulette to St. Mark's Hospital and waited until her mom and the cops showed up. Nobody wanted to hear "Landry MacElroy" and "rape" in the same sentence, but I didn't give a damn. At least the Sheriff's Department sent Ariana Roldán, the county's lone female deputy.

I didn't perform that night's removal till nearly four o'clock, not that the dead care. The next morning, while I stood bleary-eyed in line at Cuppa Jo, Sheriff Turnbull himself informed me no charges would be filed. "Paulette insists it was just a misunderstanding," he said as he cut ahead of me. Then, grinning as if being a goddamn line jumper was the worst thing you could say about him, he added, "Busy day. You don't mind, do you, Mellie?"

Only my brother Fitz is allowed to call me Mellie.

So now—two weeks later—it's another late-night call to Crest-view, another fire at the crossroad. I check my phone. At the edge of the tableland, the signal is good. Down below, it's spotty until you get nearer town or the ski area. I'd call 911 from here if I thought it would do any good.

"What's it gonna be, little sister?" Fitz died when I was eight, and his voice has rattled around in my head ever since. For seventeen years he's been the angel—or the devil—on my shoulder.

Short of options, I roll down Shatter Hill, headlights off and rid-ing the brake. I try to imagine Mrs. Crandall's Pomeranian, instead picture Paulette's bleak gaze. Ahead, something leaps across the road, a deer maybe. As the shadow passes, the fire splits into two orange smudges. Both look like they're in the road.

Not a party after all.

I hit the headlights and see two hulking shapes in the intersection, a third beyond. At the gleam of chrome, I paw for my phone in the center console.

The signal is down to one bar. I tap digits and jam the phone against my ear.

"Nine-one-one. What's your emergency?" The operator's voice sounds like it's being transmitted on a string between two tomato cans.

"Accident at the crossroad. Route 55 and Wayette Highway. Foot of Shatter Hill." The flames seem to leap toward me.

"Can you . . . kind of . . . —dent? How . . . —hicles are invol—"

"I don't know yet. Two cars at least—" I almost drop the phone as I swerve to avoid a small boulder or a chunk of wreckage. "Send everything. Fire, ambulance—"

The call drops. I can't tell if she heard me, but before I have a chance to worry about it, a horse clatters onto the road and rears.

"Jesus!"

As I slam on the brakes, the afterimage of the object I swerved to avoid resolves in my mind's eye.

Not a boulder at all.

"If we're lucky"—Fitz laughs—*"that'll turn out to be Landry's head."*

TWO

The Rancher

Out on the desert, the horse lopes around in circles, each hobbled step punctuated by an explosive snort. Hurt, but I don't know how badly—or how to help. Ever since I arrived from Massachusetts, Uncle Rémy has given me a crash course in life in central Oregon, but his advice hasn't included equine care.

The horse isn't the only one beyond my help. From the looks of things, we'll have a busy next few days at the mortuary. Plenty of learning opportunities for an apprentice mortician.

I pull the Stiff off on the right side of the road and get out. I spot a gold Cadillac Eldorado first, across the intersection in the oncoming lane. The disembodied head apparently belongs to the man behind the wheel. I check off *closed casket* on the funeral planning worksheet in my mind. A second figure lies in a pool of blood on the road, a piece of twisted steel protruding from his chest. One arm seems to be straining for a shattered cell phone just out of reach.

Nearer but off to the right, a red Subaru Outback tilts out of the ditch. The driver's side has been sheared off from front fender to rear wheel, exposing the engine and passenger compartment. Under the bumper is a slight-framed, pallid teen, who looks almost as if he's sleeping. Except no one sleeps with his neck bent that way.

"How fast were they going, you think?"

"Pretty damn fast."

"NASCAR fast."

Fires smolder in the cab of an F-350 on the far side of Subaru, as well as in the bunchgrass near the roadside. The rest of the big truck is burned out, as if the gas tank ignited. A horse trailer lies on its side, thirty feet off the road. Somehow, the trailer hitch is sticking up from the roof of the Eldorado. I have no idea which way any of them were going when they collided. Wreckage is scattered all over the crossroad.

The air reeks of burning oil and hot metal. This catastrophe couldn't have happened more than ten or fifteen minutes ago. If Mrs. Crandall had died just a little bit earlier, I might have been a witness.

"Or part of it."

"No such luck."

My phone informs me it's "Searching for Signal." I look toward Samuelton for flashing lights, listen for sirens. All I can hear is the horse in the dark and the crackle of flames. If they're lucky, whoever drove the truck died before the gas tank blew.

We're about as isolated as you can get in Barlow County without leaving pavement. Samuelton is twelve miles away, with the village of Crestview, on the slope of Lost Brother Butte, only a little nearer. But aside from Crestview Assisted Living, there's not much there—a couple of bars, a general store surprising for the quality of its wine selection, a small private school, and three motels, two of which won't be open till hunting season. Behind me, Shatter Hill rises to a broad plateau, and the open tableland is interrupted only by the Pioneer Cemetery and Old Mortuary until the Trout Rot overlook. There's more pronghorns than people that way.

I'm on my own.

I'm going to be late for another removal, but no point in freezing my ass off until help arrives. As I head back to the Stiff, I kick a chunk of wreckage and send it skittering across the road. It smacks into a rolled tarp, or maybe a duffel bag. I stare at it in the uncertain light.

Not wreckage. A gun.

And not a duffel bag. It's another body. A man.

Ice water pools in my bowels when he lets out a rattling cough. The decapitation is less unsettling.

Another wracking cough draws me across the pavement. In a way, the gun—a steel-gray automatic—is the least surprising thing about this whole mess. Half the county is armed at any given moment. If anything, the gun serves as something solid and comprehensible. I know what to do about the gun. Uncle Rémy taught me the basics after a removal where we found a handgun under the decedent's body. *Always assume a firearm is loaded. Keep your fingers away from the trigger,* and so forth. I kneel beside the man and retrieve the gun. I engage the safety and slip the weighty piece into my jacket pocket. Gravel digs into my knees.

"Sir? Can you hear me?"

Eyes half open, he lets out another wet cough. A local rancher maybe, dressed in worn work boots and Carhartt coat. A jagged, bloody gash on his forehead switchbacks into his hairline, but I can't tell if he has any other injuries. For all I know, his insides are jelly.

I learned CPR and first aid in high school health class, ten years ago. A previous life. The gash on the man's head looks like a problem, but at least he's breathing.

"Now what, Mellie?"

Stop the bleeding. Treat for shock. I remember that much. When I rise to go get supplies, the man reaches out, clutches at my pant leg.

"I just need to get some things, okay?" I hope he can't hear my panic. "I'll be right back."

He groans, and I sprint to the Stiff. Unlike the hearse we use for funerals, the van is nothing fancy. The cargo area has room for one body transport cot, with four gear bins mounted to the wall next to the rear doors. The top bin holds miscellaneous straps, tags, and bungee cords. Body bags and sheets in the next. I keep an emergency change of clothes in the third, and the bottom has nitrile gloves, deodorizing spray, paper towels and trash bags, and a drugstore first aid kit barely adequate to treat a paper cut. "A little late for emergency medical gear in a mortuary transport," Uncle Rémy likes to joke. I tuck the handgun in with my clothes, grab the first aid kit and the sheets—skipping the body bag for now— and run back.

I tear a strip off one of the sheets and bind the rancher's head. Then I double up the remaining sheets and cover him up. His breath mists, pale in the glow of the Stiff's headlights. *Still alive.* Over the last year, I've grown more comfortable with the dead than the living.

I put two fingers on his clammy neck. His pulse is weak, but I don't know if it's dangerously so. My own pounds at my temples.

"Sir?"

His lips move, but all I hear is a faint wheeze.

My phone shows no bars, but at least it's stopped searching for a signal. I try 911 again.

Nothing.

The old rancher brushes my hand with his own. "Did you . . .?" I see the reflection of firelight in his eyes. His gasping breath is dense with tobacco.

"Help is on the way," I tell him, hoping it's true.

Barlow County Fire and Rescue has only two paid staff, plus maybe fifteen volunteers. This time of night, the on-call team could be coming from anywhere in the county. I wonder if my ex, Deputy Jeremy Chapman, will be with them. I grimace. Of course he will. Bottom rung in the tiny Sheriff's Department, an outsider like me. He's always pulling lousy shifts.

Jeremy is the last person I want to see in the middle of all this.

"Did you see her?" The rancher coughs again. Red foam collects at the corners of his mouth. "She was . . . there . . ." His head rolls toward Lost Brother. The dark tree line starts several hundred yards away, juniper and sagebrush bleeding into ponderosa pine as the land rises. I can't tell if he's talking about an actual person or if he believes in the ghost of the crossroad.

"They're coming." *I hope.* "Just hang in there."

"She was right—" His eyes close and he seems to stop breathing. I fumble again for his pulse. Still there. Barely. He lets loose a strained gasp.

"She was . . . I saw . . ."

I scan the desert again. For all I know, someone else *is* out there—injured . . . or dead. Or maybe he's delirious. I take his hand in mine, feeling helpless. The horse clomps around in the dark. Dying flames crackle in the grass. The wind shifts, and I catch a whiff of evergreen.

Head flopping side to side, the rancher squeezes my fingers. "There, near the trees . . ." A low moan comes out of one of us as I spot a pale figure out on the desert.

Who—?

I blink, and the figure vanishes in a flash of red and blue on the road from Samuelton.

THREE

No Bars

I'm trapped inside a bubble of light. The Barlow County Sheriff's Department can barely field a softball team, but with all hands on deck, first responders plug the crossroad in every direction. I'd like to head to Crestview, but the Stiff is blocked by a fire and rescue truck. No one will move it out of my way. The EMTs are busy with the rancher. Deputies put up work lights on telescoping stands. Voices chatter, live and via radio, but I can't make out the words.

Jeremy Chapman appears from behind the F-350, fire extinguisher in his hand. I wonder what the fire and rescue guys are doing if he's putting out fires. He stows the extinguisher in the trunk of his car, then catches me looking at him. My stomach knots as he crosses the road.

"How you holding up, Mel?"

He's my height, which makes it hard for me to ignore his dark eyes and brown, dimpled chin. There was a time when I liked gazing at his fine, smooth features, when I appreciated the strength in his arms and the warmth of his resonant voice. Now, frowning, I look past him. From inside the bubble, the sky is black velvet. Somewhere out beyond the lights, the horse puffs and stamps. "Why are you standing here? Someone needs to take care of that horse."

He laughs, nervous, and runs a hand over his short hair. "What do you think I can do, except get my ass trampled?"

We were together six weeks, long enough for Jeremy to reach the "story of my life" phase of our relationship. I got to hear all about how he grew up in Portland, how he'd always dreamed of being a cop there, but an associate degree in criminal justice wasn't enough. His job with the Barlow County Sheriff's Department is just a place-holder while he finishes an online bachelor's degree. After that, it's back to PDX.

My friend Barb had to explain to me PDX is how Portlanders refer to the town. Far from home is about all Jeremy and I actually have in common.

I listen to the horse, to the EMTs and the other deputies. Some-one complains about the lack of cell reception. Jeremy clears his throat. Nearly two weeks ago, when we last spoke, he tried to make excuses for why Landry wouldn't be charged. Tonight, he picks up where he left off.

"It was out of our hands, Mel."

"Was it?"

"She recanted. She and her mom refused the rape exam. What can I tell you?"

"You can tell me who pressured them so I can cut his dick off."

"Mel, you don't know that—"

"I checked out the Barlow Con team website. It's a love letter to Landry MacElroy. Now tell me again no one put the squeeze on Paulette."

"What do you want me to say?"

"That you lost my fucking number."

I'm rescued, if you can call it that, by the arrival of Sheriff Hayward Turnbull and his chief deputy, Omar Duniway. In attitude, they're two of a shit-kicking kind, though Duniway is a head taller and rail thin next to the burly Turnbull. They park on the shoulder, then mosey into the light bubble. All my instincts tell me to walk the other way, but I force myself toward them, Jeremy following in my wake.

Duniway notices me first. "Well, if it isn't Melisende Dulac." He edges too near and grins. "You sure know how to stir up trouble at the crossroad."

I ignore him and face the sheriff. "The injured man said he saw someone out here, a woman maybe. It's possible I saw her too, though it's hard to . . ." My voice trails off when he starts grinning.

"Was she dressed all in white, Mellie?"

The hackles rise on my neck. Jeremy is a thermal presence at my side. He looks embarrassed—on my behalf, I suppose. "I'm just saying it might be worth a look around."

"For what? A ghost?" The sheriff's grin widens. Beside him, Duniway chuckles, the sound sharp as breaking glass.

Through my teeth, I say, "Fine. Then could you have someone move that truck? I've got to get going."

Hayward Turnbull is the kind of man I worried about on the long train ride from Massachusetts to Oregon—loud, florid, full of brash affability tempered by condescension for mere peasants like myself. That, and he looks like a man suffering a perpetual attack of the meat sweats.

Fortunately, I rarely have to deal with him. Most of my department contact is with the half-dozen deputies at Jeremy's level. But Turnbull must see a three-car crack-up at the crossroad as worthy of his supervision.

"You in a hurry, Mellie?" His voice makes my teeth hurt.

"I have a removal at Crestview."

He looks past me toward the Stiff. "How many cots you got?"

"Sheriff—"

"Because I've got three dead bodies and only two ambulances, and one of those is leaving any second with our survivor. I'm not leaving the others out here while you're off after some fellow who died in his bed. Call Crestview and tell 'em it'll be a while."

"I'm already late."

"You can be later. This is your job, Mellie. *Bouton's* job. Unless you want me to call your aunt and tell her why the county is switching to Swarthmore for contract removals. Makes no difference to me who mops up the road kill."

Much as I'd love to hear Aunt Elodie rip Turnbull stem to gudgeon if he tried to cancel our contract, she'd tell me the old blowhard is right. County jobs come first.

Lips pressed together, I tick off a backward ten count in my head. "Can you at least tell me how long it's going to be so I can inform Crestview?"

"A *while*."

I catch Jeremy looking my way, his expression dripping with sympathy. That pisses me off, so I stomp into the desert. Once past the ring of emergency vehicles, the stars return, faint and indifferent. Off to my right, a voice tries to soothe the horse. I veer left toward the distant tree line, thinking about the figure I saw. Had to be all in my head, hopped up on adrenalin and tweaked by a local's overwrought imagination.

Cold and seething, I put distance between the crash and myself. *Focus on what you can control, Melisende.* I pull out my phone and scroll through my contacts to the Crestview entry.

No bars.

Jeremy could get a message to the facility over the radio, but damned if I'm going to ask him for help. I'd sooner trek all the way to Crestview on foot and haul Mrs. Crandall back over my shoulder. That won't be necessary though. A short walk to higher ground should get me a signal. Might work off a little irritation too.

But I make it only a few dozen paces through the desert grass before I nearly kick the baby.

FOUR

Née Dulac

I accepted this life. Fifteen months earlier, when my cell phone rang and a stranger offered me a job and a place to stay, I'd said yes.

Without hesitation.

"Impulsive," Fitz murmured, his voice a tickle in the back of my head.

Desperate was more like it. When I got the call, I was on the street in Boston—ninety miles from Amherst, where I'd been living, and fifty miles from Lowell, where I'd grown up. Not that it mat I'd lost my apartment, had no friends. Another day and my cell phone would have been disconnected. My husband, Geoffrey, was gone; my grandmother had been dead four years; and my parents had changed the locks at their house while I was in psych hold.

"My name is Elodie Bouton," the woman said. "I'm Geoffrey's aunt, which makes me your aunt too. We may not be blood, but we're still kin."

My husband wasn't her blood either—he was her nephew by marriage. But that didn't matter. I had no one else. Even Helene wouldn't take my calls.

"I'll buy you a train ticket to Oregon," Elodie went on. "Flying is quicker, but the train will give you time to settle in to the idea of the work."

"What will I be doing?" Not that I cared.

"Officially, you'll be an apprentice funeral service practitioner, but we don't stand on ceremony. Around the shop, we're all just undertakers."

I tried to picture myself in a long black suit. "I don't have anything to wear."

Elodie laughed. "We'll work it out. How soon can you leave?"

"Today. I can leave today."

Despite my lack of options, I second-guessed myself the whole three-day journey. In Chicago, where I had to change trains, I almost stayed behind. The only thing that kept me on board afterward was the unfathomable emptiness of the western landscape. During the long miles and oppressive vistas, I heard Fitz nattering on about how we were following a modern-day version of the Oregon Trail, or oohing and aahing about cows or prairie dogs or some shit out the window. Not even my attempts to lose myself in the books I snagged from the lounge car library could silence him.

When I got off the train at Portland's Union Station, the man who approached could have been anyone. Tall and slender, he wore a white Oxford shirt and tan chinos. He parted his gray hair on the left. If he'd handed me a religious pamphlet or offered me twenty for a blow job, I wouldn't have been surprised. Either one.

Instead he said, "I'm Rémy Bouton, Geoffrey's uncle." His voice was quiet, with a faint Western twang. "You must be . . ." He paused, then sounded out my name. ". . . *Mell-ee-sond*. Is that correct?"

He didn't try to touch me, not even to shake my hand. He just stood and waited to hear what I had to say. His expression was warm, but cautious.

"Melisende, yes," I said, repeating his pronunciation. Most people don't get it so quickly.

"I'm happy to meet you."

A flood of voices swept past us. The funk of bodies pouring off the train, the *skrrr*-ing of luggage wheels on the hard floor—it all made me a little dizzy. I felt as old and worn as the station's sandstone walls.

At last Rémy said, "What would you like to do?"

The moment of truth. "I don't know."

A shadow passed over his face. Had he turned around and left me there, I'm not sure I'd have been upset or surprised. His wife, Elodie, a faceless woman on the other end of a long-distance phone call, had paid for me to travel three thousand miles. But that didn't mean she or her husband were eager for me to come the last hundred and fifty. If I turned back now, would they feel anything but relief? Would anyone?

"Don't be stupid, little sister." Fitz's voice was so loud in my head I half-believed even Rémy might hear. I winced, but he didn't seem to notice.

"Are you hungry?" he said. "All I've had this morning is coffee."

My ticket had included meals in the dining car, but as the train neared Oregon, I'd been too anxious to eat. The night before, somewhere in Montana, I'd poked at my dinner plate but couldn't bring myself to even attempt breakfast after a long, sleepless night.

"There's a nice place close by," he added. "Great pancakes."

I had nowhere else to go. If he turned out to be a deranged killer who left my violated corpse in a ditch, at least my troubles would be over.

At the promised "nice place," we sat across from each other in a booth. I could see a shaky resemblance to Geoffrey in Rémy's gray eyes and sharp cheekbones. He didn't try to make small talk. When the waitress came, I found myself ordering eggs, bacon, hash browns, pancakes, orange juice, and coffee.

"Train grub wasn't so great, I'm guessing."

I felt myself flush. "It was fine. I just . . ." I didn't want to tell this man who'd driven so far to get me I wasn't sure I'd made the right choice.

Rémy set down his coffee cup as I finally sopped up the last of my eggs with a crust of toast. "You're anxious, and I can't say as I blame you. Did Geoffrey tell you anything about us?"

One of the few things Geoffrey and I'd had in common was a disinterest in our personal histories. But I'd learned a few things from his sister Helene. "Your family is from Oregon going way back, but your brother left to attend Harvard and never returned." Rémy was a few years older than Verdell, Geoffrey and Helene's urbane, well-kept father.

"Not even to see our parents." Rémy nodded sadly. "Though Geoffrey and Helene would visit summers. You know Helene, yes?"

I nodded. Just hearing her name made me want to cry.

"Verdell opposed the visits, as did his wife. But our folks wanted to see their grandkids. After Mama passed and Papa slipped into his memories, Verdell again tried to stop the children from coming to visit. But by then they were old enough to make a fuss."

"When did you last see Geoffrey?" I asked him. Part of me hoped he'd say, "Oh, last night for supper." Another part of me feared precisely that.

"Eight years ago—the summer after his first year of college. Too long, not that I fault him. He was pulled in so many directions. I know he wanted to bring you to meet us."

That was news to me. Until Elodie called, I didn't even know if the Oregon Boutons were alive or dead. They were hazy figures from a soft focus past rarely mentioned.

Rémy finished his coffee and held his hand over the cup when the waitress came around with the pot. "There's no rush to get going," he said. "Would you like to see a little of Portland before we hit the road? It's a long drive. Stretching our legs first is a good idea."

For three long days, my only exercise had been to walk from one end of the train to the other. Now, I found trudging half a step behind Rémy oddly soothing. The pavement was firm beneath my feet, the city sounds comfortably anonymous and ordinary. Rémy pointed out Portland landmarks—a statue of a man holding an umbrella, a fountain that once flowed with beer. At one point, he nodded toward a dozen or so teens sitting together in the grass near the river, sharing cigarettes. One of them wore a blue plastic tarp like a poncho.

"Homeless," he said. "Seems like there's more every year."

I wondered if he thought I belonged with them.

"Mr. Bouton," I said after we'd visited a bookstore the size of a city block, then found ourselves in a narrow park, "you don't want me to come with you, do you?" I was ready for him to say no—half-hoped he *would* say no.

"It's not that at all." He sat on a bench facing a small playground. The morning was cool, the air cleaner than I had known back east. He patted the bench, and after a brief hesitation, I joined him. Neither of us spoke. I watched the shrieking children climb colorful play structures and argue about turns on the swings. They were alien creatures, a life form I'd never known. My own childhood ended when I was eight years old.

"I admit, at first I wasn't sure Elodie should call you." Rémy said at last. "And once she had, I thought it would be just as well if you chose not to come." He studied my face as if waiting for a reaction.

"Do you blame him?"

One of the many questions troubling me on the long train ride was why she'd called at all. Another time, in other circumstances, I wouldn't have answered a number I didn't recognize. But she'd caught me at just the right moment, and now here I was. Pressure grew in my throat.

"I didn't know what else to do."

He nodded. "Desperation is forebear to many an unconsidered decision."

"Are you saying I shouldn't have come?"

His lips formed a tight smile. "I can't speak for you."

"Mr. Bouton, how did your wife even know to call me?"

He took a long time considering his response. "You should talk to her about that. Elodie is closer to Geoffrey than I am. Don't get me wrong: I love that boy, but those two always had something special."

"Do you know where he is? Does she?"

He shook his head. "No more than you."

In the first days after my husband's disappearance, I'd cycled through worry and fear to bitterness and rage—with myself as much as Geoffrey. But the psych hold had worn my raw edges down to a muddy uncertainty. At least Rémy and Elodie shared my ignorance.

"Okay," I said. "So why are we here?"

He drew a breath, then reached into his shirt pocket for a folded piece of paper. "This is my idea, not Elodie's, just so you know."

It was a cashier's check for ten thousand dollars. Made out to me.

"I know you're in a bad place. Elodie reached out because she believes it was the right thing to do, but you don't know us, and you don't know where I may be taking you."

"Mr. Bouton, I can't accept this."

"You most certainly can. Your husband abandoned you with nothing. Only he can say why." His hands clenched and unclenched in his lap. "It's not much, but it's something. And it gives you options. It's money to live on while you get back on your feet. You can return to Boston or go somewhere new. Whatever you like. It means your only choice isn't limited to getting in my car and riding into a life you didn't ask for."

"Take the money," I murmured, half to myself, "or go with you."

"The money is yours either way. But at least if you have it, you can come with me because you want to, not because you have no other choice."

I held the check in my hands. Pay to the order of Melisende Bouton née Dulac, ten thousand dollars and no cents, drawn on the Rolling Sage Bank, Samuelton, Oregon. I think the *née Dulac* settled it, that and the careful way he'd pronounced my name. This man—this stranger—had made an effort to learn something about who I was. It was a small thing, maybe, but showed a degree of consideration I'd received from no one except perhaps Helene since my grandmother died.

I took a breath. "I'd like to come with you, sir."

He stood and for the first time offered me his hand. "Please," he said. "Call me Uncle Rémy."

FIVE

Undertaker's Apprentice

Somehow I manage to drag myself through the long, weary day after the crash. Only Tuesday and already I want this week to be over. I've been running on adrenaline and Red Bull ever since sunrise.

Paperwork soaks up most of my time, along with two trips to the hospital to retrieve bodies. I'm pretty much on my own. Carrie Dell—our embalmer—is on vacation, not due back for ten days. Aunt Elodie is in Bend with Uncle Rémy for his hip replacement, too busy or distracted to answer when I call with a status report. Wanda Iniguez, Bouton's funeral planning specialist and unofficial den mother, is expert at sitting with weeping families and discussing funeral arrangements or acting as hostess for services, but she won't get near the remains until they're fully prepared and in a casket. Quince Kinsrow, the old scarecrow who had my job before transitioning to semi-retirement, sticks his nose in just long enough to see there's work to be done, then bolts.

I eat my lunch in the hospital morgue with the deputy medical examiner, Aaron Varney, while he examines the bodies and agrees they're dead. "Cumulative trauma to multiple body regions consistent with high-speed vehicle collision," he tells me in a bored tone. When he finishes, he rests his butt against the metal counter. "I heard about the baby."

The baby remains the biggest mystery of the crossroad. A girl no more than a day old, lying on the ground, wrapped in a hooded sweatshirt. "Not a half-bad swaddle," one of the EMTs said. No one knows where she came from or whom she belongs to. Almost certainly not to the rancher, Zach Urban, who was on his way back from the Sweet Home Rodeo.

It's anyone's guess. There was no diaper bag, no baby seat in the wreckage.

The sheriff hoped Zachariah Urban would explain everything, but by midday, the old rancher had been air-transported to Portland, intubated and under sedation. No telling when—or if—he would be well enough to answer questions.

I don't know what to say about the baby. Aaron raises one well-groomed eyebrow. "I take it you don't like kids?"

"I thought it was a rattlesnake."

That nets me a laugh, followed by an absent wave toward the two autopsy tables. "We've got IDs on all the bodies now." I'm glad he lets the subject of the baby go so readily. "Headless is Uriah Skeevis and the other man is Tucker Gill, per their driver's licenses and confirmed by fingerprints. The boy is one Trae Fowler, age sixteen. All from the Portland area. The kid's parents had no idea he drove out here. They thought he was spending the night at a friend's. Long way to come just to crack up at the end."

"Hmm."

"Not curious what he was up to?" There's a twinkle in his eye. Teasing or flirting—maybe both. But I'm too tired, even if I had any interest to begin with.

Carrie thinks I should play nice with Aaron Varney, whom she deems a good catch. In his mid-thirties, he has ensemble TV character good looks and a career arc on the rise. In Oregon, many DMEs are cops or criminalists with specialist training, but Dr. Varney is also a physician at the county health clinic and has a growing private practice. Pillar of the community and all that. I could do worse, Carrie insists. Well, I *did* do worse, but I keep that thought to myself.

He studies me like he's trying to determine my own cause of death. My face grows hot and I look away.

"It's none of my business."

"There's nothing wrong with a little curiosity, Mel."

One of the first things Aunt Elodie taught me was that we don't stand in judgment of the dead. How and why they come to us is irrelevant to the work we do.

"All I need to know is his name and contact info for next of kin. Wanda will get in touch with his family."

He smiles and shakes his head a little, then hands me a folder. "Everything's in here." He leaves the bodies to me.

‽   ‽

It's after five when I trudge three blocks, through stifling July heat, to the Whistle Pig Saloon. Barb Ellingson is waiting for me in our usual booth under the mounted jackalope. I suspect there's a statute dating back to the Oregon Territory requiring all high desert dives to have a jackalope on display. Probably purchased from the same catalog as the sawdust on the floor.

"I ordered for you," Barb says as I slide into the booth. She's the kind of woman who draws attention, with jade eyes; burnished, luxuriant hair; and the golden skin of someone who gets just the right amount of sun. With my own unruly hair and shapeless figure, I consider myself a troll doll next to her.

"IV caffeine, I hope."

"Don't be absurd."

The waiter approaches with food and drinks and sets a sangria in front of me. I push it across to her. "Bring me a quad-shot iced Americano."

Barb makes a face like I ordered the veal.

"Ridiculous. How long have you been awake? I won't allow it."

I prop my head up with my arm, inhale the aroma of her sweet potato tots. There are three things I like about the Whistle Pig: the tots, the broken jukebox, and that the house sangria is made with bourbon.

But no sangria for me tonight. Barb accepts my glass. "It's extra stiff, just what you need."

"I'm still on call."

"And I have mid-terms to prep for and curriculum planning for fall term." Barb teaches math at Barlow County Community College, a job she loves or hates depending on the kind of students she gets each term. This summer, her students are all resentful teens from Dryer Lake Resort whose wealthy, helicopter parents are making them take calculus and statistics for college credit. "We're both allowed a break."

"Sure, but you know we're shorthanded at work, with Carrie gone and Uncle Rémy in the hospital. Hell knows, I can't count on Quince."

"There's only like ten people in the entire county. We've used up our quota of dead bodies for the year."

Barlow isn't the smallest county in Oregon, but it's close. Not counting the part-timers with second or third homes at Dryer Lake Resort, we have barely fifteen thousand residents, more than half in Samuelton. The rest are scattered throughout the high desert and foothills rising to our one real mountain. We have a Walmart, but no Target. A McDonald's, but no Burger King—yet somehow two Taco Bells. Timber, ranching, and farming form the backbone of the local economy, but anymore the real money is in tourism—hikers and campers, hunters and fishermen, skiers, and—with the recent growth of the resort—golfers.

Last fall, Barb and I found each other through the college. With Uncle Rémy's encouragement, I'd decided to study mortuary sciences, but I needed several courses to meet the program's prerequisites before I could even apply. Barb was my algebra instructor. We barely exchanged a word outside of class, but she approached after the final and asked if I would be taking any more math.

"Depends," I said. "Did I pass?"

"Hah. Let's go get a drink."

During class, it never occurred to me we'd become friends. She's in her thirties and nearer Dr. Varney's orbit than my own. But, like me, she's from somewhere else—Maryland by way of Chicago. "I had this image of myself as a distinguished professor, but after my PhD, I couldn't land a postdoc to save my life. I was teaching high school when I saw the job notice from BCCC. Continuing contract, which was the closest to tenure track I was going to find. In a fit of madness, I accepted it, and here we are."

The Whistle Pig was where we would be most nights after work, from then on.

Barb sips my sangria. "I heard about the baby."

Everyone has heard about the baby.

"You just left her lying there?"

I stab a tot into a puddle of chili aioli and refuse to answer. But Barb is no Dr. Varney. She's tenacious.

"Right out on the desert?"

"It wasn't like that." Not exactly. "I took a few steps maybe and yelled for help."

"And left a newborn rolling around in the dirt."

"I don't think newborns can roll." Not that I would know. The only baby I've ever held was made of plastic.

"But the critical point is you just left her lying on the ground."

"I didn't know what to do."

"Jesus, Mel. It's a baby. You pick it up. You snuggle it and tell it it's the cutest thing ever. You don't flee into the night."

"Now you tell me."

The saloon is middling busy, everyone on their second wind, with the workday behind. I used up my first second wind twelve hours ago.

"You should see what just walked in," Barb says over the rim of my sangria. Her hobby is ogling tourists. Usually they ogle back.

"Do I have to move my head?"

"He's worth the effort."

I turn. The object of her attention stands at the entrance, scanning the saloon. He's fortyish and fit—long and lean, with hair the color of ripe barley. His tie and linen suit stand out in a room full of denim and sun-bleached poplin.

After a moment, he sees us looking at him and strides our way. I freeze, one hand in the tot basket, when he stops at our booth. "Are you Melisende Dulac?"

"Who wants to know?"

If he senses my indifference, he doesn't let on. "Kendrick Pride." He presents his hand. "I'm here about the boy."

"Trae Fowler?" Suddenly, I'm conscious of salty grease on my fingers.

During the afternoon, Wanda spoke with Trae's father, who told her he was sending someone to handle the arrangements in person. Kendrick Pride must be the someone. I hadn't paid much attention. I don't deal with clients. He glances down at my hand, still knuckle-deep in tots, and withdraws his own.

"The woman at your office told me where to find you, but I've interrupted your dinner. I apologize."

I pull my hand out of the basket and grab a napkin. I don't understand why Wanda would send him looking for me—I don't speak with the bereaved. The weight of the long day is making my thoughts sluggish. I struggle for something to say, finally land on the oldest platitude in the undertaker manual. "I'm sorry for your loss."

"Thank you." He glances from Barb to me. "I'd like to see him."

"You'd like . . . what?" Wanda is so much better at this.

"His mother's a wreck. I have to be sure—for her." His chin drops, but his eyes, brown flecked with moss, hold onto mine.

"I thought his ID had been confirmed."

"Put yourself in my place—in his family's place. Some stranger comparing him to a photo in an email? I need to make sure."

"Uh—"

Barb looks on, breathless. From all around, boozy chatter washes over me in waves. I find myself thinking back to the baby, to my vision of the girl at the tree line. Fitz, ever looming, chitters between my ears. *Do it, Mellie. Do it.* I clench my teeth, wishing he'd bug someone else.

"The thing is, the body isn't ready." Aside from washing, no preparation has been done. Trae Fowler lies naked in a drawer, a pulverized mess.

Pride frowns. He's put me on the spot, but I'm less annoyed than confused. It's hard to meet his gaze, but I refuse to look away. Aunt Elodie says we must maintain eye contact. We don't do anything to be ashamed of.

"I'm sure you have procedures." His tone is earnest. "I respect that. But I'd like to call his family as soon as possible."

Aunt Elodie would give Kendrick Pride the once-over and make a decision on the spot. Is this a man who could handle a trek from the folksy cheer of the Whistle Pig to the cold tile and stainless-steel underbelly of the New Mortuary?

If I refuse, no one could fault me. I'm just the apprentice after all.

I exhale compressed air. "Okay. Let's go."

He offers me a ride, but I tell him I'll meet him at the mortuary. I note he drives a little blue Honda Insight—a car Barb would sniff at. She likes men with muscle under the hood—so long as they drive away in the morning.

I cover the four blocks from the saloon to the New Mortuary in less time than it takes him to navigate Samuelton's needless maze of one-way streets. As I wait for him to park and join me at the service entrance, sweat gathers on my face and neck.

The back door is unlocked, a fact I'd like to blame on someone else, but I *was* the last one out. I lead Pride down a short corridor and grab nitrile gloves from the box next to the wide fire door leading into the preparation room. Then I hesitate, my hand on the door handle.

"Is there a problem?"

"I just don't normally do this, Mr. Pride."

"Call me Ken."

Another Aunt Elodie rule: Don't get too familiar with the bereaved. Maintain compassionate boundaries. I give him a tight-lipped smile and open the door.

"This way, Mr. Pride."

The air smells of disinfectant. The counters are bare, all the equipment clean and in its place. We run a tight ship.

I double-check the clipboard hanging from a hook on the refrigerator, even though I already know who's in which drawer. "You realize the wreck was pretty bad."

"What are you saying?" One corner of his lip curves, a grim shadow of a smile. "Is it a blood bath in there?"

"Of course not. I've cleaned him up, but no other preparations have been performed."

"Okay." He draws a breath. "Show me."

There's no easy way to do this. Viewing a prepared and dressed body is like sharing dolls with a friend compared to opening this drawer.

"I'm sorry. He's not covered."

"It's okay. Just . . . show me."

I open the refrigerator door.

A rush of cold air boils out, but it hardly registers. Beside me, Pride makes a sound, a question dying on his lips.

"Uh-oh, Mellie."

The drawer is empty.

SIX

Ursus Americanus

The one bit of good news is Mrs. Edna Crandall is still safe in her own drawer. Unfortunately, Sheriff Turnbull isn't interested in her. He sits across from me in his office in the Sam Barlow Building, fingers laced on his old-fashioned desk blotter. Sweat gleams on his forehead despite the air-conditioning.

"Weren't you hospitalized for a psychiatric condition?" he asks.

"I was just going to ask you the same thing."

"There's no need to be difficult, Mellie."

"My medical history is none of your business."

"It is if it has bearing on the current situation."

"It doesn't."

He nods, but not at me. His mind was made up before he sat down. Three bodies missing, and the last person to see them is the girl with a history. I could explain what led to my psych hold, but nothing I might say would derail his train of thought.

"Who has keys to the mortuary?"

"Besides you?"

He grunts. Because of Bouton's county contract, a set is kept at the Sheriff's Department. Dr. Varney has a key as well. During business hours, the service entrance is rarely locked anyway. When he happens to be in, Quince Kinsrow leaves it open so he can slip out for a smoke every two minutes. Not that the lock would stop anyone determined to get in. Bouton Funerary Service isn't Fort Knox.

"How long were you there today?"

I can't remember when I last closed my eyes. "All day."

"You never left?"

"I drove to Crestview and then to the hospital for the two bodies. Three trips."

"Which bodies?"

"You know which bodies. You're the one who had me bring the headless horseman directly from the scene to the shop." Cause of death was clear enough, and the sheriff probably thought he'd get to me, sticking me with the gore. Like I care.

"So, during the day, you moved the boy and the second adult from the hospital morgue to mortuary."

"Yes."

"When did you last see the bodies?"

"I finished washing them around three thirty."

"What did you do with them then?"

"I put them in the fridge."

"Next to the yogurt?"

"Yes, I keep my yogurt in a fucking morgue cooler."

"Language, Mellie."

"*You* don't have permission to call me that."

He smirks and leans back in his chair like he's won a point. I can hear the whoosh of the arctic air conditioner, and voices from the hallway. Ignoring him, I scan the room. Turnbull's office is brash and masculine, a monument to himself and his stature in Barlow County. Beneath a hardwood plaque carved with the emblem of the Loyal Order of Ursus Americanus are three rows of framed photos. Turnbull at the Bear Lodge Pancake Breakfast and the Kiwanis "Stuff the Bus" Food Drive. Turnbull holding a trout; Turnbull grinning next to carcasses of elk, deer, and antelope. Sometimes alone, sometimes with others. The mayor and the county commissioners, other cops. Jeremy is in the group shot of the sworn deputies in their dress uniforms.

Pressure forms behind my eyes as I catch the sheriff scrutinizing me. Searching, perhaps, for signs of a crazy girl who snapped and made off with a trio of cadavers. Wondering if I don't remember doing it or if I remember all too well.

"I got back from the crossroad with the first body about eight o'clock this morning." I'd like to point out how long he kept me waiting, but that'll just get me a lecture about how investigations of death scenes work. "I left messages for Aunt Elodie to let her know what was happening; then, when Wanda came in, I ran out to Crestview. After I returned, I was in the prep room all morning."

"Were you alone this whole time? Or did Wanda join you?"

"Wanda never comes into prep, but Quince stopped by to ogle the head and tell me horror stories about removals gone haywire. I told him if he was going to talk my ear off, he had to work, so he scooted right out of there. Said he had trout to clean."

"A man with priorities."

Which don't include helping me. "After Quince left, Dr. Varney texted that he was done with the bodies at the hospital. I picked them up, then got them washed and stowed. Two trips. Then I did paperwork in the break room till about five."

"And after that?"

"Went over to the Whistle Pig."

"To tie one on?"

"To have dinner. That's where Mr. Pride found me. Wanda told him where to look."

"Anyone could have told him that."

A couple of weeks after I arrived in Barlow, I borrowed the Stiff to drive into town from the Old Mortuary, where I live with Uncle Rémy and Aunt Elodie. That was the day I discovered the Whistle Pig's sangria. On my way back to Shatter Hill, Sheriff Turnbull himself pulled me over. "The center line isn't a suggestion here, young miss." He didn't have the decency to arrest me or drop me at the county line with a stern warning to never return. He called Aunt Elodie and Uncle Rémy to come get me instead.

Tonight, I'm too tired to be baited.

He lets it go. "How long between when you left and when you returned with Kendrick Pride?"

"I left around five and called you guys a little after six."

He nods. "Wanda says she went home at five thirty, so whoever took the bodies would've had to move fast."

Perhaps, but probably not *that* fast. The way the New Mortuary is built, you couldn't hear a Cremulator in the next room with a stethoscope. SEAL Team Six could shoot their way in to grab the bodies, and Wanda would be none the wiser. Plus, I wasn't kidding when I told him Wanda never went in the back. Her demeanor could calm any storm, but when it came to the actual remains, she couldn't be more squeamish. She's even avoided the supply room since the time she'd come in while I was unpacking a refurbished embalming machine and made the mistake of asking me what it did.

"Ask him if he has any leads, Mellie." Fitz's voice is like wind through tall grass. *"That's what they do on TV. They talk about leads."*

I point my chin at the sheriff. "Do you seriously think I had anything to do with this?"

"It's not a theory I can dismiss out of hand."

And that's not a point I can argue. "So am I under arrest?"

"You in a hurry to get somewhere?"

"Yes."

The sheriff gives a little shake of his head. "To think, I could've been home watching the Mariners break my heart again." He sighs, and with a wave of his meaty hand, I'm dismissed. On my way out, he says, "Don't leave the county."

There's a chuckle in his voice, but I fail to see the joke.

Where the hell would I go?

∻   ∻

The Sam Barlow Building dates back to 1910, but a few years ago they gutted and redid the interior, a restoration that modernized but retained its historic character. The high ceilings feature brass pendant lighting. The walls are the color of sweet cream. The Sheriff's Department itself takes up half the second floor, sharing a waiting area at the top of a broad staircase with the county commission. I'm down the steps and rounding the hardwood banister on the first landing when I all but slam into Jeremy Chapman on his way up.

"Mel." He smiles sheepishly. "How you holding up?" Exactly what he asked at the crossroad. Dude needs new material.

"Peachy."

"You wanna maybe grab a beer? I'm off-duty."

The vein in my temple pulses. I don't reply.

"Another time then." I expect him to step out of my way, but instead he looks at his shoes. He smells of leather and perspiration, strangely alluring in the confinement of the stairway. "Something else about that baby, huh?"

My lips compress, but he doesn't notice.

"We still haven't found the mother. Even checked with the schools. Barlow Con is out for summer, but that girls' school up in Crestview is in session year-round. No go." He inspects the cuticles on his right hand. "Could be there's no one *to* claim her."

An image of the figure at the crossroad flickers through my mind. "You think the mother's dead?"

He shrugs. "Or the boy drove the infant out here to abandon her? Some Portland girl didn't want to be a mom, and her boyfriend offered to take care of the problem."

"He wouldn't have to drive a hundred and fifty miles for that." I can think of a dozen ways to dispose of a body that small without having to leave the house—the marvels of a little mortuary education. "Stupid."

"Maybe he thought no one would find the body out here or connect it back to Portland if they did. He didn't plan on getting plowed into by Zach Urban."

"You think he was leaving the baby at the crossroad when he got hit?"

"Hard to say. All we know is the boy's Subaru was stopped when Urban slammed into it at upwards of seventy-five miles an hour. We're not sure what, if any, connection there is to the men in the Caddy, but it was stopped too. Whatever the situation, if not for the wreck, the coyotes might have found the infant before anyone else."

"Huh."

I start to move and Jeremy puts a hand on my forearm. I glare until he pulls back. He knows as well as anyone I don't like to be touched. "You sure you don't want to get a beer?"

"Depends. You gonna charge Landry MacElroy?"

Before he can make another excuse, I push past him down the stairs and make my escape.

SEVEN

Internet Mattress

That first drive from Portland to the gray stone edifice I would come to know as the Old Mortuary took us three hours. The original location of Bouton Funerary Service was built by Uncle Rémy's great-great-grandfather, he explained, an 1890s replacement for an earlier wooden structure that had been more workshop and bunkhouse than funeral home. The long drive took us first up the forested slope of Mount Hood to a small village above the snow line, still busy with late-season skiers. From there, the two-lane highway turned south and dropped into a landscape I'd only ever seen on television. The tall firs gave way to a red-brown plain broken by sudden gorges, irrigated farmland, and a vast range dotted with grazing cattle. High desert, Uncle Rémy called it, dry compared to what I was probably used to, but rich and fertile for those who understood the land. Sparsely populated with strong people.

The woman who met us outside the Old Mortuary and opened my car door looked to be one of them. She was stout, with broad shoulders and short salt-and-pepper hair, dressed in a sky-blue polo shirt and tan pants. The afternoon was chilly, but she wasn't wearing a jacket and didn't seem to care. Like her husband, she didn't try to touch me.

"Welcome," she said. "I'm your Aunt Elodie."

I'd never had an aunt or an uncle. My parents used to joke they'd broken a long tradition of only children on both sides of the family when they had me. Then Fitz died, and I guess it wasn't so funny anymore.

"You must be exhausted," Elodie went on. "Come, let me show you to your room."

"You have a room, Mellie?"

Three days of weary travel had left my back sore and my head throbbing. The desert sky was high and gray and too bright. A dry breeze attacked my eyes. I blinked, then nodded.

With Uncle Rémy in our wake, Elodie led me up wide steps and through the oaken front door. Inside felt colder than out, dim and silent as a mausoleum. My eyes struggled to adjust. I felt like I was draped in shadows.

"We live on the second floor," Elodie said. "Down here is all mortuary space, though empty and mostly unused now. We have the newer facility in town, as Uncle Rémy probably told you." Upstairs, she pointed out a small family room and then a large kitchen with ceramic trivets on the walls and copper pans on hooks above the six-burner stove. The bedroom she and Rémy shared was adjacent to a sewing room she didn't get to use as often as she liked.

"Do you sew?"

I shook my head, suddenly conscious of the weight of my own inadequacy.

At the end of the hall, Aunt Elodie opened a door onto a bright room with white plaster walls and buttery wainscoting. In one corner, a brass reading lamp overlooked a leather club chair beside a bookshelf. In another stood a vanity table with a mirror and cushioned seat. A tall armoire faced a four-poster bed set between two windows.

"The furniture is old, but the mattress is new. I ordered it off the internet."

Somehow I dug deep and found my voice, tiny and broken and no louder than a squeaky shoe.

"Thank you, Aunt Elodie."

For a second I thought I would have to say it again, loud enough to be heard. I didn't know if I could.

But Aunt Elodie rewarded me with a smile. "We'll leave you to get settled in. Perhaps you'd like a nap. I don't imagine the train was too restful." She pointed out a door in the opposite wall, my own bathroom, and said she'd picked up a few things for me to wear until we could go into town and shop. I didn't want to ask how she knew my size, afraid I would sound ungrateful.

When she and Uncle Rémy left, I went into the bathroom—
almost as big as my old studio apartment in Amherst. I found a robe
hanging on the back of the door, secondhand or maybe even Aunt
Elodie's, but soft and clean. Too clean, I realized. My whole body
felt like it was coated in grime.

Taking a bath in the claw-foot tub, as old and well used as everything else in the house, felt like too much of an extravagance. I took
a quick shower instead, then slipped into pajamas I found in the
armoire. When I crawled into bed, the new mattress swallowed me
up. I slept like the dead for twelve hours.

☙ ❧

When I woke, I sat up in a panic. I thought I was back in the hospital. But it was too quiet, too dark to be the hospital. The atmosphere
felt heavy. I was somewhere far stranger, a room in the old funeral
home belonging to my missing husband's family.

"I don't deserve this," I said aloud.

No argument from Fitz.

I dressed in the predawn dark, grateful for the jeans, button-
down shirt, and clean underwear Aunt Elodie had gotten for me.
Then I slipped into the kitchen, afraid of disturbing anyone. A note
on the counter told me to make myself at home, and there was a
covered plate in the fridge. Chicken and pasta, the dinner I'd slept
through the night before. I carried it to the table and ate it cold.

I felt restless, like I'd overslept and missed something important.
I thought about the sewing room and wondered if I would have to
make an accounting of myself.

"Well, what do you do, Mellie?"

Nothing. I had nothing to show for myself. Grandma Mae had
encouraged me to leave Fitz and my old life behind. But after she
died, my only accomplishment had been disappointing Helene.

To distract myself from the certainty I'd be a failure once they
got to know me, I started leafing through a catalog left on the
kitchen table.

Mortuary supplies.

As the kitchen filled with morning light, I found myself lost in
everything from body fridges and embalming tables to urns and cas-
kets. Reconstruction materials and cosmetics fell between sanitation

supplies and transport cots, all with descriptions written in an upbeat tone that emphasized quality and performance—as if a biological waste sluice basin was just part of a mortician's jolly good time.

And yet, wasn't this what I come all this way to do?

"Around the shop," Elodie had said, "we're all just undertakers."

At the back of the catalog was a garments section. The first spread featured aprons, coveralls, and face masks, but after that came printed T-shirts, sweatshirts, mugs with morbidly humorous captions like, "Not Just Hot—Open Casket Hot!" and "I love the smell of embalming fluid in the morning."

I actually laughed a little.

"Coffee?"

I started and looked up, saw Uncle Rémy in the kitchen doorway. He was dressed in boots, canvas pants, and a striped shirt with leather elbow patches. He smelled like the Pinaud aftershave Grandma Mae had kept around to remind her of my grandfather, a man who'd died before I was born.

"You like that stuff, huh?"

I glanced down at the catalog, then back up at him. Gave a little nod.

"I have a ball cap around here that says, 'Last Responder.'" He smiled and made himself busy at the counter, filling the coffee maker and taking a pill from a prescription bottle in the cupboard. "Bad hip," he said absently.

When the coffee was ready, he brought me a cup. "Half-and-half in the fridge, if you take it that way." I was pleased and a little surprised he thought I was up to the task of getting my own cream. He blew into his cup and took a sip, then said, "Up for a little walk?"

My first thought was that he wanted to trot me into the desert and bury me in a shallow grave. But if the Boutons wanted me dead, they could have just left me on the street in Boston. I shook off the thought and drank my coffee, black. When we both finished, I took my plate and our cups to the sink and washed up. Then I followed him downstairs. He had to loan me one of Aunt Elodie's coats.

"Later, we'll run into town and get you fixed up with some proper clothes."

"You don't need to do that," I said. I had his ten thousand dollars in my pocket, after all.

"Don't worry. We'll put you to work."

"I still don't know what my job will be."

"Oh, all kinds of things," he said with a mischievous smile, "but we'll start you slow." He didn't elaborate, and I let it go. There was time, I figured, and he seemed more interested in venturing out into the cool morning.

We headed down the long driveway, away from the house. The air was clear, with a crisp, earthy scent. I felt like I could see for miles, but almost at once my attention was pulled nearer. The gravel crunching under our feet startled a small, gray-brown bird that darted off, tail high.

"Sage thrasher," Rémy said. "Lucky. We don't see them much around here."

We crossed the road, then stopped to allow him to knead his right hip. "Stiff in the mornings, but it'll loosen up." When we moved on, it was at a slower pace. He described things along the way: spiky ball cactus and tufts of wheatgrass, yellow woolly sunflowers and gnarled juniper. Once, he pointed to a bird circling overhead. "Golden eagle." How he could tell, I had no idea. To me, it was a dark squiggle. A couple of times he kept me from stepping in old, dry cow manure, and then a short tower of oval, green-brown pellets steaming in the chilly air.

"We're getting close." When I asked to what, he said, "You'll see."

A hundred yards farther, we crested a short rise. Ahead, in a gray-green depression, a herd of animals looked up at us, their black faces inquisitive. They had ruddy brown backs, with white rumps and white flashes on their cheeks and necks. A black stripe ran up the snout to their foreheads, and their curved black horns grew up above their eyes a foot or more.

I took a sharp breath.

"They're called pronghorns. A lot of folks think of them as antelopes, but they're more closely related to giraffes."

I felt like I was in the middle of a wildlife documentary. "They're beautiful."

We watched them graze for half an hour as Uncle Rémy described their behavior and habits. "This herd is mostly adult females, with a few juveniles. In the spring, the adult males break off to live alone and fight over who's boss." He said we'd see them from time to time working their way across the Shatter Hill plateau.

Slowly the pronghorns moved away. When they disappeared over the far rim of the depression, we took a wide loop on our way back to the Old Mortuary. Uncle Rémy wanted to show me a bobcat den.

I didn't realize it at the time, but it was the start of my education in the life of the Oregon high desert, and of Barlow County. Under the guidance of Uncle Rémy, I would come to learn the difference between rabbitbrush and desert sage. He taught me to distinguish a vulture from an eagle in flight, and a turkey feather from a red-tailed hawk's on the ground. Together, we watched prairie falcons catch cliff swallows on the wing and dug mouse skulls out of owl pellets. He told me about the Columbia River Flood Basalts, a deluge of lava that covered northern Oregon and southern Washington in spasms between fifteen and seventeen million years ago. The vertical rock columns along the lip of Shatter Hill were remains of the formation, which in places can be three thousand feet thick. Sometimes alone, sometimes with Aunt Elodie, we roamed the county from Trout Rot Creek to the irrigated plateau north of Dryer Lake. We spotted elk and mule deer in the Brother Drop National Forest. We watched chinook and steelhead return to the Palmer River and followed ancient wagon ruts the pioneer Sam Barlow himself may have once trodden.

"A hard man," Uncle Rémy said. "Killed a fellow with an ax."

Sadly, over time, our treks would grow shorter, even after Uncle Rémy took to using walking sticks. The pain in his hip could make him irritable, even forgetful. But he never stopped finding something new to show me.

҉ ҉

The next day, Aunt Elodie took me to Samuelton and the New Mortuary for the first time. I was anxious to start work. The check, the room with its old furniture and new mattress, the clothes, and the train ticket—they all weighed on me, debts I wanted to repay. Hell, I'd have worked for free, though over dinner the night before, Aunt Elodie had dismissed the idea. I'd be doing a job, and I'd receive a salary.

"It's not much," she admitted. "A starter's wage, less a bit for room and board."

That was fine with me. Left unmentioned was the escape that big check gave me—gave us all—if things didn't work out.

But as we pulled into the parking lot outside the one-story stucco building with its meticulous landscaping, a tremor of anxiety swept through me.

Aunt Elodie turned off the engine and looked at me, her eyes kind. "You don't have to worry. No remains today. Not till you're ready."

"It's not that." I wasn't worried about seeing or even handling the dead, even if the only body I'd ever really seen was my grandmother's. Though I still missed her, Grandma Mae had suffered a long, painful decline, and her death had been a mercy in the end. What remained behind when she finally passed seemed no more the person she'd been than her clothes or the furniture in her tiny apartment.

"What is it?"

A question. Two questions, really—though one led to the other. Before I went inside, I needed to understand how I came to be here and who I was expected to be.

I'd asked Uncle Rémy the first before we left Portland. He told me to ask Elodie. But after we arrived, I'd put it off. First I told myself it didn't matter; then I told myself the question might only make them rethink the decision to bring me here in the first place. They'd offered me a place, a job, a chance.

I should be grateful.

But sitting in the car outside the New Mortuary, I suddenly felt like everything was happening too fast—as if after a long journey I'd hit the end of the road and fallen off a cliff. I was about to meet strangers, people with whom I lacked even the tenuous connection I had to Rémy and Elodie. They had no reason to accept me.

"We can go home, honey," Elodie said quietly, misunderstanding my hesitation. "We'll try again tomorrow."

I shook my head. My tongue felt thick and dry. "What made you call me?"

Her eyes grew distant, then she pulled the keys out of the ignition. I thought she was going to get out without answering, but she only fiddled with the keys in her lap before dropping them in her purse.

"We got an email from Geoffrey's family, asking if we'd heard from him. We didn't even know he was missing." Her lips formed a thin line, and I wondered if she was thinking of Geoffrey's parents. I'd only met them one time, after he'd disappeared. The encounter hadn't gone well. "Once we'd heard the whole story, and learned of your situation, well . . ."

Her voice trailed off, as though she didn't want to raise the specter of my abandonment in Paris, or my involuntary hospitalization after my return. That was fine. I didn't either.

"You don't even know me," I said.

"We know Geoffrey," she said, as if that settled things.

At least someone did.

I looked at the white stucco building, felt as if it was looking back. I wondered what the other people who worked at the mortuary would think. Aunt Elodie had shared their names over dinner: Carrie Dell, the embalmer. Wanda Iniguez, funeral planning specialist and office manager. Quince Kinsrow, body transport and general assistant—the man I'd be replacing. That was its own source of anxiety, but Aunt Elodie assured me Quince had been ready to retire for a while.

"Are you going to tell them about me, about my . . . situation?"

"Nobody's business, unless you want it to be."

I shook my head. "No."

"Long-lost niece then, twice removed or however it goes." She gave me a conspiratorial smile. "Anyone asks, we'll say you found us online."

As if I could order a new family, a new life, like an internet mattress. I didn't mention I didn't have the first clue how to find a long-lost relative online. In the end it didn't matter.

No one ever asked.

EIGHT

Town Common

For all the space of the Oregon High Desert, Samuelton proper is tucked into a glen between two long spurs of Lost Brother Butte. Anchoring the small downtown is the grandiosely named Town Common, a nine-square-block business district smaller than the campus on College Ridge. The compact area is home to restaurants, pubs, touristy shops, and the Barlow Building, all surrounding Memorial Park, center square of Town Common.

Once I'm sure Jeremy hasn't followed me out, I pause on the front steps of the Barlow Building to inhale the scent of sage carried by the night breeze. Now after ten on a Tuesday night, Town Common is quiet. Barb texted earlier to say she was going home, so I'm on my own. I zip my jacket, then, without thinking, pull out my phone and thumb a familiar name in my Contacts. Tap "Call." Get voicemail.

"It's Melisende. What else is new, right?" I let out a breath. "I'm sorry for calling so late. It's been a long day. I hope you're okay." I tap "End" and exhale.

Helene never answers, and she never calls back. I look up at the dark sky. The moon is just climbing above the horizon. Only a fraction of the stars seen in the desert are visible. Outside the Whistle Pig, half a block up to my left, a guy steps out to smoke under the neon Pabst sign in the window. Light and chatter stream through the door, propped open to let in the cool night air. I'm only half-tempted to stop in for a nightcap. It's been forty hours since I slept.

I want my bed, but I can't face the long drive out to Shatter Hill. I'll settle for the supply room casket at the New Mortuary.

I drag my feet through the park toward the fountain, an imposing affair with a broad sandstone basin and a central column topped by a statue of Sam Barlow himself. Seven names of locals who died in the Great War are listed on the bronze plaque affixed to the near side of the plinth—similar plaques at the cardinal points list the dead from World War II, Korea, and Vietnam. Among the names is a Bouton—perhaps one of Geoffrey's ancestors. At that thought, I close my eyes.

When I open them again, Landry MacElroy is there.

"You still talking shit about me?"

He stands in a puddle of light cast by a vintage lamppost illuminating the fountain. His T-shirt—"Barlow Football Battering Rams"—strains to contain his bulk.

"I *said*, you in there spreading lies about me again?" He gestures toward the Barlow Building with a balled fist.

I inhale slowly, conscious of the night chill on my face and neck. "We talked about how distraught your mother must be."

"About what?"

Calling Landry a fish in a barrel would be an insult to fish.

Two more boys saunter out of the shadows beyond the fountain, both familiar from the crossroad. *The team that plays together, preys together.* The New Mortuary is three blocks away. With three blockheads in between, it might as well be three miles.

The larger of the newcomers grunts. "Don't matter what she says, Lan." I don't know his name, but I remember his position from when I looked up the team website after I found out no charges would be filed against Landry. Offensive guard. Seems appropriate.

The smaller one, a tailback, grins. "She batshit, yo. Dumb slut says she saw the Spirit."

"Off the rails, man."

"You hear about the *baby*?"

That draws a bark of laughter. "Fuck me, bro. *Everybody's* heard about the baby."

"Who *does* that?"

"Even Riblet would know what to do if he found a baby."

"Well, Riblet would probably eat it."

"At least he'd pick it up."

"This is some kinda whack ho."

"Bug-*ass* slag."

"How many dead bodies you think she's fucked?"

"All of them?"

"Chicks too? Gross."

"Dyke for the dead, brah."

Zero to necrophilia in under sixty seconds. Their routine has gathered enough momentum that I half-suspect I could slip away without them noticing. A breeze sweeps through the park, carrying with it the aroma of the Whistle Pig's deep fryer. I glance that way. The smoker has gone inside. Some remote part of me thinks I should be worried.

"Can you smell that, Mellie?" Fitz's voice tickles the back of my head. I answer without thinking. "Smells good."

Landry and his crew bust out in sneering laughter. "What in hell you on about?"

They think I was talking to them.

"Sweet potato tots." My head feels like it's pivoting on a ball joint. "From the Whistle Pig."

The three boys stare, bug-eyed, Landry's mouth agape. "You *are* crazy."

Maybe I should have kept my mouth shut, but staying quiet has never been one of my strengths. Growing up, it didn't matter. No one was listening anyway. But now, still a newcomer in a small town, I'm on display every waking moment. By tomorrow, everyone will have heard. *Saw the Spirit . . . left the baby . . . babbled about sweet potato tots in Memorial Park.*

The tailback prods Landry with his elbow. "We should take her out to the crossroad or up to the old graveyard."

"She'd fit right in with Molly Claire's Girls," Landry says, nodding. The way he says it makes me wonder if Molly Claire is another name for the Shatter Hill Spirit—not that I'd ask fucking Landry.

Out on the street a car goes by. The taillights vanish around a corner. I'm on my own, with nothing going for me but the beer in their bellies. The big guy, the guard, sways like he just took off his training wheels. The tailback isn't much better, with wayward eyes and head wobbling on his muscled neck. If I hurt Landry fast,

I might be able to get away before the others realize what happened. I'm still in my work boots. A steel-toe to his rape tackle could solve no end of problems.

But before I can act, Paulette Soucie appears from beyond the fountain.

"Landry, where'd you go?"

Her voice is kittenish, but there's strain in her eyes.

"Paulette—" I can't hide my disappointment, but Paulette only frowns and shuts me up with a sharp shake of her head. When Landry turns, she shows him her teeth and holds up a beer can. "Come back, sweetie. I'm getting cold." Tension lingers in her smile.

Two more girls lurk in the shadows behind her. I've interrupted a party.

"You're lucky I got better things to do, bitch," Landry says to me.

I want to tell Paulette she doesn't have to be here. That I can teach her what Helene tried to teach me before I met Geoffrey and forgot it all in a heedless rush of sex and booze. But before I can shape the thought into words, a patrol car stops on the street across from the fountain, and Jeremy climbs out.

"What's going on here?"

"Whoa." Landry waves his hands and takes a step back. "We were just hanging—"

"Underage drinking," I say. "Menacing. Another rape or two in the works."

"Yo, *bitch*—!"

Jeremy shuts Landry up with the beam of a Maglite into his bloodshot eyes. "Mel, are you saying he threatened you?"

"He thinks he did."

Grim-faced, Jeremy stares at the three boys. "Fellas, hand over your keys and then go home. Walk, call for a ride—I don't care. Just get moving. I'll be around soon to check on you and give your keys to your folks. If you're not home, the next time I see you I won't be so friendly."

"What about our dates?"

"You let me worry about them."

The boys hesitate, calculation in their eyes. Three on one— them favored sons; Jeremy, an outsider, blind to the layers in Barlow

County strata. Landry is the one who says what they're all thinking. "I don't think you realize who you're dealing with, Deputy."

To Jeremy's credit, he doesn't waver. "Don't test me, kid."

For a minute, Landry seems ready to go off, counting on his backup to help him take down a cop. But not even Landry MacElroy is that stupid. He puts up his hands, then digs for his keys. The others follow suit. But before the boys leave, Landry stares at Paulette and growls, "You got nothing to say to this bitch."

"I said move it." Jeremy spins Landry and gives him a shove. I think we're all surprised when Landry keeps walking. Jeremy doesn't relax until the boys cross the street and round the corner. Then he turns to me.

"You okay?"

"I thought you were off-duty."

"On my way home."

"So now you're standing up to Landry? Where were you two weeks ago?"

"Can we do this later?" Jeremy steals a glance at Paulette, who refuses to meet his gaze. I just shake my head, annoyed and exhausted.

"Can I at least give you a ride home, Mel? It's no trouble. I've got room for everyone."

"I'm not getting in a car with *her*," one of Paulette's friends says. I give the girl a look, daring her to make a crack about babies, ghosts, or necrophilia. She withers. I'm tempted to take Jeremy up on his offer, just to see the look on her face. But he'll want to stay if I do. I'd rather sleep in a coffin than deal with his wheedling right now.

I eye the three girls. Paulette looks resigned, but the other two continue to stare daggers. Over Jeremy's shoulder, St. Mark's Hospital looms, the tallest building in the county—a sudden beacon.

"No thanks, I'm fine."

Before he can say another word, my third "second wind" of the day carries me out of the park, past a block of dark shops, and through the front door of the hospital to check on the damn baby.

NINE

Family Birthing Center

I usually enter St. Mark's from the back, so when I step into the lobby, it takes me a moment to get oriented. The hospital is small, three floors divided into two wings. To the right and through a security door is my typical haunt: the morgue. A sign points left to an unfamiliar destination.

```
← FAMILY BIRTHING CENTER
  PEDIACTRIC CARE UNIT
```

"I heard about the baby."

The refrain of the day, with lots of laughs at the apprentice undertaker's expense from the fine folk of Barlow County.

I stare at the sign. The baby should be through the pair of double doors I've never given a second thought. Why should I? I don't have a baby—and never will. I put a hand on my belly. The only things that will ever live in my womb are the spiders weaving cobwebs.

"You just left her there?"

That I was yelling for help from the moment I realized what I'd found doesn't matter—not even to Barb.

"You are a little weird, Mellie."

"Shut up, Fitz."

He laughs me through the doors to a warm space the size of the New Mortuary's lobby. On the wall behind the nurses station, back-lit letters read "Welcome to the Family Birthing Center."

Off in the corner of the waiting area, a man on his cell sits next to the window, wild-eyed and breathless. Nearby, a couple I assume are expectant grandparents speed-talk to a younger woman, whose wide grin looks manufactured by Mattel. Behind a second pair of double doors, past the nurses station, mothers will be squeezing out offspring. *Push—scream, push—scream*, if *Lifetime* movies are any guide. Out here, it's all barely restrained happy time.

The place smells like a cage made of baby wipes. I'm too god-damn tired to face this, but I can't back out now. Someone will recognize me. If I flee, the talk tomorrow will double down on the crazy girl afraid of babies.

In the distance, I can still hear Fitz laughing.

"May I help you?"

The voice jolts me out of my thought spiral. A nurse rises from a chair behind the counter. She looks to be in her thirties yet is dressed in pink scrubs printed with teddy bears. Her black hair is bound up in a bun, and her dark eyes are veiled with suspicion.

"Are you friend or family?"

"Of who?"

Her brow furrows. In Barlow County, it's easy to think everyone is familiar. Odds are, you've at least traded nods at Cuppa Jo or Ray's Thriftway. But she doesn't recognize me. This part of the hospital is as far from the morgue as you can get without going outdoors. "Are you here to see one of our birthing families?"

"No." *Jesus.* Barb would have a field day with this. I consider turning around and leaving, gossip be damned. But I lift my chin and look her in the eye. Like you're supposed to. "There was a baby brought in. From the desert. A newborn."

She inspects me, eyes lingering at my midsection. "What is your relationship to the child?"

I force my lips into an uneasy smile. "I'm the one who found her."

"Ohh. Of course." Her expression softens. "She's not here. They have her in NICU."

"What?"

"Neonatal Intensive Care. It's a secure unit, staff and immediate family only."

"I just . . ." If I'd kept walking past the hospital, I could be climbing into my coffin by now. "I . . . wanted to see how she was doing."

"I'm sorry. We can't give out any information. Confidentiality, you know."

"Sure."

"I can understand why you'd want to check on her."

Really? I wish she'd explain it to me.

"You're not alone. People have been calling all day. The sheriff, a couple of reporters. Heck, even Lydia Koenig came by."

"Lydia Koenig?"

"From the girls' school in Crestview."

I've heard gossip about the isolated facility, a private school for troubled girls supposedly on their last stop before women's prison. But since no one's died there—yet—it hasn't been on my radar.

"Does she know something about the baby? I heard they ruled out the schools."

"I wish it was that easy." She sadly shakes her head. "Miss Koenig was just concerned, same as all of us."

Same as all of us. Right.

I turn to go.

"You work at the funeral home, right?"

She recognizes me after all, the mad undertaker who ran away from the baby.

This is the moment when people do one of two things: shrink away in horror or smile uncomfortably and pretend like it ain't no thing. But the nurse surprises me.

"I think you know my sister, Danae. She usually works Med-Surg, but she floats to the morgue when necessary."

"Oh"—I steal a quick glance at her ID badge: Danica Wood, RN. Danae and Danica. I bet they've got a brother named Dane—"yes, Danae."

"She tells me you're very professional."

"I try to be." I usually save my undertaker gag shirts for off-hours or cover them with a jacket or button-down work shirt when I have to interact with the living. After a long pause, I realize the nurse is waiting for more. I manage a weary smile. "Danae is good. She always has her shit together." I don't know if it's true. My contact with the morgue attendant has been limited, but she does have one thing on me. To my knowledge, *she's* never lost a body.

Danica glances around the waiting area, then leans forward. "Listen, I haven't heard the latest status, and this is nothing official." Her voice is low and conspiratorial. "While I can't offer specifics, the baby is doing well. Honestly, she wouldn't be here otherwise. Our NICU is hardly worthy of the name. We're neither equipped nor staffed to handle serious cases. We'd airlift your little girl to Bend or Portland if she had any major issues."

I have to swallow a bitter laugh. *My little girl.* Still, relief overtakes me. "Thanks," I murmur. "I should get going. I'm running on fumes."

She smiles and leans back. "Go get some rest. I'll tell Danae you said hi."

I seem to have made a friend.

TEN

Spent Cartridges

"You can't call yourself a mortician till you've slept in a casket."

Aunt Elodie shared that folksy wisdom one morning last November after a late-night removal when I stayed over at the New Mortuary rather than drive home through freezing rain. My nap casket is a display model with a cutaway at the head to show the construction layers. It's been in our storage room for years.

Since my arrival, no one else has used it. Elodie is a fearless driver in all conditions, and Wanda lives six blocks away. Carrie says she'd sooner sleep on the embalming table. But cold stainless steel isn't my idea of a proper resting place, not while I'm drawing breath. Not that the casket is much better. The padding is more for appearance than comfort—the dearly departed have yet to complain. Even without the lid, it's claustrophobic, and if you turn wrong you can crack an elbow hard enough to draw tears.

No surprise, I awaken too early Wednesday morning, stiff and grimy. The staff bathroom has a shower, but a long, hot soak in a deep tub is what I really want. That means going to the Old Mortuary. Carrie is still out, and Aunt Elodie isn't due back from Bend with Uncle Rémy till late Thursday or maybe Friday. I'm free—at least until the next demise. I leave a note for Wanda, pocket my cell—and make damn sure to lock up on my way out.

The sun has cleared College Ridge, pushing before it a crisp breeze. By eight o'clock I'm in the Stiff. As I drive through Town Common, my eyes linger on Memorial Park, but all I see are a few empty beer cans near the fountain. Outside Cuppa Jo I slow but don't stop. The whole county will have heard about the missing bodies. The baby was bad enough—now, I'm a ghoul too. Even a much-needed caffeine fix isn't worth the grief.

A minute later, I turn onto Route 55 under a cornflower sky. It'll be hot later, but for now I lean into the gas pedal and let the cool morning air pour through the open window. The desert smells fresh and clean, and the drone of the tires on pavement is soothing, almost hypnotic. As distance grows between Samuelton and me, tension bleeds out of me. At the Old Mortuary, a claw-foot tub the size of a twin bed awaits. I can doze while I soak. If I'm lucky, my phone won't ring for a week.

"Who's that?"

A quarter mile ahead, there's a car at the crossroad, parked next to the fire ring. I jerk my foot off the gas. I recognize Kendrick Pride's blue hybrid just as his lanky form rises from behind the car. He's moving back and forth, pausing to snap pictures of the ground with his phone.

"What's he doing?"

"How the hell should I know?"

"You should talk to him, little sister."

"I think I'll pass."

But when I turn onto Wayette Highway toward home, Pride gestures for me to stop. I let out an exasperated breath and pull onto the shoulder a little way up from his car. I take my own damn time getting out of the Stiff and walking back to him.

"What can I do for you, Mr. Pride?"

"This is where it happened, isn't it?"

Like he needs me to answer that question. "Here, yeah." I gesture at the obvious tread marks in the middle of the intersection, at the Subaru's scar in the opposite ditch. "And there . . . and there." Scorched pavement. Glittering glass fragments. We could even see hoof prints out on the desert if we looked. He follows my pointed indications and nods solemnly. He seems more interested in the bonfire clearing. He walks over to the ashes and nudges the unburnt end of a pine log with his wingtip.

"Must have been quite a mess."

For a second I wonder if he's referring to the rape. But how would he even know about it? I consider the rim of Shatter Hill above us, and the moment I spotted the firelight. I wonder what Pride would think if I told him a group of dead strangers was preferable to Landry doing whatever he damn well pleased to Paulette while his buddies cheered him on.

"Lots of parties out here?"

"If you want to call them that."

I see a question in his eye, but he turns his attention to the ground at our feet. "Did the police search this area?"

"I don't know. Why?"

He takes a pen from his jacket and points downward. A metallic gleam draws my eye. With practiced ease, he crouches and lifts a bullet casing with the tip of the pen. On the base, I can just make out the letters SIG 40 S&W. "Someone was shooting."

The laugh pops out of me before I can stop it.

"Something funny?"

"Sorry. It's just that . . ." I shake my head, remembering one of Uncle Rémy's many lessons about life in the high desert. "Every road sign for hundreds of miles has bullet holes in it. You'll find more spent casings than empty beer cans along these roads."

"I'm sure. But look how clean this is. It can't have been here long." He pulls a Ziploc bag from his pocket. "Possibly no longer than about thirty-six hours?" In other words, since the time of the wreck. My lips tighten as he inspects the casing and drops it into the bag. "Forty-caliber handgun round, which might be helpful." He smiles grimly. "Or, as you say, not connected to the crash at all."

Then why are you collecting the brass like it's evidence? Pride moves close. I edge back, but he stops and crouches again for another bullet casing between my feet.

"I wish the medical examiner had done an autopsy," he says. "At least for Trae."

"Now he can't."

"That's not your fault."

"Isn't it?"

He gazes out across the desert. "I have no reason to believe you've got anything to do with it."

"You don't know me."

"True." he concedes. "But you could have put me off last night. Cited funeral home procedure or deferred to your supervisor.

Instead, you brought me right into the facility. When you opened that drawer, you were as surprised as I was."

"Maybe I'm a great actress."

"If you try hard enough, I suppose you could talk me into adding you to the suspects list."

"You have a list?"

"Just a figure of speech."

Now it's my turn to study him. "Why not let the sheriff handle it? Or don't you trust country cops?"

"The Sheriff's Department strikes me as competent."

My lips purse. Not the word I'd choose.

"You have reason to think otherwise?"

I doubt Sheriff Turnbull would do a proper investigation of a pie stolen off a windowsill unless he was guaranteed a slice on the back end.

Pride doesn't press me for a response. "I understand Deputy Chapman will be canvassing the area around the funeral home for witnesses."

I suppose it's possible Jeremy could turn up a witness, but I'm doubtful. Except for the high school football stadium across Sixth Street, the rear driveway of the New Mortuary isn't visible from the neighborhood. An arborvitae hedge hides the service area from the houses whose yards adjoin the mortuary grounds. Even if someone saw a truck, would they have any reason to remember it? We get deliveries a couple of times a week, more when we're busy.

"Good luck with that."

As I turn to go, he says, "Would you join me for lunch? I'm trying to get a sense of the area, and I hoped I might pick your brain." He smiles. "My treat."

Somewhere nearby an eagle calls, the shrill cry riding my nerves like an electric shock. I examine the ground near my feet, my mind on bullet casings and missing bodies. On how I'm not in the mood to get hit on. On how I just want to go home.

The eagle calls again, and an ache grows behind my eyes. I pinch the bridge of my nose.

"I've put you on the spot, Ms. Dulac." He folds his hands before himself, the plastic bag tucked between his fingers. "Please accept my apology."

Damn it.

He gets points for not wheedling the way Jeremy would, the way almost any guy would. But I'm still irritated. I need an Advil . . . and a stiff drink.

"As I said, I don't believe this situation is your fault."

"Tell that to the sheriff."

"I'm sure he can see this wasn't some random crime of opportunity. Someone went there intending to take those bodies."

"I bet the Shatter Hill Spirit took them."

"I really need to go."

"Of course."

He offers me what looks like an old-fashioned calling card, stiff linen with "Kendrick Pride, Esq." in raised ink. His phone number and email, in smaller type on the second line, break the nineteenth-century spell.

"If you change your mind about lunch, give me a call."

Wheedling after all.

Out on the desert, I spot the eagle, a golden, in some open ground near a broad basalt outcrop. A pair of vultures alight nearby, wings spread and heads thrust forward. They're arguing over something, but what, I can't see. For several seconds the birds hop and flap along the ground in a display that's more bluster than battle. A third vulture watches from a juniper branch nearby. It's a standoff until the third vulture drops to the ground. The eagle retreats, pulling itself heavily aloft. The vultures strut around until the eagle flies off, then vanish into the sagebrush crowding the outcrop.

With a start, I realize I've been holding my breath.

"Is something wrong?"

I head for the outcrop at a trot.

Pride follows, his footsteps thudding behind me. "What is it?"

Something's dead, obviously.

Out here, could be anything. Deer, coyote, even a stray steer. A pronghorn down from Shatter Hill. Scavengers might even mix it up over a jackrabbit.

I hope.

But the other night I came this way in search of a cell signal—and found a baby instead. The basalt outcrop is farther, a hundred yards or more—perhaps far enough to fall outside the sheriff's search radius.

I stop at the edge of the sagebrush clump and put my hand on Pride's arm. "Hold up. Let me check it out."

"What do you expect to find?"

"Just wait here."

I don't get more than a couple steps into brittle scrub before a fourth vulture pops up and hisses. The others join in, flapping around in bare patches among the sage. I clap my hands and shout. The angry birds hold their ground. "Yah! Get outta here!" I reach down for a dead juniper branch, but between my stomping and clapping, the birds get the message. With a final threatening hiss or two, they launch themselves into the air.

I continue forward, eyes scanning the ground. The outcrop looks like a toppled pillar, twelve feet high and twice as broad, dipping away for thirty yards until it disappears into the earth. A wind-scooped hollow has formed under the near edge, shelter for rattlesnakes from the midday sun—or for a person. Between a couple of stunted junipers, I spot two legs in filthy jeans. Dead. Even without the vultures, I'd know. The dead possess a stillness the living can't fake.

Pride's shadow falls across me.

"I told you to wait."

He pushes by, and I follow, annoyed. We move carefully, making sure we don't step on anything the cops would care about—footprints, bullet casings, newborns. My first body in the desert was last fall, a rancher out looking for stray cattle when his four-wheeler tipped into a gully and crushed him. He wasn't discovered for three days, long enough to swell and ripen to the point we could smell the body from fifty yards away. This body is more recent—a boy, mid- to late teens, jammed up into the hollow like his dying wish was to become one with the stone itself. His T-shirt is bloody and torn at the site of a wide, ragged gash where the scavengers got started. A few ribs are exposed, and one eye is gone. His skin is the color of concrete. I can't be sure how long he's been dead, but not long. The vultures haven't done enough damage, and the smell of putrefaction isn't strong.

Pride crouches and cups his chin in his long-fingered hand. Far off now, the eagle cries. The circling vultures continue their vigil far above. I watch their odd, wobbling flight and imagine myself soaring with them.

"His name is Nathan Harper—Trae's best friend."

Pride's voice drags me back to earth. "You knew him?"

He nods, his expression grim. I look at the boy. One more piece of a puzzle I wish I wasn't part of it. "What's he doing out here?" Sticking to pavement would have been the smart bet, but I don't suppose he was thinking straight. Maybe he was looking for a damn cell signal. "We're a long way from nothing."

"Trying to get away, maybe." Pride stands and peers back toward the crossroad. "The question is, from what?"

ELEVEN

Old Mortuary

Pride insists on waiting with the body. "I won't touch anything, but I do need to stay here until the police arrive." Maybe he's worried Melisende the Body Snatcher will make off with another prize. Alone, I trudge back to the road through rising heat and drive up Shatter Hill to find a cell signal.

After I describe the situation, the Sheriff's Department dispatcher puts me on hold. Tinny music plays in my ear as I sit on the back bumper. From atop the steep slope, Pride is distinguishable only by his motion, a looping circuit around the outcrop. Looking for bullet casings, I assume, stowing them in plastic bags. Photographing footprints, collecting fibers from juniper branches. Swabbing for DNA.

"Who are you anyway, Kendrick Pride?"

"Just ask him, little sister."

In my ear, a great-lunged country songstress ain't gonna let me go it alone.

Sure.

After an interminable wait, a car appears on Wayette Highway, coming from Crestview. A moment later, two more approach from the direction of Samuelton, materializing out of distant, shimmering heat waves. The dispatcher returns and asks me to hold a moment longer for Sheriff Turnbull. She doesn't give me the chance to object, but fortunately the singer only manages one more chorus before the sheriff picks up.

"Where are you?"

"The body is in the desert near the crossroad—"

"I know. Where are *you*?"

I chew the inside of my lip as I count to ten. "Up on the hill."

"Good. Stay there."

"What about the body?"

"I've sent Deputy Roldán and the EMTs—"

"This kid is way past EMTs."

"—to take care of the scene and transport the body."

He's cutting me out. "Sheriff, I'm perfectly capable of doing my job."

"I didn't say you weren't, Mellie." His voice is surprisingly soft. "You should talk to your aunt." The call drops before I can tell him to stop calling me Mellie.

It's all I can do not to scream into the still air. Down below, the three vehicles converge at the crossroad. The lead car and what I now see is an ambulance pull off onto the shoulder. But the car from Crestview continues through the intersection and heads my way, covering the distance in a quick half minute. I spot Jeremy behind the wheel and clench my teeth. Just past the Stiff he stops, his car straddling both lanes. I glare at him as he opens his door and plants his feet on pavement.

"Did they send you to keep me away from the scene?"

"Sheesh, Mel." He takes his hat off. Sunlight gleams on his neck. "I need to talk to you."

Christ. "Not interested."

"It's not that." He licks his lips. "Chief Deputy Duniway is at the Old Mortuary."

"What are you talking about?" I look down the hill, wondering why Duniway isn't among those walking to the outcrop.

But only half-wondering.

"You need to understand, Mel—he has to look."

"For what? My secret stash of corpses?"

He sighs. "Don't make this difficult."

A trickle of sweat falls between my breasts. Steam is about to shoot from my ears. "Well, he better have a goddamn warrant."

He hesitates before answering. "He has Elodie's permission."

That freezes me. "Impossible. She's in Bend with Uncle Rémy."

"She's . . ." He runs his hand over his buzzed hair. "She's actually at Crestview right now. I was just there."

"Wait."

"She asked me to find you."

He won't meet my eyes. If Aunt Elodie is at Crestview, she came back from Bend without telling me. "Why didn't she call me?"

"She tried. It just went to voicemail."

I pull out my cell phone. The phone app displays a tiny numeral 3. She must have called while Pride and I were talking bullet casings and investigating vultures. Without another word to Jeremy, I call her cell.

She answers on the first ring.

"It's so good to hear your voice, honey."

"Jeremy says you're at Crestview." I look across the valley at the rising slopes of Lost Brother Butte. The village is hidden by trees and changes in elevation. Above, the sky is a bowl; below, the desert—a spill of cracked mud and broken glass. "I thought you'd be gone a couple more days."

"Things have changed." She sounds exhausted. "I'm afraid I'll be here all day—and overnight too. I need to get your uncle settled."

"Why? I don't understand."

Her exhalation is like a dying breath. "The hip replacement went well. But I've been worried about him for some time. You know how he's been, forgetful and irritable."

I feel a sharp guilt about all the hikes we've been on. "I thought that was from the pain."

"So did I. Or I hoped it was only from the pain. But something changed. Maybe during the surgery—or maybe before, and we just didn't recognize the signs. He's not himself. He can't . . . well, he needs a level of care we can't provide at home."

"He'll get better though, won't he?"

"One can always hope." But there's no hope in her voice. I think back over the last few days, about how I couldn't reach her on the phone. She's didn't want to tell me.

Jeremy looks at me like Uncle Rémy is already dead.

I look out over the escarpment. The vultures ride the thermals high above the crossroad. A faint scent of decay seems to hang in the hot air. "What can I do, Aunt Elodie?"

The line is quiet. Then I hear a breath. "It's a lot to ask, honey, but someone should be at the house while Omar performs his search. Could I trouble you to go?"

I hate the very thought. "Sure."

"After, come out to Crestview." She hesitates, then adds, "Uncle will be glad to see you." She doesn't sound convinced. The call dies.

I turn to Jeremy. "How long has Duniway been there?"

"Thirty minutes, maybe."

It's a half mile to the grounds of the Old Mortuary, an unexpected swath of green and gray appearing like a vision out of the brown Shatter Hill tableland. Mossycup oaks shade the columned, two-story main building, with the detached garage, tool shed, pump house, and windowless crematorium behind and to the right. My bedroom looks out over the old Pioneer Cemetery adjacent to the grounds, where some of original settler families in Barlow County still have plots. At times I like to wander among the Sierra granite gravestones, picking out names and dates and imagining their lives in a land and time so different from what I knew before I came to Oregon. Now, this intrusion by Chief Deputy Duniway threatens to disrupt the unexpected peace I've found in this monument to the dead.

Duniway's department Tahoe is parked on the grass near the front steps. The Old Mortuary entrance stands open. I park in the gravel lot the Chief Deputy couldn't be bothered with. Jeremy approaches from his own vehicle as I get out. I slam the Stiff's door and elbow past him.

"Mel, please . . ."

His voice fades as I hurry across the lawn, onto the porch, and through the front door.

The interior is framed in twelve-inch ponderosa pine timbers hauled fifteen miles from the slopes of Lost Brother. The first floor is all mortuary space. Two large chapels, plus a parlor and work areas. The preparation room has long since been stripped of equipment, but the flower room and caterer's kitchen still get used for the dozen or so services held here each year. Upstairs is the office, now empty and gathering dust, and the family quarters.

A deep, welcoming quiet greets me. The fading wallpaper and worn carpet hints at a prosperity the family hasn't known for half a century, but the place feels opulent to me. Maybe it's the furniture and fixtures—antiques of the kind my parents stalked back in New England. Maybe it's the sense of place and time, authentic in a way I never knew before I came here. My mother and father were endlessly buying objects to fill their emptiness—often more valuable than the Victorian settees in the Old Mortuary reposing and viewing rooms—but in the end their acquisitions felt sterile and forced. Bouton Funerary Service, last stop for Barlow County's dead, is more alive than the house I grew up in.

I take a long breath in the hall, then, with a start, sense Jeremy behind me. "What are you, a goddamn puppy?"

He takes a step back. "How do you stay pissed for so long?"

"Holding a grudge is my superpower."

"Mel. *Please.*"

I can guess. He wants to clear the air. To win me back or maybe get closure after I cut things off. I'm pissed I let things get this far, let him get close enough to think I owe him something. An even angrier part of me still finds him attractive—physically at least. Barb would tell me to go with that. Have my fun and put in earbuds when he opens his mouth. But I don't need the grief right now, not with cops crawling around the Old Mortuary.

"All I'm asking is a chance to talk. It doesn't have to be now. Just pick a time, meet me for coffee or a drink."

There it is: the wheedle.

"If I say yes, will you back off?"

Before he can answer, Omar Duniway steps through the door into the foyer. "Kind of you to grace us with your presence, Miss Dulac."

"It's *Ms.* Dulac."

"As you like." His tone is friendly, but that just sets my nerves on edge.

Thin and worn, with skin weathered into deep, dendritic crevices, Omar Duniway is the skeletal counterpoint to Sheriff Turnbull. His neck is too narrow for his starched collar, and his standing purple veins look like they're trying to leap from his flesh. His breath stinks of menthol cigarettes.

"Are you finished?"

"Almost. One question though." He shows me his gray, narrow teeth. "Any idea who's been using the oven?"

❧ ❧

A sheltered breezeway runs between the house and the crematorium, screened from public view by privet hedges. The interior of
the building is overheated by air boiling out of the crematory. I peer
into the retort. "You opened this?"

Duniway nods. "I did."

"You're lucky you didn't get a face full of exploding ash and
molten bone."

The chief deputy squeezes his lips together and steps back. I have
to suppress a smile. At cremation temps, bone doesn't burn or melt;
it desiccates. Nor is opening the door particularly dangerous. As a
matter of procedure, we take a peek at least once every burn. The
primary flame shoots down at the center of the retort, and we often
need to reposition the body with a bone rake to ensure complete
cremation. Whoever started this cremation hadn't bothered, just lit
the fire and left. The result is an unfinished burn and a fuel gauge
reading zero.

Jeremy examines the valves controlling airflow and the gas feed
to the burner, and the gauges indicating temperature and fuel pressure. "How hard is it to work one of these things?"

"It's not like preheating the oven to make cookies." New cremation machines are computerized and automated—load the body
container onto the conveyor belt, click a mouse button, and go grab
a coffee. But this unit, a beast built to handle anything up to large
animal cremations, dates back to the 1960s. If there ever was a user
manual, it's long gone. The procedure is documented only in memory now.

I don't volunteer that Uncle Rémy has passed this knowledge on
to me, one of many lessons he shared with infectious zeal.

Duniway clears his throat. "Did you have a cremation scheduled
for today?"

"I doubt it." Not likely, in fact, with everyone gone but me.

"You're not sure?"

"No reason I should be." My job is to perform removals and
assist with everything from body prep to hosting events at the New
Mortuary. I may live out here at the Old Mortuary, but I work in
town. Though I've assisted a few times, cremations are Uncle Rémy's
responsibility. A sudden wave of uncertainty passes through me.
They *were* his responsibility. But now, who knows? With everything

else she has to deal with, Aunt Elodie might just decide she doesn't have the bandwidth to continue the Melisende experiment. After the last two days, I'm not sure I'd blame her if she patted me on the back and said, "Sorry things didn't work out."

"Who would know?" Duniway says.

"Talk to Wanda." If she had something on the books, in Uncle Rémy's absence she might have called Quince. Though past seventy and technically retired, he still does the occasional odd job and maintenance—even a removal if I can't. He'd once tried to rattle me by describing how he had to dismember some cowboy's beloved roping horse in order to fit it inside the crematory.

"Do you know where Quince is?"

"Knowing him, fishing."

"Where were you last night?"

"I stayed at the New Mortuary."

"Anyone with you?"

Wanda doesn't get in 'til nine, and I was out the door before then. "Nope."

I can't tell if they believe me. Jeremy does. At least, his expression suggests he wants me to think he does. But Duniway looks at me sidelong. "You must admit this is curious."

I don't have to admit anything. Inside the open retort, the partial burn has left a heap of ash, charred flesh, and heat-splintered bones—too much for any ordinary cremation. I stand mute, waiting for Duniway to state what I already know.

Inside are the cremated remains of the crossroad dead.

TWELVE

Crestview Assisted Living

I need a long, hot bath. I settle for a quick shower and clean clothes, and skip drying my hair. Deputy Roldán and the others are still working the scene at the outcrop when I blast through the crossroad a few minutes later. No one seems to care when I run the stop sign. Kendrick Pride's hybrid is nowhere to be seen.

Shatter Hill to Crestview is nine miles as the surveillance drone flies, eleven by mortuary first call vehicle, the last four climbing twelve hundred feet through pine forest. Lost Brother Butte is to my left and five thousand feet higher, a looming presence from anywhere in the county. In the winter, Crestview serves as base camp for the cross-country and downhill skiers who can't afford the Brother Drop Resort or Dryer Lake chalets. In the fall, hunters take over, while in spring and summer it's campers and hikers. But for me, year-round, the mountain village is notable only for the body count. I do more removals from Crestview Assisted Living than the rest of the county combined.

They've put Uncle Rémy in a private room. Edna Crandall's, I realize as I slip through the door. Stripped and sanitized, ready for a new tenant even as the previous one still chills in our fridge. Edna died of cancer, but I hope she didn't also suffer from some undiagnosed contagious wasting disease.

Aunt Elodie smiles from an overstuffed wing chair in the corner. She's been cross-stitching, but stows her embroidery in her craft bag when I come in.

"Welcome, honey." Her eyes turn to Uncle Rémy, who dozes under a colorful afghan on the bed. "He'll be asleep for a while. They just gave him something."

The room is small but comfortable in its way. Her wing chair has a mate under the wide window. A painting of trout leaping in a mountain stream hangs over the bed. On the opposite wall, Gene Kelly dances on the flat screen TV, the sound muted. If not for the IV, blinking monitor, and urea-tinged air, we might be in a pleasant, if unassuming, hotel room.

I manage a strained smile. "He looks comfortable." I feel like an idiot as soon as the words are out of my mouth.

Aunt Elodie, in contrast, looks haggard. Her salt-and-pepper hair, usually clean and well kempt, has a frizz more typical of my own head. Her clothes are wrinkled, and shadows ring her eyes. I want to find a bed and tuck her in, but—as always—she's more worried about me than herself.

"You've had to deal with so much without any support."

I drop into the empty chair. "I'm fine."

"When the surgery got moved up, I should have asked Carrie to delay her vacation."

Originally set for September, everyone had been grateful when a slot opened for Uncle Rémy's hip replacement this week. With Carrie out, the timing wasn't great, but Aunt Elodie didn't expect to be gone long, and Swarthmore's embalmer would help if a rush job came up. All I'd had to do was not fuck up for two or three days.

So much for that.

My fingers twist in my lap. Carrie wouldn't have lost three bodies, that's for damn certain. "I'm sorry, Aunt Elodie. I screwed everything up."

"Oh, honey, no, no." She reaches out for my tangled hands. "You're not to blame." A sharp, electric sensation leaps through me at her touch, but I resist pulling away. Aunt Elodie needs physical contact like most people need oxygen. I give her another tight smile and will myself to relax. Anxious for something else to focus on, I stare at the monitor at the head of Uncle Rémy's bed. Heart rate, oxygen saturation. Both hover around ninety-five. I can't remember if either value is good or bad.

"How long before he gets to come home?"

Sighing, she releases my hands and sits back in her chair. Peaceful, I realize, was the wrong word for Uncle Rémy. Torpid is more like it. His skin is dry and translucent, his eyes sunken, and his lips cracked and dry. He's asleep, but he doesn't appear to be resting so much as crushed by the very atmosphere. I've washed decedents who looked more alive. The thought sends a shudder through me, and I turn back to Aunt Elodie. She's watching Uncle Rémy, her gaze remote, as if she's seeing a memory rather than the man himself.

I wish I knew what to say. I'm not used to caring about people. Helene, maybe. Geoffrey doesn't count; despite our marriage, he was more distraction than object of devotion during our brief time together. Elodie and Rémy have become more like what my grandmother tried to be before she died: an island of security in a sea of indifference. But even with Grandma Mae, there had been distance. My parents, Cricket and Stedman, all but cut her off after Fitz died. I rarely saw her until I was old enough to make the forty-mile bus trip from Lowell to Framingham on my own. She had been wheelchair bound for as long as I could remember, and her declining health meant she could only handle an occasional overnight visit.

Aunt Elodie's chair squeaks. "I heard about the baby."

Of course she has. I draw a sharp breath but don't say anything.

"That was very lucky."

For the baby, maybe. "Yeah."

"Had you and Geoffrey any plans to have children?"

My body stiffens again, but this time there's no willing myself free of the tension. "I would make a terrible mother."

"You don't know that."

I don't want to argue with her. In her mind, Geoffrey and I were husband and wife, but in fact we were together almost no time at all. It was less than two years ago that he'd first arrived unexpectedly at his sister's. I don't know what he saw in me—maybe just a willing partner in excess. I was enrolled at UMass but mostly living with Helene in Holyoke. I skipped more classes than not. Helene was a second-year law student by then, busy and absent much of the time. Geoffrey and I spent our nights pub-crawling and our days in bed, first at Helene's and then—when she kicked us out—in my shitty Amherst apartment.

He got the idea we should marry after Thanksgiving. Why I agreed I can only attribute to a growing anxiety that I was running

out of options—with no one to blame but myself. The tiny inheritance from my grandmother that let me attend college, however
fruitlessly, was almost gone. I had no job, no skills. As for Geoffrey,
he spent like his own money would never end, and for all I knew it
wouldn't. Like everything else we did, he was the one who came up
with the idea for our spontaneous trip to France. "We'll stay until
the cherries bloom," he grandly proclaimed when we landed on a
cold February morning.

I would see my first cherry blossom through the window of a
Paris police station as I explained that my husband had gone out for
croissants and never returned.

"You didn't answer my question."

Aunt Elodie blinks, as if stirring from her own reverie. "What's
that, honey?"

"When can he come home?"

She takes a long time to answer.

"You never knew us when we were young. Rémy was so strong,
so sure of himself. I don't think I've ever known a man so forth-
right." She looks at Uncle Rémy as if she's going to cry. "Now I
don't know who's going to be there the next time he wakes up."

"Dementia. What a bite."

It doesn't seem possible. Not Uncle Rémy, so vital, so full of
curiosity. A memory surfaces of one of our outings at the end of last
summer. As we hiked the eastern rim of Shatter Hill, he told me
about twin sisters, originally from Samuelton, who'd died within
minutes of each other, one in California, the other in Georgia.
"They'd chatted by phone earlier that day, and though they were
elderly, both seemed in fine fettle."

At the time, I'd been at Bouton Funerary Service four months
and had settled into a routine that felt strangely normal. Get a call,
drive out to pick up a decedent—still under Quince's guidance, but
that wouldn't be for much longer.

When Uncle Rémy finished the story of the twins, now buried
in Pioneer Cemetery, I said, "I was thinking I'd use that money to
go to mortuary school."

Neither of us had spoken of the check since that day in Portland,
but his eyes lit up then, and I felt a rush of pleasure. He would be

a source of constant support as I worked through the prerequisites, and wrote a letter of recommendation to accompany my mortuary sciences application. A month ago, when I got the acceptance letter, he said, "I'm proud of you, Melisende. You'll be a credit to the program."

I can't stand the thought he might not be with me, with *us*, as I continue down a path I couldn't have started without him.

Elodie's joints pop as she gets to her feet and moves to the edge of his bed. She strokes Rémy's forehead. "They make him walk, you know. I know it seems too soon, but the doctor says it's necessary for his recovery." A faint, anxious smile twists her lips. "I go with him, of course, and try to be encouraging. But even a few steps down the hall wears him out."

"I'll walk with him next time."

"I appreciate that."

She gives Rémy one last caress, then returns to her chair. Her shoulders slump as she sits. When she looks up, her face is grave. An unexpected chill sweeps through me.

"Melisende, honey, I'm afraid the county has suspended you from performing contract removals until the investigation into what happened to those bodies is complete."

All the air bleeds out of me. Yet, despite the gut punch, I'm not surprised. I almost ask who made the decision—Chief Deputy Duniway, Sheriff Turnbull?—but it doesn't matter. What matters is I've become a burden at a time when Aunt Elodie is crushed with worry for Uncle Rémy.

Unsure what to say, I finally manage a monotone "I understand."

"You'll continue with our private clients, but Fire and Rescue will handle county removals for the time being." I nod, but she's not finished. "And after what's happened, Edna Crandall's family decided Swarthmore would work better for them."

Out in the hall a woman calls for someone to come hug their grandmother. The piercing voice reminds me of Cricket's.

"This is all my fault."

Elodie's hand snakes back into my own. I've become too numb to flinch. "Honey, don't think that."

What I'm thinking is how we can ill afford to lose the business, especially now.

"I'm sorry." In the corner of my eye, Uncle Rémy's monitor ticks away: ninety-four . . . ninety-five . . . ninety-three. "I'm so, so sorry."

"It's okay. We'll get through this." She smiles unconvincingly. "But I do need you to do something."

"Of course, Aunt Elodie."

"Swarthmore is sending their driver. Someone has to get Edna ready for transport."

I want to apologize again, a hundred times over. I know she'll just shush me. "When is he coming?"

"Not till four." She glances at her watch. "You've got time, but—"

"I should go." I rise heavily to my feet.

"Rémy will be sad he missed you."

I let her hug me, wishing I could be sure that was true.

PART TWO

Rubble

THIRTEEN

Iced Coffee

Late Friday afternoon, I'm in Cuppa Jo, gazing out the broad front window at Memorial Park. Demographically, Barlow County tilts hard toward one foot in the grave, yet no one has called for a removal in the three days since Edna Crandall. If Fire and Rescue made any calls, they took the remains to Swarthmore. My phone rests on the table, silent. An hour or a day ago, I called Helene, left another message. One of many. "It's been a long week. I hope you're okay."

Nothing from her either.

From where I sit, I can see from the Barlow Building to Dailie's Grille, including the Whistle Pig on the other side of the park. Outside, the locals are inured to the merciless sun. Now midway through my second summer in the high desert, I've come to prefer the dry heat to the crushing humidity of New England in July myself. Campers and kayakers from farther afield wear hats and carry water bottles.

As the fluorescents buzz overhead, a black Ford Excursion with tinted windows drives past, making my undertaker sense tingle. Oversized SUVs are hardly a rare sight around here, but this one is too clean for an off-roader or a working vehicle.

Unless the work is transporting the dead.

"Who we losing this time, Mellie?"

I've been here three hours, occupying myself with the view outside and in, and with a copy of this week's edition of the *Samuelton Ledger* someone left on the table. The story about the crash doesn't mention me by name, but the one about the bodies does. Explains why customers glance my way with wary curiosity. Only the owner, Joanne, has anything to say to me. The baby, she's heard, is doing well, and has been released from the hospital and placed with a foster family. "That's good," I'd managed to respond, my voice flat. Since then, Joanne has left me to stew in my juices.

If only Fitz would give me the same courtesy.

"You just gonna sit around, little sister?"

I can all but feel him prod my shoulders.

"Get out there!"

And do what? I don't dare say out loud.

I recall the dry mouth and wooziness from the antipsychotic cocktail they gave me in psych hold as the SUV continues toward the hospital. A block farther is the New Mortuary, but there's no one there to transport. In the days since the Swarthmore driver took Mrs. Crandall, three preplanning clients have decided to move their business to a funeral home that doesn't lose decedents. Even with the hummingbird energy of Wanda working damage control, the New Mortuary feels hollow and fragile. And the Old Mortuary—it's so hard to be there I almost called Jeremy last night and asked if I could stay with him. I didn't want to bother Barb, who's been grading her midterms between curriculum meetings. Instead, I read Isabel Allende and drank Carménère from a sippy cup.

"Excuse me, Miss Dulac?"

A figure has appeared next to the table, as vague as the watercolors of alpine meadows—this month's featured artwork—on the café walls. I blink, expecting her to melt away like the specter of the girl at the crossroad. Instead, she gathers form—not some phantom, but an ordinary girl in shorts and sandals and a sleeveless white blouse. Her raven hair is pulled back from her face, her brown arms are clasped over her breasts.

Paulette Soucie.

"May I sit down?"

A slick of perspiration gleams on her cheeks and forehead. Her nervous eyes drop to my chest, and a line forms between her eyebrows. I look down and see I'm wearing my "I ♥ Dead People" T-shirt.

"I mean, if you're not busy . . .?"

I give her the chance to remember she has somewhere else to be. Instead, she looks at my chest again, and a ghost smile steals across her lips.

"Sure."

Her eyes flicker with gratitude as she drops into the chair across from me. "I'm not supposed to talk to you."

"Oh?" I suppress a laugh. "According to who?"

"Way to put the poor girl on the spot, Mellie."

I wave my hand as if I'm shooing a fly away. Paulette, perhaps entangled in her own thought, doesn't notice.

I know the feeling. I've been like a moth bouncing between porch lights. Old Mortuary to New, out to Crestview, and back again. The moments I've spent with Uncle Rémy feel the most worthwhile, but Aunt Elodie isn't eager to share him for long. Wanda has nothing for me to do. The Old Mortuary is an empty tomb. Cuppa Jo is as good as anywhere, I guess. But I didn't ask for company.

"I, um . . ." Paulette lets out a heavy breath. "I'm sorry about Landry the other night."

A huff pushes between my teeth. "It's not on you to apologize for him."

"He just gets very emotional," she continues, as if she didn't hear me. "He was upset for days after what happened at the crossroad."

"I'm more worried about you."

"I'm fine."

My face must betray my skepticism.

"People at school say I'm lucky he'll have me." There's a tremor in her voice. "There are prettier girls."

Paulette is lovely, with a round, open face and large, kind eyes. Far too kind for the likes of Landry. I remember her desolate gaze when she sat up in the back of his pickup. "Then let one of them put up with him." Not that I'd wish Landry on anyone.

"I wish it was that easy." Tears well up in her eyes. "You don't know what it's like."

I open my mouth, but she's right. I don't. Not for her, not for anyone. When I was in high school, the other kids all kept their distance. My first boyfriend, if you can call him that, was some guy whose mother made him help me carry my things when I moved into the frosh dorm at UMass. Awkward and anxious, after she left he made some excuse and fled. I was used to being alone. But Grandma Mae said college was a chance for a fresh start, to try new things. So during the dorm mixer, I let him lead me into an unoccupied study carrel, where I learned the one way I like being touched. He avoided me the rest of the term, but there would be other boys and girls. Girl.

Paulette dabs at her eyes and laughs a little. "You must think I'm stupid."

Without prompting, Joanne sets an iced coffee on the table. Paulette gives her a grateful smile and takes a quick sip. The ice in my own glass has melted, leaving me with watery, beige-flavored fluid. "What I think is that Landry's an asshole."

"Sometimes, sure."

"And I think you deserve better."

"My mother says I'm a slut." She exhales heavily as she speaks, as if each word has tangible weight. "She says I got what I deserved for drinking."

In the park across the street, a pair of blackbirds fight over a hot-dog bun. Cars pass, idlers on foot. Here in the café, two guys in coveralls conspire over a chessboard. At the next table, a white-haired woman drinks hot tea and thumbs through a puzzle book. Beyond her, a young Latino couple discusses life insurance with a man who looks like he sells jewelry on TV.

"I didn't want to lie." Paulette lets out what sounds like a dying breath. "My mother said—"

"To hell with your mother. She should be looking out for you, not making excuses for a piece of shit like Landry."

I regret the words the instant they spill from my lips. Around us, the café goes quiet. Even if Paulette doesn't know these people personally, they may know her. She was on the homepage of the *Samuelton Ledger*, after all, with the golden boy of Barlow Consolidated High School.

"Paulette, listen. I shouldn't have—"

"It's okay. I understand." She edges forward on her seat. "The thing is, I don't want to be the girl you brought back from the crossroad." She wipes her eyes and shakes her head again. "I appreciate what you tried to do, but it's enough."

Aside from pulling her out of that truck bed, I haven't done anything. I wish Helene were here. She's so much better at this. "Paulette—"

"Please. You've done enough."

Helene used to say the reason most women don't report assaults is because it takes a bad situation and makes it worse. I never quite understood that, but Paulette's stricken face brings it home in ways Helene never could.

"Sure, okay." I still want to punch Landry in the dick.

Her ghost smile returns for a fleeting instant. "That's not why I wanted to talk to you anyway." She glances down at her hands, fingers tangled in knots on the table. I can't tell if she's still thinking about Landry or is chewing on some new trouble.

"What is it?"

"Probably nothing—"

A shadow falls across us from outside and we both turn. A half-familiar figure fills the window frame, and Paulette jumps to her feet, hip checking the table. Tepid iced coffee splashes onto the tabletop. "Sorry. I have to go."

"Paulette?"

With a jangle of bells and a sudden slam, she's out the door. I race to follow, but when I yank the door open, a fog of stale tobacco envelops me.

Quince Kinsrow looms before me. He does a double take, his eyes popping like a cartoon animal. "Mel! Just the lady I was looking—"

"Not now."

Paulette is dashing into the street. I try to push past Quince, but he fills the doorway, arms akimbo, a scarecrow posing as a bouncer. I'm left to watch helplessly as Paulette climbs into a familiar yellow pickup. Behind the wheel, Landry scowls, then punches the gas and peels away.

FOURTEEN

Roman Orator

I'd like to drown Quince in embalming fluid. Maybe I say so out loud.

"Calm down, Spooky." He elbows past me into the café, his bony arms sticking out like a pair of worn ax handles. His terra cotta face has a two-day growth of white, wiry whiskers and wrinkles as deep as the river gorges he likes to fish. "Nice shirt, by the way."

I roll my eyes. His shirt looks like a wad of filthy rags strung together with fishing line.

"Miss me?"

"Somehow I've managed."

That gets a chuckle out of him. He goes to the counter and orders a coffee, black. Joanne asks if he wants it iced, and he laughs again. It sounds like a joke they share, though I'm not sure what's so funny. When she hands him his steaming mug, he takes a noisy slurp, then sets it on the counter and turns to face the café.

"You'll never guess where I been all afternoon."

He may be talking to me, but he directs his words to the room. Sudoku lady purses her lips while the chess players and the insurance agent look on with amused expressions. They've all seen this show before.

Quince draws himself up, hand extended like a Roman orator. He speaks in the sonorous drawl I'd never heard until I came to the high desert. "I was just at the sheriff's. Can you believe Omar

Duniway pulled me over up on Shatter Hill? Since when do they speed-trap the Trout Rot Bridge is what I wanna know?"

When I came to Barlow, Quince "mentored" me—his word— by standing around for hours sharing mortuary horror stories while I cleaned gear or moved decedents. He's been with Bouton since before Uncle Rémy took over from his father, fifty years or more. Still, while he may be older than dirt, when he bothers to work, he can lift a body twice his own weight without breaking a sweat.

"Turns out it weren't no speed trap."

I look helplessly at Joanne, who gazes back with pointed indifference. She's witnessed enough of these little performances to know all you can do is ride it out. For all his ridiculous declaiming, Quince is always building up to something.

"The bastard was actually looking for *me*. Can you believe that?"

Outside, the black Excursion returns, headed back toward the highway. It must be picking up the dead boy. Nathan Harper has been in the hospital morgue for the last two days. Under normal circumstances, the hospital would release the body to us, and we'd hold it until disposition. Not this time.

"Turns out he wanted to know where I was Tuesday night."

Kendrick Pride, I assume, is leaving with Nathan—if he hasn't gone already. I wonder what's become of the bullet casings.

"Apparently, he wanted to make sure I wasn't doing a little freelance undertaking." That's worth a belly laugh. "But all I was undertaking was a determined effort to hook me a rainbow."

"So you're a leprechaun?"

He ignores me. "Crazy what happened, though." He throws his shoulders up in an exaggerated shrug. "But don't you worry, Spooky. This isn't the worst thing that ever happened at Bouton's, not by a long shot." He starts a story about a family feud boiling over at the funeral of some old Barlow patriarch. Gunfire in the Old Mortuary chapel, a brawl that spilled out the front doors and into the cemetery itself.

His piercing drawl is giving me a headache. "Quince, is there a point to all this?"

"Don't you wanna know the rest?"

"You didn't come here to discuss trout or tell some overblown yarn about a fight that never actually happened." Uncle Rémy hosted the funeral in question and told me the real story. Tensions were high, he admitted, but the brawl consisted of the estranged granddaughter of the deceased puking Boone's Farm into the casket, followed by her grandmother clocking her over the head with her walnut cane. Uncle calmed the frayed feelings of the bereaved and closed the casket. The funeral proceeded without further incident.

"Christ on a cracker. You know how to sting a man." When Quince's pout fails to move me, he adds, "In any event, when he finished with me, Omar mentioned he had some questions for you."

"Questions? What questions?"

"How should I know?" His face crumples into an expression somewhere between bafflement and mirth. "Why?"

His tone makes clear he knows why.

"What did you say to him?"

"Me?" He throws up his hands in mock innocence. "Why do you think I said anything?"

"You never stop talking."

"He wanted to know where you were is all."

"What does that mean? He knows where I was." Unless, for some reason, he doesn't believe me. Alarm bells sound in my head. "What did you say to him?"

The others in the café have grown rapt with attention. Even the old lady has quit pretending to work on her puzzles. In the sudden quiet, the fluorescents sound like a bone saw.

"Just that I saw the van up at the Old Mortuary when I drove by Wednesday sunup."

Jesus. I can only draw a ragged breath.

"Criminy, Mel. What?"

"You did *not* see the van." The Stiff was parked outside the back door at the New Mortuary—thirteen miles from Shatter Hill. "You must have seen the hearse."

"You think I don't the know the difference between the hearse and the van?" He blows air dismissively. "Do I gotta remind you who slung bodies before you showed up?"

No, Quince. You do not. I know who's the outsider here. Everyone is staring, this roomful of strangers. Of course they've heard—stolen bodies, the Bouton retort filled with ash. I'm sure the drama has been discussed and dissected many times over, rumor and innuendo stirred into fragmentary knowledge. Now Quince has dropped a salacious piece of misinformation into the overcooked stew.

"That Dulac girl was up at the Old Mortuary the whole time, right when the bodies were being cremated," I can imagine him saying.

Even Joanne, usually friendly if not exactly a friend, looks on with new misgiving.

"What was I *supposed* to do, Mel?"

"Try telling the truth for once, asshole."

I bang through the jangling door. Without pausing, I cross the street and pass under the trees. The park offers no refuge. The dry fountain is a looming reminder of Landry and his friends, of their jokes about the necrophiliac who sees ghosts. As if in confirmation of what everyone believes—that I'm crazy—Fitz's voice buzzes in my head.

"Melisende!"

I don't know where to go. Maybe I should walk straight into the chief deputy's office. Call Quince on his bullshit before it calcifies into settled fact in Duniway's head. But if I go barging in there full of fury, he'll give me the hysterical-girl treatment, maybe even arrest me on the spot. I glance in the direction of the Whistle Pig. Barb would help me think things through. But it's still early, even for a Friday.

"Mellie, look."

Off to my left, across the street, Duniway walks toward his SUV, parked in an angled space in front of the Barlow Building. He pauses when someone calls to him from the top of the steps. That side of the park has no trees. All Duniway has to do is turn around.

And then what?

"Just tell him Quince was mistaken."

"Like he'll believe me over the man he's known for a hundred years."

I circle behind the fountain, my shoulders hunched up around my ears. After darting between a couple of parked cars, I jaywalk to the far sidewalk. Looking back to see if I've been spotted, I manage to collide with someone rounding the corner.

"Oh, hi, Mel. I didn't see you."

I find myself faced with a half-familiar woman in scrubs.

"How are you?" she asks.

The nurse. From the maternity ward. "Oh, hi, Dan—" Wait. Not the maternity ward. The other sister. Morgue tech. "—Danae. Yeah, I'm okay." We're steps from the entrance of Dailie's Grille. Behind me, the chief deputy looms like a thunderhead.

"Say, you want to grab a drink?" My voice sounds shrill inside my head.

"Uh—"

"I've had a week and then some." I edge toward Dailie's Grille and attempt a grin that probably comes off as a grimace.

She looks like she'd rather go for a pap smear. I'd like to think my T-shirt wouldn't bother a morgue tech, but the talk around town might have. Or maybe she just has somewhere else to be—a husband, a girlfriend. Two kids and a dog. Spin class. Chinchillas. A sex dungeon—

"Good grief, little sister. Give her a chance."

Fucking Fitz, but damn if she doesn't smile and say, "Sure. That sounds nice." Next thing I know, we're ducking through swinging, saloon-style doors to temporary safety.

FIFTEEN

Dailie's Double

The main thing Dailie's Grille has going for it is no jackalope.

It's a place meant to appeal to the kind of people who arrive via the fifty-five-hundred-foot runway at the small airport between Crestview and Dryer Lake Resort. The interior is polished walnut and creamy plaster, with tasteful sketches of desert bunchgrass, boot spurs, or coils of rope in gilt frames. The piped-in music tends toward restrained string quartets or cool jazz. The bartender wears a bowtie and a black apron over his tuxedo shirt. The menu drips with folksy charm, offering appetizers like Pig Stickers or Hambone Hash, and entrées like Chucky's River Steak. If the names suggest ass-end-of-nowhere eccentricity, the prices are all big-city shakedown.

Barb says it's a good place to pick up well-heeled weekenders. The one time I joined her here, the most interesting thing I saw was Aaron Varney at the bar, drinking himself into a sack. Barb left with a Silicon Forest entrepreneur. I left with an empty wallet.

But today it's just what the doctor ordered. Danae and I are the only customers. As we slide into a deep booth, the bartender brings us ice water in tumblers heavy enough to serve as blunt objects.

"Welcome. My name is Chet." He places a sheaf of menu pages on the table. "Happy hour doesn't start for about twenty minutes, but for you two lovely ladies, what say we start the party early?"

Oh, brother.

"I'll have a double bourbon," I say. "Your cheapest red-eye is fine. It's medicinal."

Danae giggles. "Boy, sounds like you *did* have a week." She looks up at him, wide-eyed. "What the hell, Chet. Same for me."

"Very well." He nods stiffly, no doubt worried we're too cheap to leave a decent tip. "Will you be having dinner? Or may I interest you in a starter while you decide?"

I glance at the menu, but the old-timey Western text is hard to read. "Do you have sweet potato tots?"

"I'm afraid not." His fake frown would never fly at a Bouton funeral. "Perhaps I could interest you in our beer-battered Camp Fries."

I recall the limp shoestring potatoes, their crust flaking like eczema.

"No, thanks."

When Chet leaves, Danae's expression shifts from giggly girl to serious morgue tech. All I can do is meet her frank stare and wonder what happens next.

In the time I've worked at Bouton, we've crossed paths maybe twice a month. What I know about her would fit on a business card. Medical-surgical nurse who floats to the morgue. Thinks I'm very professional, according to her sister. She looks younger than Danica, thirty maybe, but shares her black hair and long, oval face. Red-framed glasses with oversized frames magnify her brown eyes.

"You know, I don't think we've ever really talked," she says, breaking an uncomfortable silence. "You've always been polite, but I never got the sense you wanted to be friends. And Lord knows the look on your face outside wasn't delight at running into your pal from the morgue."

"Danica told me—" The words tangle in my throat.

"My sister's a dear, but she's too naive for her own good." Danae leans forward, her hands clasped in front of her. "It must be one of two things. Either you want to know about the dead boy, or you're hiding. Given how fast you hustled me in here, the second option seems most likely." She cocks her head. "Am I your lookout?"

Somewhere deep inside me Fitz laughs.

"I'm sorry. I'll go."

I start to slide out of the booth, but she waves a dismissive hand. "Don't be silly. You got twelve bucks worth of bourbon coming. Might as well enjoy it."

"Twelve dollars. Jesus."

She laughs, a deeper, more natural sound than the giggle she used on the bartender. "This ain't the Whistle Pig, honey."

After a glance to confirm no one can see me from the entrance, I slump back in my seat.

Chet arrives with our drinks—caramel liquid satisfyingly deep in crystal lowball glasses.

"We'll need another round," Danae says before he can make his escape. Then she raises her glass. "Rest in peace, later rather than sooner."

She tosses back her whiskey like it's tap water. I can't taste my own. The bite is barely enough to let me know I've had something to drink, nothing like the alkali burn accompanying the solvent they serve at the Whistle Pig. I take another sip and, as a warm ball grows in my belly, surprise myself by finishing the glass.

"So I assume you're ducking Jeremy Chapman?"

And just like that, the soft warmth twists into an icy knot.

"Heard you two broke up." She laughs at the expression that must be on my face. "No secrets in Samuelton, sweetie."

I know she's right. Gossip is the local currency, more valuable than dollars or debit cards. In line at Cuppa Jo, at the Whistle Pig— when voices grow hushed, I have a pretty good idea they're talking about me. Probably the same everywhere, but I'm still not used to anyone caring what, how, or who I'm doing. Even more troubling is the realization that if people are talking about me and Jeremy, it won't be long before the chatter reaches Aunt Elodie and Uncle Rémy. To me, he was little more than a diversion, but they might not see it that way.

Chet returns with our second round. *Dailie's Doubles.* I peer into my glass as if escape can be found in the refraction of light through whiskey. Others have begun to come in. Some at tables, some at the bar—all speaking in hushed tones. Tourists. Chet seems to be working alone, his cheeks glistening with sweat as he takes orders and mixes drinks, delivers those deadweight tumblers of water.

"What do"—I let out a breath—"people say about me?"

She sits back, considering. "You're from back east. *Bahs*-ton, maybe. People think you're on the run, like you killed someone. An abusive boyfriend or husband maybe—some kind of burning-bed thing." Her eyes take on a laser focus. "But I don't think that's it. You're so steady, I doubt a mere killing would fluster you."

A sharp laugh pops out of me. Would she say that if she'd seen me the night I checked myself out of the hospital? My involuntary psych hold had expired, so I banged on the ward door and demanded to be set free. The graveyard-shift charge nurse made me sign a piece of paper with "AMA" in block letters in place of Discharge Instructions. *Against medical advice.* Outside, alone in the cold and dark, I collapsed, bawling, in the gutter until an old woman prodded me with her umbrella and threatened to call the police.

"If I'm so steady, why am I hiding in here?"

"Oh, the living are another matter." Her fingers drum the table. "Remember that fire in Wilton last December?"

I nod, thinking back. "Those kids and their grandmother." The mother and father had been out Christmas shopping. Near as could be determined, a spark from the open wood stove caught the Christmas tree. The first responders found the bodies in the front hall a few steps from the door.

"Fire and rescue guys blew chunks while you went in and collected the remains, coolheaded and respectful. You held your shit together."

That's not how I remember it. The only person who threw up was a boy from the fire science program at the community college, a first-year student. Everyone was outside when I lifted the grandmother's body and saw how she'd shielded the two children, safe from the flames but not from the smoke. A boy and a girl.

Oh, but I held my shit together.

"I don't remember seeing you there."

"I wasn't. But I heard all about it."

"Because people talk."

"They do indeed."

"They probably think I'm a freak."

She swirls her whiskey and sips, then looks over the rim of her glass. "Are you?"

I open my mouth but can't seem to form words. What would I say anyway? That, sure, I *am* a freak? That my parents were right for locking me up, that Rémy and Elodie made a mistake bringing me here?

That I'm the one who should have died in that Vermont lake when I was eight years old, not Fitz.

Me.

I swallow bourbon and then cough—the second glass unexpectedly caustic.

Worry lines gather on Danae's forehead. "You okay?"

I smile weakly. "Someone came for the boy today, didn't they?" Before she can call me out on the clumsy deflection, I add, "I saw the body transport vehicle." If she's heard about my suspension and Bouton's fleeing customers, she doesn't admit it. "I'm surprised it took so long to move him."

She taps her nails against the rim of her glass. "Well, we didn't release the body until this morning."

"Why not?"

"The sheriff ordered a complete forensic workup with labs, internal and external exams—the works."

"For a car wreck?"

"Exactly my thought. The last time we went whole hog was winter before last—but that was for an actual case. Some entitled brat dosed his mom and dad with Xanax and turned the gas on in their chalet up at the lake." She shakes her head. "The kid tried to claim abuse, but he stood to get a nice inheritance."

It never occurred to me to murder Cricket and Stedman. Maybe if their treatment had risen to the level of physical abuse—but in some dim way they recognized a measure of responsibility for me, not as their child so much as items on a to-do list. A new toothbrush at intervals, meals in the fridge: protein, starch, vegetable—two minutes in the microwave. Once, Cricket gave me a half-dozen pairs of white socks and a six-pack each of briefs and T-shirts. Boys'.

Come to think of it, maybe I should have killed them.

"That man from Portland hung around the morgue during the autopsy, asking questions I couldn't answer."

"Mr. Pride?"

She nods. "But when the autopsy ended, the sheriff blew out of there with samples for the state crime lab in Bend. Mr. Pride went after Dr. Varney then, bugging him about the boy's personal effects, when the autopsy report would be available, and so on. Got a little snippy, if you ask me." Nails on the glass again, *tink-tink-tink*. "Doc referred him to the district attorney and left."

I try to picture a snippy Kendrick Pride. Fail. "What do they think happened out there?"

"Wish I knew, but I didn't get to assist."

A quiet descends between us. In the lull, as if he was waiting for this moment, Chet slinks up and asks if we'd like the check.

"I think Chet wants rid of you, Mellie."

Danae smiles as if she heard Fitz, and nods Chet off. Chin resting on her laced fingers, she scans the room. Every table is in use now, the dull rumble of conversation all but drowning out Kenny G.

Then she sits up, eyes on the front of the restaurant. I twist to see, but she grasps my forearm. "Keep your head down."

"Jeremy?"

"You said it. Not me." A smile flickers across her lips. "I'll run interference so you can escape out the back. Okay?"

"You don't have to—"

"We're friends now, right?" I can't tell if she's being sarcastic. I shrink against the back of the booth. She pulls a twenty and a ten from her purse and drops them on the table.

She gestures toward the rear of the bar. "You know the way?" I nod, and with that she slips out of her seat and sashays off.

I match her cash, my last three tens, begrudging Chet the change. Later, I'll mourn the jumbo order of sweet potato tots and six Whistle Pig sangrias this sidetrack with Danae cost me. Panic whispers about safety in stillness, as if a cocoon of polished walnut, soft jazz, and dread can hide me.

I peek around the edge of the booth. Danae's at the host station, chatting up a bemused Jeremy. Though a head shorter, she manages to have greater presence. With a deft hand and a brash laugh, she turns him toward the saloon doors.

"Now!"

Shoulders hunched, I weave between tables to the wide passage leading past the restrooms. After a quick turn into an unlit corridor, I crash through the fire door to the parking lot.

Chief Deputy Omar Duniway is waiting.

SIXTEEN

Disturbing the Peace

"Why are you in a such hurry, Miss Dulac?"

Behind me, the door clicks shut. Duniway leans against his Tahoe, looking cool and relaxed in the evening swelter.

"Home?"

"Allow me to drive you." He steps away from the SUV and opens the back door.

A bead of sweat runs down my neck. He knew right where to find me and used Jeremy to herd me like a steer into a cattle chute. The parking area is a rectangle of asphalt surrounded by buildings and accessed via a narrow alley. The windows looking out on the lot are closed, most home to wheezing air conditioners. I'm boxed in.

"I just have a few questions, Miss Dulac." Duniway inspects me like I'm a crime scene. "But if you want to be difficult, I could place you under arrest." He pointedly looks at the oversized watch on his wrist. "It's after five. You won't see a judge till Monday morning."

"Jesus." The door is hot against my back, and a dull ache is forming behind my right eye. "Quince doesn't know what he's talking about."

One corner of his thin lips turns up. "If you've got something to say, get in. No need to make this unpleasant."

"It's already unpleasant." Would he really put me in jail? It's my word against Quince's. We should cancel each other out, but I know

it doesn't work that way. After what Duniway found in the crematory, I have all the credibility of a coyote with a mouthful of chicken
feathers.

"Could be worse. Per department policy, anyone we transport
is supposed to be handcuffed, but I see no need to be a stickler."
He raps the window of the open door. "I could change my mind,
though."

Feet heavy with dread, I plod over and climb in. The interior
smells of cigarettes and vomit. I leave one foot hanging out the door.
His fingers drum the doorframe. His hands are thin, with knobby
joints.

"You're not a very trusting soul, are you?"

"Not if I can help it."

He nudges the door against my knee. "Please." It's not a request.

Teeth clenched, I lift my leg, and he shuts me in. I reach for an
arm rest that isn't there. No interior door handle either. The mesh
screen mounted between the front and back seats vibrates when he
climbs behind the wheel. I press against the right side door.

He drives down the alley to Dryer Street and turns left, away
from the jail—a fact that should reassure me. He continues past the
hospital and a block later pulls into the driveway at the New Mortuary. The big Tahoe comes to a stop at the main entrance as if he's
a hearse awaiting the pallbearers. I glance through the glass doors.
Dark. Past business hours, with nothing on the evening schedule.
Even Wanda will be gone by now.

"See?" Duniway stares at my reflection in the rearview mirror.
"Home."

I can't tell if he knows about the nap casket or he's just being a
dick. Home is thirteen fucking miles away. But I left the Stiff over
by Cuppa Jo, so this is just as well. "Are you going to let me out?"

"You gonna answer some questions?"

I'm sure there's only one real question: *Why did you lie about where
you were Tuesday night?*

With the engine still running, the vents discharge cold, faintly
mildewed air. Ahead, across Sixth Street, looms the football stadium.
For the last couple of weeks, I've watched members of the football
team come and go in the afternoons. Some kind of conditioning, I
think. They arrive full of piss and come out an hour later sweaty and

limp. To my right, across Dryer Street, children dash around a small neighborhood playground. Their wilted mothers and fathers look on from benches shaded by drooping linden trees.

Duniway watches the kids for a minute, then turns to face me through the mesh. "What did Quince tell you?"

I don't want to answer, but even less do I want to stay in this puke-smelling truck. I meet Duniway's gray eyes through the mesh. "That he's a liar."

Duniway's face doesn't change. "Was that the exact word he used?"

Goddamn Quince. "He claimed he saw the Sti—the van up at the Old Mortuary around when the bodies would have been burning. But that's impossible. It was here in town. With me."

"Did he say anything else?"

"That wasn't enough?"

"Enough for what?"

I press my hands against the hard seat. "Jesus."

"We have your signed statement. Would you like to amend it?"

"Obviously not."

"He's messing with you, little sister."

I shiver, but whether from anxiety or because the goddamned air conditioning is set to liquid nitrogen I don't know. I look out at the sky, craving the heat on the other side of the glass. "May I go now?"

"First tell me when you last spoke with Kendrick Pride."

I don't say anything. The question seems almost nonsensical.

"Miss Dulac?"

Helene always advised against talking to cops without a lawyer. But Helene isn't sitting in the back of Duniway's Tahoe.

"Not since"—*we found the body,* I won't say—"Wednesday morning." I don't know why I can't acknowledge the dead boy. Maybe I don't want to remind Duniway of the bodies I lost—like he needs reminding.

"But you did speak to him then. Out at the crossroad?"

"I just said so, didn't I?"

"Did he tell you why he was in Samuelton?"

"Sure." I try to keep my tone neutral. I don't understand where this is going. "He's representing the family of the boy who died in the crash."

"Both boys' families, so he claimed." Duniway's emphasis on *claimed* is subtle, but unmistakable. "Have you spoken to him since Wednesday morning?"

"What did I just say?"

He gives me a flat gaze. "We can sit here all night, you know."

I count backward from ten, my eyes swinging from the stadium to the damned playground.

"Miss Dulac."

"Ms."

"*Mizz.*" He exhales. "I asked you a question."

"What do you want exactly? I've only spoken to the man a few times."

He pulls out a pack of cigarettes and shakes one into his mouth.

"Please, don't."

He gives me a look out of the corner of his eye. "You're one of those."

I don't know what I am. Helene used to smoke after sex; that never bothered me. But there's a lot of terrain between Omar Duniway and Helene Bouton. "Open the window at least." His jaw clenches, and it's almost like he's counting down himself. But rather than open the window, he pulls the cigarette out of his mouth.

"How about you describe your conversations with Mr. Pride."

"What's this about?"

"It's about my need to know what Mr. Pride said to you. Now answer the goddamn question."

I've never heard Duniway snap. Sheriff Turnbull may bluster. Jeremy will wheedle. Most of the other deputies can be overbearing dicks, but Duniway has always been an ice sculpture.

What's made him so fucking testy?

"There wasn't a lot to it. He's handling arrangements for the deceased."

"That's it?"

"He wondered why the boy—boys, I guess—drove here in the middle of the night." I could say more. About Pride collecting brass, for instance. But Duniway's manner keeps my mouth shut. I don't understand the fixation on Pride rather than Quince. I guess I should be glad he's not doing a bright lights and rubber hose routine on me. "Where were you the night of—?" But the fact he isn't only makes me suspicious.

In the playground, the reedy sound of a kid crying reminds me of the baby in the desert. Jeremy thought the boys intended to abandon the infant, but I don't buy that. In any event, Pride hasn't mentioned the baby, so I don't either.

"This afternoon," Duniway says at last, "I spoke with Trae Fowler's father. He and Kendrick Pride have known each other for years." He shakes his head, mulling. "Mr. Fowler admits he allowed Mr. Pride to handle things for him. The sort of thing a friend would do."

"So . . .?" I shift as the silence stretches. "There you have it."

"Right. There I have it." He raises the cigarette again, then gives me a sour look. "But why come here when he could make arrangements by fax or phone? It's not like he was gonna haul the kid back to Portland in the trunk of his car."

"Have you tried questioning *him*?"

He ignores my sarcasm. "He's not answering his phone."

"Maybe he went home."

"Perhaps." He shakes his head again as if he doesn't believe that. "Mr. Fowler also suggested he could be something of a nuisance to the local police."

"How so?"

Duniway doesn't answer. Waiting for my thoughts on the matter? I suppose I could tell him about the bullet casings, but that would only invite more questions I can't answer.

"Are we done?"

"You didn't, by chance, invite Mr. Pride to town, did you?"

A sudden metallic taste fills my mouth. "I never even *heard* of him before—" I swallow and press my tongue against the roof of my mouth.

Duniway's lips stretch into a thin smile, then he climbs out of the car. Welcome heat blasts me as he opens his door. He circles the Tahoe then, outside my door, lights his cigarette. After a couple of deep drags, he opens my door as well, and steps aside. I catch a face full of smoke as I climb out.

He offers me his business card. "If you think of anything, give me a call."

I accept the card—as if I don't have the department number saved in my phone—and flee before he can change his mind. As the engine revs, I slip inside the New Mortuary, latching the door behind me. The lobby is cold as a tomb and suffused with the scent of old flowers.

At first, all I do is breathe. I'm struck by unexpected relief that Duniway cared more about Pride than me—even as memory of his last question stirs the unease in my stomach. It had all seemed like an elaborate performance—the trap, the drive to the New Mortuary, the questions. But why? If he thought I would confess, I have news for him. Him and Quince both.

The lobby credenza draws my eye. We keep it clear except for flowers and, during events, a guest book or display in memoriam of the deceased. Now, a sheaf of pages lies on the polished wooden surface beside the vase.

Search Warrant and Seize Order
County of Barlow
State of Oregon

For probable cause shown and supported by the attached affidavit, sworn deputies of the Barlow County Sheriff's Department are hereby commanded to search the premises of the Bouton Funerary Service, Samuelton, Oregon, with particular attention to the areas assigned to and frequented by Melisende Dulac, including lockers or work areas where she would have a reasonable expectation of privacy, and to seize any and all effects belonging to or associated with the decedents Trae Fowler, Uriah Skeevis, and Tucker Gill. Officers are further commanded to search, test, and/or analyze these items and their contents for evidence relating to the crimes of Burglary I (ORS 164.225), Abuse of a Corpse I (ORS 166.087), and Abuse of a Corpse II (ORS 166.085).

So ordered by a judge whose name I don't recognize and stamped "Executed" with today's date and Chief Deputy Omar Duniway's signature.

SEVENTEEN

Lost and Found

There's been another death.

People are talking about it at the Whistle Pig when I stop in to score some overdue tots. About the time I was talking to Paulette this afternoon, a man opened his door and collapsed into the arms of a UPS driver. Heart attack, probable occlusion of the left coronary artery. The Widow Maker.

The body will be held in the hospital morgue until Swarthmore makes the pickup. For all I know, the fellow had preplanned with them, but it feels like another nail in the Bouton coffin.

"Good grief, Mellie. Have a drink."

The Whistle Pig is full of noise and earthy pigment, but there's no sign of Barb. In response to my quick text, she says, "Still grading. These kids couldn't find the derivative of a function if their parents hid it in their liquor cabinets." I place my order to go. I'm still a little mossy from Dailie's bourbon, but I order a sangria while I wait for my basket of deep-fried solace at one end of the bar. Too near, a troop of hikers—sunburnt dudebros crusted with dirt—drink and laugh at random strings of grunts and woofs—a cipher I don't understand.

Every time the cowbell on the door clanks, I expect Duniway, reconsidering jail, or Jeremy, making excuses for his part in the trap. Or Pride himself. For what, I can't begin to guess. Duniway had said it. Pride could have made the arrangements from Portland, with Wanda handling things at this end.

So why drive all the way out here? To collect bullet casings like empty returnables?

"You should find out, Mellie."

"Give me a break."

Notch, the bartender, plunks down my sangria. "Talking to ghosts, Mel?"

Thanks, Fitz. I try to laugh it off. "Just babbling to myself."

I can see by his expression it was the wrong thing to say. Notch has been brusque with me since the Landry thing. That I can handle, but this is my first visit to the Pig since the bodies found their way from the New Mortuary to the Old. I'm treading uncharted ground.

"Wait!" The shouted word hits me like a sonic boom. "Wait a frakking minute!"

Against my better judgment, I glance sideways.

"Are you *her*?" One of the hikers, shaggy and reeking of trail funk, eyeballs me. "Seriously, are you the chick who saw the Shatter Hill Spirit?"

I shake my head and hunker down over my sangria, my little glass cauldron of regret. Notch's lips curl into a nasty grin as the guy points with both hands. "She saw the goddamn Spirit!" His voice is a jubilant singsong, a kid who's discovered buried treasure in his backyard. "We're out there days and frakking *nights* and don't see *nothing*." His friends, bleary from beer or sunstroke, don't seem to care about me. One of them calls for another pitcher.

"You gotta tell us, man. Did you shit your pants?"

Notch's smirk is like a needle in my eye. "You shouldn't believe everything some dickhead bartender tells you."

Dudebro just laughs. "Prolly scarier for you. Ain't no one gonna confuse *us* for Molly Claire's Girls." Exuberant, he drapes an arm over my shoulders.

The touch is like an electric shock. "Hands off, asshole."

With another beery laugh, he starts to wrap me up. Electricity flares into heat. I twist free and push him, hard.

He stumbles back against one of his buddies. "Whoa, girl—" His friend lets out a bark and shoves Dudebro back hard enough to pinball me into a group of women crowding the bar.

I keep my feet and manage to catch one of the women before she falls, but her margarita soaks her blouse.

"Sorry. This guy—"

"Back off, bitch!" Her face—local, nameless but familiar—twists into a snarl as she throws a glancing punch into my chin. I fall against the dudebro, and his hands fly into the air like he touched a hot stove. "Whoa, *whoa*," he's saying. "I just want—"

Just wants, sure. Just wants to talk, just wants to know what I saw, to hear about the ghost. Just wants to grab me, to claim a share of my life. Like he's *owed*. Voices clamor all around. I wish it would all stop. But *no* is a word from a dead language. *Leave me alone*, mere gibberish. He and his buddies searched for the goddamn ghost for *days*. Came from Corvallis for some high desert color, don't you know. He'll buy me a beer. "Just tell me the story." His voice burrs like a swarm of yellow jackets. "You owe us that much." The woman calls me crazy, a lowlife, a skank. Everyone knows it. Someone says Landry's name, and then she punches me again. I pitch up against the bar.

"Who ya gonna call, Mel?" Notch's lips peel back from yellow teeth. "Ghostbusters?"

I want to throw cash on the bar and storm out, but I emptied my wallet at Dailie's. As voices crash around me in waves, I wait for Notch to run my debit card, skin burning at the touch of so many eyeballs. How long does it take the Barlow Telegraph to broadcast from one end of the county to the other? I already see faces bent over screens, thumbs probably tapping out the news. When Notch brings the slip at last, I scrawl "Fuck you, Asshole" on the tip line.

Halfway up Route 55, I realize I never got my tots.

～ ～

The sun is doing its slow mosey toward the shoulder of Lost Brother Butte when I reach the crossroad. Before I realize what I'm doing, I've pulled off next to the fire circle. I'm still riding the adrenalin crest from the Pig, and all I want to do is inhale the cooling desert air and let the tension bleed out of me.

Christ. I might have to find somewhere else to drink.

A semi going at least seventy rips past. The wind whack in its wake shakes the Stiff and leaves behind a gasp of diesel exhaust. Had he been the one to run up on Nathan, Trae, and the Cadillac, there'd have been no bodies to steal from the Bouton fridge—just bags of jelly and crushed bone.

If only.

Eyes on the outcrop, I try to imagine another life—one where Fitz lived and I died, and Cricket and Stedman somehow learned to live with it. The thought of oblivion is more appealing than their unassailable indifference. My hands clench the steering wheel. I've forgotten to breathe. My parents are three thousand miles away. I repeat it in my mind. *Three thousand miles . . . three thousand miles.* Shadows of sage and rabbitbrush lengthen across the desert floor, a canvas of buff and brown. A harsh, empty refuge.

Except it isn't empty. Something is there. An upright figure out beyond the place where Nathan Harper died. Vaguely human, wavering and uncertain.

I count backward from ten.

Pride?

In the two and a half days since we found Nathan Harper, he's had plenty of time to search the area.

"Maybe it's the ghost."

"It's not the ghost."

"Only one way to find out, little sis."

"I hate you."

"No, you don't."

Right now I do. But I get out of the Stiff, making sure the door doesn't slam. Whoever's out there—Pride, some stranger, or the Shatter Hill Spirit—I don't want them to know I'm coming.

Orange-fingered clouds reach through the deepening blue sky. Sun and shadow cast a confusing spell of light and dark. The diesel exhaust has given way to the scents of earth and sage. I follow the wheel tracks left by Fire and Rescue's gurney. The hollow where we found Nathan Harper is smaller than I remember. In the darkness after midnight, it must have seemed like a cavern to a boy who only wanted to hide.

It's too early for the moon. With twilight deepening, I've lost sight of the figure, unless it's somewhere still ahead. Distance in the desert is deceptive, especially at sunset. I look back toward the crossroad. The Stiff is a dark hump. No cars have passed since the semi.

I'm alone.

"You sure about that?"

Empty talk has filled my thoughts with phantoms. Head pounding, I rub my temples and look toward the hills rising toward Crestview. A glimmer flits between the dark trees.

"Definitely the ghost, Mellie."

I drop my hands. "It's not the fucking ghost."

A sudden shadow looms, and a breathy snort breaks behind me. My foot catches on a stone or root, toppling me onto my ass as a mule deer leaps out of the juniper. Before I can even suck in a breath, the thump of its hooves fades. I'm left gazing up at the first stars as my heart pounds in my chest.

"Jesus."

"You didn't see that thing coming? It was huge."

The sun drops behind Lost Brother Butte, darkness chasing after it.

"Go home, Melisende," I tell myself.

As the night's chill settles around me, I roll onto my hands and knees. In the dirt where I fell, there's a faint, metallic gleam. I scrape the soil, exposing a pendant on a silver chain. I get to my feet, letting it dangle from my fingers to catch what little light lingers after sunset. Then I wake my phone and tap the flashlight icon, illuminating an oval locket an inch wide and half again as tall. I brush away the clinging soil to reveal an ornate monogram engraved on one side.

K&S.

I trace the fine filigree with my fingertips, then, with a click, pop the locket open. Inside are two photos—formal shots of a white man and woman in their early twenties oriented to face each other across the hinge. The man seems familiar, but the woman, fair-haired and smiling, could be anyone.

I switch off the light. The pale figure in the trees is gone. If it was ever there.

"Which initial is hers, do you think? K or S? S or K?"

My headache has spread to the base of my skull. Fitz starts to chant in my head, a singsong earworm.

"K and S, sittin' in a tree, K-I-S-S-I-N-G"
And then it hits me.
K.
The man in the locket is young, almost boyish, but without a doubt—Kendrick Pride.

EIGHTEEN

The Shatter Hill Spirit

"Melisende. What a lovely sight to wake up to."

"You've got a strange idea of lovely, Uncle."

"I'm not so far gone I don't know a pretty woman when I see her."

The surprise must register on my face. He waves a bony, dismissive hand. "I know why I'm here."

"Your hip—"

"My hip, right." He scoffs. "The damn thing is better now than it's been in ten years." He taps his temple. "My noggin is what's gone catawampus."

"You're going to be fine." But my voice lacks conviction. The day has barely started and I'm ready to surrender.

I'd awakened with the magpies and hit the road before seven—before Aunt Elodie could intercept me. Last night when she came home from Crestview Assisted Living, the hollows under her eyes were so deep I didn't have the courage to mention the search warrant. Instead, I insisted she let me look after Uncle Rémy today.

"You could use the break, Aunt Elodie." She's been staying overnight there. While the overstuffed wing chair might be fine for cross-stitch, she doesn't look like she's slept well.

I think she was too tired to argue.

I arrived at Crestview Assisted Living as Uncle Rémy's breakfast tray was being delivered. Under the morning light from the window, his sharp gaze makes me feel guilty Aunt Elodie isn't here to see it.

After he eats, I set his tray on the counter near the door. "Do you want to walk now?"

"No, but I suppose I have to." With a groan, he swings his feet off the bed and into his slippers. At least he no longer has to contend with monitors or the IV.

"Let me help you, Uncle."

"I can help my own goddamn self." I flinch, and his expression softens. "I'm sorry, Melisende. I just . . ." I wait, but he doesn't finish the thought. Instead, he reaches for his walker and pulls himself to his feet. His lips draw back from his teeth, but he mutters, "I'm fine, I'm fine." He shuffles into the bathroom and closes the door. A few minutes later I hear a flush and running water. When the door opens, his face is red.

"Everything okay?"

"Christ, yes. Let's do this thing."

This *thing* is a full lap from one end of the floor to the other, part of his graduated walking program. He moves with grim determination, a firm grip on his walker. I keep pace beside him, watching his feet rise and fall in time with his breathing. As we pass the nurses station, he manages a wave and tight smile, but doesn't pause. At the end of the corridor, he taps the window looking out over the facility grounds and the forest beyond.

"Tag, I'm it."

The only sound is the chatter of the nurses. "They sure as hell jabber a lot around here, you notice?" As if she heard, the charge nurse emits a loud cackle.

"Have you been eavesdropping, Uncle Rémy?"

"What the hell else do I have to do?" His eyes twinkle. "They say you got in a ten-car pileup the other night, then you kicked a baby."

"Actually, it was two babies."

"That's my girl." He's quiet for a moment. "I'm guessing the tale has grown with the telling."

"A bit, yes."

"So." He raises one shaggy eyebrow. "Did you really see her?"

I think of the figure who led—or lured—me onto the desert last night. My fingers feel for the lump in my jeans, the locket. The most likely explanation is Pride lost it when he was out there poking around, except Pride doesn't seem like someone who's careless with personal keepsakes. Nathan Harper was the only other person out there, and he seems unlikely.

Unless it was the Spirit.

"I probably imagined the whole thing," I say to Uncle Rémy.

In the distance, a long, unbroken spine of stone peeks above the ponderosa forest surrounding the Crestview grounds. For the first time, I realize you can see Shatter Hill from here.

A faint wheeze, reminiscent of the injured rancher at the cross-road, pulls my eyes back inside. Uncle Rémy's eyes have gone glassy. I wonder if he's still with me or if his mind has drifted into the darkness he's increasingly inhabited since the surgery, if not before.

But then he draws a breath and blinks. It's like a light coming on.

"You know the story, don't you?"

"There's a story?" I say with a little smile. There's always a story, whether it's about the natural history of the high desert or some piece of Old Barlow lore. It's one of the things I cherish about Uncle Rémy.

"What makes this one interesting is, it's part of our family history."

I don't remind him I'm only a faux-Bouton, a hanger-on. "Don't you want to finish your walk?"

"Talking will help." He turns his walker and starts trudging back the way we came. I fall in beside him.

"It all happened on an Oregon Trail expedition led by my great-great-grandfather, Eugène de Bouton, in 1866."

"The one who built the Old Mortuary."

"The very same." His lips compress with an impatience I'm not used to seeing from Uncle Rémy. But it quickly passes. "At St. Joseph, the expedition was joined by an ill-tempered fellow named Silas Maguire and his young wife. The marriage, Eugène would learn, had been offered by the girl's father for the forgiveness of a debt. While the union had produced a pregnancy, the couple shared no affection. The child wasn't due till fall, but the poor girl fell into labor in July, not long after the expedition turned south short of The Dalles. They were taking an unusual route to allow a group to break off toward Canyon City, or else they never would have been near

Lost Brother Butte. As a period of unexpected rain set in, Eugène ordered they make camp near where the crossroad now lies. That night, Molly Claire Maguire delivered a stillborn boy."

A trill runs through me. Both the rape crew and those assholes at the Whistle Pig had mentioned "Molly Claire's Girls." From Landry's mouth, the phrase had been almost a threat.

Uncle Rémy doesn't seem to notice my reaction. "Silas blamed his grief-stricken wife for the death of his son and left the expedition in a fit of rage. Eugène had never cared for how Silas treated Molly Claire. Now, with her husband gone, he took it upon himself to comfort her, and she responded favorably to his attentions. Once she was able to get around on her own, she would even join him on walks through the wet grass—something they had time for since the party remained encamped to rest and wait out the rain before making the final push to the Santiam Wagon Road and the Willamette Valley. Soon the sky cleared and the wagon trail dried out. As the expedition made ready to set out, Silas Maguire returned. He'd lost his horse while crossing the Deschutes away to the south and intended to reclaim both his wife and his place in the expedition."

Uncle Rémy grimaces, and I reach out. But he just shakes his head, and I realize he's reacting to his story, not to the pain in his hip.

"Silas arrived after dark on the night of a full moon. In those days, the hill was called Ragged Top, owing to the way the grass grew between the fingers of basalt on the north rim. Molly Claire and Eugène had climbed up to walk on the moon-silvered tableland. According to family lore, Silas came upon them at the very moment Eugène professed his love for her. Some claim he saw them share their first kiss—arguably an apocryphal embellishment. What is certain is Silas shot Eugène in ambush. He then attempted to shoot his wife, but either the cartridge failed to fire or the cocking mechanism of his Colt seized up—accounts differ—and Molly Claire fled with Silas fast in pursuit."

We've reached the other end of the hall. He reaches out to tap the glass, but hesitates.

"Are you okay, Uncle?"

"Old as I am, this was still long before my time. And yet . . ." His voice trails off, and his eyes water.

I put my hand on his shoulder. "Let's go back to your room. You can finish the story some other time."

"I'm fine." He raps the window. "You're it."

Head down, he begins to retrace his path. I walk alongside, matching his short, labored strides. After a few steps, he takes a deep breath and lifts his chin.

"Down in camp, the others heard the gunshot and Silas shouting up above. Then they heard Molly Claire's scream. In the confused mingling of moonlight and shadow, she lost her footing among the basalt pillars and fell into the draw where the road now runs. At the sight of her shattered body, Silas fled back south, never to be seen again. Some say he suffered the same fate as his horse, though no one knows for sure."

Uncle Rémy stops. I listen to his heavy breathing and look up the hall, glad we're almost back to his room. I'm just about to suggest he take a rest on the seat of his walker, when he starts moving again.

"Uncle, are you sure—?"

He ignores me. "Eugène was hurt but alive. Unable to continue without its guide, the expedition made its way to The Dalles. Eugène recovered—though he would lose his leg at the knee to gangrene. For several years, Eugène searched for Silas, but in time he returned to Barlow County, where he became its first undertaker. Before migrating West, he'd been a carpenter and had made coffins for those who died during the journey. At first, he meant to establish his business at the spot where Molly Claire fell, but lack of water forced him to the current location further south, where a spring rose. Early on, hard rock mining camps south and east of Shatter Hill provided much of his business."

I'm surprised I haven't heard this story before. It explains why the Old Mortuary is so far from Samuelton, and suggests why the family never sold the place off after they opened the New Mortuary. Lucky for me. I like my room full of old furniture in the old house.

Back in his room, Rémy eases into one of the wing chairs and lets out a long, slow breath.

"How do you feel?"

"Like a hot turd on cold toast."

I take the other chair, worried he's overexerted himself. His head tilts to one side, and his rheumy gaze settles on me.

"A sad story, yes?"

I nod.

"Eugène would go on to have a family, of course. I wouldn't be here otherwise. But his devotion to Molly Claire's memory never faded. It's said he was the first to see her spirit at the crossroad, weeping for her dead child and her lost chance at love. Many reported seeing him after dark, walking the ridge line on his finely crafted wooden leg in the company of Molly Claire's spirit, though in a letter late in life he insisted the apparition was a myth. In any event, Ragged Top came to be known first as Molly Claire's Shattering, then simply Shatter Hill." Uncle Rémy's liver-spotted hands clench the hem of his sweater. "Some say she claims young girls, the spurned or the forlorn, to share in her grief. Others say if such girls stand in the crossroad and call for retribution against those who've wronged them, Molly Claire's specter will appear."

He falls silent. A haunted look darkens his face, and I wonder if he believes the old legend. "Have you . . . seen her, Uncle?" The instant I say the words, I feel stupid.

"Long ago . . . I used to . . . you know . . ." He seems to search for the memory. "Have I told you about my cabin?"

I smile. "You still owe me an overnight there." Because the cabin was accessible only via a steep trail, we'd put off plans to visit more than once. The closest we'd ever gotten was in April, around the first anniversary of my arrival in Barlow County. He'd pointed to a tree-covered ridge overlooking the hanging valley where we'd come to see wildflowers. "The old place is up there. You can see the whole Palmer River valley from the doorway." He wanted to climb up, but we'd already come as far as his hip would allow that day. The trek back to the car was almost too much for him.

"But I thought . . . we used to go when you were young."

My smile falters. Until fifteen months ago, I barely knew this man existed. When I was young, the only places I visited were my parents' shadows.

"Of course I took you to the cabin. You're misremembering."

My eyes grow damp. "I'm sure that's it, Uncle." I take his cold hand in my own. "Why don't you rest?"

He pulls away. "I'm fine." It takes him several struggling breaths to collect himself. "You were such an active girl."

From outside, I hear a grinding like a failing engine. I try to think of something to say, a way to laugh it off. I'm afraid anything I say will be wrong. He looks out at Shatter Hill for a long while, then his chin drops. "Why ask me?" he snaps. "Talk to your father."

Uncle Rémy has never met my father. He thinks I'm Helene. A hollow forms behind my heart. He's returned to wherever he goes when the shadows close in around his thoughts. I reach for his hand again, but he doesn't want to be touched. I know how he feels.

NINETEEN

Near Miss

Aunt Elodie arrives about noon. When they bring Uncle Rémy's lunch tray, I offer to run and pick something up for her and me.

"I ate at home." Her tone is flat, and her hands tremble as she fusses over Uncle Rémy.

I'm not sure if she hears me say goodbye.

Outside, the noon sun hits me like a hammer. The Stiff's door handle is almost too hot to touch, and the interior feels like a crematory. Leaving the door wide to release the heat, I take out my phone. The call goes straight to voicemail.

"Helene, hi. It's me, Melisende. Jesus, why do I always say that?" Saliva catches in my throat. "Listen, I get why you don't return my calls, and I won't ask you to now. But please call Aunt Elodie. I think she needs you." I hesitate, then add, "I hope you're okay."

Moments later as I nose onto Wayette Highway—destination unknown—a yellow pickup blasts around the tree-lined curve from the direction of Shatter Hill. I slam my brakes as the truck swerves, horn blaring, missing the Stiff's nose by the thickness of its waxed finish. Landry MacElroy glares from behind the wheel, Paulette Soucie beside him. In the space of a gasp, the vehicle is gone.

Nerves abuzz, I back off the road and throw the Stiff into park. The air conditioner whispers into the electric stillness inside the van, carrying with it the faint scent of decay. An afterimage of Paulette's face lingers like a reflection in the windshield. I couldn't tell if she was a passenger or a hostage. "Please. You've done enough," she'd said. A chill shudders through me. I reach for the center console, but the familiar climate controls only confuse me. Instead, I hit the button to lower my window. The hot, dry air clears my head until a sudden lethargy floods through me. I sag onto the steering wheel.

"Hey, you all right?"

With a start, I realize there's a man beside the Stiff, car keys in one hand and a cigarette in the other. He's wearing gray scrubs with a Crestview Assisted Living badge clipped to the collar that gives his name as Erlen. His hair is black and slicked back, his face tanned. A hint of dark stubble peppers his chin. Aviator sunglasses hide his eyes.

Erlen nods in the direction Landry went. "I don't think that guy even saw you."

"I almost didn't see him, so we're even." I attempt a chuckle but sound like I'm choking. Erlen takes off his sunglasses and looks me over. His unexpectedly pale eyes stop at my chest. I doubt he's reading my T-shirt.

"You okay, sweets?"

"I just need to catch my breath."

He gestures toward a shiny black 4Runner pulled up behind the Stiff. "I'll give you a ride if you're not up to driving."

"Seriously, I'm fine." I put the Stiff into gear, and Erlen gives up. More easily than most. In the rearview mirror, I watch him amble back to his car. I'm not quite ready to drive, but I don't have many options. Across the road is the full extent of Crestview's business district: the Downhill Motor Lodge, a seedy bar, a heli-ski operation—shuttered till winter—and the East Slope Mercantile.

Two thoughts hit me at once—the East Slope's surprisingly good wine selection and the fact that Barb lives only a few miles away in a cottage at Dryer Lake. Like me, she's an outsider, but she's been in Barlow longer and actually communes with the living. Maybe she knows something about Molly Claire and her girls, and why Landry thinks I'd make a good one.

"If anyone's spurned and forlorn, it's you."

"Fitz, just stop."

Depending on how her Friday went, Barb may still be asleep, but a bottle of wine should lure her out of bed. We can sit on her deck and talk about ghosts—and Duniway and the search warrant. Even if Barb doesn't know what to do, she'll have brash opinions.

I think I could use a little brash right now.

Behind me, Erlen honks. I shoot across the road and dart into the cool Mercantile before the sun fuses my shoes to the pavement. The wine section is like a sanctuary. As my nerves settle, I get lost in the handwritten descriptions on the shelf tags. Aromas of red berry fruits with a leather base note. Or plum, cherry, and cassis. Delicate florals.

"Who writes this stuff, Mellie?"

"People who've sampled way too much of the product."

Juicy, silky, lively—Old World spirit or New World energy from places with names out of a fairy tale: Calchaqui Valley, Roquefort la Bedoule, Lodi. I'm no more familiar with Argentina or Provence or even the California wine country than I am with the far side of the moon, but the words have a mysterious allure—imagined refuges for when Aunt Elodie decides the Melisende Experiment has run its course. Surely Argentina could use an apprentice undertaker.

"Having a hard time making a choice?"

There's a presence at my back, someone substantial, tall, and smelling of Irish Spring. I spin and find Kendrick Pride behind me.

"What luck, Mellie! You can give him his locket."

TWENTY

Downhill

"I apologize if I startled you, Ms. Dulac."

Today, Kendrick Pride is wearing khakis, a short-sleeved shirt with epaulets, and Rockport walking shoes. In lieu of plastic bags, he's carrying a legal-sized portfolio pad with a leatherette cover—the adult's Trapper Keeper.

"What are you doing here?"

"I saw you come in." He nods in the direction of the motel next door. "I'm staying nearby."

"Sorry to hear that."

The Downhill Motor Lodge's only plus is its proximity to the ski area. Last updated before I was born, the rooms feature carpet the color of vomit and walls held together by water stains. I had a removal there last November, a septuagenarian who stroked out on a sprung bed with a nineteen-year-old blonde on his lap.

Unbidden, I picture Pride in the same room—the only one with a clear sight line all the way to Lost Brother. The view rates an extra five dollars per night. Lost Brother Butte lacks the spectacle of Mount Hood or the Three Sisters, but in Barlow County it's what we've got.

"Can I buy you a coffee, Ms. Dulac?"

"The cops are looking for you."

His expression doesn't change. "I wasn't aware."

"Maybe if you answered your phone."

"Cell service is spotty out here." He raises one eyebrow. "Did you call?"

"Not me. Chief Deputy Duniway."

"I'm sure he'll find me if it's important." His eyebrow drops. "What do you say about that coffee? They have tables with a view of the mountain over there."

"What do you want, Mr. Pride?" He may be avoiding the county cops, but I'm starting to understand what Duniway meant when he said Pride could be a nuisance.

"Just to discuss a couple of things. I promise I won't keep you long."

He's not the type to give up, and sometimes saying yes is easier than saying no. Between the Mercantile's iffy coffee and my own one-word responses to his questions, maybe he'll lose interest. Go back to Portland. Leave me in peace.

Helene would have a few choice words about the chances of *that* happening.

He asks what I'd like, then suggests I find a table. Feeling contrary, I pick a spot looking out on the parking lot.

"You gonna give him his locket, little sister?"

I consider the search warrant and Duniway's hinted suspicions about Pride. "I haven't decided." If I give him the locket, he'll want to know where I found it. Describing the bubbling soup of suspicion and possible hallucination that drew me into the desert isn't an option. But even if I lie—even if he *believes* me—

I shake my head. He won't believe me.

"Don't you want to know how it got there?"

The answer would probably be boring. Hole in his pocket. Slipped clasp. Flung away in a rage. I could just have Wanda mail it back to him.

Still, I slip the locket out of my jeans and let it slide through my fingers onto the seat between my legs. Keeping my options open, I guess.

Pride appears with an iced latte for me and a coffee regular in a chipped mug for himself. My latte is grainy and weak—typical for the East Slope. I don't even bother feeling disappointed. He drops a couple of napkins on the table between us and sits, sliding the portfolio off to the side. He doesn't mention the view.

"How long were you behind me?" I say before he can speak.

"I'd just walked up." A wisp of a smile steals across his face. "I do it too," he adds, "talk to myself. I'm just thinking out loud, but it helps if I imagine I'm conversing with someone else."

I wonder who else is aware of these little chats I have with Fitz. Sheriff Turnbull did my background check, but I don't think he learned the specifics of my psych hold. If anyone at the mortuary has heard me prattling away, they haven't mentioned it. Carrie sings country ballads as she embalms.

Pride lifts his cup but doesn't drink. "For me, it's John Lennon."

The name reminds me of my grandmother. During my too-rare visits to her little apartment in a continuing care community in Framingham, not so different from Crestview Assisted Living, she liked to play her vinyl records. "He was a Beatle."

"*The* Beatle, one might say." He manages to laugh without changing expression. "I still remember when he died. That was before you were born."

Along with most of human history.

"I was just a little kid, but I'll never forget the first time I heard 'A Day in the Life' on the radio. Do you know it?"

"I saw the news, something, something," I say tunelessly. A napkin finds its way into my hand. I start mopping condensation off the sides of my glass.

"Close enough." His lips curl. "Anyway, when the song ended, the DJ said he would be playing the Beatles all day in memory of John Lennon, who'd been shot the night before."

I'm not sure what to say.

"Talking to John Lennon has become my way of organizing my thoughts."

A heavy silence falls between us. My fingers twist the damp napkin into shreds. My eyes steal around the Mercantile. Cleaning supplies in one direction, wine in the other. Fishing tackle in the middle. You can buy groceries, or camping gear and ammo. Rent DVDs or skis. Fill out a wilderness permit so the rangers know where to look for your body. Today's lunch special at the deli is a meatloaf sandwich with your choice of fries, whipped potatoes, or coleslaw. The soup of the day is tomato, probably from a giant can. Tastes good, though. Better than the coffee.

"I talk to my brother," I finally say, and shrug again. "He's dead too."

"I'm sorry."

"It was a long time ago."

"Still."

I nod. *Still.*

"May I ask what happened?" Before I can decide what to say, he shakes his head. "Forgive me. It's none of my business."

"It was a long time ago," I say again, my voice at the threshold of sound.

I realize, too late, what that sounds like. With a throwaway line, I've dismissed Fitz as old news. His memory is a pressure at the base of my throat. I want to apologize, but I doubt Pride will be so understanding of the voice in my head if I start talking to it right here in front of him.

"Maybe you should change the subject," Fitz seems to whisper. He deserves better of me.

I toss the wad of shredded napkin into my half-empty glass. "What did you want to talk about, Mr. Pride?"

"The accident."

"I didn't see the accident."

"I understand that. But could you describe what you did see?"

"Haven't you read the crash report?"

"It hasn't been made public." He shakes his head. "The investigation is ongoing."

I wonder if he knows the sheriff ordered a full forensic workup on Nathan Harper, not just an external exam. If not, I won't be the one who blabs. Not that I feel obligated to keep the sheriff's secrets, but he and Duniway don't need another reason to get up in my shit.

"Whatever you can remember," Pride says, "would be a great help."

With what, exactly? But I go ahead and describe the scene, sticking to details I saw in the *Ledger.* Two cars in pieces and the pickup burned out on its side. I read they had to put the horse down.

Pride bows his head. "I understand the survivor died last night."

"I hadn't heard." He must be another Swarthmore client. A part of me feels guilty that I'm more concerned about who's handling his funeral arrangements than the fact that he's dead.

116 | W. H. Cameron

"Did you know him?"

I rub my eyes. "Mr. Pride, fifteen thousand people live in Barlow County."

A faint bloom appears in his cheeks. "I just thought—someone in your position must meet more than the average number of—"

"Dead, Mr. Pride. The people I meet are dead." That's not strictly true. Someone has to answer the door—survivors usually, in various stages of grief. I've encountered screamers, gigglers, quiet weepers, and stoics as expressionless as Pride himself. Whatever their state, making friends with the undertaker's apprentice isn't high on anyone's list.

"Of course." He sips coffee. "I don't suppose he said anything at the scene. Maybe something about how the wreck happened?"

My mind flashes to the bloody gash on Zachariah Urban's forehead, to his rattling cough and his plaintive, "Did you see her?" as his head lolled in the direction of the pale figure on the desert.

"I think he had other things on his mind."

"I understand." His eyes lose focus as if he's thinking. "You said there were lots of parties at the crossroad. Are we talking high school parties?"

Rapist shitbag parties. "Yeah," I say through my teeth. "Mostly."

"Because of the Spirit?"

I could be sipping wine with Barb by now. "Because of the isolation and easy escape, more likely."

"People say you saw the ghost."

"People say a lot of things."

Outside, a guy with a Santa Claus beard comes out of the dive bar that shares a parking lot with the motel and the Mercantile. He straps a thirty-pack of Busch to the back of his motorcycle. The bike's exhaust pipe sounds like gunfire as he heads toward Dryer Lake. Even a crap beer would be welcome at the lake on a hot day like this. I watch until he disappears, wishing I hadn't agreed to this conversation. Wishing I'd locked the New Mortuary door the other night. Wishing I'd taken Uncle Rémy's money and run, or never gotten involved with Geoffrey. Or fucked things up with Helene.

As the proverb says, if wishes were horses we'd drown in manure.

"Were any kids out there that night? Besides Trae and Nathan, I mean."

"Christ, you're unrelenting." I yank the napkin out of my glass and drop it, sopping, on the table. I don't drink, though. The translucent liquid has a sickly blue hue.

He swallows, and for the first time he seems unsure of himself. "I've been trying to find anyone the boys might have known around here. I even asked at the schools, for all the good that did me."

"Well, they sure as shit didn't know me."

"Of course not." He put his hand on the leatherette portfolio. "Just one more thing, if I may."

Like I could stop him. Fitz whispers, *"Locket"* as Pride opens the portfolio. Inside is a hand-drawn diagram of the crash site, with rectangles for the wrecked cars and dotted lines to indicate their likely positions when all hell broke loose.

"I worked this out from the skid and yaw marks at the crossroad," he says. "I believe Trae's car turned from Wayette Highway onto Route 55, westbound, then stopped. The Cadillac was in front of them, at an angle across both lanes, blocking the way. Does this look correct?"

"Everything was already in pieces by the time I got there."

He doesn't seem to hear. "The pickup driver must have been going very fast. He tried to swerve, too late, and rammed the Cadillac into the Subaru, then spun out and rolled. The Subaru was thrown from Route 55 into the ditch on the Shatter Hill side of the highway, and the Cadillac ended up to the left, at the opposite corner of the intersection."

"Sounds about right."

His lips pinch. "We found Nathan more than a hundred yards away. One of the men and Trae were out of their cars too. Why?"

"I don't know."

"And what about the baby? Where did she come from?"

I don't know.

He stares at the diagram, then uses a pen from his jacket to point out two lines running across the intersection. "These are the Cadillac's tire marks." He taps. "The Subaru's are here, and this third set show how the horse trailer fishtailed before it detached and rolled into the desert. Lot of speed there."

"NASCAR fast," according to Fitz.

"There's one more thing," Pride says.

Isn't there always?

"Another set of tire marks." He sketches two lines running perpendicular to the Subaru's skid marks and crossing over them. "They're fresh, darker than the others." He makes a little *hmm* sound.

"They aren't mine."

"I didn't think so. They're not from a braking skid. I'd say they're from a rapid start."

He studies the diagram as if he can divine hidden truth by going over it again and again.

"You think another car was involved?" I say, curious in spite of myself.

"Involved? Or a witness? Impossible to say without more information." He looks up. "If another vehicle *was* present, it couldn't have been badly damaged."

"How sure are you?"

"I'm no expert in collision analysis, if that's what you're asking."

His tone tells me he's pretty damn sure.

"Have you told the sheriff?"

But I know the answer even before he shakes his head no. *Spotty cell service.* Wednesday morning at the crossroad comes to mind, when I asked if he trusted the cops. They struck him as competent.

Competent isn't the same thing as trustworthy.

Pride rests his elbows on the table and steeples his hands. "Is there anything else you can tell me?" His eyes drop onto me like falling stones. "Anything?"

A couple at the deli counter is asking about vegan options for their sandwiches. An electronic tone sounds at the entrance as someone else exits. I wish it were me.

"What are you afraid of, little sister?"

Maybe I'm sick of having to explain myself. Pride has buried me with questions, and the locket will only raise more: "Where did you find it? What exactly were you doing out there again? How did you spot it?"

"Did the Spirit guide you?"

Reluctant, I reach between my legs for the locket.

"Just give it to him, Mellie."

The fine chain is cold in my fingers. I take a deep breath, exhale. "I found something of yours."

Pride raises a quizzical eyebrow. "Of mine?"

"I think so. In the desert near the crossroad." I raise my hand, allowing the locket to dangle from its chain. The oval pendant spins as I lower it to the tabletop, well clear of my coffee-soaked napkin. The engraved letters catch a gleam of sunlight through the window.

K&S.

The color drains from Pride's face. Hesitant, almost as if he doesn't believe it's real, he touches the locket with the tip of one finger. Then, abruptly, he sweeps it up along with the portfolio.

"Please excuse me."

His chair scrapes as he pushes away from the table. An instant later the door tone sounds. Just like that, he's gone.

TWENTY-ONE

Solve for X

When she's home, Barb knits. It's a quiet, almost unthinking act. Just the faint tick of the needles or the hushed glide of yarn from the bag at her side. She never loses the thread of the conversation, never passes up the chance for a sharp retort. And she never misses a stitch.

Her current project is gathered in her lap. Something delicate, knitted with fine, emerald wool.

"What are you making?"

I've been speed-talking my way through the last twenty-four hours. Quince and Duniway, Jeremy herding me at Dailie's, the search warrant, Pride's belief there was another car at the crossroad, and his abrupt exit after I brought out the locket. To my disappointment, Barb has never heard of Molly Claire's Girls—she didn't even know the Spirit had a name. She was more interested in how Notch reacted to my tip.

When I ask about her knitting, Barb's eyes don't stray from her needles. "It's something pretty."

"I figured that much."

"It's for you."

We're sitting in the Adirondack chairs on her deck, surrounded by potted tomatoes and peppers. I grab my wine glass from the table between us. "What makes you think I need something pretty?"

"Oh, honey." Now she looks up. "Because you think you don't."

It sounds like something Helene would say. Nearby, a gray jay screeches in the currant hedge screening Barb's cottage from her neighbor's. A breeze carries the scent of water from the lake, a fifteen-minute stroll downhill through xeriscaped plots surrounding log houses, stone cottages, and A-frame chalets. Sailboats dot the blue expanse beyond, and fishing boats bob up near the dam. On the far shore, the unexpected green of the golf course shimmers, too far to see if anyone has braved the day's heat to play. In the distance, a private jet descends toward us, on final approach for the airport. Aliens arriving from another world.

"I just think you should treat yourself sometimes," Barb continues. "You can't spend your life draped in mortuary quips."

I cross my arms over the "You'd Look Better Embalmed" printed across my chest. "It's not all mortuary quips."

"Let me guess. You've got one that says 'Girl Raised by Wolves.'"

"Wolves would have been an improvement." I've never discussed my parents with Barb, and for a second I worry she'll start asking questions. But she just shrugs.

"Thank god you have a sad tale of childhood woe like everyone else."

"*Your* mom is great." Barb once let slip that her mother was why she could afford to live at Dryer Lake on an instructor's income.

"My *mother*, sure." She leaves that floating there like a turd in a punchbowl. I don't ask. "My point is you're allowed to look pretty."

"Who am I supposed to impress?"

"No one but yourself, sweetie."

"I'm impressed by my 'I Put the FUN in Funeral' tee."

She goes back to knitting. "You're impossible." I watch the jay hop from stem to stem in the hedge. The closest I've ever come to calling somewhere home has been here in the Oregon high desert. I have a place to sleep and a closet to store my droll undertaker wear. But for how much longer? If Uncle Rémy was well, I might weather whatever Duniway throws my way. Keep my head down, focus on the work. Learn from Carrie and Wanda and Aunt Elodie. Grow up to be a real mortician.

"Every little girl's dream, right?"

Why not?

But with Rémy fading and Elodie seemingly following him into the dark, I feel adrift. I wish the bodies were still missing. Then, at least, Duniway would have a mystery to solve. As it stands, the bodies disappeared on my watch and reappeared in a spot I had ready access to. For him, the question isn't who stole them, but how to tie me to the theft. He must have enough circumstantial evidence to arrest me. That he hasn't suggests he hopes to find something more damning.

"Maybe you should talk to your lawyer, little sister."

"I don't have a lawyer."

"What's that?" Barb says.

"Sorry. Just thinking out loud."

She lowers the needles. "It's worth considering—a consultation, anyway."

"I guess it would be handy to know how many years I'll get for Abuse of a Corpse, One and Two."

"I thought there were three corpses."

I give her a look. How much would a lawyer cost? Most of Uncle Rémy's gift is still in my savings account. I'm careful to budget my sangria and sweet potato tots from my modest Bouton earnings and have tapped into savings only to pay tuition for my prerequisites. What's left will just about cover the two-year program when it starts in the fall. Assuming I'm still here.

"What I don't get is why Duniway thinks I'd have any interest in the remains of those three strangers anyway."

"Should I drag out my whiteboard? We can do a brainstorming montage like a TV legal drama."

Whiteboarding makes me think of Helene. That had been her way of breaking down problems in the old days, pre-Geoffrey. Colored markers, circles linking circles, goals and dependencies. For her, it was all about activism. Setting up a counterprotest at the women's health clinic, confronting the administration about campus sexual assault. Her personal life—aside from me—never seemed to spin out of control. Now that I think about it, I may have been one of her whiteboard projects. We'd met when she walked me out of an off-campus party.

"That asshole put something in your drink," she'd said. I didn't know who she was, but I liked her immediately. She took me back to my place and held my hair while I threw up, then put me to bed. The next day, when I awoke, she was still there. I thought she had the melancholy gray eyes of a French film star.

I lift the wine bottle. "We're almost empty."

"No points for the clumsy attempt at changing the subject."

"I just don't know what to do."

"With my students, one of the first things I teach is to iden-tify what you already know and work from there. Solving for x has to start somewhere. So what do you know? Three bodies from the crash—"

"Four, actually."

"That kid in the desert. Right. And Kendrick Pride. He's a vari-able. Tell me about him."

"He's the only man in a hundred miles who doesn't own a cow-boy hat."

"Do you want detention?"

I add a splash of wine to my glass. "He collects evidence like a TV cop."

"Maybe he is."

"A cop? Seems like he would have mentioned it."

"Unless he's undercover. Did you ask him if he was a cop?"

"No."

"You should ask him."

"And if he says no?"

"He has to tell you if you ask him. It's a rule."

"I'm pretty sure that's not true."

"It should be." She sips from her own glass. "Google him, then."

"What would that tell me?"

She shakes her head. "Sometimes I think H. G. Wells brought you here, not Amtrak. Give me your phone."

I thumb the home button to unlock it and hand it over. She taps the screen, still shaking her head. "Why don't you have any apps?"

"I've got apps."

"Just the preloaded ones. Where's Candy Crush? Where's Toon Blast?"

"Those are games, right?"

"Jesus. Whose grandmother are you?"

It never would have occurred to Cricket and Stedman to buy me a cell phone growing up, but *my* grandmother gave me one and added me to her plan as a graduation present. By then I was already a decade behind everyone else. I didn't stream video or use social media.

Helene used to flip out when I ignored her texts, but I honestly hadn't noticed. My first Christmas in Barlow, Aunt Elodie and Uncle Rémy upgraded me to a smartphone, but the only app I've bought is an anatomy and physiology reference. Until recently, I thought Angry Birds were the ones fighting over dead boys in the desert.

"Well, there you go," Barb says after a moment. "Your problems are solved."

"What? Why?"

"He's an attorney." Eyes on the screen, her thumb sweeps up every couple of seconds.

"That actually makes sense."

"Family law, according to his website."

"He has a website?"

"His firm does. He's a partner."

"Let me see."

She hands me the phone. On screen is an About Us page for "Anders, Harper, Milton, & Pride, Attorneys-at-Law." Sure enough, there's an image of Kendrick Pride, fourth in the list of partners and ahead of a dozen or so associates, paralegals, and staff. His bio is remarkable only for how bland it is. Graduate of the University of Oregon and Willamette University College of Law. Husband, father. In his spare time, a youth soccer coach.

"Maybe I should hire him." I return the phone to Barb.

"He's the wrong kind of lawyer." She taps a bit more. "Sits on the boards of several foundations. Member of some church. Blah blah blah. You need a high-powered defense attorney—or maybe the consigliere for a mob boss."

I stick my tongue out, then finish my wine. It's had no effect on me. The gray jay, perhaps realizing we have nothing worth stealing, flies away over the house.

"If he's got skeletons, they're not the kind I can find in two minutes with a cell phone." She shrugs. "The family lawyer thing at least fits with his claim about working for the dead kid's parents."

"Yeah." Though it doesn't explain him collecting bullet casings like he's investigating a crime. Good thing, I guess, since otherwise, we wouldn't have been loitering at the crossroad at the right moment to spot the carrion birds fighting over a boy's remains.

With that thought, a vague feeling of recognition tugs at me. "What did you say the name of the law firm was?"

Barb looks at the phone. "Anders, Harper, Milton, and Pride."

"Nathan Harper."

She taps. "No, it's Howard Harper."

"Nathan Harper is the dead boy we found."

"Oh?" One eyebrow arches. "But when Pride came into the Whistle Pig—"

"He was there for Trae Fowler."

"Then the next day you find a second dead kid who is what? His law partner's son?"

I gaze into the empty air between us. "I suppose."

"Be a hell of a coincidence otherwise." Her eyes gleam as she works the phone again, tapping and humming. "Here you go—a Facebook page for a Nathan Harper from Gresham."

"Is that near Portland?"

"Suburb." She studies the screen. "A lot of his info is set to private, but you can see his profile pic. Looks about the right age." She holds out the phone. "Is that him?"

The muddy snapshot shows a boy in what looks like a family room, laughing and flipping off the photographer. Late teens, with short brown hair and a wide jaw. "Might be. By the time I saw him, he'd been dead half a day and gnawed on by vultures."

"Gross." She goes back to tapping the screen. "He doesn't mind us knowing his favorite movies are the *Fast and Furious* series and that he goes to Centennial High School. But his feed is private and so's his friends list." She shakes her head. "How did Kendrick Pride react to the body?"

I picture the juniper, the basalt outcropping, the vultures taking flight.

"He wasn't surprised." I remember Pride crouching, chin in hand. "I wonder if he expected to find him."

Barb hands me my phone. "When solving for *x*, start with what you know." Her knitting needles begin to click.

What I know isn't much.

Kendrick Pride is a family lawyer who gathers evidence like a cop. He'll talk to John Lennon, but not Omar Duniway. He's cautious, volunteering almost nothing, including his likely connection to Nathan Harper's father. Only the locket seemed to rattle him.

But why? And why is he still here?

Nathan's body left yesterday. Trae is ash and scorched bone, undifferentiated from the other two men from the crossroad. By Pride's own account, no one here knew either of those two boys. If he wants to learn why they came to Barlow, he'd have better luck talking to their friends back home.

Could he be looking for something else?

I think about his self-possession as we came upon Nathan's body, then the white figure I saw near the same spot. An image of the Cadillac driver's disembodied head chases the ghost away. Those boys weren't alone at the crossroad.

My phone still displays Nathan Harper's grinning face. He remains a cipher. But there are other names to search—names I bet Pride has already investigated.

Maybe I *should* hire him.

The front doorbell sounds. "Expecting someone?"

Barb lowers her needles. "Probably the deranged scold from the home owners association who likes to bitch about my petunia baskets." She tips the last few pathetic drops from the bottle into her wine glass. "She thinks they're too leggy."

"Sounds like I should have brought two bottles."

"Two bottles of what?"

I flinch and my phone clatters onto the deck between my feet. Barb and I spin in our chairs.

"I rang the bell," Jeremy says from the corner of the house. "But no one answered."

TWENTY-TWO

Skip the Coffee

"You're driving around looking for me now?" Not that Jeremy would need to check many spots. Old Mortuary and New, Whistle Pig. The possibilities taper off pretty damn fast after that.

He closes his eyes, and I wonder if he's counting backward from ten like I do. But when his lids rise, he doesn't look angry. "I know you're avoiding me," he says, "but we really need to talk."

Barb and I exchange a look. "I'll go low and you go high," her eyebrow semaphore seems to say. Tempting, but as long as I'm part of Bouton Funerary Service—however long that lasts now—I'll have to face him sooner or later.

"It's okay, Barb."

She glares until his chin drops. "Fine. I'll be inside binging *Orange Is the New Black*." She tucks her yarn bag and knitting in one arm and the wineglasses and bottle in the other. An instant later, the sliding door shuts with a pneumatic whoosh.

Jeremy is dressed for work in gray and green. Uniforms do nothing for me, but when he climbs the steps onto the deck, the play of dappled sunlight on his face reminds me why I was first attracted to him. Hard to believe it's been less than two months since we met at the site of a single-car crash on Route 55 outside Antiko. A driver had lost control and slammed into the concrete footing of a billboard. No seat belt. His two daughters, strapped into booster seats in back, survived. Jeremy was comforting them in the ambulance when I arrived in the Stiff to take their father away.

Later that day, I saw him again at the Whistle Pig, eating alone. He looked at me then like he does now, sad and lonely. I suppose his melancholy attracted me. I joined him and ate tots while he talked about the injured and dead he'd pulled from other mangled vehicles. His voice was quiet and soothing, and his dark eyes never left my own. Fitz stayed quiet. A few hours later, we went to Jeremy's apartment in a rundown complex south of the highway. I silenced his apology about the mess by helping him add to it.

That was then.

"Not here." This space belongs to Barb and—in a small way—me. Before he can argue, I grab my phone and dart off the deck. He follows me around the house to the front, where I find his patrol car parked nose-to-nose with the Stiff at the end of the driveway. I lean against the van's passenger door, in full view of the house.

"Okay," I say when he catches up. "I'm listening."

He glances at the nearby houses, only partly hidden by trees. "We could go somewhere private. I've got some time until my shift starts."

A shadow moves in the window behind the hanging petunias. Barb standing sentry. "This is fine." At least he's guaranteed me an out: start of shift, the girl escapes.

He nods, resigned. He seems to be chewing on his thoughts.

"The other night," he says at last, "after I dropped her friends off, I tried talking to Paulette."

A band tightens around my heart. Jeremy continues, oblivious.

"I told her it wasn't too late to do something about Landry. We have a witness, after all." He nods at me, as if I need reminding who he means. "I tried to let her know people had her back."

I swallow a bitter laugh. Sheriff Turnbull claimed it was all just a misunderstanding. Paulette's mother called her a slut. No one who matters has her back. .

I force myself to look at him. "So what did she say?"

"Nothing." He laughs without humor. "She got out of the car and went into her house."

After what she said at Cuppa Jo, I'm not surprised. The desire to call Helene swells in my chest. To listen as the distant ringing goes unanswered. Leave a message after the tone. *Hey, it's me. I've made a real mess of things here. I tried to be you, but only you can be you. I hope you're—*

"—okay."

Somewhere, Fitz snorts. I didn't realize I'd spoken aloud.

A crease appears between Jeremy's eyebrows. "That's it? Just . . . *okay?*" He begins to pace side to side, his gear belt squeaking. "I'm not a magician, Mel. I just don't know what you want."

I want to believe he spoke with Paulette out of a desire for justice. But he seems more worried about what I think.

"Thanks for trying." I push off the van, ready to be anywhere else.

"Damn it, Mel. Wait."

Nearby, the gray jay shrieks.

A war rages behind Jeremy's dark eyes, hurt and frustration fighting against—I don't know. Whatever he thinks he feels for me? I don't want to know. He inhales, exhales. Inhales again. Then he tilts his head back and I contract, worried he's going to start shouting. Instead, he gazes into the sky.

When he speaks at last, Jeremy's voice is soft. "Do you ever wonder what they see in this place?"

For a long moment, the only sound is the whisper of hot air through the pines.

"Who?"

"Them." He points up at a small jet making its approach, the second one today. "They fly in from all over. For this?"

He gestures at the chalets and cottages on the slope below us, at Dryer Lake and the country club on the far shore.

"Maybe they like the isolation."

"I guess." He sounds as if the concept is alien to him. "Do you remember the big fight over extending the runways so jets could land here?"

"Not even remotely."

"I guess that was before your time."

"Everything was before my time." I steal a glance at Barb's front window. "Jeremy, was there something else?"

"I'm just . . ." He licks his lips. "I'm worried about you is all."

"Well, you can fucking stop."

His sudden, wet gaze stings me. I can tell he's remembering those postcoital confessions of his dreams and aspirations. Bachelor's degree, big-city police gig, maybe even law school.

I only ever responded with silence. He's probably thinking about that too.

"Damn it, Jeremy." The shine in his eyes makes me want to punch him. Or take him back to his apartment. I can't do either. It occurs to me Paulette was an excuse, an easy, obvious reason to walk away. "You know I can never be what you want."

He puts a hand on his forehead, a gesture I associate with my mother. A tremor runs through my legs. I suppress the urge to bolt by grinding my heel into the gravel at my feet. He saves me the trouble by walking up the driveway, gait stiff and shoulders hunched. The soles of his shoes scrape against concrete.

As he paces, I stare down the hillside. Out on the lake, the fishing boats have moved away from the dam. High above the water, a bird tips and banks on the thermals. The wobble of its flight tells me it's a vulture—one of Nathan Harper's, maybe.

Jeremy returns down the driveway and stops in front of me—half a step too close. He's smiling now with his old, familiar sadness.

I reach behind me, one handed, for the Stiff.

"I know I'm just a diversion, Mel. I never expected some great romance." His voice has gone husky. "But I hoped you'd at least let me be your friend."

Christ.

"They don't listen," Helene once said. "They hear the one word or phrase that fits the little love story they've cooked up, and everything else is white noise." Back then, before Geoffrey, I didn't understand what she meant. She'd had actual experience with relationships. I had fuck buddies.

But now I get it.

I meet Jeremy's gaze with blunt anger. "Which part of what happened at Dailie's was being my friend?"

He looks away, but in shame or guilt I can't tell. "I didn't know he was going to ambush you."

"Bull. *Shit.*"

His eyes dart around as if seeking a lifeline. "Mel—"

"He stuck me in the puke-smelling backseat of his goddamn Tahoe. He threatened me with *jail.*"

Before I can add, *And you helped*, all the air goes out of him.

"Duniway pinged me and said you weren't answering your cell. He said your van was parked over near Jo's and asked me to look around. I knew you wouldn't respond if I called or texted." He laughs a little. When I don't react, he continues. "Anyway, I stuck my head in the Pig, then worked my way around the square. But, hell, I never even saw you in Dailie's."

"He never tried to call me."

"What can I say, Mel? I think he's kinda making it up as he goes."

"You expect me to believe that?" Duniway's actions have seemed damn well choreographed—from Quince to the search warrant on the New Mortuary credenza.

But Jeremy presses his point. "This just isn't the kind of thing we deal with. DUIs and bar fights, domestic calls, drug stuff, maybe a tourist gets ripped off—that's what we're used to. Body snatching? Not so much."

"So somehow I'm the mastermind behind Barlow County's crime of the century?"

"When you put it that way . . ." His shoulders rise and fall. "It's just—everybody was chalking it up to a motor vehicle collision. A bad one, sure, but an accident. Then the bodies walked away and turned up out at Bouton's, and Quince came in and . . ." His voice tapers off.

"I'm the common thread."

"Well, think about how it looks."

"Pretty damn convenient." Unless you're me.

"It's all Duniway's got, Mel."

I glance at my phone, but instead of checking the time, I think about Barb's internet search. And the search I was contemplating when Jeremy arrived.

Jeremy can tell me things I won't find with Google.

"Start with what you know, little sis."

What I know is that if someone hadn't taken the bodies, my part in this farce would be over. There might be details for the cops to sort out, but I'd just be the girl who called it in and transported the remains. Even when the bodies disappeared, the worst that could be said was that I was negligent—the dumbshit who didn't lock the door. It took finding bones and ash in the Old Mortuary retort to make it all about me.

Melisende Dulac, first on the scene. Found and all but fled from the damn baby. Transported the remains, and even discovered another body the next day. But Crazy Melisende wasn't driving the pickup with the horse trailer. Have the cops stopped to wonder why two adult men were in an apparent midnight standoff at the crossroad with a couple of teenaged boys when Zach Urban plowed into them?

I look at Jeremy, thinking of Dr. Varney's DME report. "Tell me about the guys from the crash. Tucker Gill and Uriah Skeevis. Dr. Varney said he confirmed their IDs by fingerprint. Did they have records?"

"Mel, I can't really—"

My lips compress. "You want to be my friend or not?"

He grimaces. "The thing is, I don't know anything."

"Why not?"

"I've been on Duniway's shit list ever since the sheriff moved me from jail to patrol a year ahead of department policy." His hand goes back to his forehead before dropping to his side. His fingers start drumming the seam of his uniform pants. "He's got me doing civil forfeitures and interviewing backpackers about food stolen from their campsite. Like I can arrest a bear."

"I thought you were canvassing the neighborhood around the New Mortuary for witnesses."

His twitchy hand goes still. "Did Kendrick Pride tell you that?"

The question is like the clatter of stones ahead of an avalanche. "What makes you think he told me anything?"

"You had coffee with him."

"Wait." A sound like rushing wind fills my ears. "You're *spying* on me now?"

He breaks eye contact. "No one is spying on you."

I can't tell if he actually believes that. Danae's round face pops into my head. "No secrets in Samuelton, sweetie."

"What the hell do you call it, then?"

He ignores the question. "What do you really know about the guy, Mel?"

Not as much as I'd like, I think, *despite Google.* But I won't give Jeremy the satisfaction of knowing his question was on the mark. "You brought him up. What do *you* know about him?"

"I know he's been all over the county asking questions and stirring the bees, but no one knows why."

"What does that have to do with me?"

"There's something off about him. Hell, for all we know *he* took the bodies."

I stare at him. "And then stuck around all week 'stirring the bees'? Why would he do that?"

"I don't know. Some kind of misdirection, maybe."

"Who's he supposed to be misdirecting? The crack investigators of the Barlow County Sheriff's Department?"

Jeremy scrubs a hand over his face and scalp before dropping it to his side. "I'm just saying next time you run into him, maybe skip the coffee."

The sky darkens, as if a cloud passed before the sun. "Do not think for one second," I say, jabbing a finger at his chest, "that because I fucked you, you get to tell me what to do."

I turn away, but he grabs my arm. The glare I throw at his hand is hot enough he lets go immediately. "Goodbye, Jeremy."

"Where are you going, Mel?"

There's a note of warning in his voice. I glance back at Barb's window, but only for a second. I won't use her as a human shield. Not that she'd mind, but I've got questions piling up around my feet like cremated ash and bone, and I won't find the answers here.

What I know is I'm sick of all the insinuations, of being treated like a criminal on the one hand and a helpless child on the other. I know my questions won't get answered if I don't ask them myself. And I know of only one other person who seems to care what actually happened at the crossroad.

I fix Jeremy with a hard stare. "I'm going to speak with an attorney."

PART THREE

Ruin

In Memory of the
GIRL IN BLUE
Killed by Train
December 24, 1933
"Unknown but not forgotten"

—Gravestone
Village Cemetery
Willoughby, Ohio

TWENTY-THREE

Nancy Drew I'm Not

I'd like nothing better than to leave Jeremy in a cloud of dust. But the Stiff was built for hauling bodies, not ass. I'm stuck with a sense of peevish satisfaction as he slowly falls away in my rearview mirror. In the heat of the moment, I'd let my anger do the talking, but I have no reason to think Pride will tell me what he's learned. On my own, I don't know where to start. Set up a whiteboard? Buy myself a leatherette portfolio and a box of Ziploc bags? Nancy Drew I'm not. I'm no more qualified to investigate body snatching or what happened at the crossroad than I am to pilot a sailboat on Dryer Lake.

I'd love nothing more than to return to the Old Mortuary, lock my door, and soak in the tub for the rest of my life. But momentum born of anger and desperation is what I have working for me right now. I don't know if Pride will help me, but for now he's my best option.

"Wait. Did you just make a decision?"

"Shut up."

Barb's house is on the north side of the lake, and the quickest route back to Wayette Highway is through the resort village. The area is an alternate reality when compared to the rest of Barlow County. According to Uncle Rémy, fifteen years ago there was little more here than a boat ramp and a few tumbledown rental cabins. Then a developer with big ideas and an even bigger budget bought the desert surrounding the lake. Within a few years, a planned community and resort with a destination golf course rose out of the desert, anchored by Dryer Lake Village. Home to a hotel, chichi eateries, and pricey boutiques with names like Sunstone and Diaphaneaux, Dryer Lake Village fills a spit of land that juts into the lake below the golf course. It's basically an open-air mall, with brick walkways and cast bronze sculptures of leaping trout or pronghorns. Strings of lights thread among bristlecone pines, grape holly, and inexplicable palm trees. The buildings are all rough-pointed basalt and earth-tone stucco, as if assembled from a kit. Barb once described the place as the zombie spawn of a *Sunset* magazine focus group.

One thing the village has going for it right now is the Paiute Crossing Coffee Bar—and no chance of running into anyone I know. It occurs to me I could use a moment of peace to come up with a plan, and some caffeine to fight off half a bottle of wine. I take it as a good sign that I'm able to score an empty parking space right outside the door.

Inside, a green-haired pixie makes a hard pitch for the summer special, a black cherry mocha. "All ingredients fair trade or locally sourced!" Her chin crinkles when I instead order an extra-large iced coffee. As I wait, a tall, slender blonde woman at a table near the door scrutinizes me. From the looks of the purplish-brown scum on her half-empty glass, she fell for the black cherry mocha.

She's well put together in the way Dryer Lake women always are, a High Desert Barbie in beige capris, silver and turquoise jewelry, and an Indian cotton blouse unbuttoned to the top of her cleavage. She doesn't seem amused by my "You'd Look Better Embalmed" T-shirt, despite the cheerful yellow fabric and cartoonish red printing.

"Tell her to take a picture, Mellie. It'll last longer."

I laugh in spite of myself. That seems to confuse her, and she looks away. When the pixie calls out my drink, I make for the door. Better hot air than cool judgment any day.

I'm tempted by one of the benches along the village walkways, but end up back behind the wheel of the Stiff. I take a sip of coffee, then wake up my phone to call Pride.

Of course I don't know his number.

"Fitz, don't you dare laugh."

Pride gave me his card the morning we found Nathan's body. I check around in the Stiff, under the seats and in the center console. No luck. Nor is it in my purse, a small leather satchel with backpack straps. It holds my phone, keys, wallet, and a couple tampons, but no card.

Where have I seen Pride? At the Whistle Pig, the crossroad, finally at the Mercantile earlier today. "I saw you come in," he'd said as he nodded toward the Downhill Motor Lodge.

When I tap my phone's browser to look up the Downhill's number, Nathan Harper's Facebook photo is still there, giving me the finger. A week ago, he was a boy. Now he's a corpse, his face disfigured by vultures. Distantly, I wonder how Carrie would tackle Nathan's preparation for an open casket.

I tap back to Google, but rather than "Downhill Motor Lodge" I find myself typing "Uriah Skeevis" into the search field.

"You sure you're ready to try this on your own, granny?"

Despite Barb's needling, it's not like I've never done online research. It just tended to be stuff like the Compromise of 1877 for school. I tap the search icon.

And have no idea what I'm looking at.

The first result is "Heavy Metal Rage: Page 7." I tap the link, just in case. It's a list, 121 through 140, of bands I've never heard of, including one called Uriah Heep. I tap "Back" and scan the other results.

There's a page of usernames from some online community. *Rusty_teh_Faggot . . . trav3l3r . . . Elvenslag . . . Detesticulator.* I scroll down until I see *Uriah* and *Skeevis.* Two different members. I don't care to know of what.

The other results are mostly links to Bible sites. Uriah, it seems, was an Old Testament character murdered by King David. Probably not the same guy, unless David chased Uriah all the way from ancient Israel to the crossroad.

The results for "Tucker Gill" aren't much better. There's a fishing guide in Montana, a college wrestler for Iowa State, and a high school football player in Texas. An online phonebook lists eleven nationwide, but if one happens to be the Tucker Gill from the crossroad, it's not like he can answer his phone.

Then an item catches my eye, a link to the Washington County, Oregon, Jail Roster. The current roster, updated that morning, includes no Tucker Gill, but that gives me an idea. In the search bar, I type "Tucker Gill Washington County OR."

The first two results point back to the jail roster, but the third is for a year-old news story: "Domestic Dispute Turned Violent Leads to Multiple Prostitution Arrests." Police, responding to a call at an apartment complex in Aloha, Oregon, broke up a fight between three sex workers and their pimp—a man named Tucker Gill. He'd punched one of the women, then had his ass handed to him when all three jumped him at once.

Could he be the same Tucker Gill? If so, what brought him to the crossroad? Maybe he relocated to Barlow after his ass whipping. In my experience, teenage boys are looking for any chance to get laid, but would they drive from Portland to central Oregon for the chance? It's a long way to come for something that shouldn't be that hard to find in the city.

A shadow falls across the phone, followed by a rap on my window. I glance up, half-expecting that creep from Crestview with the shiny 4Runner. Instead, it's a cop. He makes the universal "roll down your window" gesture. I hesitate, but when his movements get more forceful, I hit the button on my armrest.

"What brings you here today, Miss?"

He has the face of a man who was born old and never got over it. His crew cut and brushy eyebrows match his starched gray shirt, similar to the Sheriff's Department uniform. But his badge might have come out of a cereal box, and his nameplate is orange plastic. The Dryer Lake Resort logo is engraved next to his name, "X. Meyer." He's a rent-a-cop.

"What is your business, ma'am?" He peers into the Stiff, his eyes casting to the back where the cot is locked in place. Too bad I don't have a body.

"I'm just drinking my coffee." I raise my cup.

He considers me, and for a second I see Duniway in his icy glower. "Well, Dryer Lake Village is private property, so I'm going to have to ask you to vacate."

My neck stiffens. "Why?"

"You're illegally parked." He gestures toward the curb, where I see a signpost. Fifteen-minute parking.

"I haven't been here that long." Not that I've checked the time.

"According to the report I received, you have."

"Report?" I glance at the coffee shop. From the window, a smug High Desert Barbie looks back. "Are you fucking kidding me?"

He straightens, and suddenly I'm glad he's just a rent-a-cop. The only thing on his belt is an old-fashioned cell phone holster.

"Ma'am, if you don't move along, I'll call the Sheriff's Department and have you arrested for trespassing."

No wonder Barb doesn't like the resort village. I'm tempted to pull out the "Official Business" placard I keep in the center console, the one issued to Bouton by the very department he's threatening to sic on me. It's supposed to be for removals under our county contract.

But if he calls me on it, I'm shit out of luck. Suspended from contract removals. Not even Jeremy would back me up.

I raise my hands in surrender. "Sure. Fine. Whatever."

Google was getting me nowhere anyway.

I navigate to Crestview on autopilot and pull in at the Downhill Motor Lodge. There are only a few cars parked outside the two wings of rooms that stretch left and right from the motel office, none of them Pride's. It's a little after four, too early for dinner unless you're a fogey. How old is Pride? He said he was just a kid when Lennon died, which my phone informs me happened in 1980. So, up there—but not lining up at the Old Country Buffet just yet.

The Downhill's lobby smells of bleach and scorched coffee. Behind the counter sits a white-haired man in a tattered "Ski Brother Drop" T-shirt, hypnotized by his phone. I remember him from the night I transported the elderly stroke victim last November, but he doesn't seem to recognize me.

"I need to leave a message for one of your guests. Kendrick Pride?"

He shakes his head without looking up. "No one here by that name."

"Did he check out?"

"Never checked in."

"Are you sure?" No answer. "Could you double-check?"

His lips purse. "Trust me, lady. It's been a slow week." He shoos me away with one hand, then twists his whole body in response to whatever's happening on his phone. I flee the reek and stand next to the Stiff, door open to let the heat out.

Had I misheard Pride? Next door, the Mercantile is doing a steady business. Hikers and campers, plus a couple of wiry women from an SUV with kayaks on the roof, stop for a cold drink or a snack after a day on the trails and streams. "I'm staying nearby," Pride said. Nearby doesn't include a lot of options. Of the three Crestview motels, only the Downhill is open during the summer. Maybe he rented a place.

I go back to my phone. The contact page for Pride's law firm includes direct lines and cell phone numbers for several staff members, but Pride isn't among them. I call the main number, only expecting to reach voicemail on a Saturday afternoon. To my shock, an actual human answers. "Anders, Harper, Milton, and Pride, Attorneys-at-Law. How may I help you?"

"Uh—you're a person?"

"Yes, ma'am. How may I help you?"

"Sorry. I didn't think anyone would be in the office. I was going to leave a message." My superpower.

"You've reached the answering service." The man's voice is crisp and formal. "I can take a message for whomever you'd like to reach."

I guess legal trouble can happen any day of the week.

"I'm trying to reach Kendrick Pride. My name is—"

He cuts me off. "Mr. Pride is on sabbatical. Ms. Anders is taking his calls."

"Sabbatical? For how long?"

"I don't have any information on when he'll return. But Ms. Anders should be able to help you."

I hesitate. "It's something of a personal matter. Is there any way to get a message to Mr. Pride?"

"I'm afraid I can't help you there. Perhaps Ms. Anders can."

Trae Fowler's father confirmed to Duniway that Pride was representing him. Being on sabbatical could explain why he's been free to lurk in Barlow County for days on end.

"Ma'am? Would you like to leave a message for Ms. Anders?"

I barely know Pride, but I definitely don't know Anders.

"Never mind." I start to pull the phone away from my ear. "Wait."

"Yes, ma'am?"

"Do you know how long Mr. Pride has been out?"

There's a brief pause. "Since March."

Four months. "Thanks."

Kendrick Pride's sabbatical can't be connected to the crossroad, can it? I don't see how but add it to my growing heap of questions. Why is he avoiding the cops? Because he doesn't trust them to do their job properly? Or maybe he doesn't trust them, period?

I return to the motel office. The desk clerk looks up from his phone, annoyed now.

"Sorry for bugging you. I know the other motels in town are closed for the season, but is there a hotel or a lodge nearby?"

"Christ, lady."

He meets my stare. I focus on the red lines in his eyes.

"Try the Long Grass Bed and Breakfast." When I shake my head, he sighs. "Go up to Hensley Drive and turn right. It's just a little ways up. If you come to the girls school, you've gone too far."

TWENTY-FOUR

Hensley School

The first time I saw the green sign on Wayette Highway, I took the place for a historic site, a one-room pioneer schoolhouse preserved to enthrall families of car campers.

```
┌─────────────────────────┐
│    HENSLEY SCHOOL        │
│      NEXT RIGHT          │
└─────────────────────────┘
```

Eventually I'd hear about the private school for girls, but until now I've had no reason to take that right onto Hensley Drive.

It's easy walking distance from the Downhill for those foolhardy enough to brave the highway shoulder. I drive, and before I get out of second gear, I'm idling in front of a pristine, three-story Victorian house with turrets at the corners. "The Long Grass Bed and Breakfast," the sign says. The windows are curtained with lace, the exterior paint fresh and multihued. But the gravel parking area is empty except for a rack of bicycles under a wooden awning.

Nobody home.

To my left, at the end of a short cul-de-sac, several houses cluster among the trees. Straight ahead, Hensley Drive narrows into a broad lane and curves left—presumably to the school.

Jeremy said they checked the school for the baby's mother, and Danica Wood said pretty much the same. But right now I'm thinking more generally. Girls attract boys. They also attract other girls, but it was Nathan and Trae at the crossroad.

Tall pines crowd the roadside, with just enough shoulder for me to get over if a vehicle approaches from the other way. After a quarter mile or so, a wide clearing opens, and the lane ends at a pair of parking lots, the school grounds beyond.

Pride's car is in a small gravel lot on the right side of the lane. Beyond, separated by a strip of green lawn, is a larger paved lot. I let the Stiff idle forward, then brake behind the blue hybrid. Curious spot to park, considering the main lot is a quarter full.

I roll forward into a space shaded by an ash tree. Ordinarily I wouldn't expect school staff to be available on a Saturday afternoon, but Pride has a way of getting people to sit down with him. Whether I can intercept him here is another matter.

The Hensley School is a far cry from the one-room shack I'd half-imagined. A path of stone pavers cuts through the grass, circling a dry fountain before continuing to the front steps. The fountain reminds me of the one in Memorial Park, though instead of Sam Barlow, a bronze girl stands atop the plinth, an open book in her hands, her head and shoulders gray with bird droppings.

The three-story school is reminiscent of the colonial architecture I knew as a kid, with red brick walls, a slate roof, and gray stone lintels. I climb the steps to the broad porch, conscious I have no real business here. I hesitate outside the entrance, wooden double doors propped wide with whitewashed cinder blocks. The foyer is carpeted, with high ceilings and openings on each side into what appear to be sitting rooms. At the far end, a plain metal desk stands guard before a corridor that goes off to the left and right.

"Can I help you?"

I spin and spot two girls staring at me with frank appraisal from a swing at the right end of the porch. One is pale enough to pass for the Spirit, with wispy hair the color of dead oak leaves and suspicion in her ultramarine gaze. The other girl's dark brown skin sets off the silver bangles on her wrists and silver hoops in her ears. Both wear blue blouses with billowy sleeves and open collars.

The dark-skinned girl shoots me a grin. "Nice shirt. I know a boy in Springfield who would look hella better embalmed."

I cross my arms over my chest. She laughs.

"My name's Celeste." Awkwardly, she pushes herself off the swing. "I'm on the desk, so if you're visiting, you gotta go through me." She walks with her shoulders back as if her center of gravity isn't quite where she expects. Her belly bulges inside her blouse like she's trying to shoplift a soccer ball.

My eyes pinball from Celeste to the other girl, round-bellied as well. "What is this place?"

The white girl's stare becomes a scowl. "It's Hensley School." Based on her tone, the *bitch* is silent.

"I know that. I mean—"

"It's a school," she snaps. "Just a damn school."

"But—"

"That's right, lady. As you're about to point out—gasp—we're *with child*."

Celeste rolls her eyes in an exaggerated manner. In a stage whisper, she says, "Please excuse my friend. She thought she was doing anal."

Her friend huffs, then emits a braying laugh.

Under other circumstances, I might have laughed too. Now, I force myself to draw a deep breath. "This is going to sound weird, but did anyone here lose a baby?" Jeremy can say what he wants, but I'd like to hear it from someone nearer the source.

"Not me." Celeste pats her round belly. "Gemma?"

The girl on the swing examines her nails. "Still working on it."

Celeste shrugs. Then her eyes widen with recognition. "Wait. I heard about you." She breaks out in a broad grin. "You're that undertaker lady who found the newborn."

My skull suddenly feels like it's full of bees.

"You probably want to talk to the director. She was in her office a little bit ago."

I latch on to the word *director* like a castaway to a life ring. "Yes. Thank you."

Celeste guides me through the doorway. A girl is reading on a couch in one of the sitting rooms, a baby in a sling on her chest. There are changing stations everywhere I look. The air smells of pine cleaner. On the wall behind the desk is what I guess is the school's motto, rendered in party-store letters.

Make Motherhood a Mother-Habit

We continue into a long hallway. Somewhere in the building, an infant cries. Wall posters encourage healthy sleep habits and pre-natal exercise. We pass recessed doors marked "Group Study," "Quiet Study," "Media," and "Lactation Clinic."

Halfway down the hall, Celeste raps on the frame of an open door. "Ma'am? I have a lady here who thinks she found one of our babies."

A slender woman with white skin and brown hair pulled back in a ponytail appears.

"Come in, please." She smiles at my guide, then inspects me top to bottom, her eyes pausing on my T-shirt. There's nothing printed on her plain, white one. "Thank you, Celeste."

"No problem." With a quick wave, Celeste returns the way we came.

The woman leads me into an office with an oak desk and three walls of bookshelves that stretch to the high ceiling. Stacks of papers and folders cover the desk, almost hiding a laptop and telephone. In the corner, two chairs face each other across a small round table.

"I'm Lydia Koenig." I remember Danica mentioning her name. She offers me her hand. Her fingers are smooth and cool. "Excuse my appearance. I wasn't expecting company."

"I wasn't expecting to be company."

She laughs as if I've made an actual joke. "You must be Melisende Dulac."

I go stiff.

"I read about you in the *Ledger*."

I hold my breath, waiting for her to add, "You just left the baby lying there?" But she smiles like I'm an old friend she hasn't seen for too long.

"I'm hoping my fifteen minutes are about up."

That nets me another laugh. "Please, sit down."

I drop into one of the chairs as she takes the other. The wide window behind her desk looks out onto a courtyard between two wings of the school. A trio of girls sits at a table, one breastfeeding an infant.

Koenig follows my gaze. "I take it you're not familiar with the Hensley School."

The seat cushion feels a little sticky. "I'm starting to catch on."

"Well, as you can see, we're a school for teen moms. Specifically, we offer a year-round residential education program for high school girls who are pregnant or have recently given birth."

"So you must be crawling with babies."

"Not so many that we'd misplace one."

"Not even on purpose?"

Her lips tighten. Then her smile returns, if not so wide. "All our girls are here voluntarily. Some will offer their children for private adoption, but many intend to keep them. Whatever they decide, we help them stay on track with their education through the process. Our goal for our girls is on-time graduation, with each well prepared for whatever she chooses to do next. They're not just young mothers, but young women with a future."

She sounds like she's reading from a brochure. "Do they ever change their minds?"

"Sure. And when that happens, we address the situation according to the needs of the individual. But before you ask, no, they don't sneak off to abandon their babies in the desert. They attend Hensley so they won't feel the pressure to do something like that."

"Maybe that wasn't the plan. Maybe one of your girls called her boyfriend, and he came to get her, but on the way out, something went wrong. She went into labor, or . . . I don't know." That might explain why their car was stopped, and even why the Cadillac was there. Hell, maybe Tucker and Uriah pulled over to help.

Her lips remain upturned, but the smile leaves her eyes.

"We're no more missing one of our students than one of our babies. As for your boyfriend theory, well, our girls have limited, well-monitored access with the outside world. No cell phones and no internet except for what's required for school assignments. The girls write letters or have scheduled phone calls with their parents or guardians only. Visitors must be preapproved, and boyfriends rarely are."

She sighs. "Listen, I understand. As you put it, we're crawling with babies. Our current census is fifty-eight students, about half postnatal. We also have strict procedures. We're a state-accredited facility, with many girls here under an Oregon DHS contract. If one of our young moms snuck off or somehow lost track of her baby, we'd know—and so would the authorities. For what it's worth, the sheriff came here the morning you found the infant. I believe we were his first stop after he left the scene of the accident."

Just as Jeremy claimed. But something still troubles me.

"Don't you think it's weird, though? About the baby at the cross-road, I mean."

She nods thoughtfully. "And tragic, though thanks to you an even greater tragedy was averted."

She means it as a compliment, but all I can think about is how everyone reacted afterward. I change the subject. "What will happen to her? The baby, I mean." As if I could have been talking about anyone else.

"They'll try to find the parents, of course. If they do, what happens will depend on the circumstances under which the child came to be left in the desert."

Jeremy thought the baby had been dumped.

"So they haven't found anyone."

"Not that I've heard. But there's no reason to inform me if they had. Just because I'm director of this school doesn't mean I'm responsible for every baby that passes through the county." I listen for the reproach, but her tone is bluntly factual. "I'll read about it online, same as everyone else."

"Right." My fingers tangle in my lap.

"Is there anything else?"

"Uh, yes, actually." The original point of my visit had slipped from my mind. "I was looking for someone who came to the school. Kendrick Pride? He's an attorney from Portland."

She looks up, thinking. After a few seconds, she shakes her head. "The name isn't familiar, but I've been away at a conference and just returned this morning." She glances at the desk. "In fact, I should get back to work. The only reason you caught me in the office on a Saturday is I needed to catch up on a few things."

"I expected to find him here now," I say before she can rise.

"I assure you, I haven't seen him." Her tone has taken on a peremptory edge. "And my staff would have informed me of any visits by attorneys."

"His car is in the parking lot."

Her brow creases. "By chance was it the outer lot?"

"Yes."

"There's a trailhead out there." She nods as if that settles it. "The outer lot belongs to the Forest Service, not us."

I wouldn't peg Pride for a hiker—not that Lydia Koenig would know that.

"Is there anything else?" Her tone carries a note of finality. I'm being dismissed.

"I guess not."

She escorts me all the way to the front door, as if to ensure I'm really leaving. We pass a long row of photos on the corridor wall, formal eight-by-ten portraits, under a plaque that reads "Hensley School Trustees." All but one are men. Helene would have opinions about a girls' school run by dudes, but Lydia Koenig strikes me as a woman who can stand up to them just fine.

TWENTY-FIVE

No Distractions

When I step out onto the porch, Celeste waves from the swing.

She's alone now, with a book propped on her belly—*Watership Down*, one I've read myself more times than I can count. I feel dizzy from the scent of baby lotion and the distant sounds of babies and their mothers. How many, I wonder, are here because they want to be, and how many because they had no other choice?

Celeste sets the book on the swing. "Well, what do you want to know?"

I consider the question, then say, "What's the name of the boy who would look better embalmed?"

She smiles. "Trae."

My face grows hot. "Fowler?"

"No. Alcobendes."

Of course. Her Trae is from Springfield, not Gresham.

She arches one eyebrow. "Is Trae Fowler the daddy of that baby you found?"

Good question. "I don't know. He was one of the people who died in the crash at the crossroad." Her expression is blank. "Where I found the baby."

"We don't get much news. I mean, the other day cops were here for hours asking about your baby. But no one mentioned a wreck."

Lydia Koenig said the girls had limited access to the outside world, but Celeste makes it sound like they're completely cut off. I shake my head.

She seems to read my thoughts. "It's cool. We're supposed to focus on school and our babies and learning how to balance the two. No outside distractions."

"'Make Motherhood a Mother Habit.'"

"You saw the sign!" She grins. "Ms. Koenig says we're here to learn a new set of skills and priorities. Childcare, self-care, life care. We can figure out if there's room for Snapchat or Xbox when we get back to the world."

"When will that be?"

"I graduate in December. My little guy will be around three months old, depending on when he decides to pop out."

"You're—" I stop myself, but she guesses my question.

"Yeah, I'm keeping him. Nobody's lining up to adopt mixed-race black and Latino babies." Her smile takes on a hint of sadness. "My mom's gonna help, though. It'll be good."

"Have you picked a name?"

"Clinton. It's my mom's maiden name."

Definitely not Trae. I smile, then have another thought. "Do the girls have their babies here at the school?"

"Most, sure. There are birthing suites in the clinic wing. Some have to go to the hospital in that little town, though."

At first, I think she's referring to the urgent care in Munro, but she must mean St. Mark's in Samuelton. After more than a year here, the county seat feels like a big city. But it's small compared to Lowell where I grew up, a blip next to Boston. "Samuelton is a long way if something goes wrong."

"We've got nurse-midwives here twenty-four-seven and a doctor on call. They keep an eye on us."

For all her confidence, the school's isolation leaves me uneasy. The drive from Crestview to Samuelton takes at least twenty-five minutes, and that's in addition to however long it takes Fire and Rescue to get here. But I don't want to worry her. Besides, what do I know? The school has been around longer than I have. With sixty girls at any given time, no doubt they've seen it all.

I shift gears. "Earlier you said you were on the desk. What does that mean?"

"Bell desk in the front hall. Someone is on duty during open hours in case of visitors or emergencies. That's eight to six most days, and till nine on Fridays and Saturdays. Sometimes girls go out with their families for dinner or whatever."

"That seems like a lot to put on you."

"There's staff around. Floor mothers, the duty nurse." She reaches under her blouse and retrieves a small walkie-talkie. "Bell desk helps us learn responsibility."

Like Lydia Koenig, she sounds like she's reading from a brochure. "Do you get a lot of visitors?"

"Sometimes."

"Baby daddies?"

That makes her laugh. "Parents, mostly. My mom and Gram come out at least every other weekend." She regards me. "You think your Trae tried to visit?"

"Maybe."

"Well, I've been here since April, and I've only seen one or two sperm donors."

Helene would like this girl. "The fathers aren't popular, I take it."

"Not with me." She makes a face, but then forces it back to a smile. "To be honest, I try not to think about Trae. He was such a prick, claiming the baby couldn't be his, calling me a slut, that kind of thing. I got news for him, but he won't believe it till we do the paternity test."

"Do all the girls feel that way?"

"I guess."

"You don't talk about it?"

"Oh, sure. But, you know, just among friends." She spreads her arms. "It's like any school. We're all teen moms, but that doesn't make us all besties."

I can count the besties in my life with my thumbs, and one of them won't take my calls. Back in my student days, high school and college both, I barely spoke to anyone. Not even the ones I had sex with. Even with Barb and Helene, I've withheld more than I've shared. Why should these girls be any different? Still, Celeste seems like a girl others might confide in.

"Are you sure you never heard the name Trae Fowler? Or Nathan Harper, maybe?"

"Sorry. Now, if you said Assface or Dickless, maybe I could help."

"Dickless?"

She rolls her eyes. "Sometimes you just don't want to know."

I smile. My gaze strays to the Forest Service lot. "Do you know if a man came to the school? Tall, dresses nice?" I point at Pride's little blue hybrid. "That's his car."

"What did Ms. Koenig say?"

"That she's been away."

"I don't have class with her, but she did miss dinner in the dining hall the last couple of days." She nods, as if that settles something. "Anyway, I don't remember any tall guys, but this is my first desk shift since Wednesday." She chews on her lip. "We aren't supposed to talk to the hikers."

She picks up her book, universal symbol for *done talking*. I wish I could join her. The swing looks comfortable, and a breeze through the trees has eased the stultifying heat. I'd give almost anything for the chance to lose myself in the adventures of Bigwig, Hazel, and Fiver, to forget stolen corpses and search warrants. But I'd have to be ten years younger and "with child." Not even *Watership Down* is worth that.

Besides, I still need to find Pride, and his car is my only lead.

"Good luck with your baby, Celeste."

At the foot of the steps I cut straight across the lawn. A mix of pine and oaks grow right up to the Forest Service lot. The ground at the edge of the forest is thick with leafy shrubs and alive with the chatter of birds. The sections of ponderosa forest Uncle Rémy walked me through were much more open and airy. Here, I can see only a short way down the steep hillside between the crowded trunks.

It's only been four or five hours since our awkward coffee klatch, yet Pride's car looks like it's been here longer. A splash of bird shit, cracked and dry, covers part of the windshield.

Is it possible, in the middle of his investigation, he just up and decided to take a forest stroll? The idea seems unlikely, but the About Us page for Anders, Harper, Milton, and Pride hardly counts as in-depth biography. For all I know, he really is an avid hiker.

According to the info sheet stapled to the plywood notice board under the trail marker, this is the Hensley Stand of the Brother Drop National Forest—mixed ponderosa pine and Douglas fir with patches of white oak at the margins, last harvested in 1973. There's a trail map beside the info sheet, along with sun-bleached warnings about cougars and black bears. From the parking lot, a short connector leads to the Palmer-Getcham Trail—a sixteen-mile "challenging" trek with a twenty-two-hundred-foot change of elevation. Or, if that's too daunting, the Cerise Creek Trail splits from the Palmer-Getcham and loops around Crestview until it pops out of the trees behind me. Seven and three-quarter miles, with a four-hundred-foot change of elevation and breathtaking views.

I'm not dressed or geared for a hike. Uncle Rémy always insisted we carry water and emergency supplies, even for short jaunts. I've got none of that, and even if I did, the chances of me finding Pride in the woods are slim.

I return to the car and try the doors. Locked. I'm not sure what I'd do if I could get inside. Rifle through the glove box, feel around under the seats? If he's anything like Helene was in law school, he's a prodigious notetaker. I might learn a lot if I could get my hands on his portfolio.

"You're supposed to be clearing yourself of a crime, little sister, not committing one."

Looking through the windows, I don't see the portfolio, but he did leave a manila folder on the passenger seat, a five-by-seven photo sticking partway out. The subject seems to be a girl. Her yellow top with rolled collar reveals light skin and slender collarbones. A fine silver chain around her neck disappears inside the collar. What little hair I can see is blond and straight, hanging off her shoulders. The backdrop is the blotchy bluish-white hallmark of school pictures everywhere.

A friend of Nathan and Trae?

Distant movement draws my eye, a figure coming out of the trees at the far end of the school lot. For half a second, I imagine it's Pride. But when the figure moves from shadow to sunlight, my heart drops into my stomach.

It's Landry MacElroy.

I drop behind Pride's car. After a few quick breaths, I peek over the hood. Landry is trotting across the parking lot toward the Stiff. He's dressed in shorts and a singlet—Barlow Con red and white—with a matching nylon waist pack. At the Stiff, he cups his hands to peer through the glass. After a moment, he straightens and looks toward the school building. One hand goes to his chin, then he turns my way, as if he senses my presence.

I drop back into a crouch. I do not need this right now.

In the distance, a Jake brake grumbles as a semi rolls into Crestview, the sound ratcheting up my nerves. I feel exposed, without options, too aware of the Hensley School's isolation. If he comes my way, he'll spot me. If I make a break for the Stiff or the school, he'll just cut me off. As I recall, linebackers are fast—faster than apprentice morticians, anyway. I could try calling 911, but by the time help arrived, they might find a new client for Bouton.

What would the local worthies say if their football star outright murdered me? "Aw shucks, boys'll be boys"? It's not a question I want put to the test.

I lift my head and peek through the windows of Pride's car. Landry is scanning the school grounds and the margins of the forest. The instant his head turns away, I dart across the gap between the little blue hybrid and the trail sign, and into the forest beyond.

TWENTY-SIX

Je Suis Désolé

My work boots are great for long hours on my feet, moving bodies from one flat surface to another. A headlong flight down a steep trail is something else. My heels skid out as I pass the trail marker, and I land hard on my ass, with a grunt. Startled, a magpie explodes from the brush near my head and screams off through the trees.

"Next time, send up a flare."

I'd barely given the map a glance, so I have no idea where the trail goes. All I remember is it's either seven and three-quarter or sixteen miles. But I can worry about where I'm going once I've put some distance between Landry and myself.

I scramble up, brushing gravel from my hands. The trail plunges to the left, with bends and dips that limit how far I can see to thirty or forty feet ahead and behind. The undergrowth and trees grow thicker on the uphill side, perhaps due to runoff from watering that big green lawn. Through gaps, I catch sight of an eave here, a window there, but mostly it's all oak leaves or brushy pine boughs.

After a few hundred feet, I pause at some split-timber steps that descend into a narrow draw, dry this time of year. I follow the draw up the hill with my eyes, head cocked. I can't see the school now. Or Landry. The only sound is an insectile hum—unless it's my own trilling nerves.

My phone shows two bars. There's a cell tower on the grounds of the assisted living facility, so I should be fine for some distance. As I drop the phone back into my purse, a voice sounds from above.

Another answers, too faint for me make out the words. Male or female? I can't tell. Could be teen moms strolling around the school grounds.

Or Landry calling a friend.

"You don't even know if he saw you."

Well, I don't know if he didn't, either.

I cross the draw over a dry bed of water-rounded stones and climb to a shoulder of the hillside. Beyond, the trail continues down and left, more gently now. The oaks end, leaving only ponderosa pines. The undergrowth gives way to patchy grass pushing up through carpets of pine needles. I keep moving, alert for the thump of pursuing feet. Soon, the magpie returns, raucously complaining. Unseen but near, a woodpecker hammers away at a tree trunk. Aside from the birds, nothing stirs in the forest. Whatever Landry was doing in the parking lot, he hasn't followed me. Maybe he was sniffing after Hensley girls. Hell, maybe he's a sperm donor. I wonder what Paulette would say about that.

A short way ahead, an inviting splash of sunlight falls across the trail. I continue on and come to a clearing above a long slope of dark, broken rock—an ancient lava bed feathering into the trees some distance below. Further still, another section of trail winds toward what can only be the Palmer River Valley.

I stop to catch my breath. The clearing above the lava is thirty feet across and half as deep, surrounded by smaller, younger pines. At the back of the clearing, a bench made from a split log is tucked under a lone white oak. The magpie has moved on, but from down the valley comes the distinctive whistle of a varied thrush—Uncle Rémy's favorite bird. Suddenly lightheaded, I cross the clearing to the bench and sit, letting my hands dangle between my knees. A thread of blood, already crusted over, runs down my right palm. I must have cut myself when I fell.

"I didn't know you could move that fast, Mellie."

"So graceful too."

I start gathering cigarette butts from the ground around the bench. On our many hikes, Uncle Rémy would pick up trash from the trails—a task rarely necessary. Most hikers, he said, were good about cleaning up after themselves. Leave only footprints, and all that. This clearing seems to be the exception.

I pile the butts on the bench. I wish I had something to put them in. Uncle Rémy always carried a trash bag. Pride has his Ziplocs. I suppose I can just scoop them up. The way back isn't far. Besides, I suspect there's a more direct route to the school, one the teen moms use when they sneak down here to smoke. No doubt Lydia Koenig would have an opinion on the matter if she knew. I laugh quietly. Not all habits can be changed by slogans on a wall.

"Were you scared?"

More than anything, I was fed up. "I'm just sick of Landry."

"Je suis désolé."

I recoil, scattering butts, as Landry MacElroy saunters around the bench. Almost languid, he sidles past me. His hands hang loose at his sides, and his gaze wanders as if he's taking in the view.

Of all the things I thought might spill from Landry MacElroy's mouth, a doleful phrase in a foreign tongue isn't it. There's no anger, no bluster or threat. I don't know what he said, but his tone brings to mind Paulette's desolate expression that night at the crossroad.

Seeing Landry now in his singlet and shorts, it's clear how lucky I was when I dragged him off Paulette. If he'd known I was coming, he might have torn me in half. In the light of day, his shoulders and chest stand out in high definition, the flesh marred only by a peppering of zits. His biceps are so bulbous they force his arms away from his body.

I back away—matching him step for step until I glance over my shoulder to make sure I don't stumble backward onto jagged lava. Landry stops before I'm forced to make a dangerous choice. His eyes flutter like someone coming out of anesthesia, the air between us thick with hormonal musk.

"My mom is making me take French for my language requirement." His eyes fall onto my chest, but I'm not sure he sees me. "I flunked last semester, so I have to retake it in summer school if I want to play next season." He looks at his hands and seems surprised to find them empty. "I guess some of it's sinking in."

"That's good, I guess."

The words feel stupid, but he just looks through me again. *"Je ne pas . . ."* His tongue darts over his lips. *"Je ne vais pas . . ."* He smacks his palm against his forehead. "Maybe it hasn't sunk in that much."

"Huh."

His cheeks inflate with a sound like wet shoes crossing a tile floor. "I'm not going to hurt you. That's what I was trying to say." He looks me in the eye as his voice gains urgency. "I'm not going to hurt you."

The words seem genuine, but for all I know his mother made him join the drama club too. "Okay." I take half a cautious step to the side—a test. "How about you let me by then?"

"I said I wasn't going to hurt you." He spreads his arms, palms up. *"Je ne vais pas te faire de mal."* The words spill out so suddenly his eyes bulge. "I don't know if that was right."

"It sounded fine."

"Really?" He grins like a kid who just did his first cartwheel. "Do you speak French?"

Helene does, along with Russian and German. To keep herself linguistically limber, she also studied Mandarin while in law school. Before Geoffrey showed up, she was even teaching me to swear in different languages. I've forgotten it all, along with my high school Latin.

As if Landry would care. I shake my head.

He deflates a little. "How do you know it was right then?"

I swallow. "I just mean it sounded good."

He seems to consider that. "I don't know why I have to take French. If I knew Spanish, I could yell at the illegals in their own language."

I take another step to the left.

"Don't go." He reaches out for my arm, then seems to think better of it. "Please?"

My pulse pounds in time with the nearby drumbeat of the woodpecker. "Someone is waiting for me." He obviously doesn't believe me.

"I just want to talk."

"Don't you have friends for that?"

His head jerks as if I hit him. I hear that wet shoes sound again as his cheeks puff in and out, and realize he's sucking spit between his teeth. His skin is sallow and drenched with sweat.

"Christ, Landry. What is going on with you?"

His gaze wanders back out over the valley. I have to stifle the paranoid urge to look behind me. *"Pourquoi—"* He drums his fingers against his damp thigh. *"Pourquoi est—*no. Damn it." He balls his fist and strikes his leg hard enough to bruise. "I want to know why you're so fucking *important!"*

Spit sprays me as his voice rises. I stumble backward, my left heel catching a root or stone. I twist to find my footing. My right heel comes down on nothing. For a split second my mind flashes to the jagged lava below.

"Breathtaking view, Mellie!"

Eyes big, Landry lunges to grab my flailing right arm below the elbow. Then he rocks backward and catches my other arm at the wrist. The sudden change in motion slams my organs against my ribs. With surprising grace, he swings me around until my feet find purchase on solid ground. When I jerk free, he holds on a second too long.

"Damn, lady. I said I wasn't going to hurt you."

Without responding, I head for the bench and sit again, head down and fingers tingling. The ground is still covered with cigarette butts. Soon, my breathing steadies, and my heart rate settles back into double digits. I raise my head. Landry looms in front me, his face as red as a baboon's ass. He opens his mouth but then stamps to the edge of the clearing. Pacing, his feet land perilously close to the drop-off.

"I'm no linebacker," I say. "If you trip, you're on your own."

"Who cares?" He kicks a rock into the gulf. "She dumped me."

"Paulette?" I grip the bench as if to keep from flying into space.

He spins toward me. "She got all pissy after dance team because she wanted to ride with Chelsea, but I *always* drive her home from dance team." He says it like it's his job. "And then, boom, like ten minutes later, she's texting me to fuck off forever."

Just yesterday—though it feels like another lifetime—Paulette seemed resigned to an existence in Landry's sweaty grasp. I'd like to think I had something to do with whatever changed, but that's probably too much to ask.

"When did this happen?"

"Right after you tried to T-bone me with your corpse wagon. I knew something was up, because she got all mad at me—like it was my fault." He sags. "I guess you already knew."

I shake my head. "Paulette doesn't confide in me."

162 | W. H. Cameron

"Then what were you talking about at Cuppa Jo?"

She'd gotten into his yellow pickup yesterday, but I hadn't noticed how long it was there before she ran out of the café. He must have seen at least part of our talk. I force my expression to go blank. "She was only there for a few minutes. We barely had time to say hello."

"You didn't talk about me?"

His face is blotchy. He's trying to work me for sympathy or pity. He deserves neither. If Paulette decided to scrape him off, despite the obvious pressure she's getting from every football fan in the county, good for her.

"It's not like Paulette and I are close."

"Then why is she on about you all the time? Lately, you're all she talks about." His voice squeaks with wretchedness. "She was even thinking about calling the funeral home or whatever."

My instinct to pull away gives way to a niggling thought. Yesterday, right before Landry interrupted us, Paulette had wanted to tell me something. Not about Landry, not about the rape. She'd already shut those topics down.

There's only one other possibility.

"Was it about the crash?"

"What crash?"

"At the crossroad." If she didn't want to talk about what happened with Landry, what else was there? "Did she know something about those boys from the wreck?"

"The dead guys?" His tone grows sullen.

"Yes. The *dead guys*."

"Who cares about some dumb fuckers that don't know how to drive?"

They weren't even in their car, dipshit. But Landry's callous ignorance doesn't matter. All that matters is Paulette. Is it possible she actually knew Nathan or Trae? If so, she might also know why they came to Barlow and why they stopped at the crossroad with Uriah Skeevis and Tucker Gill. Maybe even why someone would steal their bodies.

"Where does Paulette live?"

I know I sound overeager. He gets a cagey look in his eyes.

"If I tell you, will you talk to her for me?"

Unbelievable. "Forget it." I'll find her on my own.

"Wait." He reaches out as if to grab me again. I jerk away, and he throws his hands up. With his chin, he points up the hill. "Just up there. I could see you at Long Grass from her porch. When she didn't come to the door and I saw your van at the end of her street, I thought she was with you."

So he hadn't been looking for me *or* visiting Hensley. Landry had gone looking for Paulette—and found me instead. With this kind of luck, I should buy a lottery ticket.

"Well, if I see her, I'll tell her how terribly sad you are." Maybe we could share a laugh, girl to girl.

His bottom lip starts to quiver. "Wait."

"Jesus, now what?" My frayed patience is fast unraveling.

"Could you just remind her of this?"

He raises his left hand, palm out. A sharp white line runs at an angle across his palm.

"It's our *serment d'amour.*" He turns his hand over and contemplates his palm almost reverently. "We did it together."

It takes a moment for the words to sink in. He cut himself, and apparently so did Paulette.

Did she have a choice?

"I really need to go."

But before I make it even one step, he reaches into his waist pack and pulls out a wooden-handled folding knife. "This is what we used." With sure-handed grace, he flicks the blade open, tip pointed my way.

A liquid chill floods through me, and a tremor runs down my legs. Last fall, I was called out for a removal on a similar trail in the hills above Wilton. But when I arrived, they weren't ready for me. "Wrongful death," a deputy told me. "You can wait, but it'll be awhile." A woman had been a victim of multiple stab wounds.

As Landry's blade sways in front of me, I can't help but remember the wounds on the woman neck and chest, or the long slash through her coat and shirt that opened her stomach and exposed her intestines.

Someone screams, the sound an electric lance up my spine. Only when a second scream echoes the first do I realize it's not me. Landry flails and spins, both arms flying. The blade passes below my chin as I catch sight of three girls, all in blue, crowded against the white oak behind the bench.

164 | W. H. Cameron

Teen moms. Hensley girls.

Landry's eyes bulge. "Oh, fuck, I didn't mean to—" He totters toward me, knife still in hand, shaking his head frantically. "I'm sorry. *Je suis désolé.* I'm *sorry.*" His eyes bulge and the color drains from his face. Behind him, the three girls are a frozen tableau of open mouths, their eyes fixed on my chest.

I look down as a sharp pain flares at my throat. My yellow shirt with its cartoonish printing is splashed with vivid red.

He cut me. The fucker actually cut me.

With Fitz's laughter ringing in my ears, I kick Landry in the goddamn rape tackle.

TWENTY-SEVEN

Asylum

Somehow Landry manages to keep his feet, but his sudden tears and the howl in his throat tell me I've hit my target. I try to slip past him toward the screaming teen moms uphill, but he throws himself across my path. His long arms swing toward me, so quick all I can do is throw myself backward. I can't tell if he's trying to cut me again or tackle me, but I'm not sure it matters. When he lunges, I turn and bolt the other way.

Heedlessly, I hurl myself through the forest. The path cuts ever downward, first through pines, then across a second lava flow. About the time my lungs begin to burn, the trail zigzags at a switchback. Seconds later, I'm back at the lava field, maybe thirty yards below where I just crossed. Panting, I skid to a stop.

Somewhere above, Landry screams, "Fucking *bitch!*"

I want to scream too. I've evaded Landry, but now I'm cut off from the trailhead and the Stiff.

Farther down, the trail crosses the lava again, suggesting a second switchback ahead. From there, it disappears into the forest for good.

The lava field offers no cover. If he spots me, I'm sure Landry will have no problem angling down the broken slope to catch up.

And I'm already feeling spent.

I retrace my steps back through the forest, scanning downhill. At the switchback, I find what I'm looking for. A game track, half-carved by snowmelt, leads away from Landry and the exposed lava field. Without hesitating, I push through a clump of pine saplings and down the track.

Branches snap against my arms and face. I hurtle from tree to tree, catching myself on rough-barked trunks and half-sliding through dirt and pine needles. Sweat pours into my eyes, and a burning stitch shoots up my side. Somehow, I keep my feet, and before I know it, I blunder into a small clearing and skid to a stop, gasping.

Firs and larch grow among the red ponderosa. An ancient wooden sign nailed to a tree reads "DHA ½" with an arrow pointing out a path. Not the groomed Forest Service trail, but something rougher—perhaps an older track abandoned when the switchbacked route was built. Whatever DHA is, my guess is it's half a mile ahead.

Down trail, the forest canopy closes in. A comforting cover—should Landry come after me with a goddamn drone. The thought makes me laugh, and his screams seem to burn away like an old memory. Left behind is a vague sense I've overreacted, though the pain on my neck and blood-streaked shirt might suggest otherwise. I look back, but the hillside behind me is empty except for two bickering Steller's jays in the trees.

I don't want to go much farther, but I'm not eager to return quite yet—not until Landry has had time to give up on me. I don't know what DHA is, but a half mile doesn't seem too far to go to find out. Maybe the main trail connects there.

The path winds over tangled roots and rock extrusions, around the occasional fallen tree. Though the air feels overly warm and thick, my breathing calms and the stitch in my side eases. Still, a heaviness tugs at my legs. Just as I'm starting to regret coming this way, the forest opens up at a vertical cliff ahead. Relieved, I let gravity pull me down the trail and out of the trees.

It's like walking into a hot retort. The white sun hangs above the tree line, a disc of molten light in a diluted sky. Insects hum as I blink to clear the sun's purple afterimage. When my vision returns, the cliff resolves into an old stone wall.

Twice my height and built of lichen-encrusted basalt, the imposing barrier stretches twenty or thirty yards in both directions from where the path exits the forest. Clumps of grass and a few ambitious saplings break through a berm of gray, fist-sized rocks extending thirty feet out from the wall. A dilapidated water tower stands on the other side, the sun-bleached shadow of an "H" on its wooden tank. My curiosity aroused, I pick my way along the stony berm. The wall makes a right at the point where a river flows out the trees—a lot of water for these high dry hills, suggesting headwaters at or near Lost Brother's snow line. From there, the wall parallels the river for forty or fifty yards to the next corner. Another fifty yards further, a narrow, dirt road crosses the river on a flat stone bridge, perhaps a Forest Service road. Past the bridge, the river falls precipitously through the largest lava field yet before disappearing into the forest. In the distance, the trees thin as the terrain descends, eventually giving way to a high hanging valley overlooking desert and rangeland, and the Palmer River far below. With a jolt, I recognize the hanging valley as the spot Uncle Rémy and I once hiked to view wildflowers. Somewhere to the east must be his cabin, though exactly where or how far I couldn't guess.

From the bridge, the road curves up to a cast iron gate in the eastward wall of what seems to be a large, square compound. I find the gate secured with a chain and padlock. Through the rust-streaked bars, I look into a deep courtyard that may once have been as green and well kept as the Hensley School grounds. Now, only tangled thorns and patches of dry bunchgrass grow among crumbling benches and lampposts. A drive loops in front of a three-story building built of the same stone as the wall. The narrow windows are covered with weathered plywood. The steep, galvanized roof is topped with a cupola surrounded by stone crenellations like battlements on a medieval castle.

"Looks like a prison."

Affixed to the lintel over the front doors is a corroded plaque.

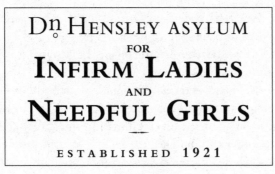

DⓇ HENSLEY ASYLUM
FOR
INFIRM LADIES
AND
NEEDFUL GIRLS

ESTABLISHED 1921

The DHA from that sign in the forest, I realize. Short for Dn. Hensley Asylum.

"What's a 'needful girl,' Mellie?"

"1921-ese for 'teen mom,' I think."

Asylum, prison. *You say potato* . . .

I assume this was probably the original Hensley School, from a time when an unwed mother was a thing to conceal, warehoused away with doddering grandmothers. No doubt all ate from the same vat of gruel. I'm glad Celeste didn't have to face this version of the Hensley School.

I tug the heavy, gleaming chain securing the gate. The padlock has a shank as thick as my thumb. I continue on along the outer wall of the compound. Past the next corner, the broad flat area extends into what I at first mistake for the upper reaches of the lava flow, though with oddly regular stones. But no. It's a scene as familiar as the one outside my bedroom window at the Old Mortuary.

A cemetery.

If the Hensley Asylum is a curiosity to me, its cemetery is a magnet. I pass between a pair of weathered gateposts in a fence that's now a memory. The ground is hard as stone, and the air smells of dust—as if I've entered a long-forgotten attic. The insect hum, quiet when I circled the asylum, returns, punctuated by the sharp cries of forest birds. Dead grass pushes up through drifts of gray oak leaves and pine needles. Unlike those at the Pioneer Cemetery, which still sees a few burials each year, the small, unadorned tombstones here are old and eroded. On most, the engravings are unreadable. Here and there I make out a name or a date. Girls and women. Died 1927, . . . died 1931. The most recent I see is from 1941. Toward the back, grave sites lie among the trees, as though the forest has begun to claim the cemetery. The place has a sad, forgotten air. These grounds haven't received the attention of an Uncle Rémy, not for a long time.

Most of the grave markers are small, with little or no decoration. But one ornate column topped by a granite Virgin Mary draws me to the rear of the cemetery. The rising ground exaggerates the monument's imperious height. Of higher quality stone than the other grave markers, I'm not surprised to see the name "HENSLEY" engraved in eight-inch letters. Beneath, surrounded by carved flowers, is an inscription.

> IN LOVING MEMORY
> ALICE ASTOR HENSLEY
> ARRIVED ON THIS EARTH – NOVEMBER 1, 1878
> PASSED UNTO HEAVEN – NOVEMBER 11, 1918

Just forty when she passed unto heaven. Below Alice's, a second name is partly obscured by a dead vine.

> GRACE FINOLA HENSLEY
> JANUARY 16, 1902 – NOVEMBER 2, 1918

Sixteen years old. No flowery phrases describe Grace's coming or going, no loving memory. Just the dates. The two might have been victims of the worldwide flu pandemic—Uncle Rémy once pointed out the disproportionate number of graves from 1918 through 1920 in the Pioneer Cemetery. But I have a feeling it was something else.

Alice and Grace, I'd guess, were wife and daughter of the eponymous Dn. Hensley of the Asylum for Infirm Ladies and Needful Girls. Given the dates and the prominence of the monument, their passings may have inspired the founding of the institution behind me.

I look back at the abandoned institution. From here, the roof and upper stories are visible above the wall. The plywood has fallen from one window on the third floor. The inmates had a view of the cemetery, though they may have felt differently about it than I do my own.

A memory springs to mind of Landry's sidekick invoking "Molly Claire's Girls." There can't be any connection between the actual Molly Claire Maguire and the Hensley Asylum—by 1921, Molly Claire was long dead. Still, I wonder if the tenuous thread of myth-making somehow wove her story in with this old ruin. The Asylum—and its cemetery—must fuel no end of bonfire tales. Its isolation and lichen-veneered creepiness make it the perfect spot for a haunting.

As calming as this visit to a forgotten cemetery has been, I've lingered long enough. Landry has had more than enough time to hobble off, and I'm still no closer to finding Pride. I return the way I came, stopping at the iron gate to look into the asylum court-yard again. I half-expect to see spirit girls and haunted old women, but there's only a crow poking the ground beneath one of the old benches.

A low rumble rises behind me, an oversized SUV with a light bar on top. It crosses the bridge and rolls to a stop about ten feet away. The passenger-side window slides down.

"Hey, Mellie!" Sheriff Turnbull's jowls quake as he calls out. "Heard you had a little problem up the trail. Hop in and we can talk about it."

TWENTY-EIGHT

Skull Fragments

At least he lets me sit up front.

The sheriff drives a Ford Expedition. I saw one rigged as a first call vehicle at the National Funeral Directors Association Expo last fall. Uncle Rémy wasn't impressed. He thinks an SUV is a poor choice for first call—overpowered yet cramped even in the long wheelbase models. "I don't need zero-to-sixty or luxury trim, just a working van with elbow room," he'd said.

The sheriff must prefer luxury. The Expedition's interior is awash with cool, fresh air. Aside from his cell phone in a cradle on the gleaming dash, there's no gear. No computer, no shotgun locked to the center console. When I shut the door, the sound of the idling engine fades to a whisper. The soft leather seat seems to draw the ache from my legs. I could almost nap—if anyone other than Turnbull was driving.

"I wondered when your turn would come," I say.

"Dunno what you mean."

"Right." First Duniway, then Jeremy, now the lord of the manor himself. The question was never if, but when.

"I'm just making sure you're okay, Mellie."

The leather seems to harden against my back. I close my eyes and count back from ten. When I open them again, we're moving up the rutted road. I hadn't even felt the vehicle start.

"You want me to take you to the hospital?"

My hand jumps to my neck, gritty with dried blood. I lower the visor to check the mirror. The cut doesn't look too bad, though a little deeper and Landry might have left my carotid exposed for Carrie when it came time to flush my remains with embalming fluid.

I flip the visor up. "I'll live."

He grunts. The sheriff is driving like he wants the trip to last. I look out at the passing trees, younger and more uniform the further we go. Soon, nothing but Ponderosa saplings grow among gray stumps.

"Would it help if I told you Landry is on his way to jail?"

A sudden void forms inside me. "Oh, great."

"Isn't that what you want?"

Like Turnbull could begin to understand what I want—or what I've faced since I pulled Landry off Paulette. He doesn't have to deal with the whispers and the sidelong glances, with the veiled threats and being knocked around the Whistle Pig. If I go after Landry again, who knows what'll happen. Once is an accident, a misunderstanding of the unwritten rules. Twice—three times if you count our encounter in Memorial Park—and I'll be forever labeled an obsessed harpy out to get an All-American hero.

"I'm not pressing charges."

"May not be up to you." He scratches his meaty chin. "I have three witnesses who saw him attack you with a knife. We can charge him on the basis of their statements, but it'll be a lot easier to convict if you play along."

I laugh bitterly. "Oh, so *now* you want to take down Landry?"

The sheriff frowns. The funny thing is I truly don't think Landry meant to hurt me. He's cruel and self-absorbed, but today all he wanted was an audience for his performative act of self-pity. *Poor me. My girlfriend dumped me, wah wah.*

All my signature on a police report will do is ease the sheriff's guilt and give the fine citizens of Barlow County yet another grievance against me.

"Do what you have to do, but keep me out of it."

I expect the sheriff to go all paternalistic autocrat on me. He only sighs. "Something else I wanted to discuss with you anyway."

"Pride?" I fold my arms over my chest. "Or the missing bodies?"

He seems to chew on the question as he stops the SUV. We've come to a road—Wayette Highway north of Crestview I'd guess, though I don't spot any obvious landmarks. Between the village and the airport, there's little except the rare house, a couple of bridges, and a lot of trees.

The sheriff twists to lean against the doorpost, fingers laced across his belly. "How about you decide."

Some choice. I take a different path entirely. "You get a lot of calls to bust parties at that old place?"

If he's annoyed by my deflection, he doesn't show it. "Not as many as you'd think. Of course, the old grounds are still property of the Hensley Foundation. School security keeps a weather eye on things. How else do you think I knew where to find you? There's a pair of security cameras on the front of the old building. Motion activated, sends a text when anything approaches the gate. Like a bear, or a Mellie." He glances my way. "How'd you end up down there? Bit off the beaten path."

"I was sightseeing."

He chuckles.

"What's the story behind that place anyway?"

"Product of the times. Dalton Hensley was an old-timey land baron who got religion late in life. He was born poor on the Oregon Trail but made a fortune in the county. Timber and mining mostly, along with selling shovels and beans. Back then, Crestview was called Mudbath and was bigger than Samuelton. The old ghost town behind the nursing home is all that's left of it. Anyway, when Dalton built the house that's now the Long Grass Bed and Breakfast, he decided the town needed a more respectable name. That was in 1910."

"Did he get religion before or after his wife and daughter died?"

"You saw the graves."

I nod.

"After. Tuberculosis took the wife, though it was believed the daughter's death hastened her demise." Sheriff Turnbull looks grave. "Supposedly the girl was ravished by a logger, but talk around town was the fellow was in fact her beau, whom she bedded freely and frequently."

"She died in childbirth?"

"Officially, complications after a miscarriage." He shakes his head. "But according to the gossips, she hemorrhaged during an abortion. Alice passed a week later."

"And that inspired Hensley to build an asylum in the woods."

"The man had money to burn and torches to carry. But he died in 1929, and though his will established a foundation to keep the work going, the place shut down during World War II. After the war, the trustees decided the two missions were incompatible in a single, isolated institution. The asylum itself never reopened. In the sixties, the Hensley Foundation licensed the ladies' rest home to some East Coast health-care operation that changed the name to Crestview Assisted Living and opened the doors to gents. But the Hensley Foundation still runs the new school directly."

It's strange and a little disquieting to think Uncle Rémy's current home was once part of an institution that started out as confinement for pregnant girls and their heartbroken mothers. The more I pull at the threads of recent events, the more entangled they all become. It *can't* be coincidence I stumbled across a newborn baby so near a twenty-first-century asylum for needful girls.

I look at the sheriff. "How sure are you that baby didn't come from Hensley?"

His eyebrows go up, then he smiles a little. "Pretty damn sure. And not just me either. Before we even finished our investigation, a case manager from state DHS showed up. Between us, that place got inspected up one side and down the other."

"You couldn't have missed something?"

"Mellie, you are one suspicious young woman."

"I have my reasons, especially when it comes to the Barlow County Sheriff's Department."

He side-eyes me. "Are you ever *not* nettled about something?"

I squeeze my arms tight against my chest to keep from punching him. Outside, the lowering sun has fallen behind the trees. The cab feels cold. A semi-rig whips past, throwing a tremor through the vehicle.

"Are we done here?" I feel a sudden need to visit Uncle Rémy and Aunt Elodie. Maybe pick up grilled cheese sandwiches and tomato soup from the Mercantile. Pretend none of this is happening.

"It's Omar, isn't it?" When I don't respond, the sheriff adds, "He's pursuing all possible avenues of investigation. It's nothing personal."

"Feels pretty fucking personal to me."

Disapproval rumbles deep in his chest. "You in jail?"

"You *suspended* me. And I had to find out he'd been rooting through my shit from the search warrant he left on the credenza."

"Would you have given him permission to search if he'd asked?"

My silence is all the *no* he needs.

His hands unlace. "Chief Deputy Duniway has acted with the diligence of a responsible investigator." He could be reading from a teleprompter. "The investigation is ongoing, but had he found evidence implicating you in the theft and destruction of those bodies, the district attorney would have acted quickly."

The sheriff himself ran my background check when I was listed as a removal specialist on Bouton's county contract. He asked far too many personal questions—with a laser focus on those parts of my life that didn't show up on a computer report. He was particularly interested in the circumstances surrounding my departure from Paris and what effect my medical history might have on my ability to do my job. I never felt like my answers were good enough. Nothing I say now will be good enough either.

"Whatever you think you know about me, I would never do anything to hurt Aunt Elodie or Uncle Rémy."

He nods a fraction of an inch. "Glad to hear it, Mellie."

"Jesus." I run my hand over my face. "How many times have I asked you to stop calling me Mellie?"

"I might need to take my shoes off to count that high."

"And yet you keep doing it."

He's quiet for a long time. "I thought it was a little game we were playing, but I see I was being obtuse. For that, I apologize. What would you like me to call you?"

I look for a clue in his eyes that this is another a joke. But his expression is contrite.

My legs are sore and my head aches. I'm too damn tired for this. "Mel is fine."

"Mel it is."

We're both quiet. Finally, I draw a breath. "Are we done?"

"In fact, new information related to the missing bodies has come to light. I was hoping you could run down the day for me again."

A couple of southbound cars pass, followed by a pickup towing a boat. Then the driver of a bright yellow convertible tosses out an empty coffee cup onto the shoulder near the Expedition. "You going to let that asshole get away with that?"

He folds his hands across his belly, a big old toad. "I left my citation pad at the office."

I shake my head imperceptibly. "I've told you everything."

"So tell me again."

I'm trapped like a bug in a jar. All I can do is summarize the fateful day, starting from when I transported the first body and finishing when Pride and I opened Trae Fowler's empty drawer.

"And then you did what?"

I embarrassed myself in front of Pride is what. "This is not happening," I'd said, yanking open the other drawers. "This is not happening." Pride had kept his cool and called 911.

"Mrs. Crandall's body was unmolested?"

Not the word I would choose. "Untouched, yes."

"And you had no other bodies at that time."

"No."

"Maybe someone Quince brought in?"

"Quince doesn't transport without me. Besides, our fridge only has four drawers, and I needed all of them. I'd have noticed a double-booking." There's a three-drawer portable unit in the storage room, but it was unplugged and empty. "Why are you asking all this?"

"We've completed our preliminary examination of the cremated remains."

My muscles clench. His tone has taken on a troubling note.

"Imagine our surprise when we found fragments of a fourth skull."

"What?"

"I've sent everything to the state crime lab for more detailed analysis, but we also found two spare femurs, a lower mandible—you name it."

Our crematory is roomy, but it would have been tough maneuvering three bodies at once in the retort. With four, it's a wonder the gas jets didn't get blocked. I shudder. It would have to be someone small—or young. Another teenager?

The photo in Pride's car. The baby in the desert. *Jesus.*

"It was a girl, wasn't it?"

"What makes you say that?"

The sheriff leans forward as if he expects a revelation, but I can only speculate.

"Maybe Nathan and Trae had someone with them. The mother."

He nods as if the thought already occurred to him. "Where was she when we were scraping bodies off the pavement?"

In the fourth car? If Pride hasn't mentioned his theory about a fourth car to the sheriff, he must have his reasons. I feel the weight of a secret I didn't ask for. This is my chance to unburden myself. Give the cops someone else to fix on—and leave me the hell alone.

"The cremated remains of the stolen bodies aren't the only thing you sent to the state crime lab."

It's a clumsy attempt to change the subject. He raises an eyebrow. "And how would you know that?"

I hope I haven't gotten Danae in trouble. "No secrets in Samu-elton, Sheriff."

His eyes go sharp. "This isn't a matter of public record, Melisende."

Not Mellie, not Mel.

Melisende.

Phlegm collects at the back of my throat. It's another secret, but one I need to hear. Diffident, I attempt a bland smile. "Who would I tell?"

"Your math teacher friend, for one."

He has me there. I start to make a promise I won't keep, but he cuts me off.

"Dr. Varney pulled a bullet out of Nathan Harper's back."

The cab of the Expedition seems to grow painfully cold. A bullet means Nathan Harper wasn't fleeing some ordinary motor vehicle collision. So who was doing the shooting? The men from the Eldorado? Or whoever was in Pride's mystery car?

"You gonna tell him, little sister?"

A siren wails from the road to our right. Light bar flashing, a patrol car blasts past, heading for Crestview. At once, the sheriff's cell phone rings. He gives me an unreadable look as he snatches the phone from its cradle.

"Turnbull."

He listens, then lets out a low whistle. "You're sure? . . . Okay, where?" He nods, then adds, "Tsokapo Gorge, got it." His eyes steal my way, unreadable. "Be there in five."

He plunks the phone back in its cradle. "Got a situation."

The last week has been one endless situation. I need time to think. "I'll walk back to town." I reach for the door handle.

"Oh no, Mellie." He activates his light bar, throws the SUV into gear, and hits the gas. "We're not done yet."

TWENTY-NINE

Cerise Creek Trail

My first New Year's Day in Barlow County, a married couple from Portland went missing while cross-country skiing on Lost Brother Butte. They were experienced hikers and skiers with an intimate knowledge of the region, so friends were surprised when they didn't appear for dinner at the lodge that night. Fearing the worst, Fire and Rescue was called out, but a winter storm interrupted the search almost before it began. By the time the weather cleared, the high country had received twenty inches of snow. For all their experience, the couple hadn't carried a locator beacon, nor had they told anyone their planned route.

By May, most had forgotten about the missing couple. Then some fifth-graders from Eugene, visiting for outdoor school, found a ski boot near the Salt Creek trail. The foot was still inside. A search for additional remains was led by a wildlife expert and a state forensic anthropologist. They turned up skis, pieces of a down jacket, and bones—including two partially denuded skulls. Within a day, investigators confirmed the remains belonged to the missing couple. The best guess was that they'd become disoriented when the storm closed in, and presumably had died of exposure.

Though not involved in the recovery of the remains, Uncle Rémy brought me out to the site to observe. I'll never forget seeing the woman's decomposed torso pulled from a rocky hollow under a cliff. Much of the flesh and organs had been stripped away by scavengers. What remained seemed less a person than a prop from a cheesy horror flick. But as the team moved the torso to a body bag, something glinted and fell from the ribcage. I drew a sharp breath when the crew member picked up a blown-glass pendant in the shape of a hummingbird.

Uncle Rémy noticed my reaction but misjudged its cause. "This sort of thing is always a possibility," he said. "In our business, you need to be ready for anything." He spoke in the same sincere tone he used to tell the bereaved he was sorry for their loss.

I'd nodded, but I wasn't really listening. I was thinking about a glass hummingbird I'd bought at an arts fair in Provincetown—a gift for Helene. I never gave it to her, afraid she'd think it silly or sentimental. I suppose my parents sold it, along with the rest of my meager belongings, to pay my back rent after I was evicted from my apartment.

As Sheriff Turnbull pulls out onto Wayette Highway, a heavy foreboding settles over me. I find myself thinking about the dead woman's pendant. The sheriff isn't bringing me along because he enjoys my company. Something has happened. In our business, you need to be ready for anything.

He tears down the winding road, indifferent when I grab the handle over my door. Within seconds we pass the turn-off for the Hensley School, and then we're through Crestview in the space of a breath. Trees whip by in a gray-green blur until we cross a bridge, then make a sharp turn onto a paved ramp. The sheriff coasts back toward the bridge for a few hundred feet, before stopping beside a Barlow County Fire and Rescue ambulance and two department patrol cars. Dr. Varney's silver-gray Escalade is one of several other vehicles in the gravel lot.

The sheriff kills the engine and opens his door. "Come on, Mel."

"I can wait."

"I said come on." He slides out with unexpected agility. "That wasn't a request."

At least he called me Mel.

Worry shadows me like a cloud as I follow. Behind a row of pruned junipers, a small, shady clearing overlooks the gorge under the bridge. There are a couple of picnic tables, a hitching rail next to a trough and spigot, and a cinderblock latrine. The Forest Service kiosk informs me we're at the Tsokapo Gorge Wayside on the

Cerise Creek Trail—another section of the same trail I fled down not so long ago. Here, the path hugs the lip of the gorge, climbing through trees to my left, dipping under the bridge to my right. The easterly wind smells of sand and pine, as well as something acrid and unpleasant.

Deputy Ariana Roldán waits with a tan, dark-haired young girl—maybe eight or nine—at one of the picnic tables. Tears streak the trail dust on her cheeks. Her mother sits with her, one hand stroking her neck. The gesture stirs an ancient memory in me of a time before Fitz died, before my mother became merely Cricket Dulac. A pink-faced man nearby rounds out the family. He rubs his face, then reaches out to his wife. His hand hangs in the space between them as if grasping for something in the dark. Head bowed over her daughter, the woman doesn't seem to notice. They're dressed for the trail—boots, cargo shorts, and blousy cotton shirts. A large day pack lies on the table beside three insulated water bottles. Uncle Rémy would approve.

Deputy Roldán speaks to the couple, then goes to huddle with the sheriff, away from both the family and me. I listen to the wind in the gorge, to birds squawking in the trees. I peer up at the arches of the bridge, at the high blue sky. I don't need to hear what the sheriff and his lone female deputy are saying. I don't need a formal callout to tell me what's going on.

"Aren't you still on suspension, little sister?"

"I'm not here to remove a body." I don't care if anyone hears. "The sheriff wants to see how I react to one."

☙ ❧

Sheriff Turnbull leaves Deputy Roldán with the family and leads me beneath the bridge. A stream winds among boulders and fallen tree trunks in the bottom of the gorge, twenty feet below the trail's edge. Beer bottles and other trash have collected at the high-water mark halfway up the gorge walls. The unpleasant odor grows stronger.

We pass the Fire and Rescue volunteers, standing to one side of the trail, smoking and talking with Dr. Varney. Jeremy is with them. The doctor nods a greeting, but I hurry past, uninterested in chitchat.

Tsokapo Gorge slices through basalt and welded ash threaded with ancient magma intrusions. At its bottom runs a stream, ankle deep and calm. Cliff swallows emerge from mud nests on the gorge wall to feed on flies buzzing above the water's surface, squeaking and churring as they swoop.

Below the bridge, the stream falls down a steep decline to a blue-green pool fifty or sixty feet below. During the spring snowmelt, this must be an impressive waterfall, but in high summer it's a gentle burble. The trail descends beside the falls via hewn-rock steps and a series of natural terraces, with walls on either side. At the bottom, the trail curls around the pool, then crosses a wooden bridge and continues into the pine forest.

At the top of the falls, Turnbull gestures toward a puddle of vomit on a rock ledge jutting out from the bridge embankment—the source of the stench.

"The father puked when he came to see what upset his daughter."

Ten feet below, a body lies facedown on the first terraced ledge, arms splayed at his sides, palms up. My foreboding hardens into a numb certainty. I know it's Pride without seeing his face. Tall and lean, hair the color of ripe barley. I recognize his shirt with its epaulets, his khaki pants, and the Rockports he was wearing this morning at the Mercantile.

"No wallet," the sheriff says. "We haven't moved him, and it may not help when we do. We're pretty sure who it is, but you saw him last."

"It's Kendrick Pride." Behind his right knee, his pants are dark with blood, the lower leg bent at an unlikely angle. "The little girl found him?"

The sheriff's eyes are hollow. "The family is staying at Brother Drop, visiting the fish hatchery, doing vacation stuff. They were hiking the trail loop and passed this spot about an hour ago. He wasn't here then. But the little girl wanted to come back, wade in the pool and chase salamanders." He inhales sharply. "She was so excited, she ran ahead."

"Jesus." A small dark pool of congealing blood surrounds Pride's head, a grim corona.

"Poor kid was scared out of her mind."

Anyone would be. Yet the scene is inexplicably tranquil—the buff gorge walls, the murmuring stream, the blue sky above. Though half-closed eyes, you might just convince yourself the prone figure is resting. But I've seen it too often. Not resting. Not even a man, not anymore. Remains—what's left when our animating spark fades.

I wonder about Pride's family and whether he's made his funeral wishes known. Open casket is out of the question. The distance from the bridge is tough to gauge, but Pride is lying facedown. His facial bones would have shattered on impact.

The rest of the damage may be manageable. Carrie and Aunt Elodie would know. As I study the purplish blue skin on his palms and the exposed skin on the backs of the arms, something Carrie once said tugs at me, something about another body. I reach for it, but the memory flees as a raven lands near the body. The bird's croak jerks me from my reverie. Its head pivots side to side, sizing up Pride's scalp. With another rumbling croak, it bounces toward him.

Without thinking, I jump down the wide, uneven steps. The sheriff shouts, and from the corner of my eye I see him reach out to stop me. I dodge his grasp, skirting wide of the blood haloing Pride's head, and throw a kick at the huge black bird.

"Git! *Shoo!*"

The raven aims its thick beak at my foot, striking the steel toe without effect. I holler again and clap furiously. The raven launches into the air at my face. With a shriek, I throw my arms up, feel wings beat my scalp. I duck sideways and catch myself on the gorge wall. When I look up, the raven is already banking in the open air beneath the bridge. It croaks one last time, then glides toward the forest downstream.

Heart in my throat, I lean against the rough stone to catch my breath. A thread of silver catches my eye. Hanging from the fine chain caught in the cracked rock is a gleaming oval pendant.

The last time I saw Pride, he blanched at the sight of this very chain. The locket wasn't just any piece of jewelry. I should tell the sheriff it's here, where it came from. But then what? Pride could have shared his speculations with the sheriff, but didn't. He was a lawyer on sabbatical, representing the interests of Trae Fowler's family and perhaps Nathan Harper's—yet from the start he'd acted like he was working a criminal investigation.

"What in hell are you thinking?"

The sheriff's voice makes me nearly jump out of my skin. I twist as his shadow falls over me. He looms at the top of the trail, hands on his hips.

"Well?"

Pride's law firm bio described him as a husband, a father. If the locket was important to him, wouldn't it be important to those he left behind? And if I alert the sheriff, might it simply disappear into the evidence locker in the Barlow Building, to be ignored or forgotten?

I try to smile. "I didn't want the bird to disturb the remains."

Casually, I drop my hands, snagging the silver chain and slipping it into my jeans pocket as I move away from the wall.

"You didn't touch anything, did you?"

The locket feels hot enough to burn a hole through my skin. "I'm not an idiot."

He studies me. "No, you're not." If only he knew. The glare fades, replaced by a faint smile. "You have something of your Aunt Elodie in you, don't you."

I listen for the reproach in his tone, but there's none. I flush and look away.

"Now, please, Mel, get back up here."

The sheriff has never said *please* to me, let alone offered any praise. An unexpected sensation floods through me, one I associate with Uncle Rémy and Aunt Elodie. But just as quickly, it dissolves into a disquieting guilt. Aunt Elodie might defend the dead from a scavenger, but she would never pilfer their belongings.

I join the sheriff and the others under the bridge. Jeremy frowns as if he knows I'm hiding something. The others straighten up and stub out their cigarettes, attentive vassals in the presence of their lord. If it were up to me, I'd keep walking. Back to the rest area, up the ramp to the highway. Stick out my thumb, accept the first ride offered. To Reno, Tijuana. Timbuktu. Anywhere but here.

But just like that night at the crossroad, I'm stuck.

THIRTY

Ass to the Wind

The sheriff asks the Fire and Rescue volunteers to wait with their ambulance until he's ready for them to transport the body. They shuffle past me, avoiding eye contact. Everyone knows why I'm not on the job.

"We'll need to make an official identification," the sheriff says when they're gone, "but Melisende agrees the dead man is Kendrick Pride. The evidence tech is on her way, though the situation seems clear enough." My hand steals into my pocket to finger the oval locket. The sheriff turns to Dr. Varney. "Our witnesses give us a window for time of death. What are your thoughts?"

"I think he fell off the bridge." Varney stretches a pair of nitrile gloves between his hands. "Long way down."

"Died on impact?"

"At the very least we can assume massive brain trauma. If not instantaneous, it was quick enough." He shrugs. "I'll run a tox screen to see if he was impaired and do a more thorough visual at the morgue, but I see no reason to cut him."

"You're thinking accident?"

"From up top, the gorge is something else."

Jeremy nods. "It's a wonder this hasn't happened before. I've lost count of the hikers I've caught sitting on the guardrail up there, ass to the wind, admiring the view. As if the bridge doesn't shake like a mofo when trucks go by."

"The lack of a wallet has to be considered."

"Robbery?"

Everyone looks at Varney, who raises his hands uncertainly. "There's no obvious defensive wounds or contusions, but I'll know more after I get him back to the morgue." He peers up at the bridge. "Anything up there?"

The sheriff looks at Jeremy, who shakes his head. "No watch, but no tan line to indicate he wore one," he says. "His keys and phone were in his pockets, along with about forty bucks. Phone's busted all to hell." Jeremy holds up a plastic evidence bag. No bullet casings. The phone looks like it was hit with a hammer. "As for his wallet, some guys stick it in the console when they're driving. Maybe he forgot it."

"His car is at the trailhead by the Hensley School," I say.

The sheriff gives me a quick nod, then turns back to Jeremy. "Check it out." He takes his chin in his hand. "Why leave the cash, though?"

"Wayette isn't I-5 at rush hour," Jeremy says, "but Saturday afternoon during camping season makes it a risky spot for a robbery. The woods would make more sense."

"Which puts us back at accident."

"Unless you turn up a suicide note," Varney says.

I make a face. Pride no more killed himself than he hiked the Cerise Creek Trail. He was too focused, too driven. I also can't picture him sitting on the guardrail, ass to the wind. "Where's his gear? The trail between here and the school has to be long enough he'd at least bring a water bottle. Maybe a trail map and an emergency kit too." A flare gun wouldn't surprise me.

"How would you know?" Varney says. "Were you two close?"

They all stare at me, Jeremy the hardest.

We had three uncomfortable conversations, none a basis for friendship. "I barely knew him. But the few times we did talk, he didn't come off as a total idiot."

Varney frowns. "Well, I only met him the one time"—he lifts his chin toward the sheriff—"after that boy's autopsy, you remember."

The sheriff nods.

"He was pretty agitated, but I can't say I thought him likely to harm himself. I'll request his medical history, though."

"Maybe Mizz Dulac chucked him over." The voice comes from the direction of the wayside. We all turn to see Chief Deputy Omar

Duniway laughing as he tramps toward us. The lowering sun silhouettes him, but I can feel his eyes on me. He pushes into the group, elbowing Jeremy aside. "Sorry I'm late, Sheriff," he says, eyes still on me. "A word, please?"

"Of course."

The two move down trail to the top of the falls. Duniway glances down but seems indifferent to the body.

Beside me, Varney stretches the gloves between his hands again. "I was at a barbecue. It's supposed to be the weekend." With that, he heads for the wayside.

Frowning, I strain to hear Duniway and the sheriff. The swallows darting through the gorge are louder.

Duniway is talking fast, half with his hands. The sheriff nods once or twice and kneads the sun-reddened flesh on the back of his neck.

When Duniway shuts up at last, the sheriff looks my way, his eyes grave. He waves for us to join them. I hesitate, but he gestures again.

"Come on, Mel. You too, Deputy."

All I can do is follow Jeremy.

We gather in a circle. The sheriff tilts his head at Duniway. "The chief deputy has a matter he'd like to discuss."

Jeremy's eyes bounce between his two superiors. "What's going on?"

Ignoring him, Duniway hooks his thumbs in his gear belt. "Anything you want to get off your chest, Mizz Dulac?"

Something in his tone makes my throat clench with sudden misgiving.

"Nothing? You're usually so full of sass." He chortles, a false sound from him, then pulls a small gray electronic device from a pouch on his belt. It has an LCD display and some kind of lens on one end. "Know what this is?"

No one answers.

"Laser distance meter, accurate to three-hundred-thirty feet. More than enough for our purposes today." He points up at the bridge. "From the guardrail to where our decedent struck is eighty-nine feet, seven inches. May not be important, but I like to be thorough." Quick nod to the sheriff. "For the report, you see."

"Okay," Jeremy says. "So what?"

Duniway lowers his gray stare onto me. "The way it works is you point the laser to wherever you want to measure, in this case from the bridge to the point of impact. This particular model links to your phone, with a viewfinder to help you aim. It's got zoom and everything."

"Omar, we get it." The sheriff sounds tired, which is perhaps even more unnerving than Duniway's giddy performance.

"Right. Well, a few minutes ago when I stopped on the bridge to measure the drop, I saw a curious thing in the viewfinder." He shows me his yellow teeth. "Mind telling us what you put in your pocket, Mizz Dulac?"

The ground seems to quake beneath my feet, as if it could give way any second. I attempt to laugh. "Women's jeans don't have pockets." Of course they do—too small to be that useful maybe, but adequate for a locket on a chain.

Duniway mock-frowns and swivels his head from side to side.

If I run, they'll catch me. If I jump, the shallow pool below won't save me, not on a July afternoon months after the last rainfall. Might be just as well. No one here would care. Duniway could play with his toy, measure the distance to my body. Turnbull would have a new tale to tell at the Bear Lodge: Crazy Mellie and the Locket of Doom. Jeremy would have to find a new target for his wheedling.

I wonder if any of them would stop the salamanders from disturbing my remains.

"Deputy Chapman," Duniway says, "please take Mizz Dulac into custody."

I sense Jeremy's dismay without having to look. "What are we talking about here, Chief Deputy?"

"Can I be any more plain? She removed evidence from the scene of an active death investigation. I want her cuffed, I want her in my truck, and I want it *now*." Duniway's yellow teeth are those of a predator. "It's time this little chippy explained herself."

PART FOUR

Regrets

As the flowers are all made sweeter by the sunshine and the dew, so this old world is made brighter by the lives of folks like you.

—Epitaph of Bonnie
Parker, died 1934

THIRTY-ONE

White Room

They take the locket. They take my purse. They take my boots and belt. Duniway wants to take my bra too, but the sheriff steps in. "What do you think she's going to do, Omar? Hog-tie you with lingerie?"

Only Fitz laughs. *"Maybe you'll get to wear one of those stripy prison outfits."*

They leave me in my blood-streaked T-shirt.

Duniway sticks me behind a metal table in a small room across the hall from the sheriff's office. Sits facing me. His tobacco breath could wilt flowers.

"You gonna answer my questions, or you gonna be a problem?"

Helene once gave me a wallet card. On one side, it listed what to do "If You Are Arrested." On the other, "If You Are Sexually Assaulted." They took my wallet, but I'll never forget the theme common to both sides: Don't trust the cops.

"Someone broke into Kendrick Pride's car. You were seen poking around it this afternoon. Care to comment?"

"No." That's all I can manage. Anything else and my voice might break.

His gray eyes bear down on me. I fold my hands on the table to keep them from shaking. There are red abrasions on my wrists, but at least they took the handcuffs off.

"Why'd you steal the locket? You don't seem like a jewelry girl."

Metallic light shines from a mesh cage on the ceiling. The room is painfully white and clean, as if rarely used. Can't be much call for murder interrogations in Barlow County, land of bar fights and domestic abuse. In one corner of the ceiling, a small glass globe holds a camera. No red light, but that doesn't mean we're not being recorded.

"If you talk to me, maybe I can help you. You've not been charged yet."

Yet.

But I'm not listening to Duniway. I'm thinking about what I'm going to say to Aunt Elodie. I lifted evidence from . . . what? A crime scene? If Pride's fall into Tsokapo Gorge was an accident, it didn't become a crime scene until I took the locket. The crime of idiocy, especially with Duniway already trying to implicate me in body snatching. But in Aunt Elodie and Uncle Rémy's eyes, I did something far worse—I stole from the dead. Duniway can do whatever he likes. It's Aunt Elodie I can't face.

"Is there something special about the locket? Is that why you broke into his car? Were you looking for it?"

Duniway's tone reminds me of my therapist back in the psych ward. Fifteen months ago, though it feels like fifteen years. Like him, she was firm but cajoling. Urging me to talk, to engage with my Plan of Care. She had translucent skin like antique glass. Each evening, she'd bring me to a room adjacent to the nurses station, an anonymous space with vinyl furniture and a framed watercolor of mountains like you'd see in a Hampton Inn. A window with blinds looked out on the ward. She'd leave the blinds open, close the door. To onlookers, we were a television with the sound muted.

"You seem like a night owl," she said at our first meeting.

I sat on the edge of the couch. "I don't know what kind of owl I am."

"You're up at night and sleep during the day. That's all I'm saying."

"Time has no meaning here."

She smiled like a character in a diarrhea commercial. "That's a little dramatic, don't you think? There are clocks. There are windows."

"A window is no better than a movie on a screen."

Her diarrhea smile went saccharine. "Would you like to go outside? How about lunch tomorrow in the courtyard?"

Everything was a negotiation. In exchange for lunch in the courtyard, she wanted to hear why I didn't believe my parents were trying to help me. For a visit to the library, I had to recount the ways I'd sabotaged myself at UMass. When I asked to make a phone call, she wanted to know what I missed most about Geoffrey.

She didn't believe me when I said nothing. She had notes on what had happened when his mother and father confronted me after my return from Paris. My own parents had showed up in the middle of the fray, suddenly aware of me for the first time in years—embarrassment overcoming indifference. Between my exhaustion, my frayed nerves, and too many cocktails on the flight from Paris, I'd made the slip that landed me in psych hold.

"Fitz, please tell these assholes where he is so they'll get *off my fucking back.*"

Mistake. In the week since Geoffrey had vanished, I'd already begun to think of him as a memory, someone I'd known in another life. I wasn't sure I'd even recognize him if we passed on the street. Our brief, tumultuous marriage had carved a divide between what I once was and who I might become, a chasm that bottomed out in the gendarme's office in Paris at the moment I finally saw cherry blossoms.

"What would you like to happen here?" the therapist asked my third night on the ward.

"You know what I want."

She surprised me by taking out her cell phone. "Tell me the number. I'll make sure whoever answers would like to talk to you."

"What do you get out of it?"

"This isn't about me, Melisende."

I leaned back and pulled my knees up to my chest. The painting on the wall went soft and wet. I told her the number. She dialed and listened, then lowered the phone to her lap. "It went to voicemail."

I held out my hand. "That's okay." Voicemail was better, in fact. She hesitated, but I told her I'd do whatever she asked. Talk about Geoffrey, about Cricket and Stedman. About Fitz. Dig the pus from my wounds and put it on display.

"Honesty is all I ask," she said as she redialed. I'd refused my medication that day, and my hands shook when she offered me the phone.

194 | W. H. Cameron

"Helene, hi. It's me. I'm sure I'm the last person you want to talk to, and that's fine. I just wanted to say . . ." She watched me intently. "I just wanted to say I hope you're okay. That's all. I hope you're okay."

The therapist wanted to hear about Helene, but I'd lied. I was done talking.

"Maybe tomorrow," she said.

There wouldn't be a tomorrow. My seventy-two-hour hold had expired. During the night, before the hospital could alert Cricket and Stedman, I checked out AMA. Later that morning, Cricket called my cell phone to say they had changed the locks at their house. Unless I made significant changes in my lifestyle, I wouldn't be welcome back. "Whatever. I lost my keys in Paris anyway." I tried Helene again, but she didn't answer. If Aunt Elodie hadn't called later that day, there's no telling where I'd be now.

There will be no AMA checkout with Duniway. Just questions and more questions.

"Did you speak with Kendrick Pride after the Mercantile? Maybe on the Tsokapo Gorge bridge?"

The room feels short of air.

"Was he angry with you?"

In my mind, I picture Helene's wallet card, simple declarative statements that come back to me as Duniway natters on.

You are legally obligated to identify yourself, but not to answer any other questions.

"Did you two fight?"

Do not volunteer any information.

"Did you see him fall?"

Do not argue, use profanity, or raise your voice.

"Did you *help* him fall?"

Whether detained or arrested, ask for an attorney.

"I want a lawyer," I say, my voice unexpectedly loud in the conspace.

He nods as if it's exactly what he expected. "You know what that makes you look like."

"Like someone who passed high school civics," is what Helene would say. I keep my mouth shut.

Duniway goes to the door and calls for Deputy Roldán. When she appears, he says, "She wants a lawyer, let her call a lawyer." To me he adds, "This late on a Saturday night? Good luck."

Deputy Roldán leads me to the large shared space where the rest of the staff works, a half-dozen desks in two rows behind a high counter. Town Common's vintage streetlights shine through the windows, most half open to let in the night air. I hear music from the Whistle Pig—Saturday night is live bluegrass. Dailie's looks busy, and a few people linger outside the antiques mall. I'm only a little surprised no teens loiter in Memorial Park. It strikes me how cocksure Landry and his friends must be to hold a beer bash in full view of the Sheriff's Department.

Roldán points to an empty desk. "Dial nine for an outside line."

The chair creaks beneath my weight. The phone looks older than I am, dense black plastic with a row of clear buttons below the worn touch pad. I'm tempted to call Paris and leave the phone off the hook.

"Can't I use my cell phone?" I don't remember phone numbers, not even Barb's. Everyone is in my contacts list. Tap a name, send a text. Talk only as a last resort.

"Your personal effects are secured." She taps a printed list of phone numbers, mostly staff, taped to the desktop next to the phone. "Bouton Funerary is on there. Or maybe I can scare up a phone book?" The doubt in her voice tells me how likely that is. She walks away without waiting for an answer.

The only lawyer I know is dead. The Bouton number will forward to my cell phone, then the mortuary voicemail box when I don't answer. Aunt Elodie may get the message, or Wanda on Monday morning.

I punch nine and dial the one number I do know by heart, then wait through the familiar voicemail greeting.

"Helene, hi. It's me. Jesus, you know that." I hate how predictable I've become. "I did something stupid, and now I'm in trouble." Roldán sits on one of the empty desks, her back to me. "That's not why I'm calling, though. I don't expect you to do anything. It's not your problem, and I'm not asking for help." I take a breath. "I just hope you're okay."

Roldán approaches when I cradle the phone. "Did you get something worked out?"

"I left a message."

She smiles sympathetically. "They'll call back. They always do."

Helene hasn't called back in a year and a half. There's no reason to think she will now. Especially since I didn't tell her where I was.

Roldán takes hold of my upper arm. Then she guides me to the basement jail and puts me in a cell. Cinderblock and concrete, all white—though unlike the interrogation room, the paint is scratched with profanities and crude drawings of boobs and dicks—though one talented soul scratched out a deft Pubic Hair Rapunzel. The plastic bench mounted to the wall is narrow, and barely long enough for me to lie down. A compact fluorescent bulb hums in its overhead cage. Above the steel door is the small globe with the camera. The only color is the stainless steel of the combo toilet/wash basin and inexplicable flower print on the toilet paper.

Roldán leaves me there, then reappears with bottled water and a plastic-wrapped sandwich. "Don't try to flush your trash."

The sandwich is processed cheese and white lettuce on damp bread. I drop it uneaten on the floor by the toilet but drain the water bottle in one long pull. Though the cell feels hermetically sealed, sounds filter in. Weeping and swearing, a rhythmic thud like someone knocking their head against the wall. I lie back on the bench and wrap my arms around myself, wondering if Landry is nearby or if he bailed out already. The cell isn't cold, but I shiver anyway.

"Mellie, you're going to be fine."

Fitz's voice sounds like its coming from the bottom of a steel drum.

"I'm not so sure."

"You're just feeling alone. But this isn't the first time, is it? Do you remember?"

"No."

"Yes, you do."

Yes, I do.

Nine years old, wandering the house by myself, I found a photo album in my mother's bedside table. All pictures of Fitz. None of me. He came to me that night, a voice in the dark. Dead a year, yet his voice coaxed me to bed and sang me to sleep.

He's been with me ever since.

"Sing to me, Fitz?"

He laughs. *"Only if you sing too."*

"They'll throw away the key."

"Nonsense. It'll be like Lúthien enchanting Morgoth's hordes in Angband."

I scoff at the Tolkien reference, but he insists. So we sing Fitz's favorite song, one from our grandmother's record collection about a gangster shotgunned in a hotel lobby.

I hope the whole goddamn jail can hear us.

THIRTY-TWO

Postmortem Stain

No blanket, no pillow. Not even a real bed. The noise never ends, but at some point I drift into a fitful drowse. I dream of vultures and bullets and falling, of lying on a stainless steel preparation table. Carrie leans over me, Landry beside her. "I cut her right there." He points at my neck. "She wanted it to be easy for you to find the artery."

"Too bad she hit face first," Carrie says. "Open casket is out of the question."

My eyes pop open to a white ceiling, not the satin lining of a casket. My cell smells faintly of blood diluted with embalming fluid. My mouth feels like it's caked with wax. A shooting pain runs from my neck to the base of my spine. The light hasn't changed since they locked me in. It could be midnight or noon. A cobweb hangs from the surveillance camera, still in the dead air.

But I'm not thinking about any of that. I'm thinking about remains on the New Mortuary preparation table. It was last September, a chilly morning threatening rain. Carrie met me at the back door.

I'd been working at Bouton less than five months, mostly doing setup and teardown for memorial services, and assisting caterers and florists. By then I'd decided to enter the mortuary sciences program at the community college, but I didn't expect to work in the prep room—except to mop the floor and sanitize equipment—for a while.

So I was surprised when Carrie said, "Elodie and I thought you might want to assist me this morning."

I tried not to seem too excited. "Of course."

In the prep room, the body of a young woman not yet out of her teens lay on the table. Her left side was almost colorless while her right was blotchy and purple. This, Carrie explained, was because the body had lain on its right side, allowing the blood to pool. "The discoloration is called livor mortis. Postmortem stain to us folks in the trade." She rolled the body onto its side. The darkest purple ended at the shoulder blade, but the rest of the back was also discolored, if less intensely. "It starts to develop immediately after death but doesn't become visible like this for a couple of hours. The body must have remained in one position for a few hours, then been moved or repositioned. That's why we see this secondary lividity."

Carrie rolled the body flat again. Purple stained her face and neck as well, darker and less evenly than on her back. "Those bruises are ante mortem." From before she died. The girl's mouth hung open, revealing broken front teeth caked with dried blood.

That was when I made the connection. The story had dominated the *Samuelton Ledger* website for days. A Wilton girl had been reported missing a week earlier after she failed to check in with her family. She'd been hiking and camping her way through central Oregon with her dog and was last seen at the Painted Hills in Wheeler County. Authorities didn't start to worry until the dog turned up on a ranch near Sutton Mountain—beaten to death. A day later, the girl was found at the Wheeler fossil beds. Strangled and dumped in a trench. At present, there were no suspects.

"This is the murder victim," I said.

Carrie's eyes focused somewhere below the tile floor. "Her name was Michelle Duerte. She was taking a gap year between high school and college, with plans to travel through Southeast Asia after she finished her camping trek. She's someone's daughter, someone's sister, someone's friend. Her loved ones will never forget what happened to her," Carrie said, "but when I'm finished, I hope they can see her at rest. At peace." Carrie's voice shook. "I want you to help me get her ready for her funeral."

"There's still time to apply at Walmart, Mellie."

I shook my head at Fitz, a gesture Carrie misinterpreted. "Are you up for this?"

"Yes, I'm fine."

For the rest of the morning, I stood by Carrie's side, handing her instruments, watching her apply the wax, glue, and makeup that would transform the corpse from a battered ruin into a young woman again.

Now, I swing my legs off the bench. There's crud in my eyes. My back aches and my feet tingle with the rush of blood.

"What is it, Mellie?"

If Pride hit facedown, why were the backs of his arms purple with postmortem stain?

Because he was dead before he fell from the bridge.

THIRTY-THREE

Counsel

As I bang on my door, two white guys with three-day beards appear in the cell window across from me. I recognize the dudebros from the Whistle Pig, one with a swollen, gauze-packed nose, the other sporting a black eye. When they spot me, they start hooting and making kissy faces.

I flip them off, then bang my door again.

"Anybody actually work here?"

A voice shouts for everyone to shut the hell up, answered by a drunken, "G'fug yerse'f!" Someone calls out an order for eggs over easy, bacon, and a short stack with real maple syrup.

A glowering deputy storms into view. He stops at my window. "What the hell is your problem?" His voice comes through a small grill beside the door.

"I need to speak with the sheriff."

"You and every other shitbird in this joint."

"It's important."

"I thought you were waiting for your lawyer."

"This isn't about me. But I think he's going to want to hear it."

The glower never fades. "The sun is barely up—on a Sunday no less. Wouldn't hold my breath."

He continues along the corridor, shouting for quiet and cracking doors with a baton.

"Is that a no on the syrup, Dippity?"

While he works on quieting the others down, I use the toilet and rinse my mouth with tepid water from the washbasin. My stomach feels like a sinkhole, but the uneaten cheese sandwich offers no temptation.

It's some time before the cell door opens and Dippity Glower waves me out.

"Is the sheriff here?"

He doesn't answer, just guides me to the second floor and into a conference room. The chairs are cushioned, and the windows look out over the park. The early morning sun casts long shadows through the trees. A digital clock on the wall reads 6:18.

"You gonna behave?"

"Sure."

He offers me another bottled water. "Breakfast isn't till seven thirty, but if you're lucky they'll cut you loose before—unless your thing is a cold hard-boiled egg and white toast."

"And rich creamery butter?"

"Yeah. Sure." Somehow, he manages a darker glare. "Just wait here."

Breakfast time comes and goes before the door opens again. Not Dippity Glower and not the sheriff. A tall white man in baby-blue slacks and a neon yellow polo shirt enters, carefully juggling two coffee cups and a thin leather briefcase. His smooth skin is deeply tanned, setting off his white eyebrows and the hair on his forearms. He's wearing a smartwatch and a diamond pinkie ring, without apparent shame.

"Melisende Dulac?"

"Who are you?"

"Pax Berber. I'm your attorney." He sets down the briefcase and offers me a cup. "I didn't know what you liked, so I got lattes for both of us. Quad shots since I heard they left you in solitary holding all night."

I gratefully accept the latte as he takes a seat. When he opens his briefcase, the brass latches pop like gunshots.

"I understand you asked for the sheriff this morning. Were you intending to waive your right to counsel?"

"No. It's about something else—"

He holds up his hand. "We'll get to that." He takes out a round-barreled pen as thick as my thumb, a yellow notepad, and several printed sheets. "Okay, good," he mumbles as he scans first one document, then the next, aligning each page on the table beside the pad. At last he slides the last page across the table. "This is a representation agreement. Read it over and sign. Then we can get started."

With the proffered pen, I add my scrawl and push the agreement back to him.

"Not a reader then."

"Not if it's printed in Courier."

"I've lobbied my partners to switch to Comic Sans." He adds his own signature. "Now then, you haven't said anything to the chief deputy, or anyone else, correct?"

"No." Helene trained me well. I'd like to say I'm not stupid, but I wouldn't be here if that were true.

"I'd move to suppress anything you might have said, but best if I don't have to try." He smiles, his teeth so white they seem to fluoresce. "Especially since all three judges in this county think Jesus put them on this Earth to pre-populate Hell."

I have a more immediate question. "Mr. Berber, how did you come to be my lawyer?"

"The usual. I got a phone call on the golf course. We had a six thirty tee time—to beat the heat, you know." He laughs, but it fades when I don't join in. "I've spoken with Elodie Bouton. She's your aunt?"

Strictly speaking, no, but I don't have the energy to explain. "Yes."

"Lovely woman. She asked me to tell you she's thinking about you, and she hopes you're doing okay."

I knew I wouldn't be able to keep this from getting to Aunt Elodie, but I'd hoped to tell her on my own terms. The sheriff must have called her, which makes Pax Berber one more debt on my ledger. If Elodie keeps me on, I should just work for free.

I reach for my latte and fumble instead, nearly knocking it over. Unseen, Mr. Berber presses the cup into my hands.

"If you need some time—"

I shake my head. "I'm fine." My hands tremble as I raise the cup to my lips, indifferent to the sudden heat on my tongue. "I said I'm fine."

"He wasn't arguing with you, little sister."

204 | W. H. Cameron

"You sure?" the lawyer asks.

I wipe my eyes. My face feels hot and raw. "Yes, I'm sure."

"Okay." He doesn't sound convinced. "I've read the complaint. It's ticky-tack. What did you do to piss off Omar?"

"Besides existing?"

He chuckles. "Yes, well, you and everyone else. He's been testy since Hayward took over." His expression grows serious. "Here's what we're dealing with. The chief deputy is calling it tampering with evidence at the scene of a death investigation. He wants to toss in trespassing, but Hayward did bring you there himself. Given that the incident seems to be an accidental death, we can argue—"

"I don't think Kendrick Pride died from the fall."

Mr. Berber's mouth freezes, half open. One hand finds his chin, the pinky diamond winking. "What are you suggesting?"

The words feel dangerous in my mouth, so I just spit them out. "I think he was already dead when his body fell from the bridge."

He takes his time responding. "Dr. Varney has made a preliminary determination of cause of death—massive trauma subsequent to the fall. As of this morning, I understand that will stand in his final report."

"I'm not so sure about that."

"Why didn't you say something yesterday?"

Because I had one or two other things on my mind. Bullets and babies. Mystery cars and the exact nature of Pride's investigation itself. Jeremy said Pride had been all over the county asking questions. But what, and of whom? For that matter, what happened to the bullet casings and to his portfolio with the collision diagram? Duniway said Pride's car had been broken into. All I'd seen was that folder with the photograph, but perhaps the rest was in the trunk or hidden under the seats. Was the evidence he'd collected gone?

Was the evidence he collected what got him killed?

Mr. Berber stares, waiting. If I spill all this to him, what will it get me? More time in a cell? Or dropped off a bridge?

"No, you're right. It's probably nothing."

I can see the calculation in his eyes. When he looks at me, does he see Crazy Melisende?

After a long, uncomfortable silence he says, "Best you tell me. If it's nothing, it's nothing."

Still, I hesitate.

"I'm your attorney, Ms. Dulac." His voice is soft, yet earnest. "I'm here to help you, but I can only do that if I'm informed."

I exhale, long and slow. Aunt Elodie wouldn't have called him if she didn't trust him.

"Something bothered me at the scene, but it didn't fully register till this morning. There was discoloration on the back of his arms and neck, as if his blood pooled there. That takes time and gravity." I pause for emphasis. "Mr. Pride fell face first."

He licks his lips. "It's not that I don't believe you. It's just that Dr. Varney is the deputy medical examiner. You're—"

"Someone who moves dead bodies for a living."

He nods, thoughtful, then looks at one of his other printed sheets. "Do you think there's a connection between Pride's death and the missing bodies?"

There has to be, but it's not like I can prove it. "I'm not sure."

"This situation with the locket won't lend you any credibility."

"I know." I sigh. "It was stupid."

He doesn't contradict me. "Omar also believes you're somehow connected to the man's death—though he has yet to suggest how. Turning an accident into wrongful death—or worse—does not move you into more comfortable territory."

"I'm just saying what—"

He holds up his hand. "Here's the thing. You're suggesting something very serious, not the least being incompetence on the part of the deputy medical examiner. It's one thing for me to go tell Omar you're just a young woman who, let's say, grabbed a pretty bangle on impulse—"

"I'm not a goddamn magpie."

"Nor do I think you are. Like I said, I've spoken to Elodie. She insisted you must have had a good reason for taking the locket. She has faith in you."

I clench my teeth. I don't deserve Aunt Elodie's faith.

"Anyway, to finish my thought, it's one thing for me to argue you made a foolish mistake and you're sorry. I could probably get the sheriff or the DA to tell Omar to step back. But it's something else altogether for me to allege a homicide." He rubs the bridge of his nose. "I usually advise my clients not to invite trouble."

"Do you get a lot of clients volunteering crimes the cops don't even know about?"

"You have no idea." Mr. Berber's teeth flash. "How about this? You walk me through the last few days, and then we'll figure out how best to proceed. I may need to talk to the sheriff, though that might just rile Omar up. My job right now is to get you out of this building as soon as possible, ideally without any further legal entanglements—but one step at a time."

My fingers clench in my lap. I've barely slept, I'm hungry, and I'm still wearing my bloody shirt. Unruly on the best of days, after last night my hair must make me look like Medusa's less-attractive little sister. Pax Berber seems straight, but the thought of rehashing the last week makes me want to bury myself.

I saw a ghost at the crossroad.

I press my hands against the tabletop. "You know about the crash?"

"I do."

"Okay then." I skip the crazy and focus on the concrete and confirmable. One hurt and three dead at the crossroad. The baby in the desert. The bodies stolen from the New Mortuary. Pride and I discovering another crash victim the next day even as Duniway searched the Old Mortuary, then finding ashes in the crematory.

Mr. Berber knows about the search warrant. He seems unperturbed. "Why don't you tell me about the locket?"

I'd rather not, but I give in and describe stopping at the crossroad Friday evening, how I was nearly trampled by a deer, how I spotted a metallic gleam in the dirt. I avoid any mention of the Shatter Hill Spirit.

"How did you know it belonged to Kendrick Pride?"

"It has his picture in it, his and a woman's."

He nods, making notes. "And you returned it to him when you met for coffee yesterday?"

"It was a chance encounter. He's the one who insisted on coffee."

"At the Mercantile? Must have been his first visit to Barlow County." He smiles at his own joke. "What did you discuss?"

"Just what I remembered about the crash. Honestly, I didn't tell him anything that wasn't public knowledge." This would be the time to mention his theory about the fourth car if I was going to. I don't.

"What happened after that?"

"I went to my friend Barb's house out at Dryer Lake. Around three, Jeremy Chapman stopped by to say hello."

"You're friends with Deputy Chapman?"

I only hesitate for a moment. "Yes."

It's harder to explain why I wanted to meet with Pride again. That with Duniway fixated on me, I thought Pride might be more likely to find out what happened to the missing bodies is all I can say. "Despite what Duniway thinks, the one thing I know for sure is *I* didn't take them."

"And that's when you went looking for Mr. Pride."

"Yes. I mean, I tried calling him, but I didn't have his cell number, and his office said he was on some kind of sabbatical." That led me to the Downhill, then the Long Grass, and then to Pride's car outside the school. Celeste and Lydia Koenig, Landry and my escape to the old asylum. What a fucking day, but at least there were witnesses at points along the way.

Mr. Berber takes notes, pressing me on timing. It's hard to be specific. I don't wear a watch, and I didn't look at my phone that often. "Why does it matter?"

"If you're right about Pride's time of death, knowing where you were, and when, could help if Omar pushes the idea you're involved."

"Do you know why he's so hard set on me in the first place?"

He spends a moment examining his fingernails. They're well manicured, with a clear-coat polish. Once, on a trip to Bend, Barb treated us to a mani-pedi. I did my best to relax and enjoy it as much as she did.

"The thing you need to understand, Ms. Dulac, is law enforcement has its own agenda. To serve and protect, sure, but whom? People don't go into law enforcement to fight The Man. They value order and authority. They believe the simple answer is the correct answer, because often it is. Crimes aren't puzzles to be solved, but disruptions to be eliminated."

"That doesn't explain why Duniway thinks I'd steal three bodies."

"He's got a growing file on his desk detailing a big, hairy mess, and you've been party to each new complication. The arrow of circumstance points right at you."

"The arrow of circumstance has terrible aim."

"Perhaps, but if targeting you lets him close that file—voilà, the system works."

"Even if the actual criminal gets away?"

"One might argue the criminal is whoever gets convicted of the crime."

"So you're saying Duniway is corrupt."

"Heavens, no! I'm saying he's a professional with a point of view validated by long experience. More often than not, he's right."

"Well, he's not right this time."

"That's why you got me." Mr. Berber grins. "Now you wait here. I may be awhile." He stands, adding, "Do you need anything?"

Rocket boots. "The deputy said something about hard-boiled eggs."

THIRTY-FOUR

Well, Actually

I never do get my egg and toast. Through the window, I watch the line form outside Dailie's. Tourists. People come and go from Cuppa Jo; a few filter into the Whistle Pig. The Pig doesn't serve breakfast, but you can eat off the bar menu all day. By nine, I'm willing to commit a felony for some sweet potato tots.

When the door finally opens again, it's not Mr. Berber, but Jeremy.

"How you holding up, Mel?"

"I'm hungry and I have to pee."

He rubs his bristly scalp. "I'll see what I can do." Ten minutes later, he returns with a banana, an apple turnover, and a latte from the coffee cart in the Barlow Building parking lot. Not as good as Cuppa Jo, but quicker. "I can walk you to the bathroom."

"Do you have to watch me too?"

"Jesus, Mel." His cheeks darken. "They could have put you back in a cell."

At least there was a toilet in my cell. Back in the conference room, he asks if I need anything else. I'm tempted to ask for a clean shirt, but that might be pushing my luck. I shake my head.

He pauses in the doorway. "Mel, I'm sorry about all this shit."

He looks so wounded, a squirrel of guilt churns in my belly. "It's not your fault, Jeremy." It's all mine. "Thanks for breakfast."

He smiles thinly. The second he's gone, I want to punch myself.

Not long after, Mr. Berber returns with his notes of my movements yesterday, typed neatly. "Look this over and make any necessary corrections."

It's weird to see my Saturday laid out like an itinerary.

"This all looks right."

"Great." He heads for the door. "Shouldn't be much longer."

But the door doesn't open again until noon. When it does, Duniway and the sheriff accompany Mr. Berber. The cops drop into chairs across the table while Mr. Berber sits at my side. He smells of bay rum and breath mints. The scent isn't enough to blunt the sweat and tobacco miasma creeping across the table.

No one speaks, though Duniway looks at his watch a few times. I assume we're waiting for Dr. Varney, though I don't want to risk Duniway's ire by asking. Phones ring in the outer office, voices pass in the hall. The atmosphere seems to thicken. At last the doctor arrives.

"Sorry for the delay. I was reviewing the reports and my notes from yesterday."

There's an open seat beside Duniway, but the doctor sits at the head of the table. Neutral ground. May be just as well since Duniway looks like he wants to beat him with his own shoe. Varney's skin has a gray cast. Hungover. He drops a folder onto the table, then eases into his chair like he's slipping into a cold bath.

"We ready?" Duniway drums his thumb against the table.

The sheriff turns one hand over, gesturing for Duniway to proceed. He seems like he'd rather be anywhere else, and for once we're in agreement. The chief deputy plants his gray gaze on me. "How long did it take you to think up this cattle crap story about your boyfriend?"

He's trying to get a rise out of me. It works, a little. "According to local gossip, Deputy Chapman is my boyfriend."

Duniway's nostrils flare. "I'm not having your back talk today. You're already in it up to your backside."

Mr. Berber straightens. "Could we dial it back a notch?" He shows the sheriff his gleaming teeth. "Hayward?"

The sheriff's lips push in and out. "No, you're right." He dips his head as if peering over nonexistent glasses. "Mel, I know you're tired and anxious, but we're just trying to get a handle on this situation. Okay?"

I notice he doesn't scold Duniway. Lips pinched, I nod.

"Okay, then." He turns to Mr. Berber. "Pax, how would you like to proceed?"

Based on Duniway's sour look, he's not happy about giving the floor to my attorney.

With his rich tan and blinding teeth, Pax Berber reminds me of a used car dealer pitching a lemon. "Ms. Dulac, I've briefed the sheriff and chief deputy on what you've told me about the body, but I think they should hear it from you. Do you mind?"

His tone makes me feel like I'm being worked a little. But the sheriff is right. I *am* tired and I *am* anxious. All I want is to get out of here, but that won't happen if I let Duniway goad me into a dick fight.

I swallow a gob of thick saliva. "As I explained to Mr. Berber, something bothered me at the scene yesterday, but until this morning I didn't realize what." I choose my next words carefully. "Even though Kendrick Pride's body had landed in the prone position, I saw postmortem lividity on the backs of the arms. That wouldn't be possible if he'd died from the fall."

The corner of Duniway's mouth curls. "Amazing what people will cook up after a night in a cell."

"I'm just telling you what I saw." I fight the urge to fidget. "For that kind of discoloration to be visible to the naked eye, he'd have to have been dead and lying on his back for at least a couple of hours."

"Well, I'd say an *actual doctor* is more qualified to determine time of death than the likes of you."

Duniway cocks his head like he's scored a point.

"Well, actually . . ."—Dr. Varney clears his throat—"she's right."

The sheriff lets out a faint snort. Duniway's pulse throbs in his neck. "What the hell are you saying?"

Color rises in the doctor's cheeks. "As you well know, any preliminary analysis is subject to change. I'd intended to complete my examination and write my report early this week. But when the sheriff called this morning, I went to the morgue straightaway."

Duniway looks like he wants to punch the doctor in the throat.

Dr. Varney opens his folder. "The nine-one-one call came in at 5:50, and Fire and Rescue arrived on scene at 6:07, a few minutes before Deputy Chapman. They assessed the victim and determined he was beyond hope of resuscitation. At that point, based on witness reports, the assumption was Kendrick Pride had been dead less than an hour, but per the protocol implemented by the sheriff when he took office, the boys took a liver temp. Uh . . ."—Dr. Varney taps the top sheet in the folder—"thirty-five-point-one. Given ambient conditions, time of death would have been two or more hours before the body was discovered—possibly longer. It was a warm day."

"Holy Lord, Aaron," Duniway snaps. "You couldn't have realized this *yesterday?*"

Dr. Varney ducks his head. "I didn't read the first responder report till this morning. I admit my initial exam was cursory, but I had no reason to doubt what I was told at the scene."

Duniway's head swings side to side. "Yesterday it was an accident or 'Goodbye, cruel world,' but today—on the say-so of a girl with zero credibility—you're ready to jump to what? Wrongful death, maybe murder? Because dead guys don't roll off their backs and climb over bridge railings without help."

"For Christ's sake, Omar, I was at a barbecue. I'd had a cocktail or two. Maybe I should have looked closer, but according to *your* people, it was a slam dunk." Dr. Varney rubs the bridge of his nose. "I like to think I'd have noticed the low liver temp, but honestly, we have Melisende to thank for pointing to the correct determination here. She's the one who saw what the rest of us missed." There's a subtle emphasis on *the rest of us,* as if to make clear he wasn't alone at the scene.

Duniway's lips pull back into a sneer. "Well, since we're deferring to Nancy Drew, shall we ask her who killed Kendrick Pride? I mean, if she's doing our jobs now."

"At least I can admit a mistake."

With that, the doctor sags into himself, as if he's expended his last reserves. Duniway's sneer sharpens, but before he can retort, Mr. Berber taps the table with his index finger.

"Gentlemen." He looks at each in turn. "I'm sure we all have things we'd rather be doing on a lovely Sunday afternoon. Might we stay on task?"

Duniway glares like Mr. Berber farted in church. "None of this lets her off the hook. What's the actual time of death?"

Dr. Varney takes a moment to gather himself. "Uh. Best guess, between two and four."

"Okay, fine." Duniway's hard eyes bear down on me. "So where were you between two and four, Mizz Dulac?"

I look at Mr. Berber, who slides copies of my itinerary across the table. "Her movements are well documented during the period in question, verified by your own Deputy Chapman and a citizen contact log entry by a Dryer Lake Resort public safety officer." He smirks. "And she was several miles away, with the sheriff, when Mr. Pride's body was discovered."

Duniway ignores the photocopy. "You still removed evidence from the scene of an active death investigation. I want to know why."

This is the question I dodged even for Mr. Berber. As answers go, a gut feeling the locket is linked to recent events doesn't help me. Raising Pride's speculations doesn't either. The fact is, sticking my neck out is what gets me in trouble—with Paulette and Landry, and now with this big, hairy mess.

"When I saw it stuck in the wall, I thought . . ." my voice trails off. It's a trinket filled with captured memories, lost and found in the desert. All I know for sure is in the short time I knew him, the only time Pride's self-possession cracked was when I returned it to him. The locket mattered, but not in any way Duniway will understand.

I take a deep breath. "I just wanted to make sure it got back to his family."

"What a bunch of nonsense." Duniway turns to the sheriff. "I want her charged. And given that we've now apparently decided this is a homicide, I want hindering prosecution added to the bill." To me, he says, "Your felonies are stacking up."

The room goes still. Dr. Varney eyes the door. Duniway looks like he wants to make a break too, but across the table toward me. Deep inside my left ear, Fitz *tsk-tsks*.

"Chief Deputy," Mr. Berber says at last, "if that's your position, then my next conversation will have to be with the DA."

"Fine by me," Duniway snaps. "We've got room at the inn."

Mr. Berber sighs. "Sheriff, a word?"

The sheriff grips his forehead, then scrubs at his chin. "No need. Melisende, go home. But something like this happens again, you won't find me so accommodating." Duniway opens his mouth to

214 I W. H. Cameron

protest, but the sheriff cuts him off. "I believe you have an investigation to attend to, Omar. Dr. Varney, we'll expect your written report this afternoon."

As they file out, Duniway looks daggers at Dr. Varney. As with all things Duniway, it seems excessive and misplaced. Ignoring the chief deputy, the doctor smiles apologetically at me. I guess that's something.

When the others have left, Mr. Berber grins. "And with that, you're free."

"It feels too easy."

"Oh, I wouldn't say that. We're lucky the sheriff is a reasonable man."

Is he? Or did he just not want the headache? I guess it works out the same, either way.

"The best thing you can do now, Ms. Dulac, is give the investigation time to move past you."

"How do I do that?"

"Keep your head down. Cops are like dogs. You think they have you treed, but they'll forget you the second the next squirrel comes along."

"Thank you, Mr. Berber." I'd offer to shake hands, but I don't like being touched. "I'm sorry I screwed up your golf game."

"Don't be. The call came right after I four-putted the second green, and the rest of my foursome were those judges I mentioned earlier. You saved me no end of personal and professional humiliation."

I hate to think what this long morning has cost Aunt Elodie, but I have plenty of time to run the numbers in my head. It's an hour and a half before they finally let me go.

THIRTY-FIVE

Doctor's Orders

People exhaust me. It's probably why I prefer working with the dead. After so much human contact the last few days, I'm ready to crawl into my own grave.

"And yet you linger in cafés and saloons playing the forlorn maiden."

Fitz may have a point, but when I'm out in the world, I'm not usually *with* other people—I'm in a cocoon made of noise and color. The more people, the less I notice them. And, critically, the more people, the less I notice myself.

Except that hasn't been working lately. Not before Paulette appeared at Cuppa Jo, not in the Whistle Pig later that night. Alone or surrounded, I can't escape myself any longer.

It's one thirty before they finally return my personal effects. Immediately I text Barb, who wants to mother me. "Why didn't you call me, you poor thing?" Before I can pick an appropriate emoji in response, she adds, "I'll bring you something to wear."

She insists we start with tots and sangria. "Doctor's orders."

"Notch will jerk off in my aioli."

"I'll deal with Notch."

A half-hour later when we walk into the Pig, Notch actually blushes. Barb already got to him, unless he's reacting to the out-fit Barb put me in: sandals, long pleated skirt, and plum-colored silk blouse with billowy sleeves and a scooped neck. My own filthy clothes are tucked away in the overnight bag she brought the clean clothes in. As we take our usual spot under the jackalope, I spot

Danae alone in a booth, an open book and a beer in front of her. Our eyes meet, and she gives me a smile before returning to her book. Still friends, I guess.

Our sangrias are out before Barb and I are settled into our seats, the tots a few minutes later. The only light comes from the bar and from the pool tables in back. There, two bikers play a somnolent game, the balls clacking at just the threshold of sound. Between shots, they sip beers and stare into the middle distance. I know how they feel.

Barb leaves the talking to me, but I'm content to sit in companionable silence, crunch tots, and sip sangria until a shadow falls over the table.

"Mind if I join you?"

Jeremy.

Barb lifts one eyebrow. Jeremy radiates a kind of moist heat out of place in the high desert. I'd like to tell him a turnover and a latte don't make up for my last twenty-four hours, but I'm too tired. "Fine."

"There's a toll," Barb says. "Another round, on you." That's probably not a good idea, but I don't argue. Bemused, Jeremy returns a minute later with our drinks and an expression of rapt expectation. I don't move. Barb makes room for him instead. I want to kiss her.

"You look nice, Mel." The man is incapable of being quiet.

"I look like a woman who spent the night in a cell."

He flinches but recovers quickly. "I just meant your outfit."

I squirm, suddenly conscious of the sensation of silk on my skin. The alien softness is at once luxurious and disconcerting. Barb watches me, smiling. "It looks better on you," I say to her. She has the chest for it.

"The purple brings out your eyes."

I emit the aural equivalent of a shrug. "But how are people supposed to know I put the fun in funerals?"

She cackles, but Jeremy doesn't seem to know what's so funny. He huddles over his beer like he's afraid someone will take it. Even though the Pig is cool, his face is filmed with sweat. Barb prods him with her elbow.

"Jesus, Jeremy. Lighten up."

He grabs his glass and manages to spill beer on himself. I focus on the basket of tots. Notch arrives with a couple of salads I didn't know Barb had ordered. He helps Jeremy mop up, then asks if we need anything else. No one answers.

After Notch slinks off, Jeremy tries again. "You really have them riled, you know."

"It's my superpower." I stab a tot into the chili aioli and leave half behind.

"Duniway doesn't like the wrongful death scenario."

I laugh without humor. "But it gives him what he wants—something else to pin on me."

"Oh, he thinks you're involved, but since you raised the idea, he insists it can't be right."

"What does he think happened? I hurt the man's feelings so bad he threw his own corpse off the bridge?"

"I don't know, Mel. I don't even think *he* knows."

That makes me wonder if Duniway has heard about the fourth skull in the retort. It's more ammo to use against me, but it never came up the whole time I was in custody. Fourth car, fourth skull, fourth body with a bullet in it. There are secrets everywhere.

I look at Jeremy. "How does Duniway explain Pride falling off the bridge hours after he died?"

He spreads his hands. "He thinks the Fire and Rescue guys screwed up the liver temp. Or if Pride did die earlier, the body somehow got snagged up above before finally dropping."

"That sounds plausible," Barb says sarcastically. Her first sangria a memory, she reaches for the second. "Or at least it will once I get six or eight more of these in me."

Jeremy manages a dry laugh. "The problem is there's nowhere on that bridge a body could go unnoticed for hours before falling. You got the deck, the guardrail, and open air. If he hung himself and the rope broke, where's the rope?"

"If he hung himself, his legs would look like grapes."

He nods. "And a body on the deck would have been spotted dozens of times over. Hell, I would have seen him on my way to work after we talked." He grimaces as if he reminded himself of something he wanted to forget. "Are we supposed to believe someone thought he was a dead deer and pushed him off the bridge to get him out of the way?"

"A local would have claimed the venison," Barb says around a mouthful of kale. "But what's the alternative? He gets killed . . .

somewhere . . . then hours later the murderer drives his body to the bridge and tosses it overboard? Gross. I mean, why? But gross."

With my salad fork, I fish tot fragments from my aioli. "Someone wanted it to look like an accident."

"Or suicide," Jeremy adds.

Barb nods. "They didn't count on our little undertaker unraveling their evil scheme."

"I didn't unravel anything. I noticed lividity. And it took me all night to realize what it meant."

Jeremy snorts. "Varney should have caught it anyway."

"You were there, Jeremy. We were all thinking the same thing. If Duniway hadn't stuck me in a cell with nothing to do but endlessly rerun the last twenty-four hours, I probably would have forgotten about it too."

"I still think Varney should have caught it." Jeremy stares into his beer. "With Pride asking around about those boys, I'm thinking someone might not have liked his questions."

I wonder if Jeremy believes that or if he's looking for a way to draw attention away from me. As if in confirmation, he adds, "Duniway won't give up on you, but I could check around. If I find something, I'll take it straight to the sheriff."

I make a face.

"Don't underestimate Sheriff Turnbull, Mel. He isn't just some alpha yokel ruling over the hayseeds. The man is a long way from stupid."

I'm being sold a line, and I'm not in a spending mood. "He's a tub of butter swimming with pork rinds." I finish my sangria in one long swallow and instantly regret it. A headache strikes with the force of a rockslide.

"Get you another?" Jeremy says, oblivious to the strain I can feel in my face.

"I'm tired." I've only eaten half my food, but I want to get out of there.

Jeremy lifts himself partway out of the booth. "I'll drive you home." His tone is casual and hopeful at once. I can picture him on duty last night, checking campsites for trail mix thieves as he relived our conversation outside Barb's. He's probably worked out a new tactic. The coffee cart breakfast was meant to soften me up.

Sharing dirt on Duniway shows whose side he's on. Investigating Pride's movements will prove he's serious. Now he wants to bring it home with a self-serving apology and some makeup sex.

"I'll go with Barb."

I need to retrieve the Stiff, so Barb points us toward the Hensley School.

I rest my head against the window. Outside, the sky is as empty as the desert between Samuelton and the crossroad. I register the passing landscape only for what it lacks. No vultures lurk on the basalt outcrop where we found Nathan Harper, no teen dirtbags drink beer at the crossroad fire circle. No spirit girls dart among the trees as we climb toward Crestview. No bodies lie on the Tsokapo Gorge bridge. Landry MacElroy doesn't haunt the Cerise Creek trailhead on Hensley Lane. Even Pride's blue hybrid has been towed.

But when we pull into the Hensley School parking lot, what stands out most of all is the empty space in the shade of the ash tree. The Stiff is gone.

THIRTY-SIX

The Photo

Stolen? Towed? I don't know which would be worse. There's no glass on the pavement to indicate a break-in. Not that Lydia Koenig would tolerate shattered glass on school grounds for long.

"We'll ask inside. If they had it towed, we can pitch a fit. If not, we'll add it to Jeremy's to-do list." Barb smiles at her own quip. "But don't fret. No one wants to joy ride in a hearse."

The Stiff isn't a hearse, but I don't bother to correct her. "I'm more worried Landry drove it into the river."

She has no answer for that.

In contrast to yesterday, girls roam the grounds or gather in little clots on the grass, many in the company of adults. Four generations have claimed the porch swing: newborn, teen mom, mother, and a sour-faced grandmother who sits facing away from the rest. A father and daughter—the relationship clear in their shared nose, wide-set eyes, and high foreheads—laugh together in the wicker chairs at the other end of the porch.

As we go inside and cross the foyer, the sour tang of spit-up and the reek of fouled diapers attack my nostrils. In one of the sitting rooms, a teen boy, his skin umber brown, grins as he changes a squirming newborn on a blanket between his knees. *Sperm donor?* The young mother watches from the couch beside them, her expression a mix of wonder and worry.

Confronting us at the bell desk is a petite Latina girl, her stomach surprisingly flat under her blue Hensley smock. She taps an open sign-in sheet on the desk. "Name of student?"

"Excuse me?"

"Who are you visiting?"

A baby's shriek nearby drives a wedge of pain into my skull. I struggle to find the words to explain the Stiff and why I left it here. Feeling stupid, I settle on a feeble, "Lydia Koenig?"

"The director?"

I nod.

"Hmm, I haven't seen her today, but I can try her office." She picks up the phone and dials. After a minute, she pulls the receiver away from her ear. "It kicked to voicemail. Would you like to leave a message?"

Sensing my exhaustion has caught up with me, Barb leans forward.

"That shouldn't be necessary. My friend was here yesterday for a meeting but got pulled away by an emergency and had to leave her van in the parking lot. We just returned to pick it up, but it's gone." As Barb speaks, the girl's expression screws up with concern. "Is there someone who might know what happened to it?"

"I can call security?"

"That sounds great. Thank you."

The girl dials again. The crying makes it hard to hear her. ". . . ladies here . . . something about a van . . . Okay." She cradles the receiver. "They're on their way."

"Great," Barb repeats, too brightly.

Head splitting, I move away from the bell desk. An older woman in a chair against the wall daubs her eyes with a tissue. Beside her, standing, a gray-bearded man gently swings a carrier holding the crying infant. Barb looks up at the party store letters on the wall. "Make Motherhood a Mother Habit." She once said she wouldn't have kids on a triple-dog dare.

Solidarity fist bump.

I steady myself against the cool wall, find myself facing the dour framed headshots of the Hensley School trustees. They could be store manager portraits on display at Ray's Thriftway or members of Congress.

"You again?" a sharp voice snaps. "You're like a damn canker sore."

My whole body jerks. I recognize the voice, or at least the irritation it arouses. A man in a sharply creased, Hensley-blue shirt has materialized at my back and now stands glaring from beneath a half-familiar gray crew cut and bushy eyebrows. It's the resort village rent-a-cop—X. Meyer, Lord of Fifteen-Minute Parking. Before I can tell him to fuck off, Barb slides across the hallway and injects herself between us.

"Hello, Xavier. How are you?" Her tone is casual, even a little friendly. She must not know him very well.

"You with her, Ms. Ellingson?"

"I am. I didn't know you worked here too."

"Just part time. I fill in for vacations and stuff." The sheriff mentioned some of his deputies moonlighted as Hensley School security. If they take Dryer Lake rent-a-cops too, they must have pretty low standards.

"Are you here about that van?"

"Do you know what happened to it?"

"I was on shift at the resort yesterday, but I understand the sherrif called and asked us to leave it overnight."

"We were worried it got towed."

"Been up to me, it would have been." A wave of dizziness is the only thing keeping me from cracking Xavier upside his pruned head. Good thing Barb is doing all the talking. "In any event, some-one came by for it this morning."

"Do you know who?"

"Afraid not. The vehicle was gone when I came on at eleven. Only reason I even know about it is the log entry."

Someone taps my arm. "Hey, you're back."

I turn away from rent-a-cop's sneer and find a warm, friendly face at my side. "Hello, Celeste."

Her eyes are bright and excited. "I was talking to one of the girls, Kaylee, and she told me about a man who came to the school on Friday. Tall, dressed nice. Sound like your guy?"

"Kendrick Pride?" Saying it aloud makes my stomach hurt.

"She didn't remember his name, just that he showed up while she was on bell desk and asked to see the director. Lydia was gone that day, so he ended up leaving a note."

"Do you know if he came back?"

"Sorry, no."

Not that it matters now. I manage a wan smile. Behind me, Xavier continues to grouse about the Stiff. As if it wasn't gone before he ever knew it was here.

"Anyway, the reason Kaylee brought it up was he showed her a picture of some girl, asked if she recognized her. She didn't, but he kept pushing for her to look again." Celeste steals a glance at Xavier. "He was insistent enough about it that she called security, but they couldn't help him either."

It must have been the photo I saw in Pride's car, now missing along with his evidence and notes. Another piece of the puzzle, gone. Trae Fowler was the son of Pride's client; Nathan Harper, the son of his law partner. Who does that make this mystery girl, besides the likely mother of a lost baby and owner of unexpected bones in the Bouton retort?

A sharp wave of nausea washes through me. I reach out for Barb, stumble into Xavier Meyer instead.

"Whoa! She drunk? I can't allow that here."

He backs away. Concern scrunches the smooth skin between Celeste's eyebrows. Then Barb is there, arm in mine. "What is it, honey?"

That damned photo is what got Pride killed.

THIRTY-SEVEN

Private Quarters

Barb suggests taking me back to her house for a girls' night. "We'll tuck into my California King with a pint of Ben and Jerry's and watch Lizzy Bennet eventually fumble her way into Mr. Darcy's arms."

"I'm in more of a *Fury Road* mood."

"A double feature then."

It's tempting, but after everything that's happened, a night in my own bed followed by an early start at the New Mortuary feels like the best way to show Aunt Elodie and Uncle Rémy I appreciate all they've done for me.

"Maybe next weekend."

I need the silence of Shatter Hill and the emptiness of the Old Mortuary. I need space to make sense of everything that's happened.

I need room to escape.

"Are you sure you're going to be okay, Mel?"

"As okay as a hot bath and twelve hours of sleep in my own bed can make me."

From the driveway, I watch her car disappear over the lip of Shatter Hill, then head for the house. The wind carries the scent of sage. I allow myself a couple of deep breaths. With each exhalation my headache eases, as if the very air at the Old Mortuary is restorative. At the edge of the lawn, I drop the overnight bag with my dirty clothes and boots, then slide out of Barb's sandals.

No one has watered since Uncle Rémy left for his surgery ten days ago. The grass crackles underfoot. The gasping roses, peonies, and lavender under the windows suddenly seem as unexpected on the dry, undulating tableland as the Old Mortuary itself.

The grounds have always been Uncle Rémy's thing. Quince helps, or did—but never without Uncle Rémy's supervision. Now the responsibility will have to fall to someone else.

Someone like me?

"What do you know about yard work, little sister?"

About as much I knew about undertaking before I got here.

An open padlock hangs from the hasp of the maintenance shed behind the crematorium. It's never latched. Who'd steal from the isolated Old Mortuary? Inside, rakes and shovels, hoes, and clippers hang on the walls. All tidy, everything in its place. I power up the pump, then head outside to open the spigots feeding the soaker hoses in the flower beds. The lawn sprinklers are on a separate line, a manual system Uncle Rémy installed decades ago. The grass will have to wait. "Water the lawn before the heat of the day," Uncle Rémy says. With the late afternoon sun still high, I decide to run them tomorrow morning while I'm getting ready for work.

When I circle around to the back of the Old Mortuary to make sure the soakers are all doing their job, I see the Stiff parked outside the garage. Aunt Elodie must have brought it here, though she'd have needed someone to drive her back to Crestview. Just one more burden I've put on her, and now on someone else too.

A wave of guilt drives me across the lawn to the edge of the Pioneer Cemetery. The place usually serves as a respite, but as I step from the lawn onto the buff earth and brown stone, the silence is broken by the sound of car or truck approaching on Wayette Highway. Aside from us, there's nothing up out here for miles. I can only hope it's someone heading to Trout Rot Bridge to fish, or to the state park away east. But we do get visitors to the old cemetery, the occasional mourners or history buffs in search of Old West color. I'm in no mood to share the hard-packed paths winding among native plantings of sage, sulfur buckwheat, and larkspur. I want the graves covered with raked gravel and the whitewashed boulders marking the boundaries of family plots to myself. But as the car engine dies, I know my solitude is about to be shattered.

Before I turn away, my gaze falls on a tall granite gravestone topped with a cherub, the engraving weathered but still readable after more than a century.

GRUFFYN FRESHWATER
1835–1901
DEAREST HUSBAND,
MAY I NE'ER FORGET YE

He was laid to rest among other Freshwaters, children and grandchildren. I'm struck by the similarity to Alice Hensley's monument in the old cemetery at the Hensley Asylum, and by the contrast to the many graves around it. A sudden sadness comes over me at the thought of all those forgotten infirm ladies and needful girls.

Back in front, an unfamiliar silver Lexus with Washington state plates is parked on the drive. A woman in pegged slacks, sensible flats, and an embroidered peasant blouse sits on the porch steps. Her skin is the color of antique ivory. Her dark brown hair is loosely knotted behind her head. When she looks up, the breath goes out of me. She has the melancholy gray eyes of a French film star.

"It's good to see you again, Melisende." Helene's voice might be from another era. "It's been too long."

❧ ❧

She has house keys.

"I didn't want to frighten you. That's why I waited outside."

Helene picks up Barb's overnight bag and the sandals I'd taken off, then leads me inside. Her footsteps make no sound on the deep carpet in the foyer or on the stairs leading to the second floor. I follow close enough to inhale her scent, yet afraid to. I half-wonder if she's really here. A sharp breath might dispel her like smoke. At the top of the stairs, the short hallway ends at the entrance to the private quarters.

"I thought we'd be more comfortable up here, but if you'd prefer, we can go somewhere else."

Numbly, I shake my head. We continue into the family kitchen. Through the windows I can see the crematorium and the road beyond. The chattering valves of a passing pickup disturb the desert's peace.

The chair squeaks when I sit at the old enamel kitchen table. Helene drops overnight bag and shoes beside the door. Then she moves from cupboard to fridge. Ice trays crack and cubes clink against glass. She joins me at the table, with a pitcher of iced tea and two tumblers.

"Unless you want something stronger."

"This is fine."

They're my first words to Helene Bouton in a year and a half—not counting a million voice messages. *This is fine.* Iced tea is fine. A friendly visit in the family kitchen is fine. Just drop my things anywhere—it's fine. Missing bodies and search warrants and teen rapists with knives, unidentified bones, postmortem stain in the gorge—all fucking fine. I rest my head on the tabletop. When Helene reaches out to stroke my neck, I flinch.

"I'm sorry. I know you don't like to be touched."

If anyone ever had permission to touch me, it's Helene. But I hadn't believed my eyes when I saw her on the porch. I hadn't believed my ears when I heard her speak. It took the physicality of her fingertips against my skin for me to accept she's really here. Now that I do, I don't know what to say, to think. To feel.

"You helped Aunt Elodie with the Stiff," I say, settling on the mundane. At her quizzical look, I add, "The van."

"Right." She gives me a little smile. "I followed her, then drove her back to Crestview."

"You saw Uncle Rémy?"

"Yes." From the look on her face, I don't need to ask how he was.

"So, are you a lawyer now?"

Her head tilts. "No, not yet. Until I pass the bar, I'm basically a glorified proofreader."

"In Washington." I say, remembering the plates on her car. I never pictured Helene in a Lexus or pegged slacks. Back in Massachusetts, she was a Vespa and cargo pants girl, or if she had to drive, a hybrid like Pride's.

"My firm is in Seattle, yes. The exam is in ten days. I'll know if I passed in early September."

"You'll pass."

"I should be studying right now."

I can't tell if she means that as a rebuke. "You got my messages." My words seem to pool on the cool enamel.

"All of them."

"You never called back."

She makes a production of pouring the tea, like she's performing a ritual. "You never asked me to."

Helene, hi . . . I hope you're okay. Could it be so simple that all I had to do was add a *Please, call me?*

I lift my head. "You didn't need my permission."

"I knew *you* were okay."

My numbness dies in a sudden flash of anger. The space between us seems to expand with an energy that threatens to burn me alive. I press my hands against the table . . . breathe in, breathe out. Count backward from ten.

I don't make it to seven.

"I am anything *but* okay. Half the county thinks I'm a body snatcher, and the rest want to feed me to the coyotes over a rapist football player. When I'm not kicking babies, I'm a murderer on the lam. I've repaid everything Uncle Rémy and Aunt Elodie have done for me by jeopardizing the business they've devoted their lives to. I just spent the night in jail. The sheriff thinks I'm crazy. His chief deputy thinks I'm guilty. And the hell of it is, they're not wrong. What kind of dumb bitch takes evidence from a crime scene?" Tears in my eyes, I point at myself with both thumbs. "This kind. So don't tell me I'm fucking okay."

She reaches across the table to take my hand, stops just short of touching me. "We all make mistakes, Mel. It's behind you now."

"How would you know?"

Her gaze falls to her empty hand.

"You shouldn't have come all this way for me."

"I should have come sooner."

Her tone is offhand, but the words are like pieces of a jigsaw puzzle scattered across the table. I finger them in my mind, feel for the connections.

I've called Helene far too many times and left far too many voicemails. Desperate messages, yet devoid of substance. Even last night, I'd danced around what really happened—

I'm in trouble.

It's not your problem.

And, as always, my tiresome refrain.

I just hope you're okay.

Somehow that message, of all of them, triggered the drive from Seattle to Shatter Hill.

Or had it?

Someone must have told her what's been going on, someone who mattered enough that she'd pick up when they called. Helene is Elodie's actual niece, not some faux kin by a broken marriage. She visited Barlow County when she was a kid. She probably knows the Old Mortuary and the Pioneer Cemetery better than I do. She's probably been in touch with Aunt Elodie all along.

"*You're* why I'm here." It's so obvious, I should have seen it ages ago.

"In the kitchen?" She laughs awkwardly.

"In Barlow County, at Bouton Funerary Service. Living in this house, working for your family." I marvel at the words even as they spill out of me. "*You're* why Aunt Elodie called me the day I got out of the hospital. Why she and Uncle Rémy put me on that train." Hell, even how Elodie knew what size clothes to buy for me before I got here. "Christ, you must be why she still puts up with me even . . ."

. . . *even as Uncle Rémy slips away.*

I wince, unable to finish the thought aloud.

"Mel, wait—"

"*You* called Mr. Berber on the golf course, then talked to him after the big conference."

She looks at her untouched tea as if answers float among the melting ice. "Your confidentiality wasn't violated. I promise you that. All he said was the situation had been resolved in your favor."

"Resolved in my favor." A sudden knot forms in my stomach. "Jesus, how much do I owe you?" I don't know what attorneys cost, but if I have to fork over every last penny of my savings, so be it.

Then a fresh revelation hits me. "*You* wrote the check Uncle Rémy gave me." Her strained silence is all the answer I need. "Do you pay my wages too?

Money was never an issue for Helene, or for Geoffrey. Even when his parents threatened to cut him off, he just laughed, saying he had his own means anyway. Like him, Helene always had money—for college, for law school. For a nice apartment and good wine and dinners out. She could easily launder ten grand through Uncle Rémy.

Her neck stiffens. "That money is yours."

"That's not what I asked."

"I was afraid you wouldn't accept it if you knew who it came from."

"Why give it to me at all?"

"Because of what Geoffrey did to you."

My bark of laughter is so sharp the table shakes. "He didn't *do* anything to me. Whatever happened, I played along. I was foolish, maybe. And impulsive. But all he *did* to me was leave." Went out for croissants and kept walking.

"He left you alone and penniless, thirty-five hundred miles from home."

"I still had my return ticket."

A sad expression is her only response.

We sit in awkward silence for a few minutes, then she gets up. I watch her wash our empty glasses and set them in the drying rack with the familiarity of someone who'd stood at the Old Mortuary sink countless times before we ever met. Then she wraps her arms around herself as if she's caught a chill.

"I should go."

Neither of us speak as we walk out to her car. But before she drives away, I ask her the question I'd never had the courage to voice.

"What did you ever see in me?"

I know what I saw in her. She's beautiful, yes, but that wasn't it. She sees a problem and doesn't hesitate to tackle it, no matter how intractable. "I'm not afraid of failing," she once said. "I'm afraid of never giving myself a chance to succeed." What would be a treacly platitude from anyone else was, from Helene, a confession. Her movie-star eyes may have drawn me in, but her sense of commitment kept me anchored. At least until I threw it all away with Geoffrey.

There on the gravel driveway of the Old Mortuary, she ponders my question. When she answers, her voice is full of regret. "I loved your fearlessness."

THIRTY-EIGHT

The Weeping Parlor

Across from the Old Mortuary's unused office is what Aunt Elodie calls the Weeping Parlor. "In the old days, should someone become overwhelmed by grief, they'd be led up here," she told me. In the privacy of this small, wood-paneled chamber, mourners wept and wailed to their broken heart's content. Downstairs, funerals would continue in decorum and peace.

Lit by stained glass lamps and furnished with stiff settees and marble-topped side tables, the room is now more museum than parlor. The smell of must in the air reminds me of my grandmother's house back in Lowell. Plastic runners cover the threadbare areas of the carpet. Antimacassars disguise fraying upholstery. Silk flowers, gray with dust, droop in porcelain vases. A glass case is filled with old photographs: mourning portraits from another era.

I may be the only person who still comes in here, though no one would confuse me with a weeper. I come for the mourning portraits. One in particular, of a young boy propped in a wooden chair, draws me back again and again. His name and fate are written on the back in soft pencil.

> *Aloysius Ludvik*
> *drown'd*
> *Ashwood, Ore. 1891*

His mother stands beside him. From behind, his father holds his head straight. A girl in a long skirt and high collar leans into the woman's hip. The boy's eyes are closed, but the others stare bleakly into the camera.

The boy looks nothing like Fitz. His parents are dark where Cricket and Stedman are bloodless. Their clothes are stiff and formal while Cricket and Stedman dress like New England Casual catalog models. And the girl—she belongs to them. The mother clings to her daughter like she never wants to let go. I don't need therapy to tell me why the moment Helene drove away may be when I finally understood why the mother in my favorite mourning portrait held her daughter so close. When you lose something precious, you hold on to whatever you have left that much harder. But unlike Aloysius Ludvik's mother, I have nothing left.

I'm still in the Weeping Parlor when Aunt Elodie returns from Crestview. Only one lamp is lit.

"I'm sorry you had to stay in that awful jail overnight. You should have called me."

"It's okay." In some ways, that awful jail was better than my old apartment in Amherst. "You and Uncle need your rest." Even in the dim light, I can see the weariness in her face.

"Nonsense. I needed to be down there rapping Omar Duniway on the forehead with a mallet."

I smile in spite of my mood. She points to my cup on the side table. "What are you drinking?"

"Tea." Untouched.

"I think we've earned something a little stiffer. Come on."

In the kitchen, she pours us each a generous dose of Blanton's in crystal lowball glasses. As she comes around the table, she squeezes my shoulder before easing into her chair. Though it's been hours, the air feels charged, as if Helene left something of herself behind.

I take my glass in both hands but don't drink. The whiskey's aroma, heady and warm, is enough for now. "How is Uncle Rémy?"

"Walking better." She sips from her own glass. "He told you about the Spirit, I hear."

I nod.

"Did you really see her?"

Almost exactly what he asked. "I saw *something*. But whether it was someone in the desert or in my head I couldn't say." I shrug, as if one option is the same as the other. "Have you ever seen her?"

"I haven't, no." She shakes her head slowly. "But even if I had, I wouldn't assume she's real. Tell a story often enough, and it gathers substance in our minds. Then, we see what we expect rather than what's actually there."

Though I don't think she meant any reproach, I can't help but sense a phantom of doubt behind her kind eyes.

"I'm sorry I'm so much trouble."

"Melisende, dear, if anything, I should be apologizing to you. I've managed this situation with Rémy poorly, and left you dangling as a result. I should have done more to support you. Even if it was just to tell Quince to take a break from fishing and give you some backup until Carrie got back from her vacation."

"That's not it." I doubt Quince would have made things any better. "I know it wasn't your idea to bring me here."

Outside, darkness shrouds the desert in blue-gray shadows. The mercury light on the wall of the crematorium comes on, but the silver glow doesn't banish the night so much as merge with it. Inside, only the dim bulb over the stove is on. Frowning, Elodie leans over and hits the wall switch for the pendant lamp hanging above the table. In the sudden light, the hollows under her eyes look like bruises.

"You saw Helene, then."

I nod.

"We should have told you."

If I'd known, I would never have agreed to come. I wouldn't have accepted the check. I'd still be in Massachusetts. Back in psych hold or sleeping under a tarp. Maybe dead. I'd worn out my last welcome and had nothing left. Even so, my guilt over the situation with Geoffrey would have left me incapable of accepting a cup of coffee from Helene, let alone a home, a job. A life.

"Do you miss her?" Aunt Elodie says as if she's guessed where my mind went.

I'm not sure how to answer. My feelings for Helene are too entangled with my guilt about Geoffrey. Even in this house of mourning, I can't mourn him. He threw himself into the abyss, and even if I held back at the precipice, there's no returning from some choices. The path disintegrates behind you.

"I asked her to stay over," Aunt Elodie adds quietly. "But her test is coming up, and it's a long drive back to Seattle."

"I can't stay either."

I hadn't known how to say it. In the hours since Helene left, I've rehearsed a dozen variations. But when the moment comes, blunt and without preamble seems all I'm capable of.

She smiles sadly, her expression a mask of acceptance and denial all at once. I look into my glass, but the amber liquid is out of focus.

"Where will you go?"

"I have a few ideas," I lie.

"There's no rush. No matter how it started out, Melisende, you've made a place here." Aunt Elodie takes my hand. I don't fight it. "This is your home now."

"Some grow up in the work," she'd once said, "and others grow into it. But you? You seem born to it."

"I know you'll need time to find someone to do removals and help around the shop." My voice catches as I remember the soaker hoses and add, "And someone to care for the grounds."

She tosses back the last of her whiskey like Barb at Friday happy hour, then stands. Before she leaves, she takes my hand again. She's become someone else I've granted permission to touch me. Too late, though.

Then she surprises me yet again.

"You've had a hard week, Melisende. Get some rest. Maybe tomorrow you'll feel differently." She gives me a squeeze. "Whatever you decide, I just hope you do it as the woman who pulled Landry MacElroy out of the back of that pickup."

When she's gone, I pick up my own glass but hesitate. I don't want whiskey anymore.

I take my teacup and the two lowball glasses to the sink and wash them all. Set them in the rack next to the glasses Helene washed. This has been my kitchen sink for more than a year, but while Helene was here, I felt like a guest who had overstayed her welcome.

Now, with Aunt Elodie's parting words echoing in my mind, I'm not sure what to feel.

THIRTY-NINE

Callout

I'm back at the Cerise Creek trail. The others are gone, or haven't arrived. Maybe they never will. There's no Caitlyn and family, no vomit beside the trail. Under a pale sky, the stream pours through Tsokapo Gorge with the force of the spring melt, white and foaming. Kendrick Pride's blue body floats facedown in the pool at the base of the falls. Blood threads from his fingers like dark lightning. High above the bridge, the raven rides the thermals, calling out in a familiar voice.

"I loved your fearlessness."

"She shoulda seen you scamper down that trail away from Landry." Fitz laughs as the raven drops in a narrowing gyre toward me.

"I tried to be you," I call out. "I tried to be you, but—"

The cell phone's chirp cuts me off. My eyes shoot open. A cobweb hangs from the light fixture overhead. For a second I think I'm back in the jail cell. But the ceiling is the color of brie; the fixture, a frosted globe mottled with the remains of dead flies. My body floats in clammy water in a claw-foot tub large enough to swim laps. I don't know how long I've been asleep. Last thing I knew, wisps of steam were rising from white foam. The bubbles have long collapsed into iridescent scum on the water's surface.

The ringing stops. I suppose I should see who called, but my phone lies out of reach on the marble sink. No such thing as a small room in the Old Mortuary. I toe the hot-water handle. As the warmth spreads, feet to thighs, to belly, to breasts, I let myself sink underwater. My hair floats in a tangled net around my head. Dissolved bubble bath burns my eyes. When I close them, I see the raven.

I tried to be you . . .

Aunt Elodie wants me to be the woman who pulled Landry out of the back of his pickup, but who is that exactly? A fool, based on how it all worked out.

"Where you gonna run now, little sister?"

I've been a leaf in a rushing stream my whole life. I don't know how to be anything else.

I tried to be you, but only you can be you.

A tantalizing languor overcomes me as heat infuses the tepid water around my head. I let air trickle from my nose in a stream of bubbles. As I shed breath and buoyancy, I long to float here forever. Yet the moment my back touches bottom, my tranquility is shattered by the phone. Teeth clenched, I will the damnable thing to be silent. The piercing bleat continues.

"Where you gonna run now?"

As far as the stream carries me.

The ringing stops, but not before my lungs start to burn. I press against the side of the tub and remain submerged, fighting the instinct to rise and breathe until the effort threatens to split me open. When I finally sit up, gasping, the phone starts up again.

"You still work here or not, Mellie?"

He's right. I promised Aunt Elodie. Even running away from the high desert requires me to buck the current.

Before I even step out of the tub, the phone goes quiet. They'll call back, or they won't. They'll leave a message or call Swarthmore. It has to be work, a body, a removal. Short of an emergency, Barb wouldn't call this late. I don't think Jeremy would either—though his idea of an emergency might be feeling kinda sad.

What that has to do with me, I don't know. He was never going to stay in Barlow County and—until today—I had no plans to leave. One of the first things he told me was how he'd be gone the minute he landed his coveted big-city job. *Good for you,* I'd thought at the time.

Still do.

At least he knows where he wants to be.

The phone rings again on my way into my bedroom. "Private Number," the display tells me. I note the time before picking up: ten till one.

"Bouton Funerary Service." *You stab 'em, we slab 'em,* my brain adds in echo of the L.A. county coroner's T-shirt I pull from a pile of unfolded laundry.

"Having a hard time waking up?"

The voice is familiar, but it takes me a second to place—last heard across the conference room table twelve hours ago. "Dr. Varney?"

"Yeah. Sorry. I should have said so when you answered." I can't tell if he's slurring or if the words are swimming in my own head. "Can you make a pickup?"

As if I'm a cab driver. "Sure. Where?"

"Copper Hollow. You know where that is?"

"Sort of." Paddle Creek flows east from the Dryer Lake dam through a winding ravine, eventually pouring into the John Day River. Copper Hollow is a spot along the creek Quince mourns as a good trout hole lost to development.

"It's one of the resort homes on the bluff, east side of the golf course. I'll text you the address."

Their owners are the ones who come and go by private jet— though for most, Dryer Lake serves less as home than glam-rustic weekend getaway. Barb's cottage across the lake is a hovel in comparison.

I guess I should wear a proper work shirt.

After I disconnect, I consider the idea he's doing me a favor, but if he's doing anyone a favor, it's Uncle Rémy and Aunt Elodie. More likely, he thinks the sheriff moved me off the county shit list today, if he ever knew I was on it. Although he serves as deputy medical examiner, he's a physician first. He may not have much day-to-day contact with law enforcement.

Depending on who else is at the scene, things could get awkward. But awkward I can handle, especially if it means I can give Aunt Elodie some billable time before I drift away.

FORTY

Copper Hollow

As I cross the spine of Shatter Hill, the rising half-moon paints the landscape silvery gray. There's no bonfire at the crossroad, no party—no ghosts to slow me down. The desert almost seems to be holding its breath. In Crestview, the only lights blaze at the Mercantile and the twenty-four-hour gas station. I continue on, winding through forest on the north spur of Lost Brother. A small jet takes off from the airfield as I pass.

The GPS guides me through the main entrance of the Dryer Lake Resort, then to the right around the golf course. Faux-natural rock walls and plantings of bristlecone pine help hide the sprawling houses with terraced lawns that merge into the rough and fairway.

The address Dr. Varney texted is on the desert side of the street. Still exclusive, but of a different order from the homes on the course itself. The GPS turns me onto a gently descending gravel driveway wide enough for two cars. Irrigated lawn gives way to desert landscaping. A hundred feet further, the driveway ends at a concrete pad big enough to land a helicopter. My phone announces, "You have arrived."

I can hear Paddle Creek even with the Stiff's windows up. Aspen leaves fluttering in the moonlight mark the location of the stream off to my right. Ahead, I can just make out a large, low-slung stone house behind clumps of switchgrass and a trio of spindly pines. A yellow glow softened by curtains shines from a corner room.

There are no other cars, but as I reach for my phone to call Dr. Varney, headlights shine down the driveway behind me. The doctor's Escalade passes on my left. He performs a languid two-point turn in the parking area, then comes to a stop beside me. Before he kills the engine, he lowers his window, so I open mine too.

"Hey, Mel." Out on the desert, a coyote barks as a breeze stirs the aspens. Varney looks past me into the darkness, then climbs out of the Escalade. I get the vague sense he's not quite here.

"Dr. Varney?"

He shakes his head like someone awakening from a long sleep. "Sorry." He leans through the open window of the Escalade and pops back out with a tall to-go cup, the Dryer Lake Resort logo on the side. "I almost forgot. I got you a mocha. Girls like chocolate, right?"

I can't tell if he's actually trying to flirt. "That's the rumor." As the chill night air fills the Stiff, I accept the cup more for its warmth than its contents.

He retrieves a second cup from the SUV. "Drank most of mine already."

Maybe I should give him mine. "So what's the story?" I gesture at the house, if only to get him talking. "Where are the EMTs?"

"Oh. It's not like that." He twists around to look at the house. "It's a hospice thing."

That explains the callout despite my suspension. Whoever died in this house may even be a Bouton preplan client. It also explains why we're not rushing in. Survivors aren't always ready for decedents to be moved. Inside, a son or daughter, husband or wife may be trying to make sense of a room suddenly more silent than it was an hour ago. There's no telling what they're feeling. With hospice deaths, the grieving may have started days, weeks, even months ago. But sometimes no one believed death would come until it finally did.

After the last week, I'm struck by how ordinary a mere death feels, something that happens more than six thousand times an hour around the world. In Barlow County alone, on average someone dies every sixty hours. Even with Swarthmore handling some of the work, a removal call is as common as dinner out.

"One of your patients?"

"Yeah." He shakes his head sadly.

"Were you here when—?"

"I was over at the hotel." I wonder how much he's had to drink. Word is, the hotel lounge has a large selection of artisan whiskeys.

I sip the mocha and manage to avoid making a face. "What's in this?"

"It's the summer special, the bartender said." I see a quick flash of teeth. "Is it okay?"

Tastes like cough syrup mixed with ash. I remember the green-haired barista at Paiute Crossing making a hard pitch for the black cherry mocha. Must be a resort-wide thing. "I'll just have to be grateful for the medicinal effect."

His head tilts, and then he laughs a little. "Yeah, right." He takes a big sip from his own cup. "Like a fancy truffle, right? Only hot. I think it's pretty good."

Out of misplaced courtesy, I match him. Cloying, but at least it's warm and caffeinated. Given the silence from the house, we might be here for a while.

"You want to walk down by the creek?"

"Not especially."

"We won't go far." He takes a few steps. "I have my phone."

"Congratulations."

"There's something I wanted to talk to you about." Without waiting for an answer, he disappears into the darkness. Annoyed, I climb out of the Stiff, slipping my phone into my back pocket as I push the door shut.

"Why can't we talk here?"

"I don't want to disturb them in the house."

Worried he'll fall into the creek, I follow. Under the aspens, the moonlight is more decorative than functional. Glints of reflected moonlight and the sound of water rushing over stones tell me the creek is uncomfortably near. "Dr. Varney? Where are you?"

"Stay there," he says.

Gladly.

His voice, somewhere to my left, startles me and the top pops off my cup, splashing me with warm, sticky liquid. "Jesus." The cherry smell makes me feel queasy, so I dump what's left in a clump of grass.

"Dr. Varney, how much have you had to drink?"

He laughs, though he doesn't sound amused. "Maybe more than I should have."

I may have lost bodies and looted the dead, but at least I never showed up for a removal half lit. To think Carrie once suggested this guy was a good catch.

"I'm going back to the van."

Suddenly he's right in front of me.

"It's darker out here than I thought it would be." His breath is a foggy wisp. He puts his hand on my forearm. I tense but don't jerk away.

"I just—" His mouth is a dark hole in his pale face. "I owe you an apology."

A shiver runs through me, and my head starts to throb. "For what?"

"I really screwed the pooch with that guy in the gorge, Mel." His voice hitches. "I made a terrible mistake, and now you're paying the price."

Any moment, I'll be expected to wrestle a body from the house to the Stiff. Dealing with a drunk, maudlin medical examiner isn't supposed to be part of the job.

A wave of nausea hits me. I bend over and put my hands on my knees. I'm regretting the mocha.

"Mel?"

"That drink tasted like ass. I feel sick."

"I feel okay."

"Good for you." I put the sound of the creek at my back and take a few steps, but the nausea hammers me again. "I'm going back to the van."

"Let me help you."

It's too cold, too dark, the rushing creek too loud. I look for the Stiff, but aside from the stars above and the half-moon in the corner of my eye, the darkness is all but complete. Dr. Varney calls my name, but the sound seems to come from far away and all around me at once.

Use your phone, dumbass.

Yes. Good idea. I fumble at my back pocket, get my fingers on my phone. Nearly drop it before I find the home button and squint at the bright screen. I can't focus on the icons, can't tell which is for calls, which is for looking up dead teenage boys on the internet. I tap and swipe almost at random, manage to flood the ground at my feet with light.

"What are you doing, Mel?"

Vision swimming, I lurch forward, the phone's glare dancing over thorny scrub and jagged stone.

"Slow down. You'll hurt yourself."

I turn toward Dr. Varney's voice, cringe at the sight of leaping shadows. I lunge the other away, try to run, but my feet give out. I land facedown like Pride on the Cerise Creek Trail. My mouth fills with blood and dirt.

"You all right?"

I try to rise, but all I can do is squirm when Dr. Varney kneels at my side. "I'm so sorry, Mel."

"Whuh—" My tongue is numb, my throat a knot. I want to say *wait*, to ask what he did to me. The words won't come, but a distant corner of my mind guesses. *Drugs.* Drugs in the coffee, a taste like cherry cough syrup but much stronger. Fresh panic surges through me.

Wait!

"I'm sorry. I was supposed to rule the death an accident. I was supposed to make it go away." He puts a cold hand on the back of my neck. I jerk and manage to push up onto my knees. But it's not enough. Nothing left, I slip sideways and roll onto my back, exhausted.

"You had to go and notice the lividity."

My phone is somewhere to my side, a painful spark in the black. I paw the ground, but Dr. Varney is quicker. With a grunt, he heaves the phone like he's tossing a grenade. For a long, strange moment, I watch it tumble skyward, tracking along the path of the Milky Way.

I roll onto my side and lift my head. Out of the roiling shadows, a beam of light appears, bright enough to blot out the moon.

"Watch yourself there, chippy."

The acrid stench of tobacco overwhelms me as hard hands slam me back down. Pain shoots down my spine, but with it comes a brief, fractured clarity. Dr. Varney is gone. In his place, Quince Kinsrow looms in the flashlight's glare. I writhe, helpless, as he clamps his gnarled hand over my face.

My last thought before he cracks my head against the ground is regret I won't be there in the morning to water Uncle Rémy's lawn.

FORTY-ONE

The Stiff

Someone spilled whiskey. A shot, maybe two fingers from a lowball glass. Tipped over on the bar, knocked off the kitchen table. The sweet, smoky scent surrounds me, tickling my nose, drilling into my brain. Bourbon. Not the silky Blanton's Aunt Elodie poured, nor the rotgut I usually drink. Elijah Craig, maybe.

"What, you're some kinda hootch connoisseur, Mellie?"

Barb would say anyone who can't distinguish between top shelf, bottom shelf, and the fertile bourbon midlands should stick with Long Island iced tea.

"Only if she could hear me."

My right eye feels like someone is pulling a nail from the socket with a claw hammer. My teeth taste of blood. Cold seeps into my flesh and curls around my bones like fingers of ice and fog. An awful, droning vibration burrs through me. I need to get up, need to run. But my hands, my head, my feet—all so heavy, like I've been buried in sand. I force my mouth open but can't draw a breath. The pressure on my chest is too much. I'm buried—they buried me. Fitz laughs again, yet it's not Fitz. It's a whine like a straining engine. The sound rises and falls as light particles streak through the endless darkness, and the blood rushes head to toe and back again.

Open your eyes, Melisende.

"She's right, little sister."

Who?

The answer seeps in with the fog.

Me. Melisende.

My right eye doesn't work. Nailed shut, plucked out? *Out, vile jelly.* The left flutters enough to reveal a metallic gleam, cold and close and strangely familiar. Then the world shakes and my head bounces. The gleam shatters into a million specular flashes. I gasp, and the flashes coalesce into a silver sheen against a formless gray field. Teeth chattering, gut churning, I squeeze my eye shut and force myself to breathe until all I feel is vibration. "Count back from ten," a quiet voice says. When I reach one, my eyelids separate like tearing paper. Both eyes. A straight line, a bar—cold and lustrous— slices the darkness above. I stare at it until my eyes ache.

At least I'm not dead.

And not floating, not buried underground. I'm in the back of the van. My van. The Stiff. Wedged between the wall and the legs of the cot, my head jammed against the cargo bins mounted near the rear doors. The engine growls, the tires whir on pavement. The air stinks of bourbon and puke. When this is over, I'll need to pull the entire transport assembly to clean it.

"Don't fret, Mellie. After this, the Stiff is gonna be Quince's problem again."

With the suddenness of a snapping bone it comes back to me. The dark driveway . . . the doctor and the mocha . . . moonlight glinting off the creek . . . and Quince's calloused hand on my face. I let myself be lured like it was any other removal—a hospice thing. As common as dinner out. They drugged me and tossed me into the Stiff like any old body.

Except a body would be strapped to the cot, handled carefully and with respect. Quince dumped me like a sack of garbage.

I remember falling, trying to rise, falling again. Varney put his cold hand on my neck. Quince appeared, and someone spoke.

"Watch yourself there, chippy."

Chief Deputy Duniway.

I try to sit up. It's like fighting a tangle of rope. Whatever Dr. Varney put in that shit mocha must still be affecting me. Exhausted, I sag. The Stiff rounds a curve, and inertia presses me against the wheel well.

I tilt my head and can just make out the two front seats in the glow of the instrument panel. Duniway's arm drapes over the armrest on the passenger side. Quince is driving.

The van makes a turn and starts to climb. "Slow down! You want to get us killed?"

"What I want is to get this shit over with."

"All well and good, but the idea is we're not *still on board* when this damn thing goes into the draw."

Duniway's snarled words hit me like ice water. The spilled bourbon, the girl tossed around like so much garbage. Quince and Duniway mean to crash the Stiff. Maybe stick me behind the wheel before pushing it down some steep gully. My body will reek of booze. Maybe an empty bottle turns up in the wreckage. Dr. Varney will attribute any wounds or bruises to the crash, declaring my sad end an accident, with alcohol a contributing factor. The Barlow County grapevine will note my thing for sangria. And Aunt Elodie will remember our shared Blanton's.

The only reason I'm still alive is they can't risk making the same mistake twice. I have to die in the crash, or near enough to avoid inconvenient lividity.

Before I get a chance to panic, Quince burps out a startled bleat as lights start flashing in the Stiff's rear windows, red and blue, blue and red.

"Christ on a cracker, Omar. I thought you had this under control."

"Chapman thinks he's a detective."

"The fuck am I supposed to do?" Stripped of its usual orator's warmth, Quince's drawl has slipped into a high-pitched twang.

"Punch it." Duniway's tone is sharp and sibilant like he's forcing the words through his teeth.

"This thing can't outrun him."

"That's okay. I just want him riled."

The lights brighten in the Stiff's tinted windows. Brighter and nearer. Quince knows it too.

"Ain't no one ever told me I should *try* to rile a cop."

"Stop grousing and pull off up there."

Gravel crunches under the tires as the van rolls onto the shoulder. The vibration of the idling engine makes my teeth ache. The red and blue lights keep flashing. A car door slams.

I'm in here.

The words fail on my numb, swollen tongue. I try to move, to bang the wall beside me, to make any noise at all.

"Cover your ears."

"Fuck me, Omar, you can't—"

The footsteps fall heavily, as if Jeremy's already exhausted by the encounter he expects with me when he reaches the driver's side door.

"I said *cover your ears*, Quince!"

Too late, I realize what Duniway means to do.

And then I'm rising. Too slow, far too slow. A crazy thought—*the Stiff was built for hauling bodies, not ass.* Tendons strain in my wrist. Heat shoots through my neck and my back and my arms. *I am not the Stiff.* A shadow darkens the rear window as I reach for the glass.

Jeremy doesn't see me. No one sees me. The lights oscillate, blue and red, red and blue. Forward, Duniway leans across the center console, arm outstretched. I don't need to see it to know what's in his hand.

As the gun fires, I scream and throw myself against the wall. I can't see anything, can't tell what happened. Quince is hollering, Duniway shouting. My own cries must be just part of the cacophony.

"Go, go, *go!*"

I fall against the rear doors as the Stiff jerks forward with all the pep of a petting zoo pony. Through the tinted glass, I see blue and red, red and blue. In another life, an earnest, frustrated Jeremy dropped out of my rearview mirror. In this one, all that remains is a shapeless heap in the road.

FORTY-TWO

The Draw

Fitz roars as the Stiff gathers speed. Varney's drug has mostly worn off, but lingering vertigo gives everything a sickening tilt. With a desperation fueled by fragmented memory, I tear into the cargo bins. Straps and bungee cords, sheets and body bags. Deodorizer and nitrile gloves. An emergency change of clothes.

Then I grip something hard and metallic, slightly oily, and the memory comes rushing back.

. . . *scattered wreckage and bodies . . . dying flames in the engine compartment of the F-350 . . . the horse huffing out on the desert . . . and a chunk of debris that isn't debris—but an object as common as a coffee cup in Barlow County.*

A gun.

In the heat of the moment, I had Zachariah Urban to worry about, so I tucked the gun in with my spare clothes. Any other time, I'd have discovered it again while cleaning the Stiff, but the next day the world turned upside down, and I haven't gotten into the back of the Stiff since, let alone rifled the cargo bins.

"What? You gonna shoot 'em?"

Hell yes, I'm gonna shoot them. All Jeremy wanted was to earn his degree and land that job in Portland. Whatever his faults—like I'm one to judge—he didn't deserve to die alone on a dark road.

"Stop."

My voice cracks, but it's loud enough. Duniway looks over his shoulder.

"Holy Mother!"

Jackrabbit quick, he twists in his seat and raises his own gun. Quince wails, "Don't do it—don't don't don't . . .!"

I don't know who he's screaming at, don't care. I aim at Duniway's face and squeeze the trigger.

The damn thing doesn't even click.

Duniway bares his teeth and fires.

At once, the van swerves and I tumble backward, cracking my head against the rear door. As the Stiff veers and sways, Duniway struggles to squeeze between the seats.

"Hold it together, Quince!"

One-handed, he drags himself along the cot, trying to aim as he comes. There's only one choice left to me. With my free hand, I feel for the latch and give it a yank. The back doors fly open with a rush of wind. Caught in the latch, my finger snaps and I shriek. The Stiff tilts hard to the left. Eyes like eggs, Duniway falls toward me. I lash out with my feet, connect at the spot where his neck meets his shoulder. The force of my kick launches me through the open cargo doors as he bellows. Then I smack hard and roll, tumbling to a stop facedown on pavement. Behind me, a metallic crash rings out, followed by a high, mechanical whine. Somehow, I'm still holding the gun.

My lungs feel like they're about to collapse. Every inch of me hurts. I suck air and force myself onto my side. Across the road, the Stiff hangs at a crazy angle as if it's run up onto a stump. As the engine revs and the van shudders, a figure climbs out of the back.

"Just let him shoot you, Mellie. Quick, at least."

A whimper escapes me. Somehow I make it to my feet. Heedless of the darkness, I stagger, my legs threatening to give out with each step. The useless gun is a dead weight in my right hand, but I'm afraid to let it go.

Duniway screams my name.

A gunshot lights up the night. Something hard slams against my thighs. I pitch forward, gasping. For the space of a heartbeat I marvel at sudden weightlessness. Then, with cold air rushing past, I start to fall. Before I hit, I have just enough time to wonder if some shadow of Kendrick Pride's spirit lingered as his remains plummeted from the Tsokapo Gorge Bridge.

PART FIVE

Remains

Here lies One
Whose Name was writ in Water
—Epitaph of John Keats, died 1821

FORTY-THREE

Lake Champlain

I died at Lake Champlain on a stormy summer afternoon when the electric air lured me down to the windswept shore. Thunder pressed against me like a warm, damp blanket. I laughed as the wind inflated my lungs. Waves broke against the dock, and the cool spray raised goose bumps on my legs. Hopping from foot to foot, I lifted my arms to welcome the sudden rain.

Grandma Mae later said she and Fitz looked out the cabin door at the very moment lightning leapt through my hands and tossed me into the lake. He was out the door before she could speak. From her wheelchair, she could only watch as he sprinted to the dock and dove into the turbulent water.

Somehow, she said, he found me on the murky lake bottom. Somehow, he carried me back to the surface. Somehow, he pushed me onto the dock. It was the last thing he would ever do. A wave smashed him into the piling, and he disappeared. There was no one to bring him back. Our mother and father had driven to Burlington for the day.

For a week, machines kept me alive. Tubes fed me and a pump filled my lungs. But wires recorded a chronicle of emptiness behind my eyes. I missed Fitz's burial and slept through the decision to pull my plug. They expected me to follow him into the dark.

Instead, I woke up. To an empty room.

Mother had given up on me before Fitz was in the ground. Father reached acceptance about the time I learned to breathe on my

254 | W. H. Cameron

own again. And that was that. No second chances with Cricket and Stedman Dulac. I was eight years old.

I grew up an orphan in my own home, a guest who had overstayed her welcome. There were days when all I wanted was to know if I existed—a question Cricket and Stedman would never answer. They'd forget to account for me at meals, to pick me up if I stayed after school. When they went out, I never knew when they'd return. I was nine the first time they left me an entire weekend. I ate cereal and read Katherine Paterson.

At least I never had to sweat through a parent–teacher conference.

FORTY-FOUR

Downstream

"Melisende."

A hollow emptiness surrounds me like the sudden silence in the preparation room after Carrie turns off the embalming machine. So cold, so deep.

Did he—

Pain laces my chest and back, pierces my head like a spike. I can't remember why.

"Did he hit us . . . ?"

Did who hit us?

"Duniway!"

Does it matter?

"Melisende, try to move."

I have no strength. All I have is enveloping quiet and peaceful cold. "Algor mortis, the second stage of death, is characterized by a postmortem change in body temperature until equilibrium with ambient conditions is achieved."

Equilibrium. I could stay here forever.

"You need to use your legs while you still can."

Please stop talking, Fitz.

"Wudn't me, li'l sis."

But it's so familiar, a voice I hear every day. Not that I care. I just want it to shut up. To leave me to float in the deep, so very quiet. Deep enough the cold can't reach me, this silent void. Only the pain in my legs, my back, my hand pierce the quiet. Little jabs in the dark.

I can't remember why—
Use your legs, Melisende!
"Why—?"

My mouth fills with water and I choke, spinning in the powerful current. My hip slams against rock, my hand drags through gravel. The pain makes my whole body go rigid.

"Rigor mortis, the third stage of death—" The voice drones like someone reading aloud from a textbook. "—characterized by the stiffening of the muscles due to chemical changes in the tissue—"

"You'll be with us both very soon."

Jeremy lies in a heap on the dark road—
I'm sorry! It should have been me!
Lightning leaps through my hands—
Kick, goddammit—
An explosion of light as waves smash me against the piling—
I said kick!

My feet dig into sand and propel me to the surface. I gulp air till the ropy current drags me down again. The silence has become a boiling roar. I kick against nothing, and nothing, and . . . my right foot strikes rock, and my ankle buckles. I shriek bubbles, then a piercing wail through bitter air. I claw at weeds and rock. The current pulls at my legs, but I wedge the hard metal object in my hand between boulders and heave myself onto a muddy bank. A coughing spasm overtakes me, and my arms give out.

For a long time, all I can hear is my own dying heartbeat.

❧ ❧

"How you holding up, Mel?"

An insistent whispering intrudes upon a dark dream about Jeremy at the crossroad.

"How you holding up . . .?"

Lights flash, red and blue. Flames smolder in the bunchgrass. Jeremy approaches the injured horse from behind. I try to stop him, but my tongue is a swollen lump in my mouth. The horse kicks him in the chest. He falls into a shapeless heap in the road. My eyes snap open.

". . . was out of my hands . . ."

I'm lying facedown, numb, mouth filled with mud. The whispers are like stones falling into deep water.

"*. . . you know how to stir up trouble at the crossroad . . .*"

So deep, so cold.

"*. . . batshit, bug-ass slag . . .*"

With a shudder, I jerk up onto my knees. I'm soaked, freezing. My bones ache, my muscles are as weak as wet paper. I pull my legs out of the stream and crawl. When the mud becomes crumbling earth, I flop over. Bits of gravel stab my back. My ankle, my thighs, my finger all hurt more.

"*. . . hospitalized for a psychiatric condition . . .*"

The stars overhead skitter and leap as nausea wracks me. I force myself to a sitting position. Little by little, my stomach settles and my head clears. I'm on a sandbar at the edge of a creek or small river. Out in the stream, froth surges. Around me lies a broken landscape in browns and grays. Thick darkness looms at my back. The inscrutable whispers continue to swirl around me.

"*You should—*"

"Not *now*." My teeth chatter, my breath is a fog. I may have pulled back from rigor mortis, but algor mortis still has me in its frigid grip . . . *calm down, Spooky* . . . I need to move, to get my blood pumping. Twelve hours from now, it'll be ninety degrees, but I may not survive to see daylight if I crouch beside a cold stream for what remains of the high desert night.

"*That's all I was gonna say, li'l sis.*"

I struggle upright, keeping most of my weight on my left foot. The effort leaves me gasping. Gingerly, I test my right ankle. My leg trembles, but the ankle holds. My left index finger feels worse, swollen and canted unnaturally at the knuckle. Only when I reach over to probe the injury do I realize I'm still holding the gun. Water droplets glisten dimly on the barrel. Feeling stupid with cold, I stare at it, then titter morbidly. With my thumb, I disengage the safety.

Click.

No wonder it didn't fire in the Stiff. Doesn't mean it works now. Uncle Rémy's firearms lessons hadn't covered a dunking in a mountain stream. Last fall, Quince and I transported a man whose revolver exploded in his hand. I have no idea what water or sand might do to the damn thing.

But just pointing it at someone might be enough.

For what . . . ?

Shivering, I scan my surroundings again, more clear-eyed now. The dark profile of Lost Brother puts me east of the mountain, but that doesn't tell me much. While staggering away from the wrecked Stiff, I must have hit a bridge guardrail and fallen. Not into Tsokapo Gorge. The flow is too big, too strong with late season snowmelt. I can think of at least three streams Wayette Highway crosses, and there are other roads, other streams. I could be anywhere.

The darkness behind me seems to be a natural levee topped with pines, at least twelve feet high with a base gouged by spring floods. Too tall to climb. A fallen snag near me juts into the stream, forming the eddy where I escaped the river. Beyond, water leaps over submerged rocks and plunges into noisy, turbulent holes. On the far shore, trees crowd the water's edge. Even on a warm day with proper gear, an attempted crossing would be reckless, if not impossible.

A light flashes away to my right, upstream. Duniway making his way down from the bridge, searching for me? The whispers surge along with my panic as I pick my way to the far side of the fallen tree and crouch. Above, the river shoots through a gap between high rock walls. Uncle Rémy once explained the rapids classification system. I don't remember the details and couldn't guess the degree of whitewater I survived. Class Are-You-Fucking-Kidding-Me.

"*. . . trying to get away, maybe . . .*"

I wait, leaning against the tree, for a long time. The light doesn't return—if it was ever there. My anxiety remains. The space between the high bank and water continues downstream for as far as I can see, possibly for miles through the wilderness. Risky, but it's got to be better than sitting here and freezing or waiting for Quince and Duniway to find me. If I'm lucky, I'll find a spot where I can scramble up to higher ground and get a better sense of where I am. A cabin or homestead would be even better.

"*. . . who ya gonna call . . .*"

Near the water's edge, I find a narrow track, perhaps a fisherman's path. It's a small blessing for my throbbing ankle. I move slowly, one eye on the bank to my left, the other on the foaming water to my right. My clammy clothing clings like a lead shroud. The whispers shadow me. I have to take frequent breaks, but I don't dare sit. I may never get up again. I rest with the weight on my left leg, my arms wrapped around myself. High above, the stars are bright points in a black sea.

"*. . . you in a hurry to get somewhere . . .*"

As I toil around a rightward bend in the river, the moon emerges from behind a tree-lined ridge. Half full and still rising, it reveals details in the landscape—ashen sand, tumbled silver logs and round russet stone, patches of shaggy gunmetal brush. Ahead, the river straightens for some distance before curving left again, wider and less turbulent now. Yet the opposite shore remains out of reach, and on this side the bank is still too tall to climb.

Wind rises in the trees, stirring the whispers in the chill air.

"*. . . in a hurry . . .*"

"*. . . heard about the baby . . .*"

"You're still breathing," I say to myself. "Your heart is still beating."

"*But not Jeremy's . . .*"

An ache swells in my chest. If only I'd drunk less of Varney's awful coffee, or none at all.

If only I'd found the gun sooner.

Or recognized the threat Duniway posed.

"*. . . you're one of those . . .*"

Begged Helene for forgiveness and ridden off with her in her silver Lexus.

"*. . . dyke for the dead, brah . . .*"

So many *if onlys*. But Jeremy is dead. Kendrick Pride is dead, as is everyone from the crossroad—except the baby. How many ghosts haunt these hills and the high desert below? Molly Claire Maguire must have plenty of company. Soon enough, I'll join her. The night is too cold, too dark, and I'm too far from anyone who might help me.

"*Like I've never died before.*"

Laughter bubbles up in me, becomes a harsh cough.

I force myself to move, my ankle protesting each step. I come to another downed tree, its bark stripped away by years of implacable water. The tree's crown dips into the water, its root mass tangled in a thicket of thorny saplings. I half-scramble, half-slide over the top. Almost drop the gun, unclear why I'm still carrying it. Downstream, I make out a large, dark shape, dull against forested hillside behind it. An old lumber mill or an oversized pole barn. I wonder if they have a phone.

"*. . . sorry for calling . . . I hope you're okay . . .*"

More likely, the place is locked or abandoned.

"*. . . not a very trusting soul . . .*"

A thin strand of cloud passes in front of the moon. The silvery landscape turns matte gray and vague, and for a dozen breaths I navigate by the sound of the water, by the whispers. When the cloud passes, a taller structure snaps into focus behind the first.

Ahead, across the river, is the Dalton Hensley Asylum for Infirm Ladies and Needful Girls.

I don't know whether to feel relief or despair. If I dare show my face at the gate, a text alert goes to school security, followed by a call to the Sheriff's Department. Duniway will know right where to find me. Helene used to say cops are most dangerous when they know one of their own is in the wrong.

It doesn't get much more wrong than Omar Duniway.

Beside me, the river's whispers surge and writhe, words half-remembered, half-imagined.

"*. . . for probable cause shown . . .*"

"*That's my girl . . .*"

"*. . . skip the coffee . . .*"

"*. . . held your shit together . . .*"

Melisende's greatest hits, churning and cold as the current itself, a Barlow County cascade.

"*. . . you've done enough . . .*".

"*. . . fun in funerals. . . girl raised by wolves . . .*"

"*. . . loved your . . .*"

My breath catches in my throat, a strangled sob.

I look up at the long sweep of the Milky Way, remembering how it appeared from the rim of Shatter Hill. The catastrophe I found that night at crossroad has led me straight as a bullet to this river side—cold, battered, and alone. My mother and father left me for dead, my husband left me and for all I know died. I tried to save a girl and failed. I've lost Helene—surely for good this time. Even Fitz has run out of things to say.

"*I loved your fearlessness . . .*"

Or maybe I gave up on myself when I told Aunt Elodie I was leaving.

"Some grow up in the work, like your Uncle Rémy, and others grow into it. But you? You seem born to it."

She's right. This is my home now.

"Whatever you decide, do it as the woman who pulled Landry MacElroy out of the back of that pickup."

I can't bring the dead back, but maybe I can give them justice. I'll cross the river on the asylum bridge, avoid the cameras at the gate, and find the old trail. Then I'll crawl back to civilization, if crawling is what it takes.

But when I reach the bridge, I'm too late. Quince and Duniway are already there.

FORTY-FIVE

The Bridge

I hear them before I see them—urgent murmurs obscured by the river. The sound freezes me halfway over a tree trunk. The waning moon suddenly seems bright as a spotlight, the scrape as I slide back behind the tree as loud as an ash grinder.

Someone coughs.

"Give me one."

"These things'll kill ya."

"You wish."

A lighter clicks, then a waft of smoke overwhelms the scents of water, sand, and pine. There's another cough.

Quietly, I exhale. They haven't seen me.

I ease my head up. They're on the bridge, maybe twenty-five feet away and four or five feet higher than where I crouch—twin scarecrows distinguished only by the gear belt and sidearm on Duniway's narrow waist. Motionless, he leans forward in a way that suggests restrained wrath. Beside him, Quince puffs smoke and paces, a walking nerve ending.

"Would you stop that?"

Quince ignores him. "She hadda drown if the fall didn't kill her."

"Or maybe she's hiding in the trees, planning an ambush. Why didn't you tell me they keep a weapon in the van?"

"They *don't*."

"Could've fooled me."

"This whole thing has gotten way out of hand."

"Whose fault is that?"

"Hey. I was trying to help."

"You'd have helped a lot more if you'd done as you were told. One body, Quince. One damned body. I could have handled the others."

"One *damned* body, Omar? Fuck me. You're getting a little over-het with the language there."

I imagine more than see Duniway's cheeks suck in with irritation. He turns his back on Quince and takes a few steps toward the asylum.

Between the bridge and me, the bank dips toward the road, with little cover except tussocky overhangs of dry grass. Boulders snarled with flood debris slope down to the water's edge. The river rushes under the bridge, still too fast to risk a swim. My downstream trek warmed me up a bit, but now the night's chill seeps back into me. I can't linger here, but as long as they remain on the bridge, I'm stuck.

Duniway flicks his cigarette into the river, then turns back to Quince. "Once Xavier is freed up, I want you to get your boat. You can search the river faster from the water."

"I'll have to drive to Little Cherry. Nowhere closer to put in, and there's all kinds of places a body can get snagged between here and there. Hell, she could be in a hole thirty feet below us and we won't know till the river drops."

"I'll get Varney up here to walk the banks at sunup."

"If she's not dead, maybe she still has the gun."

"So?" Duniway throws him a dark look. "Don't get shot."

"Jesus, Omar. You gonna warn him too?"

"What are you worried about?" Duniway's voice takes on a mocking twang. "*She hadda drown.*"

"You don't think she did?"

"I didn't think she'd wake up in the van." Duniway shakes his head. "Just be careful. And if you do find that weapon, make sure it disappears down the deepest souse you can find. I don't want it confusing things. Got me?"

Instead of answering, Quince turns toward a light in the trees. I drop my head as a white pickup rolls out of the forest and stops, its front wheels on the bridge. The right headlight is broken and dark, but the left catches Quince in the act of tossing his butt into the river. In the ambient glow, I see a red streak on the cracked bumper.

Trae Fowler's Subaru was red.

Duniway leans over as the passenger-side window slides open. I can see the driver's silhouette—hands on the wheel, head turned toward the open window—but the river and the idling engine drown out anything said inside the cab.

"I know, I know. You'd think the good doctor would understand his dosages."

Duniway's voice, at least, carries. "Doesn't matter," he continues. "Likely as not she'll wash up at some fishing camp tomorrow. The river's forty-four degrees up here."

I can't even tell if the figure in the truck is a man or a woman. Whoever it is seems to have a lot to say. Duniway listens for a while, his shoulders hunched up around his ear.

Suddenly he smacks the window frame. "I know it's been a week. I'm doing everything I can."

My ears perk up. It's been a nearly week since the crossroad. But if Duniway has anything more to say about it, I can't make it out. At a gesture from the pickup driver, he bends down, sticking his head almost through the open window. Whatever they're discussing, the conversation remains heated. Finally he straightens up. "Don't worry about that," he says sharply. "The dash cam will have captured everything we want it to see and nothing we don't. Even if she survived the river—"

Duniway goes quiet as a faint electronic beep sounds. He pulls out his phone and scans the screen, then turns to Quince. "Someone called in Chapman, and all hell is about to break loose. I've got to go."

Quince stares at his feet. "What in hell am I supposed to do?"

"Wait here. Shouldn't be long."

As the pickup backs up, Duniway strides across the bridge, then angles toward the asylum gate. The truck makes a two-point turn, then departs the way it came. Quince ignores them both. When he reaches the asylum, Duniway opens the big padlock and throws the gate wide. A moment later, he drives out in his department Tahoe. As he crosses the bridge, he calls out the window, "Go lock up."

But once the Tahoe is gone, Quince stays put. He jams a cigarette into his mouth, then fumbles with his Zippo, flicking it a half
dozen times before it sparks. When he inhales, half the cigarette
burns away. "Christ in a cooler," he mutters through smoke. "I did
not sign up for this shit."

I don't know what he's whining about. Duniway isn't planning
to pin Jeremy's murder on Quince Kinsrow. He's going to pin it on
me.

FORTY-SIX

C'est Moi

I'm not even surprised. I've been drugged, battered, frozen, and nearly drowned. Of course Duniway wants me to go down for Jeremy's murder too. He's had me in his sights ever since the bodies waltzed out of the New Mortuary. Ever since *Quince* took them—though it sounds like the chief deputy would rather he hadn't.

"One damned body."

The sheriff never confirmed to me that the fourth body in the retort was a girl, but I no longer doubt it. It had to be the baby's mother, carried away for unknown reasons by Pride's mystery vehicle, the white pickup. The others—the crossroad dead—Duniway could have handled, as he said. Written them off to the accident. It sounds like Quince's task was to get rid of only the girl's body, but he decided it would be helpful to grab three more.

Not that I can prove it.

I could walk into Sheriff Turnbull's office and lay it all out, including Varney's phone call and my narrow escape, but Jeremy's dash cam still points to me. Only one person drives the Stiff these days.

As Landry might try to say, *"C'est moi."* Melisende Dulac.

For my part, I can talk all I want. Pride's fourth vehicle, his collection of spent cartridges and crash diagram. Where's all that now? As for tonight—a ridiculous story. "Quince drove the Stiff, Duniway fired the shot. I was in the back, drugged by the medical examiner . . ." A good catch, that Dr. Varney—pillar of the community, though one with terrible taste in coffee.

Everyone knows Jeremy and I were seeing each other—"No secrets in Samuelton, sweetie." The newest gossip will be the juiciest yet. I'm the common thread tying together every sordid detail of Barlow County's Crime of the Century. No one will question it.

"I heard she killed a man in *Bahs*-ton."

"Claimed she saw the Spirit."

"Tried to punch me at the Pig."

"Total psycho."

"Nympho too."

"Necrophiliac."

Soon enough, the accepted narrative will be that I stole the crossroad dead to satisfy my ghoulish needs, then tried to burn the evidence. *Why those three?* is a question no one will ask—and one I can't answer if they did. People will say Chief Deputy Duniway wouldn't have arrested me for no reason. Sure, I got out, but that doesn't make me innocent—just means I have a good lawyer.

Rémy and Elodie may get some measure of sympathy. They're Old Barlow. But it'll be diluted by unspoken blame. They brought me here, didn't they?

And if Duniway's plans work out, I won't be around to muddy things anyway.

I'll die wondering why two boys and two men drove a hundred-fifty miles from Portland to Barlow County. Why they stopped in the middle of a remote intersection. I'll never know what they were doing when Zachariah Urban came tearing up the highway with a horse trailer, doing seventy-five in a fifty-five zone. Too fast, but it was nearly midnight. The only time there's traffic in Barlow County is when there's good snow at Brother Drop or if some steers get past a cattle guard.

So many dead, all for what?

The deep sky overhead has no answers.

I shift against the tree, the gun heavy in my hand. Perhaps the very gun that killed Nathan Harper.

"What's it going to be?"

Not Fitz this time. Me.

What would the woman who pulled Landry out of that pickup do?

What will Melisende Dulac do?

My legs are stiff, and my joints all throb. I ignore the pain and pull myself over the fallen tree. Only twenty-five feet away, Quince seems to only care about his cigarette. He doesn't hear me, doesn't see me. I scan the bridge, the dirt road. That way isn't an option, not with all hell breaking loose because of Jeremy. It'll be lights and sirens from Shatter Hill to Dryer Lake.

The way through the forest is my best bet. From the trailhead, I'll stick to the trees along Hensley Lane and then cut through the old ghost town to the back entrance of Crestview. Aunt Elodie will listen. Even if the cops get to her first, she'll hear me out. But first, I have to get past Quince.

He coughs a pillow of smoke. It would feel so good to shoot him in the back.

Then I have a new thought, a crazy thought.

Take him with me.

Alone, all I have is a farfetched tale with more questions than answers. But maybe I don't need to explain the whole sordid mess.

Maybe I just need to sow doubt.

I heft the gun. Quince, like it or not, is going to help me do just that.

FORTY-SEVEN

Quince

Quince sits on the downstream edge of the bridge, legs hanging off and wriggling like a troll tied to an anthill. A line of smoke rises past his ear. I remember his leathery hand gripping my face and fight the urge to shove him over the brink. Below, the river rushes down the steep gradient, a hundred yards of bucking whitewater with standing waves six feet high and woven eddies pouring into black, swirling holes. Class No-One-Gets-Out-of-Here-Alive.

I nudge him with the tip of my boot.

He jerks so hard he almost goes over anyway. The cigarette drops from his mouth in a shower of sparks. When he sees me, he scuttles away as if he knows what I was thinking.

"Christ, Spooky. You scared the piss out of me." His face is shrouded in shadow, with only dark holes to indicate his eyes and gaping mouth.

"How you doing, Quince?"

My right arm hangs at my side, gun in hand, trigger finger flat against the barrel—one of Uncle Rémy's lessons.

"Been better."

The rushing river swallows my humorless laugh. With my left hand, I gesture across the bridge. "Let's walk."

When he doesn't move, I raise the gun until the barrel catches moonlight. Quince's cavernous eyes gleam white, and he jerks like a puppet, all but hopping across the bridge. I trot to keep up, neither easy or painless. He makes for the gate.

"Not that way."

With the gun, I point upstream along the bank. In the dark, it seems unlikely the security cameras could pick us up this far from the gate, but I'd rather not take the chance. "Stay near the river."

"Where we going?"

"Just be glad I'm not pushing you down a draw."

Another white gleam sparks in his eyes. His jangly body radiates skittish energy. Mine feels like it's made of mud. If he tries anything, I might not be able to stop him. But he doesn't know that.

Shoulders slumped, he heads along the riverbank. I follow, keeping my distance should he get any ideas. The asylum's upper stories and cupola peek over the wall. Faint light leaks from around the plywood covering several of the third-floor windows.

"Is someone inside?"

Quince looks back over his shoulder. "How the hell should I know?"

I let that go. There will be time for talk when we're less exposed. "Pick up the pace." He obliges without further comment.

I'm not used to Quince doing anything without making a speech first.

Once we move under the wall, I relax a little. The shadows are inky black, and the old stone amplifies the river sounds, welcome shrouds against eyes and ears. But negotiating the uncertain footing in the dark reawakens the stitch in my side. Spikes of pain start shooting from my ankle to my knee. At the corner, I call for Quince to hold up. I'm almost surprised when he does.

"Now what, boss?" There's a smirk in his voice, as if he can see my grimace.

Here on the back side of the asylum, the forest creeps down to the rocky berm at the foot of the wall. I gesture toward a knee-high hump of stone, and he sits without argument. Behind us, the river washes through burbling riffles. He gazes at the water with longing.

"I have some questions."

Moonlight glints in his eyes. "What makes you think I have answers?"

"You always have answers, Quince."

"Not about this shit."

"Who was driving the pickup?"

He looks up at the wall, as if the answer can be found in the lichen-rimed basalt. His shoulders twitch in a marionette's imitation of a shrug. "I don't recall any pickup."

I have to remind myself everything is a game to Quince, a performance, a calculated effort to rankle or rile.

"There's still a chance you walk away from this. No one has to know you helped kidnap me."

His head lifts again, but he doesn't speak. A niggle of disquiet runs through me, and I turn, half-expecting spying eyes atop the wall. But all I see is dark stone and the old water tower.

On a hunch, I ask, "Was it Xavier Meyer's pickup?"

Quince's eyes bug out like a couple of boiled eggs. "Sorry. Can't help you."

"Yet you didn't mind cracking my head against the ground. I know we're not friends, Quince, but I had no idea things were that bad between us."

His boiled-egg gaze steals to the river. The man is tanned leather and bone strung together with baling wire. The river here isn't too rough, a section of relative calm before the bridge. If he kept his feet, maybe he could make it across. But if he stepped in a hole, he'd sink right to the bottom.

"Forty-four degrees," I say, just in case he's thinking about it.

"I've been in the water around here. Don't think I can't handle it."

"Could you handle it if I shot you in the back?"

His head drops.

I don't know what I expected. Not a tearful confession—not from Quince. But not a complete shutdown either. He's usually too much of a showboat. I expected him to tease something—a connection, a name, some small piece of the puzzle—but he's just sitting there with his chin on his chest.

It's all well and good to threaten to shoot him, but if it comes right down to it, I'm not sure I could follow through—assuming the gun even works. That incendiary moment after Duniway killed Jeremy was one thing. But here, under the eaves of the forest with the river whispering at my back? Quince goes back years with Uncle Rémy and Aunt Elodie. Hell, for all his ridiculous bluster, he taught me a lot when I first got to Barlow County.

There has to be a better way.

I let out a slow breath. "Do you remember the last county removal you and I did together?"

"You know how many removals I've done, Spooky?" He speaks into his chest.

"Not so many with me."

"Ain't like I kept a log."

My lips purse. "It was a drowning on the Palmer footbridge below the fire watchtower. Last October."

He doesn't say anything at first, then nods. "Eagles Lift." He fidgets until curiosity gets the better of him. "What about it?" Quince loves a story, even if it isn't his.

"You were in a foul mood because the river would be closed for fishing soon. While we waited for Fire and Rescue to pull the body out of the water, you complained about how in another week you'd be stuck with the reservoir or long drives to rivers with year-round fishing."

"So what?"

"'A man with priorities,' is how the sheriff described you when I told him you came by the New Mortuary that day after the crash. You couldn't help because you had trout to clean."

He shrugs. "What's your point?"

"I guess I never quite understood how important fishing is to you."

"Like you said, Spooky, we ain't never been friends."

I lick my lips. Half-turning toward the water, I gesture with my aching left hand. "Is this the Palmer River?"

He hesitates, as if it's a trick question. "Yeah. Why?"

"This must be part of your fishing grounds."

He eyes me like I've said something stupid. "Not a big fishing stream this high up. Oh, there's some good spots, but you have to hike to reach any of them. Rafters and kayakers can put in up at Ours Lake, but the whitewater is too big for drift boats. I mean, a lot of drifters think they can go anywhere a raft can, but I like my boat too much. Anyway, it's all catch and release up here."

"What does that mean?"

I can't hear it over the river, but the sigh is clear in his posture. "You'll only hook wild trout up here, but you have to let 'em go.

That's why it's called catch and release." The *dumbshit* is silent. "They stock the lower river with farm trout."

"How do you tell the difference?"

"They cut the adipose fin off hatchery trout. That's the little one between the tail and dorsal fin." In case I was wondering. "Catch one of those, and so long as it's over the size limit, you've got dinner. Mushy farm trout maybe, but it eats."

Quince isn't one to let niceties like the *rules* get in his way, but I keep that thought to myself. "So you don't fish in this part of the river?"

"Oh, I come up here a few times a year. Wild trout are wilier than farm trout. Worth the hike. But on the lower Palmer, I put in below the Goose Creek Hatchery."

I've seen Quince's boat a few times being pulled behind his pickup. Aluminum, not unlike a rowboat, but with a wide, flat bottom and a high bow. Oars, no motor. "You drive to wherever you want to put in, launch from your trailer, then float downstream?"

"Yeah. So?"

"So Duniway said he wanted you to search for me with your boat. Is it nearby?" If his boat is close, his truck is too. And that means I might not have to walk on my throbbing ankle all the way to Crestview. Quince should even know his way around the backcountry logging roads so we can avoid whatever law enforcement Duniway has rallied.

But Quince is shaking his head even before I can finish the thought. "Not sure what you think you saw or think you heard." He leans back and rests his palms on the rock. "Maybe you were hallucinating."

I close my eyes against a growing sense of futility. In the end, all Quince cares about is fishing. Crack a joke, get a few laughs, then hit the next trout hole. It's probably where he'd be right now if he thought Duniway would let him get away with it.

But thought of the chief deputy makes my eyes pop open again. Quince hasn't moved from his seat. As I stare at him, I think back to the moment when I came upon the two of them on the bridge, to the way they spoke and what they said. Duniway could barely restrain his anger. Quince, twitchy and on edge, couldn't stop pacing. What had he said after Duniway drove off? "I did not sign up for this shit."

Whatever is going on between them, they're reluctant allies. I have to hope that when Duniway shot Jeremy, the alliance suffered a mortal wound too.

I take a couple of steps toward Quince, scratching my thigh with the gun sight. He shifts, rocking his ass against the stony hump.

"You probably know I was seeing Deputy Chapman. I mean, everyone knows, right?"

He doesn't say anything, but his shoulders move up and down in acknowledgment.

"It was just a lark for me, but Jeremy took it seriously. He thought we should do things together. Date, I guess, like a real couple. That's not what I wanted, but Jeremy didn't give up easily. He said we could start simple, maybe with a picnic in some out-of-the-way place where we wouldn't run into people. As it happens, one of the spots he suggested was that lookout at Eagles Lift." I pause to let the words sink in. "He said the view was spectacular."

Quince has gone uncharacteristically still.

"I'm not really a picnic kind of girl, but Jeremy could wheedle with the best of them. Sooner or later, he might have worn me down, cajoled me into going up there just to shut him up. Did you know that about women? Sometimes we agree to things because it's just easier. I mean, you motherfuckers can be *relentless*." I make no effort to hide my anger. "But now Jeremy will never get the chance to wheedle me ever again, will he?"

"What do you want from me?"

"You can start by telling me who was in that pickup. And then you can drive me to the sheriff and tell him."

"The headlight was in my eyes."

"How much fishing do you think you'll get to do in prison, Quince?"

He has no answer to that.

"I know you stole the bodies. No one else around here knows how to fire up that ancient crematory."

"Someone coulda looked it up on the internet."

"Did someone look up how to make a murder look like an accident?"

"I don't know anything about that."

"I heard you and Duniway talking, Quince. You're in this up to your bony ass, but I'm willing to forget about that if you give up Duniway and anyone else involved." I'm making promises I don't have the power to keep, but he doesn't have to know that. "We can leave together, go straight to the sheriff, or even the state police. I was there, Quince. I know you were just as shocked as I was when Duniway killed Jeremy. You can get your side of the story on the record before he even knows you're gone."

He's shaking his head, but whether at me or the weight of circumstance I can't tell. Did he help kill Pride too? Anything's possible, but the way he was acting earlier makes me think not. Quince has always been a hired hand. Disposing of remains is one thing, even driving the Stiff. But helping kill someone is a whole 'nuther matter.

"You said it yourself, Quince. You didn't sign up for this shit. I know you're not happy about what happened tonight."

"There's a whole lot of river between not happy and stupid."

"Let's just go to your truck while there's still time."

He stands and shakes his head. "Sorry, Spooky, but I didn't drive."

As if to emphasize the point, he shoots his arm out and turns his wrist as if he's looking at a nonexistent watch. I step back, and nearly trip on a loose stone in the scree berm. "About ten minutes."

"What?"

"Response time when they see something on the security monitor." He points at the top of the dark wall. "There's perimeter cameras at every corner. Night vision and everything."

My onrush of panic seems to infuse the air with a surreal luminosity. I scan the wall as if I expect to see a glass globe with a glowing red dot.

"How 'bout that, Spooky? My ride is here."

His words are like a kick in the gut. The glimmer in the air intensifies and a car or truck engine guns, loud enough to drown out the river. Quince's teeth glow ice white beneath the shivering black holes of his eyes.

He knew what would happen this whole time.

FORTY-EIGHT

Spirit

As I lurch past Quince, I clip his forehead with the gun barrel. An accident. Maybe. He yelps and falls back, clawing at my legs. My boot heel lands on his hand, and his yelp becomes a scream.

"Now I bet you wished you'd pushed him in the river, little sister."

The long asylum wall looms to my left. To my right, the ponderosas all look the same, cracked pillars in a black void. Ankle screaming, I lumber along the shifting, rocky berm until the vehicle rounds the corner and bathes me in light. A car door slams. A man shouts. I skid on pine needles as I lunge into the trees, but manage to stay upright as the shadows close in around me.

More shouting, mostly unintelligible. "—the fuck . . . she go—!"

"—can't . . . forest—!"

Navigating by headlight, I stay just inside the trees until the asylum wall ends, then falter. I've missed the old path, but I can't risk going back. In the dark, they could be upon me before I see them coming.

Counting Quince, there's at least two of them, maybe more. Unhurt, better rested. No doubt familiar with the forest around the asylum, including the old trail. Hell, half the trees might hide surveillance cameras. *Night vision and everything.*

All I have is a gun that might blow up in my hand.

At the edge of the trees, I crouch in the shadow of a twisted oak. The wall seems to fluoresce under the headlights, but the glare drops off in the open space between the asylum and the cemetery. Beyond, the tombstones look like broken teeth in the moonlight. Where the forest intrudes among the grave sites, the ground starts to rise.

"—see her—?"

"—cutting . . . river—"

"—too far—"

The first hint of dawn is just showing in the east. In the distant river valley, people will soon wake to a long day of fishing, rafting, or hiking. Out in the rangeland, ranchers will be filling Thermoses and fueling ATVs in preparation for an even longer day performing the many tasks necessary for their precarious livings, unaware of the drama in the high country. In the days ahead, will the *Samuelton Ledger* carry a piece about Melisende Dulac, the apprentice mortician who went mad, defiled the dead, and murdered her cop lover? Or do I still have a chance to write a different story?

Keep going. Tell the truth. Don't give up.

It's all I can do.

The trailhead and Crestview are both above me. No matter what, I have to climb. In a crouch, I cross into the cemetery, feeling my way among the tombstones toward the Hensley grave and the forest beyond.

As I near the monument to the mother and daughter who inspired the asylum, the praying hands of Mary crack and a granite shard strikes my cheek. Half a second later, the gunshot sounds. With a shriek I dive behind the tomb.

"—got her! I got—!"

I scrabble through dirt and leaves, still warm from the previous day. Great spot for a rattlesnake.

"Over here!"

Another gunshot sounds, loud and too close. I spot movement among the tombstones. Without thinking, I thrust the gun around the granite column, thumb the safety, and pull the trigger.

I almost drop the gun when the shot goes off. Ears ringing, I squeeze again, once . . . twice before daring to look.

There's no one in sight, but as the echoes of the gunshots die, the unmistakable voice of Xavier Meyer hollers, "Get your goddamn ass over here!"

I crab backward into the forest. The shadows feel too thin. When I smack against the bole of an oak, I push myself up. Meyer shouts again. I jam the gun into the back of my pants, then charge around the tree. The barrel feels hot against my ass.

The ground rises sharply. Almost at once, I'm climbing as much as running, grabbing at branches I can barely see. A couple of shots ring out, but I don't look back.

"They're just trying to spook you."

It's working.

Soon the slope is so steep the trees grow at an angle out of the ground. *"Keep going. Don't give up".* I aim for the deepest shadows, hoping darkness means space between the trunks. When I guess wrong, branches tear at my face and arms. I smell blood and taste acid. My lungs burn, and every step makes my ankle scream. Half the time, I drag myself up by the roots of trees growing above my head. My left hand is useless, leaving my right to do all the work. A year of moving the dead may be the only reason I have the strength to make the climb at all.

It ends abruptly when I reach for a branch and pitch forward in darkness. My broken finger explodes with pain as my arms crumple, and I slam into the ground. For some time, all I can do is sprawl in the thick litter of crumbling pine cones and dry needles, head spinning. But little by little, my ragged breathing eases, and the pain recedes to a dull background throb.

Even then, I force myself to lie still, listening. The forest is a cold, silent tomb.

Wincing, I ease onto my hands and knees, then get to my feet. The effort leaves me dizzy. A wall of trees drops away behind me, with thick forest stretching along the rim of the escarpment. But ahead, in the distance, moonlight shines into a clearing. The overlook where the teen moms smoke comes to mind.

Could I have climbed that far?

"Don't get your hopes up," I whisper. I can't even be sure I've come the same direction.

The soft carpet of pine needles wants to slide beneath my feet. Here and there, shafts of moonlight break through gaps in the forest canopy. A crisp breeze stirs the pine boughs and drives some of the heaviness from the air. Once, I hear an owl call.

The farther I go, the lighter and more open the forest becomes. Soon, I can see ahead to an open space maybe fifty yards across and extending well out of sight to my right and left. Beyond, the forest climbs again. On the near side, a shallow bank rises just before the trees end.

Not anxious to leave shelter just yet, I pause. A branch snaps at my back.

"Hold it right there, young lady."

I wheel around to see Xavier Meyer twenty paces back, his gray hair shining in a shaft of broken moonlight. In a fumbling panic, I claw for the gun but manage only to hook the trigger guard with my thumb as he throws himself sideways behind a rotted stump. Pivoting back, I lunge toward a depression half-hidden by a tilted pine at the edge of the forest, maybe fifteen feet away. Too late, I realize my mistake. What I thought was a clearing is no high meadow, and no lava field. The depression drops into a long gully slicing down through a steep canyon wall.

Skidding too fast, I claw at the leaning tree. There's no guardrail here, no river below. My chin cracks bark and the gun spins off into empty air. I catch a limb with my left hand. A scream rips out of me even as I scrabble at the tree with my good hand.

Meyer's crew cut appears above the brink.

"Please—"

Eyes cold and empty, he brings the butt of his gun down on the swollen knuckle of my broken finger. Somehow, shrieking, I hang on. Through tears, I watch Meyer raise his gun again.

But before the blow lands, our eyes lock. His mouth gapes wide and a tiny sound escapes, a disbelieving whimper. Then he somersaults over me, the toe of his boot clipping my forehead as he flies past. His long, trailing scream dies with a sickening crunch somewhere below.

Before I can make sense of what just happened, my left hand loses its grip. I snag a trailing limb with my right but almost at once, slick with sweat, it slips . . . slips. There's nothing else to grab. I kick at the gully wall but manage only to dislodge a cascade of dirt and pebbles.

"Help, anyone, help! Quince—!"

As if only waiting for my cry, a figure appears and reaches down. Not Quince, but a gleam among shadows, spectral white and flowing like fog in the wind. Shrouded in moonlight, she flickers in and out of view like an image projected through falling leaves. Her face is made of pale gold.

Molly Claire?

"Grab me, damn it. I can't do this without your help," she says.

Her strained voice shatters the illusion. As she clutches at my shirt collar, her dirty white hoodie, "CENTENNIAL SOCCER" in block letters across the front, resolves in front of me. Not the costume of a pioneer woman dead for more than a century.

"Tell a story often enough," Aunt Elodie said, "and it gathers substance in our minds." But this is no phantom brought to life by dint of imagination or delusion. This is a girl, a living girl who's come out of nowhere to save my life.

The branch cracks. My collar goes tight around my throat. I slam against the gully wall. Clawing wildly, I grip fabric and hang on tight as she drags me over the gully's rim by the back of my shirt. We tumble into a heap with my head on her chest. She's warm and soft and smells of sweat. I can hear her heartbeat.

Gently, she pushes me off and sits up. I just want to lie there, but dread still has hold of me. I have to be sure about Xavier Meyer. Groaning, I crawl to the edge of the gully and peer down into the canyon. Far below, I can just make out his body in the shadowy gloom, bent and broken on a heap of fallen rock.

Aunt Elodie may say we don't stand in judgment of the dead, but I think I'll make exception this time. Good fucking riddance.

"There's another guy out there," the girl says when I turn away from the edge. "I heard them yelling to each other." The shadows are still dense under the boughs, but away east, morning is approaching. In the twilight I can see she's sixteen or seventeen. Her eyes are hollow and dark, and her ash-blonde hair hangs lank and tangled around her face. Her nails are cracked and filthy, her black yoga pants ripped at the knees.

As I climb unsteadily to my feet, I'm struck by a sudden feeling of familiarity. At first I think she must be one of the girls I saw at the Hensley School, one of the teen moms holding her newborn or visiting with family. Yet if she's a Hensley girl, why does she look like she's been living in a cave? Where's her blue blouse with the billowy sleeves?

"Where did you come from?" I say, my voice hoarse.

"It doesn't matter." She stands and brushes the pine needles off her arms and legs. "Can you walk?"

A little pressure on my ankle is rewarded with a lancing pain, but it quickly subsides. "I think so."

"Then we should get out of here."

"Wait." I can't shake the sense I've seen her before. "Who are you?"

The girl looks away. "If that other guy shows up, I'm not waiting around." Her resolve seems at odds with her battered, filthy appearance. *Not Hensley,* I decide as she jams her hands into her hoodie muff. The block letters on her shirt front stretch, stirring a dim memory: Nathan Harper's Facebook pic, him laughing and giving the finger to the camera. According to his profile, his favorite movies were the *Fast and Furious* series. He went to Centennial High School.

He died at the crossroad.

I look at her with growing wonder. The old rancher had pointed out a pale figure in the desert. *Did you see her?* As the flames crackled in the grass, I *did* see something, if only for an instant. A figure at the tree line, then gone. Afterward, no one believed me.

Hell, I wasn't sure I believed it myself.

"Were you there?" I say. "The night of the crash, were you at the crossroad?"

Her body goes stiff, and her eyes flash with suspicion. She takes a quick step back, then freezes. "What do you know about that?"

Only that I have more questions than answers.

I can see a storm in her eyes. A moment ago, she killed a man to save me. Maybe it's starting to sink in, causing her to question herself. And who could fucking blame her? If she was at the crossroad, she's been on the run for a week. It's possible the last person she saw was whoever shot Nathan Harper in the back.

"Listen, I was the first on the scene that night. I know something terrible happened." The fire, the wreckage, the bodies. "I found . . ."

I almost say *Nathan,* but bite it back. If she really did know him, I can't be who tells her. Not here, not like this. I don't speak to the bereaved.

But the girl's eyes flash and she surges toward me. "Who did you find?" Her voice is choked with a sudden desperate need. "A little baby girl? Is she okay?"

The mother, I think. *I've found the baby's mother.* For a second, my tongue seems to tangle in my mouth. "She's safe," I manage. Placed in foster care, according to Joanne at Cuppa Jo. "I promise."

With that, the girl sags, and for a second I'm afraid she's going to collapse. I take a painful step, not sure what I could do to help. Collapse with her? But she waves me off. For a long time she stands still in the brightening dawn, her chin on her chest. When she looks up at last, relief has replaced her suspicion.

"We should go." Her voice sounds wrung out.

"But . . ." I still have so many questions. Why did those boys came to so far that night, and what really happened when they arrived at the crossroad? If this girl is the baby's mother, who was the fourth body found in the retort? Is she who Pride was really looking for? Is she why he had to die? But I know the questions will have to wait. As the girl said, Quince is still out there. While I can't imagine him giving chase himself, surely he's called Duniway by now. Still, there's one thing I have to know.

"Please, just tell me your name."

Her head snaps around at the call of a bird in the forest. When she turns back, she lets out a noisy breath. "Shelby Pride, okay? Now can we get the hell out of here?"

FORTY-NINE

Needful Girl

When I wake up, Shelby Pride is sitting on a stool at my side, her eyes fixed on the empty space above my head. I don't know where we are.

After she led me away from the gully, we followed the canyon rim downhill, chased by morning birdsong, and crossed a groomed trail. From there the trees thinned, but I struggled to keep my feet on the uneven ground. My ankle throbbed, and the growing daylight made my head pound. Before long, Shelby was forced to half-carry me. When she finally pushed open a door and led me into a dark, airless space smelling of ash, I half-believed she'd brought me to a crematorium. She told me to lie down, and I didn't argue. I welcomed the flames.

I'm lying on a narrow camp bed with a couple of blankets for padding. My boots and socks are off, exposing my purple, swollen ankle. *Ante mortem lividity.* She hands me a tin cup. The water is earthy and metallic.

"I have to pee," I say.

"There's an outhouse around back. Can you walk?"

"I better try."

She offers me a pair of old rubber clogs. "I checked them for spiders." With her help, I hobble through the low doorway of what turns out to be a small log cabin built on a ridge overlooking the Palmer River Valley. Under the late afternoon sun, the river is a molten ribbon winding through a basin of ochre, red, and blocks of irrigated green. Another time I might find the view breathtaking.

My ankle holds up well enough on the short walk to the rickety outhouse. Flies and mosquitoes buzz around my head as I relieve myself.

Back inside, Shelby returns to the stool, and I drop onto the bed. I seem to have slept the day away, but the short foray has worn me out. In the heavy silence, I scan the cabin. There's an old kitchen table with a pair of mismatched chairs and a wooden rocker in front of a stone fireplace. Shelves hold cups and plates, an iron skillet and a Dutch oven, plus a couple of ancient paperbacks: *Zen and the Art of Motorcycle Maintenance* and *The Tao of Pooh*. A wall calendar shows a faded photo of a mountain lake. August 2002.

My eye stops on an exquisitely carved wooden leg mounted above the cold hearth. Though I've never seen it, I know at once who made it and wore it. Eugène de Bouton.

A sudden sadness comes over me. "This cabin belongs to my uncle."

"I had to break in." Shelby's face colors. "I didn't have anywhere else to go."

"I'm sure he won't mind." The Rémy who picked me up at the train station wouldn't. "How did you find this place?"

"After the crash, all I wanted was to get away, even though I could barely walk."

"Were you hurt?"

"Not in the crash." She puts her hand on her stomach and laughs quietly. Sadly. "Somehow I made it to the trees. From there, I just kept going. But every little noise scared me, made me think they—"

She shakes her head, not ready to talk about *them*, or why she'd been at the crossroad. She's telling her story backward, but I don't press. It's enough to listen for now.

"I had this idea that I should get to a phone, but who would I call? My dad, maybe, though I half-thought he'd just turn me over to the cops. I suppose that sounds crazy, but I was pretty messed up. I kept thinking how maybe I deserved whatever happened to me." Her voice breaks a little. "Not that it mattered. There were no houses, no people. Just trees."

She'd climb a hill, rest, trudge down the other side. She drank at streams, rested whenever her legs threatened to give out. From ridges, she could see the desert far behind. The distance made her feel safe, but at one point she heard a gunshot. That drove her deeper into the forest. Then, late in the afternoon she rounded a hogback and realized just how far she'd come. Across the dell, at the top of a sloping lava field, she saw the place she'd barely escaped the day before. An old building inside a stone wall beside a tumbledown cemetery.

"The Hensley Asylum," I say, almost to myself.

"I turned and ran. No idea how far, but finally I came over a hill and saw this place a ways off. No one home. I had to break the padlock with a rock." She drops her gaze. "There was a little canned food, blankets, the bed. But no power and no phone."

Afraid to light a fire, she ate cold expired soup.

When no one came that night or all the next day, she ventured out. In the woods, after dark, she came across a band of backpackers, college-aged boys. Their noise and talk made her nervous. She was afraid if she asked them for help they'd call the police, if not do something worse. What happened at the crossroad never left her mind. So once they fell asleep, she snuck into camp and raided the food bag they'd hung between two trees.

If only one of them had left out a phone.

"How long have you been here?"

She shrugs and looks away.

"Since the crash?"

"I've kinda lost track of time." She hesitates, then adds, "Are they looking for me?"

Pride was—though I don't know why he kept it a secret. I don't have the heart to tell her father is dead. I can see him in her now, that familiarity I'd half-recognized in the forest. She has the same green-flecked brown eyes. I can see the woman from the locket as well, her nose if not her smile. Shelby has little reason to smile—and may not for a long time.

I think of Duniway smacking the window frame of the white pickup. "I know it's been a week," he'd said. "I'm doing everything I can." I wouldn't be surprised if he'd sent Quince out to search for Shelby, his expeditions disguised as fishing trips. Meyer too, and maybe even Duniway himself when he wasn't pretending to investigate me.

"I saw helicopters flying around while you were asleep," she says.

"They're for me."

"What did you do?"

"I became a problem. Like you."

She looks up. "What do you know about me?"

Not much, but I can guess a little. "You've been missing at least since March," I theorize, because that's when Pride left for his sabbatical. "Did you run away?"

She nods. "It was a lot longer ago than that, though." Her face darkens with shame.

"It's okay, Shelby. Really." I try to speak with the conviction I feel, but I'm not sure she can hear it. "Why don't you tell me what happened."

She's quiet for a long time. "What did you call that place?"

"The Hensley Asylum?"

"Yeah." She examines her dirty fingernails. "You gotta understand, I *wanted* to be there." The disbelief must show on my face, because she quickly adds, "No, really. They said they'd take care of me, even *pay* me." A chuff pushes through her teeth. "Five thousand dollars if I agreed to give up the baby for adoption."

"How did it happen?"

"Nathan and I hooked up at a party." She thinks I'm asking about the pregnancy, but I don't interrupt her. "I wasn't in a very good place. My mother . . . she got breast cancer." Her voice breaks and she wipes her eyes. "They caught it too late."

Somewhere in the back of my mind, Fitz stirs but doesn't speak. I watch her fingers twist in her lap, and then I manage a hollow "I'm sorry."

She gives a little shrug, like she's heard that a thousand times. "After she died, my dad just checked out. I mean, he was *there*, around the house and stuff. But he might as well have been gone. He stopped talking to me or even noticing me. He'd get up in the morning and take a shower, put on a suit. Go to work, I guess. I'd ask him questions, but he wouldn't answer. At first I just tried to do my own thing, but the more time that passed, the harder it got to even be in the house when he was there, and even harder when he wasn't. But it wasn't until he forgot my birthday that I realized I couldn't stand it anymore. It's not like I wanted a party or anything. Mom had only been gone about a month. But I guess I hoped he'd sit me down and give me a little pep talk or something. 'Hard to celebrate, but you're still my daughter,' or some bullshit. But it was like I didn't exist. The next morning, I left the house and didn't go back."

"That's when you ran away?"

She nods. "Yep, on October twenty-second, the day after my Sweet Sixteen." Another sad laugh. "I didn't plan it, exactly. First I went and hung out with some friends, and then I ended up at that party with Nathan. We knew each other because our dads worked together, but we weren't friends exactly. He was just someone my age to hang out with at the firm picnic. But at the party he started coming on to me, saying all this stuff about how he'd always liked me. I knew he was trying to get into my pants, but I figured why not? Since Nathan's parents were away, we went to his house. He had a condom, but when it broke, I didn't even care. It was just the one time." She shakes her head. "He fell asleep like the second he finished, and I ended up staying over. But the next morning Nathan was being clingy, like we were suddenly a thing. He wanted to trade cell numbers, hang out. Have sex again. It was starting to feel like too much. I wasn't sure I even wanted a boyfriend—him or anyone else. But I said I'd think about it. Before I left, he wrote his number on my arm with a Sharpie."

"Where did you go?"

"I'd seen this crowd in downtown Portland, kids with no place to stay."

I nod, remembering seeing kids like that with Uncle Rémy, my first morning off the train.

"I started hanging out with them. Probably sounds stupid, but I actually felt better with them, sleeping under bridges, than I did in my own home. At first it was just going to be a few days, long enough to freak my dad out. Or maybe he'd call the cops and I'd get dragged back. But a few days turned into a few weeks and then a few months. Long enough to figure my dad must really not have cared where I was. Then I found out I was pregnant. I didn't actually believe it at first, but my period had stopped and my pants were getting tight. One of the other girls took me to this youth outreach place downtown. They have free pregnancy tests. I found out I was going to have a baby by peeing on a wand behind a bush."

I have to suppress the urge to shake my head. I don't want her to stop talking.

"My friends all said I should get an abortion, but by then I barely had money to eat. Just what I could panhandle. I even considered going home again, until someone hooked me up with a woman who said she could arrange a private adoption. I'd live in a facility with doctors and nurses and stuff. All hush-hush, because some parents would try to interfere, but *she* knew we young women were capable of making our own decisions."

"What was the woman's name?" I ask. I'm not surprised when Shelby says, "Lydia."

But Lydia Koenig didn't bring Shelby to the Hensley School with all the other teen moms. *Make Motherhood a Mother Habit,* my ass. Even as she mouthed platitudes about helping young woman make a future for themselves, Lydia was luring the most desperate, like Shelby, to the Asylum. The resort would provide the perfect cover for her clients. Fly in for a weekend of golf and pick up a baby, like Cricket and Stedman shopping for antiques.

The long drive from Portland in the back seat of a Cadillac left Shelby unsettled. The driver, a guy named Tucker, kept staring at her in the rearview mirror. "At least the place wasn't too bad," she said. "Old, but clean. I had my own room, the food was decent, and there really were a doctor and nurse."

I actually smile a little. "But."

"Yeah. *But.*" She raises her eyes to mine. "They had us locked on one of the upper floors with the windows boarded up. *'For our safety,'* which I guess we half-believed."

"We?"

"It was mainly me and this other girl, Alyssa. Two other girls were there when I arrived, but only for a few weeks. Alyssa called us Slut Team Six, which she thought was extra funny because there were only four of us." She smiles.

I wonder what happened to those other girls. Were they really paid off, or were they turned over to Tucker Gill, the man with a history of pandering? Even more troubling is the question of how many might've ended up in the Bouton retort.

Fitz was right. I should have kicked Quince into the river.

"I mean, it could have been worse. We had books and movies to keep from getting bored, and crafts and shit. And the nurse, Fina, was really sweet. Her office had the only open window, and during my checkups, I'd watch birds circling over the forest. She'd let me stay as long as I wanted after she finished the exams."

"What about the doctor?"

"Only saw him a couple times. He did a checkup when I first got there, said I was fine. Otherwise, he only came around for the births." She trails off, thinking. "Never even knew his name."

Must be Varney unless there's somehow another doctor mixed up in all this. "How long were you there?"

"Like four months."

Jesus. "And then you had your baby?"

"Yeah." She presses her hand against her stomach again. "That's when it all went wrong."

Her eyes lose focus. When she finally goes on, it's in a tone you might use to describe a trip to the store. *Had lunch, ran some errands. Gave birth.* Not so different from what I've been doing since I awoke in that empty hospital room when I was eight years old.

"It was down to me and Alyssa by then. We both started having contractions at the same time. At first, Fina said mine were Braxton Hicks, those fake kinds, but that idea didn't last long." Her voice trails off for a moment. "I knew something was wrong with Alyssa. We were in our own rooms, but I could hear her. I thought my labor was bad, but she sounded like . . . scary. Meanwhile, I was mostly on my own. Fina checked on me every so often, and the doctor showed for the actual birth. Like three minutes." She shakes her head. "The whole time, Alyssa was up the hall screaming."

Shelby lowers her head. "But it was worse when she stopped."

Helene used to say the most dangerous thing a woman can do is give birth. While talking with Celeste, I'd worried the Hensley School was too far from Samuelton. But at least from there, an ambulance ride was an option.

"After a while, Fina came in to help me use the bathroom. She kept saying, 'Don't worry, don't worry.' But I knew Alyssa was dead. On her way out, she didn't close my door all the way—I think she was too upset. That's when I heard the doctor in the hallway talking to Lydia. He thought they should have taken Alyssa to the hospital, but Lydia said, 'You know what would come next if we'd done that. Losing your license would be the least of it.' That shut him up. They were all quiet for a minute, then Fina asked what she should do about Alyssa. Lydia told her that was being handled. 'Prepare the infant for travel. The clients are on their way.' When she and the doctor left, Fina cried in the hallway."

Shelby doesn't remember getting dressed, but at some point she found herself in the empty hallway. Fina's office door stood half open. The nurse, perhaps in her distress, had left her keys and phone. Shelby had seen Fina enter the PIN a couple of times when she didn't realize Shelby was paying attention. "It was easy—the four corners: one-three-nine-seven." Across from the office was the room Shelby knew to be the nursery, though she'd never been inside. One of the keys worked. There, lying in a clear plastic bassinet, she found a newborn girl.

Hers or Alyssa's? She didn't know. She hadn't been allowed to see her baby. She and Alyssa looked pretty similar, just a couple of blonde girls; the wriggling infant could have belonged to either of them. As for the other newborn, Shelby figured Fina must be taking it to the mysterious clients. No matter. She wrapped the baby in a blanket, but when the baby started crying, she panicked. She fled downstairs and through the courtyard, then out the gate, dropping Fina's heavy key ring after opening the big padlock. The river made her nervous, so she went through the cemetery and into the forest. The sun was setting, but it was still light enough to see.

Once she lost sight of the asylum through the trees, Shelby stopped and dialed the only number she could think of—Nathan's. Even though she'd never called him, the digits, written in Sharpie, had taken days to wear off her arm. Without hesitation, Nathan promised to come get her. He'd been worried sick about her for months. Using the GPS app, she figured out there was a road less than a mile away through the woods. A small town, Crestview, was a couple of miles down the road. She hoped she and the baby could make it that far, even though her insides felt like they might fall out. Nathan had further to go, a hundred and fifty miles, but he promised to hurry. His best friend, Trae, would drive.

They switched to texting then. The phone battery was low, and she needed the GPS. When the baby cried, she comforted her as best she could. It was dark by the time she reached the road. She hid in the trees when headlights approached.

"Nathan and Trae found me near some motel. The baby had messed herself, but we were afraid to stop for diapers. We cleaned her up with some paper towels, then Trae wrapped her in his sweatshirt. He was a new uncle, and his sister had taught him how to swaddle. He thought I should try to feed her too. My breasts were killing me by then, but I was so tired and hurt so bad I just made another mess."

I guess the asylum doesn't have a lactation clinic.

"I kept telling myself everything would be okay once we got back home. But when we got to that intersection—" She grows still. "—they were waiting for us."

"Who was it? Did you know them?"

"Just the guy who drove me here, Tucker, and a security guard from the asylum." A shadow passes over her face. "He used to watch us when Fina wasn't around."

"Was he the man—?"

"From last night, yeah." She draws a shaky breath. "But the one who did all the talking was a cop. He said he was placing us under arrest. Kidnapping, child endangerment—you name it."

According to Pride's diagram, the Cadillac was angled across Route 55 westbound—the most direct route back to Portland. The white pickup—Meyer's, I assume—was probably blocking the road up to Shatter Hill.

"Nathan thought it was bullshit, but I wasn't so sure. I didn't even know if I had my own baby. And even if I did, I'd made a deal. Meanwhile, this cop is saying there's nowhere to run. They'd tracked Fina's cell phone that far, and now they knew what we were driving. I remember looking at the phone, then dropping it like it was on fire. Suddenly Trae jumps out of the car. His dad is a criminal defense attorney, and Trae thinks that makes him some kind of badass by proxy. He goes off about due process and wrongful arrest and how his father will sue them all. This whole time, Nathan and I are in the back seat. He's holding the baby and telling me not to worry, but it just sounds like Fina after Alyssa died. That's when the security guard pulls a gun. I think I start screaming. Nathan drags me out of the car, yells for me to run. Like, I can hardly walk and he wants me to run? But then the gun goes off and everything just . . . I don't know. It's like the world turned white and exploded."

Her chin drops.

"I fell down, and when I looked up, there was fire everywhere. And noise. So much noise. A fucking horse ran by. I looked for

Nathan and the baby but couldn't find them. I saw Trae's car torn to hell and a big pickup on fire in the road. Bodies. I think that's when I realized there'd been a crash, though it didn't really make sense to me. Then I saw headlights up the hill. I thought it would be more cops, or even Lydia, so I ran. I don't even know how, I hurt so bad. I guess I was scared. I remember praying Nathan and the baby got away." She looks at me. "But he didn't, did he?"

Aunt Elodie would take Shelby's hand without hesitation. It's harder for me, but somehow I manage to sit up, to reach out and rest the lightest touch on her trembling fingers. At first, she stiffens, but then her fingers thread into mine, her grip tight. She pulls me toward her, and I let it happen. With my left hand, I reach up and guide her head onto my shoulder. My finger doesn't hurt at all.

"You're going to be okay," I hear myself saying as she sobs against me. "I promise you're going to be okay." I wish I could be sure it was true.

FIFTY

The Way Back

I hold Shelby until she stops shaking, and then a little longer. When she pulls away, her tears have left streaks in the grime on her cheeks. She stands and goes to the door. The old hinges creak.

"I haven't seen a helicopter in a while."

"They'll be back. On foot too, I think." Duniway will have resources he couldn't use before. The dash cam will make sure of that. "We can't stay here much longer."

A part of me wishes she still had Fina's phone, though I know if they tracked it to the crossroad, they'd have tracked it here as well. It would be dead after a week without power, anyway. Our best hope is still Aunt Elodie. If we can make it to her, Shelby's prospects are much better than my own. All she wanted was to go home. As for what I want, well—Duniway in a cell with a damp cheese sandwich may be too much to ask.

Crestview should be west of Uncle Rémy's cabin. The question is how far. The way my ankle feels, I can't afford to wander around lost. At least I have no doubts about Shelby. She got here from the crossroad, a tough hike even for someone who hadn't just given birth.

Right now, though, her pensive gaze suggests her thoughts are even farther away than that. Perhaps she's thinking about her father, about what drove her away. Suddenly I want to tell her what happened to Pride, but don't know how. I perform removals, help with services, clean the prep room.

I don't speak with the bereaved.

But don't I have to learn? Aunt Elodie can't truly say I was born to the work until I can look survivors in the eye and talk to them about the one they've lost.

Her eyes meet mine, and it's as if she senses my dilemma. "Just tell me."

"Your father came. He was looking for you." I let out a shaky breath. "I'm sorry—"

"They killed him, didn't they? The guard and that cop."

"I'm so sorry."

She stares at her hands for a long time. Everyone close to her is dead. Her father and mother. The boyfriend she wasn't sure she wanted. Outside, the wind rushes up the hill. In the distance a helicopter's rotors thump. Finally, she looks up at me. No tears on her face. Something else.

"What do you need me to do?"

Resolve.

She's spent a week wandering these ridges and dells, mostly in the dark. "That town, Crestview—can you get us there without being seen?"

"I haven't gone that far, but I know where the trails are." She frowns. "How's your ankle?"

Last night, I confused Shelby with the spirit of Molly Claire Maguire. The association is more apt than I knew. Within a day of giving birth, Shelby showed herself to have the mettle of any pioneer mother in the days of the Oregon Trail. Compared to what she's been through, she's asking if I'm up for a stroll.

I smile grimly. "It'll have to do."

Using a paring knife from the jar of cooking utensils, she cuts two strips from one of the blankets. With the first, Shelby binds the first two fingers of my left hand together. Then she wraps my ankle. "It's not great, but it's the best I can do without tape."

"You've done this before?"

A ghost smile graces her lips. "*Years* of soccer."

Next, she cuts long vertical slits in my boot at the ankle. That gives me enough slack to pull the boot on. When I stand, the support feels adequate.

Before we can head out, we have to wait for a helicopter to fly out of sight down the valley. At first, we make decent progress. There are no trails near the cabin, but the light is good and the forest floor open. Soon the valley drops out of sight behind us.

The going gets tougher once we cross the crest and descend toward the juncture of two streams, one flowing out of the forest from our left and the larger from straight ahead. "The big one goes past the asylum," she says.

When the sun falls behind Lost Brother, the uncertain light makes progress more difficult. The soft ground is difficult on my ankle, and I need frequent breaks. Shelby is patient, and I don't complain. She holds my arm when the way gets steep, a sure-handed guide. As we near the stream junction, she slows and gestures for me to be quiet. We listen for a long time. The only sound is water flowing over rocks.

Eventually, we continue down to a dirt road and over a one-lane bridge. A Forest Service sign there reads, "Little Cherry Shallows." I wonder if this is where Quince would have put his boat in to search for my body.

The thought sends a jitter through me. I pick up my pace. We follow the road a short distance to a trail crossing, then turn left into the trees. After a couple hundred feet, we come to a wooden foot-bridge back across the river.

"I never went all the way to the trailhead, but I think this is the best way from here. Easiest on your ankle, anyway. If there are any night hikers, we should see their lights before they get close."

I'm more worried about the Barlow County Sheriff's Department. But the evening is quiet, with only the murmur of the two streams mingling away in the trees.

The trail winds and climbs, a manageable grade—easier than the descent from the ridge. When my foot drags, Shelby is right there to make sure I don't fall. After a grueling half hour, we reach a break in the trees. A ravine climbs away from the trail, barren and rocky with steep sides. She points midway up the far wall. With a shudder I recognize the ponderosa tilting over the gully where she saved me. From here, we can't see Xavier Meyer's remains. I think about the eagle fighting the vultures over Nathan Harper and hope the god-damn coyotes scatter Meyer's bones.

296 I W. H. Cameron

"Let's go."

There are no night hikers and no search teams. It's full dark when we reach a T in the trail. A sign indicates the trailhead is right, one mile.

"This is as far as I ever came," she whispers. "Seemed too civilized up ahead."

"We'll be careful." The path is steeper now, straining my ankle as we climb through switchbacks. I grit my teeth and power forward, anxious to reach the end. We cross the same familiar lava flow twice as the trail zigzags uphill. A short time later, we smell smoke.

Shelby balks, but I know where we are, and I urge her on. The teen moms, visible only by the glowing tips of their cigarettes, ignore us. Even so, Shelby doesn't relax until we're far up the trail.

"Who were they?" she asks when the scent of smoke fades.

"Girls from a boarding school up at the top of the hill."

"They go to school in summer?"

"It's a long story." One Lydia Koenig should have told her when they met in Portland.

I'm nearly spent when we reach the top of the trail. The Forest Service lot is empty, but there are a few cars parked at the school. We hide in the trees when a car pulls out and drives toward the village. Once its taillights disappear around the curve, we head up the narrow street, then into the woods behind the Long Grass Bed and Breakfast. I never did find out if that's where Pride was staying.

Ahead, lights shine through the trees. Now I become the guide, first through an open field, then past a few of the rickety ghost town structures, and finally into the staff parking lot of Crestview Assisted Living.

The exterior doors will be locked this time of night, but I know the code for the loading dock. Once inside, the staff elevator will take us to Uncle Rémy's floor. Shelby and I look like victims of the zombie apocalypse, but the bigger problem is the Barlow County grapevine. By now, everyone must know what happened to Jeremy. I just have to hope I can talk my way past anyone we meet.

"Is that what I think it is?" Shelby says as we slip between a couple of parked cars and angle toward the dock.

A long black vehicle is backed up to the loading dock where I've parked the Stiff more times than I can remember. Bouton's hearse.

Someone has died, an event only too common at Crestview Assisted Living. With the Stiff wrecked and me gone, Aunt Elodie would have to use the hearse to transport the remains. I run my hands over my face. Given everything she has to deal with, I'm surprised she didn't have Swarthmore handle it. Perhaps it was someone she knew, or—

"Oh, no."

"What is it?"

Ignoring the pain in my ankle, I rush past the hearse and up the steps. But before I can punch the code into the keypad, the door swings open. Aunt Elodie is there, with Barb just behind.

For an interminable moment, we all stand under the harsh glare of the loading dock lights. "Thank god you're okay—" Barb begins as Aunt Elodie rushes to me.

"He's left us, Melisende." The heartbreak in her eyes is devastating. "I'm so sorry. Your uncle is gone."

Gone? My head swims, and I stagger against the doorframe. Barb reaches out for me. Murmuring consolations, she helps me inside and up the dim hallway. Part of me looks for Shelby, but all I can see is my last memory of Uncle Rémy as he gazed out the window at Shatter Hill, his sunken gaze bleak.

Outside a dark office, we find a couple of chairs, and I slump down. Aunt Elodie takes the seat beside me. I grip her forearm. My heart feels like it's going to burst from my chest.

"What happened?"

She takes time to gather her thoughts. "He'd been looking out the window, and when he noticed me watching him, he said, 'The stars sure are beautiful tonight.' I thought it strange, because the sun hadn't yet set. Then his eyes closed, and he just"—the words catch in her throat—"stopped breathing."

"They couldn't help him? Couldn't bring him back?"

"Oh, honey. He didn't want that."

I sag against the seat back. Of course he didn't. Rémy would want to pass with as little fuss as possible. And he'd want to leave an easy job for Carrie Dell, not hand her a body cracked and bruised by the extreme measures necessary to give him a few more miserable minutes or hours.

"I'm sorry I wasn't here." The skin of Elodie's arms feels like paper. "I should have been with you. With him."

298 | W. H. Cameron

"Don't you fret, darling. He knew you loved him."

"Did he—?" My voice breaks. "Did he hear what they're saying about me?"

"Of course not, not that he'd believe it any more than we do." She steals a glance at Barb, standing nearby in the shadows. "Soon enough, we'll need to attend to him, but there's no rush. He's fine in his room. Right now, I think you better tell us what's happened." She strokes the bound fingers of my left hand, then her concerned gaze returns to my face. "You look like you've been through hell."

Understatement of the year, yet I haven't been through a fraction of what Shelby has. I turn to call her over.

The hallway behind us is empty.

"Where's the girl?"

Barb and Aunt Elodie exchange looks, confused.

"She was with me in the parking lot."

I struggle to my feet and lurch down the hall. The door swings wide as I throw all my weight against the crash bar. Outside, a white pickup makes a sharp, squealing turn out of the parking lot and disappears into the night.

FIFTY-ONE

All I Have

Barb slips up beside me, her breath like a shadow. "What is it, sweetie? What's happened?"

"They've taken her."

"Who?"

"Shelby." Her eyebrows form twinned question marks. "The baby's mother."

In Barlow County, you can count the people close to me on one hand—with fingers left over. All they had to do was park one set of eyes at Crestview Assisted Living and another in the driveway of one of the empty vacation rentals near Barb's cottage. But while I may have been the target, Shelby is the one they've been looking for. I brought her right to them.

"You found her?" Barb says, her voice soft with wonder.

"She found me." *Like an avenging spirit.* But there's no time to explain. Feeling exposed, I nudge Barb back inside and let the door close. Aunt Elodie joins us in a huddle under the glow of the emergency exit sign. I can barely walk, and I'm down one hand. I'd fall down if Barb wasn't propping me up. It would be one thing if I still had the gun, but it's at the bottom of that canyon with the remains of Xavier Meyer. My clothes are filthy and torn, my exposed skin bruised and raw with scratches half-scabbed over. I stink of sweat and dirt. My head is ready to split open. Hell, my whole body is a bruise.

It's all I have.

"Tell me what's been happening."

Barb's jaw sets. "They say you killed Jeremy. They've been searching for you all day." She peers at Aunt Elodie, who looks frail and worried. "For your body, really. They said you wrecked the van and then, injured and likely disoriented, fell into the Palmer River."

"But they don't think I'm dead anymore."

"I don't know about that, but according to a story at the *Ledger*, tomorrow they're going to expand the search beyond the river. Jefferson County is sending help. Until then, they've set up roadblocks at Trout Rot Bridge, Antiko, Route 55 east of Samuelton, and on Wayette at the county line."

I'd laugh if the situation wasn't so fucked. *Melisende Dulac, Public Enemy Number One.* I wonder what Cricket and Stedman would say. "We're not surprised." Or perhaps only, "Melisende who?"

"Where's Quince?"

They glance at each other. "No idea. We haven't seen him."

Quince must have reported the direction I fled to Duniway, even if he didn't follow Meyer and me into the forest. That today's search focused on the river must mean Duniway was able to direct official attention away from the asylum and surrounding forest. He can't risk me being brought in alive. If I end up in custody and start talking, no matter now implausible my tale, there's a danger someone might listen. But there's probably only so much even the chief deputy can do to contain the search. With the scope expanding tomorrow, especially to include outside agencies, he must be scrambling to find me first. He'd know the places I'd be likely to make an appearance. He'd just need a plausible excuse to keep his deputies from manning the stakeouts.

I can imagine him saying, "We need everyone on the roadblocks until Jefferson County gets here." Then sending the white pickup to wait for me.

The only question is, who was driving?

This time of night the facility is locked, but Duniway would know I have access to the loading dock door. If he has the manpower, he'll have someone out front too—but he's down three, including the two who died at the crossroad. I hope he's shitting himself wondering what happened to Meyer. In the meantime, I have to assume he knows I'm here.

I'm a problem, but one easily solved. *Killed while resisting arrest.* Shelby is the one who knows who was at the crossroad, who fired the bullet pulled from Nathan Harper's body. Xavier Meyer may be dead, along with those creeps from Portland, but Shelby can still identify Lydia Koenig and Omar Duniway, along with everyone else at the asylum.

That means just one thing. They're going to kill her, if they haven't already.

I shake my head. I can't let myself think like that. Not until I'm sure.

But what can I do, and who can I trust? Pax Berber, maybe, but he can't protect me from what might happen after they put me in a jail cell. The only law enforcement for miles is the Barlow County Sheriff's Department. We might call the FBI, but they'd never get here in time. Shelby will already be dead. One more body for the retort.

And why would the FBI believe me anyway? I'm a cop killer.

Aunt Elodie puts her hand on my arm. "Melisende, we can't help if you don't tell us what you need."

I look at Barb. "Somewhere around here is a vending room. Can you get me a water—no, a soda? I need sugar and caffeine. And food. I haven't eaten since the Whistle Pig." Whenever that was. While she's gone, I let Aunt Elodie lead me back to the chairs for a moment's rest. Just a moment, though. When Barb returns, I inhale the package of oatmeal cookies and two cans of Mountain Dew she brings me. My stomach clenches at the sudden onslaught of fructose and fizz. I ignore it and stand.

"I need a car."

They argue, but I'm not listening. I'm thinking about the sheriff and his little smile when he said, "You have something of your Aunt Elodie in you." He may be a tub of butter, but I have to believe he's not Duniway's tub of butter. He did order a full forensic on Nathan Harper.

If I'm wrong, I'm dead.

"I also need you to find Sheriff Turnbull. If you can't get him on the phone, try the roadblocks."

"Where are you going?"

If Shelby is still alive, there's only one place she could be.

"The old Hensley Asylum. Have him get there as quick as he can, with all the backup he can bring."

"What if he won't come?"

"Tell him I'll be there. Tell him Omar Duniway is responsible for what happened at the crossroad. He killed Jeremy, and he'll kill Shelby too unless I can stop him."

Aunt Elodie pulls at my arm. "Stay here, honey. You can tell him yourself." Her eyes plead. "He'll believe you."

"The department is spread to the far corners of the county. Even if the sheriff did believe me, he'd never get there in time unless I can slow Duniway down." I may already be too late, but I can't think about that. "Just have him come as fast as possible."

Aunt Elodie looks from Barb to me, then presses keys into my hand. "I left my car at home earlier, so you'll have to drive the hearse. Take my phone too, just in case."

"Thank you."

As I turn to go, Barb pulls me into a hug. "You still owe me that double feature."

FIFTY-TWO

Response Time

There are no landmarks and few signs of life once I leave Crestview—just the occasional house or doublewide marked by the gleam of security lights through the trees. I drive too fast, but to my relief, no patrol cars appear, lights flashing and sirens blaring.

A gap in the trees is the only indication of the access road to the asylum. I brake hard and turn, throwing gravel. Darkness swallows the headlights as I rumble down the washboard track, steering mostly by touch. A fork appears out of nowhere, and I skid to stop in front of a small sign. "River Access, Left 1 Mile." I go right.

Past the fork, the road narrows and gets rougher. I ease off the gas and lean forward, struggling to see over the hearse's long hood. Somehow I miss the deepest ruts and potholes. For what feels like hours but must be only ten or fifteen minutes, I work my way deeper and deeper into the forest. Just as I'm starting to worry I've made the wrong turn—either back at Wayette Highway or at the fork—the road widens. Ahead, I spot the flat bridge over the churning river. On the far side, the asylum seems to skulk in the shadow of the dark forest.

The cast iron gate stands open, the white pickup inside to the left. I park outside, well clear of the wall, and leave the keys under the driver's seat. Whatever happens next, I hope Aunt Elodie can recover the hearse. With the Stiff out of commission, she'll need it.

My ankle complains as I hobble through the gate and past the truck. Inside, the old building looms, its gray, forbidding wings outthrust to either side. A pair of old iron fixtures on either side of the front doors cast sickly light across the deserted courtyard. It's not until I near the steps up to the entrance that I see the camera—a small unassuming box above the door, with a faint gleaming reflection on the lens.

About ten minutes.

Somewhere, a phone is receiving a text alert, perhaps several phones. Unknown is whether Duniway receives alerts himself or if someone has to forward them. Might not do for the chief deputy sheriff to be on the distribution list for the secret forest baby lair.

If anyone sees me, there's no indication. It's been at least two minutes since I pulled up outside, which leaves me eight to save Shelby's life. Even if Duniway heard the moment Shelby was grabbed, he'll need to make a careful exit. He has to at least pretend to do his job, perhaps at one of the roadblocks, putting on a show for the troops. "We'll get her, boys." Forgetting one of his deputies is a woman. "Stay alert. I'm going to check in at the other positions." He might have a thirty-mile drive. Or he might already be tearing down the corrugated dirt road. His Tahoe will handle the ruts better than the hearse.

The front door is ajar. Someone was in a hurry. I limp inside, then pause to catch my breath. My ankle feels like it's being crushed in a vise. In my back pocket, Aunt Elodie's phone vibrates. Barb has been texting.

Sheriff isn't taking calls. Trying to get a message to him.
You should wait till we hear back.
Respond, goddammit!

As I'm finger-pecking a response, another message comes through.

I will end you if you get yourself killed.

I manage a weak laugh, glad she can't hear, then text back:

Don't worry, it'll be okay.

The foyer is dark and empty. A single bare bulb glows in the corridor to the left, the only light in the place. I lumber past doorways that open onto empty rooms. No furniture, no fixtures. The doors don't even have knobs. At the end of the hall, the bulb illuminates a heavy fire door. With a grunt, I push through to a dim stairwell, the steps worn smooth from decades of needful feet. Long, dendritic cracks run up the walls like the maps of watersheds. In spots, plaster has crumbled away to reveal the lath underneath. Bore holes indicate where handrails were once mounted.

I climb as fast as I can, one step at a time, the only sound the faint swoosh of my feet. I don't see any cameras. On the second-floor landing, I pull the door open with my good hand and peer into blackness. No lights, no open windows. No Shelby. I continue my climb. By the next flight, a dozen lousy steps, I can barely lift my feet.

"This is taking forever, little sister."

Until now, Fitz's silence has been surprisingly welcome. Ignoring him, I take one more step, then another. Shelby has got to be up there.

"I've *got this*, Fitz."

"Testy."

I am worn down to a single frayed thread. One more halfhearted yank and I'll come undone. *How about you shut the fuck up and let me concentrate, Fitz?* But I don't have to go much further. One step. Two. The door to the third floor comes into view. With my right hand, I steady myself against the wall. Step. Again. And again.

Then I'm slumped against the door. I pull out the phone and see another message waiting.

Absolutely do NOT "don't worry" at me.

Takes too long to tap out my response:

I'm going to call. Just let it go to voicemail so it records.

I wait, eyes squeezed, until the phone vibrates.

Ready.

Barb's number is at the top of the chat screen—good thing, since my contacts list is at the bottom of Paddle Creek. If I survive the next ten minutes, I vow to memorize the phone numbers of every person I've ever met, alive or dead. I tap "Call" and slide the phone into my pocket. Grab the door handle. Pull.

It swings open onto a bright hallway. I make it three halting paces before Lydia Koenig steps through a door ten feet ahead. As our eyes meet, my ears fill with a roar I realize is my heartbeat. She has a leather briefcase in her left hand and a nylon bag slung over her right shoulder. Her sharp, knee-length skirt and matching blazer shout "board meeting," but her worn sneakers suggest she'll have to run to get there in time.

"Hello, Lydia."

She makes as if to move past me. I raise my bound left hand, and she hesitates. Maybe she thinks I'm armed with something more than bitterness and pain.

"I suppose you came for that girl."

"Is Shelby here? Is she okay?"

"Of course she is. What do you think I am?"

Her head turns, and I look past her down the hall. Aside from the one she came through, all the doors are closed. Locked too, I bet.

"I think you're someone who wouldn't let Dr. Varney take Alyssa to the emergency room."

Shelby said she never knew the doctor's name, but Lydia doesn't contradict me. "We take good care of these girls, better than they were caring for themselves on the street. *I* cared for them." Her chin points up. "I wouldn't expect you to understand."

"Was there no room at the Hensley School? If you really cared, you'd have found a place for them there, or helped them reconcile with their families. Not locked them up like fucking prisoners."

Lydia flinches as though slapped. "You don't know what it costs to run a facility like the Hensley School. I have to do more with less every year. We survive on private contributions. It's not unreasonable for our donors to expect something in return."

"Oh, so *you're* the hero."

"I've done what I had to do."

"You let Alyssa die."

"No one regrets that girl's death more than I."

"You sold their babies."

"The adoptions we arranged were legal—"

This is taking too long. "Shut up."

She scowls, but she shuts up.

"You're not going to convince me, and I'm not going to convince you, so let's get back to the issue at hand."

"What issue?"

"Shelby and her baby."

"What do you expect from me?" Even as she's asking the question, Lydia answers it for herself. "No. Impossible. It's out of my hands."

"Lydia, she's a mother. Her baby is in foster care right now. Just let her go so she can take care of her baby."

"She didn't even *want* the child. She *wanted* to sell it to *me*."

"Her."

"What?"

"*Her.* The baby is a little girl."

Lydia's head twitches, as if she can barely contain her anger. *Join the club, bitch.*

"So what if Shelby didn't want her baby when you found her? She was scared, and you took advantage. You manipulated her to get what you wanted. I'm asking you, in the name of what you pretend to believe in at that fucking school, just give her a chance."

Her eyes close, and for a moment I think I may have gotten to her. But then her head shakes a little. When she opens her eyes again, they're empty. "As I said, it's out of my hands. I don't know why you're so concerned—"

"Maybe because I know what it's like to grow up without a mother."

My outburst is loud enough to rattle the old doors in their frames. How long it's been bubbling inside me I don't know for sure. Most of my life. Ever since I woke up in that empty hospital room. Reinforced every time I came home to a package of boy's underwear on my bed or an empty house and a freezer full of potpies. Fuck knows Fitz did his best, but he's just a dead little boy, a phantom of memory, no more real than the Shatter Hill Spirit. A shadow of what I really needed.

Fists start pounding on a door down the hall. A voice cries out. Shelby. I put my hand out to Lydia, but her eyes widen and she shrinks back.

Duniway has me by the arm before I can even scream.

FIFTY-THREE

Caught

With his free hand, Duniway punches me in the ear. Burning light and shattering pain rock through my skull. I collapse in his tight grip.

"Lyd, come on." He starts yanking me back toward the stairs. "It's time to go."

"We're not ready—"

Duniway's scowl shuts her up. "We're hanging by a thread here. There's still a chance I can tie things off, but only if you stop dawdling."

He's going to kill Shelby. That's how Omar Duniway ties things off. It's what he did to Jeremy, what he plans to do to me.

Lydia has to realize.

She looks down the hall, then her shoulders drop almost imperceptibly, and her empty eyes fall on me. "What about her?"

"She's going back in the river." Duniway's voice rises again as he swings me around. "I'll hold her damn head down to make sure she doesn't come up again."

Lydia edges past me. I claw at her with my damaged hand, indifferent to the pain. She jerks away so hard she hits the opposite wall.

"Move, damn it!" Duniway shouts. "I'll take care of this."

"Please, Lydia, let her go." I've been on borrowed time since I was eight years old, but Shelby shouldn't have to die. I can hear her shout and bang her door, even over my own hoarse cries. *Lydia, please.* When she darts out of sight, I plead with Duniway. "She won't say anything, I promise."

His answer is a feral grin. "I knew that girl would draw you here."

Laughing bitterly, he tosses me into the stairwell. I slam into the hard floor, knees and then wrists. My left arm collapses as lancing pain shoots through me. Duniway strides through the door. I kick at him with my good leg but miss the mark, my foot thumping harmlessly against the back of his thigh. He bends over and backhands me across the face.

"You dumb bitch, stop fighting."

Dizzily, I remember Quince clucking about Duniway's overhet language on the bridge.

As the door swings shut behind him, Shelby's cries fade. I try to lift my head, can't.

"Please, *please*—"

With his foot, he shoves me down the stairs. At the landing, I roll, grabbing for the wall, the steps below. He's too fast. He hooks my collar and pulls me after him down the next flight to the second-floor landing, drops me in a heap.

"Don't move, chippy."

He yanks the heavy door open and canters into the dark hallway beyond. The slap of his feet on linoleum fades quickly. The door shuts.

"You don't have to listen to him, Melisende."

I blink stupidly as my own muddy voice penetrates my dull mind. With a sobbing gasp, I force myself onto my belly, then to my hands and knees. My left hand is a ball of agony, but I crawl toward the stairs, squealing through clenched teeth. I'm three or four steps down when the door opens again.

"I told you not to move."

His boot slams my tailbone, and I pitch forward. Hear a loud crack. I can't even tell what hurts anymore. I curl into a ball at the foot of the stairs. He storms down after me, and then his hands paw my ass. I squirm until he rips the phone from my pocket. The cracked screen is dark. *For how long?* Did anything get recorded?

Even if it did, isn't it too late?

"Guess a cop killer can't call nine-one-one."

Shattered plastic and plaster dust rain around me as he slams the phone against the wall. Then my head thuds down step after step.

I'm half-blind and choking, and in the dim recesses of my mind I recognize the smell of smoke.

What a time for a cigarette, I think, but then the reason for his visit to the second floor hits me.

"Please, don't burn her. Jesus, fuck, *don't burn her!*"

"Shut your filthy mouth."

I scream and sob, but have no strength to fight him. He drags me to the first floor, then down the long, empty corridor. The bare bulb over the stairway door swings and spins. "You can't, you can't—"

I'll die in cold water, she'll die in flames. All tied off, evidence gone, the witnesses silenced. Barb and Elodie may speak for me, but the dash cam will overrule them. In the end, Duniway will blame it all on me. The bodies in the retort, the abandoned asylum destroyed by fire. If they even find Shelby's body in the rubble, he'll write it off as a kid caught where she shouldn't have gone.

The foyer is still dark and quiet. The fire will climb faster than it will descend. He kicks open the door and pulls me down the steps into the courtyard. Above me, flames flicker at the edges of the plywood covering the second-floor windows.

"Don't, please." My voice is a bare hiss. Useless. Gravel and thorns rake my back. My thrashing arms and legs do nothing to slow him down. One of the sheets of plywood splits and smoke pours out. I can hear the flames now, the roaring cry of burning wood.

Duniway grunts and drops me.

"Damn it."

I twist my head. The glare of headlights floods through the gate. Truck lights. "What did I tell you, Lydia? *Get out of here!*" he mutters, throwing his arm up and waving like he's shooing kids off his lawn. The lights don't move. His hand drops, shading his eyes as the door of the vehicle opens and a large figure ambles into the glare. I try to scream but can only squeak.

Duniway adapts quickly. "Thank goodness, Hayward. Look what I found. I got her."

The sheriff looks from me to Duniway, then up at the building. Firelight dancing in his eyes. I can't tell what he's thinking. I fear I've misjudged him, but then he holds up a cell phone in his left hand.

"Omar, what did you mean by 'She's going back in the river'?"

Duniway's face contorts as his eyes bounce from me to the sheriff. "I was off my head, Hay. She shot that poor boy."

"He wasn't a boy." The sheriff's face is grim. "He was my deputy."

"Of course, I just mean—"

"Did you kill him?"

Duniway's body goes very still. "Hay, don't be ridiculous."

"Omar, you dumb bitch," I mumble through blood and spit. "You're caught."

Car doors slam, people shout, feet pound the dry ground. Figures rush through the gate and past the sheriff. Fire and Rescue. Only two paid staff in Barlow County, maybe fifteen volunteers. Looks like the sheriff brought them all.

Sound and heat seem to boil around me. I slump onto my back. The gravel can cut through my spine for all I care. Deputy Ariana Roldán appears, takes Duniway by the arm. He's still arguing as she leads him away.

"We got her. We got her!" People are coming out of the building. Shelby looks my way, and our eyes meet before she's drawn away to safety. With that, the pain seems to drain out of me, displaced by a peaceful lassitude as the asylum burns.

Someone kneels beside me. A young woman lifts my head and slides something soft under my neck. Gentle fingers stroke my forehead. "Miss Dulac? They're bringing a stretcher. They had to check the building first, but they're coming back for you." Paulette Soucie.

I nod and attempt a smile. "Where did you come from?"

"The sheriff let me ride with him." Her brow creases with worry, and she looks toward the gate. When her gaze returns to me, I think I can see tears in her eyes. "I'm sorry," she says. "I was almost too late."

"Don't worry about it." I have no idea what she's talking about.

"I tried to tell you at the café, even though I wasn't sure if it even mattered. But then everyone was saying you killed that man and blaming you for all kinds of things I knew you wouldn't do. That's when I went to the sheriff."

I still don't understand. The effort to make sense of what she's saying requires more than I have left in me. I want to melt into the rocky ground. But the tears in Paulette's eyes are almost too much to bear. I lick my lips and taste blood.

"That day the bodies went missing, I'd gone to the football stadium to meet Landry after he was done lifting weights. You can see the back of the funeral parlor from the stadium parking lot," Paulette says.

She must have seen Quince. No wonder she ran out of Cuppa Jo so fast that day when he appeared.

The sheriff crouches beside Paulette. I hear his knees crack. "How you doing, Mellie?"

"Fucking great, Hayley."

The old tub of butter actually laughs.

"We're gonna get you to the hospital here in a jiff. Your aunt and your friend will meet you there. But I thought you'd want to know I have Quince in custody. When I told him we had a witness who saw him steal the bodies, he actually burst into tears. Now he won't stop talking."

"I only saw him drive in and out, Sheriff." Paulette frowns. "I mean, the time was right, but—"

"It's okay, Paulette. He confessed." He gives her a reassuring smile, then turns back to me. "He also told me all about Jeremy. Claims he had no idea what Omar was going to do."

The moment in the van returns in a crushing flood of memory. I don't want to think about Jeremy dying like that. "He was still going to help Duniway kill me."

"I figured." His eyes soften. "For what it's worth, Mel, Quince only confirmed what I already knew. You're a foulmouthed pain in the ass, but I know you didn't shoot that young man." He pats my shoulder. "I never believed you had it in you to begin with."

FIFTY-FOUR

The Apple Peddler

As promised, Aunt Elodie and Barb are waiting when the EMTs roll me out of the ambulance and into St. Mark's emergency department. I let them fuss over me until the nurse comes to roll me into the treatment area, and then I ask Barb to take Aunt Elodie to pick up the hearse. "I'm fine," I insist. "They'll keep an eye on me here."

There's some argument and a few tears. In the end, I know Aunt Elodie will want to get Uncle Rémy to familiar ground, even if it is the New Mortuary prep room. It's one of the places he'd be the most comfortable.

A couple of hours later, after I've been scanned and stitched and wrapped in gauze, it's Danae Wood—floating to the emergency department—who informs me they want to keep me overnight as a precaution. When I say I'd rather spend the night in jail, she laughs. Maybe she thinks I'm joking. I don't want to get into my issue with hospitals, so I resort to pure force of will and a little active bitch face until she sees things my way. It was hard enough to sit still while the doctor stitched my forehead and for the X-rays that led to my finger in a splint, my right leg in a walking boot. For the million cuts and scrapes on my arms and legs, I ask for the bandages with rainbows and unicorns.

"Those are for kids, Mel."

"I can be pretty immature."

Danae laughs again, then promises to return shortly with my discharge orders. I doze and dream of a forest full of ghosts and a desert full of bones. When I wake again, hours have passed. The lights are dim in the treatment room.

I'm not mad. But for the second time in my life, I leave a hospital AMA. This time I don't even sign my name—I just hobble through the small emergency department and out into the cool morning air. The sun is just peeking over College Ridge.

Twenty minutes later, when I limp into the Sheriff's Department office, Sheriff Turnbull himself, lord of the manor, is sitting at one of the desks behind the counter.

"You working graveyard now, Sheriff?"

"Just waiting for you. I'm surprised you let them keep you."

"They took so damn long to do my paperwork, I fell asleep."

He studies me for what feels like a very long time. "You needed the rest. Hungry?"

"If you offer me a cold boiled egg and plain white toast, I'll commit a fucking felony."

"I think we can do a little better than that. Come on."

On the way out, we're met in the first-floor lobby by a pair of suits. I wait, disinterested, while the sheriff steps aside to chat with them. Soon, the sheriff waves me over.

"These gentleman are with the Oregon State Police." He introduces them as they shake my hand. The names don't register, and their faces might as well belong to mannequins. Featureless, the color of putty. They'll need to talk to me, one says, but later is fine. They've just finished a long interview with Quince. They'll be seeing Shelby at the hospital next.

"Is she okay?"

"In better shape than you, I suspect." One of the putty-faces molds itself into something like concern. "They're keeping her for observation, but just as a precaution."

"When can I see her?"

They defer to the sheriff, who looks at his watch. "We'll check in after we eat."

The sheriff leads me down the Barlow Building steps and through the park, letting me set the pace. We turn down Third Street in the direction of the community college, then turn again on Palmer Street.

A half-block down, the sheriff holds the door for me at a tiny diner. We take a seat next to the window. I nod when the waitress asks if I want coffee. She offers me a menu. "Just—whatever," I say. I think back to Uncle Rémy taking me to breakfast that morning the train arrived in Portland, more than a year ago. A world away.

The sheriff waves off his menu too. "Bring us each the German apple pancake platter. With scrambled and bacon." When I don't disagree, she leaves.

"I didn't even know this place existed."

"The Apple Peddler? I think you'll like it."

The waitress brings our coffee and leaves a carafe on the table. I look out the window.

"Lydia Koenig is gone. We found the white pickup you described at the airport."

"It was her truck, then."

"The school's, actually. Maintenance vehicle."

That mystery solved, at least.

"Anyway, a private plane took off around eleven last night. Flight plan said Salt Lake City."

"Let me guess. It never arrived."

"You must be psychic."

"Why am I not surprised?"

"You probably also won't be surprised the asylum was a total loss."

As planned.

"The crew had to let it burn. We're not equipped to handle a building of that size in the middle of nowhere. We'll be weeks picking through the rubble, but they did find one body just inside. A woman." His lips pull away from his teeth. "We believe it's the nurse. Shelby says she unlocked her door after the fire started."

Shelby seemed to like Fina, and I guess freeing her counts for something. Still, I can't work up much sympathy. Fina could have helped those girls escape any time.

"Do you think you'll catch Lydia?"

"Out of my hands. This show's going federal." He stirs his coffee, even though he's added nothing to it. "I'm sorry you had to go through all this, Mellie."

We're back to Mellie. I don't correct him. Fuck it. It's fine. "When did you know?"

"About Omar? Not until last night."

"But you suspected."

"What makes you say that?"

Because of what Danae said about the autopsy, how Sheriff Turnbull personally carried the samples to the state crime lab. He didn't trust anyone else, not even his chief deputy. But I don't want to get Danae in trouble, so I say, "You told me about Nathan's bullet and the fourth set of bones in the retort. You knew something was up, but if you really suspected me, you wouldn't have . . ." I let my voice trail off, not sure how to finish the thought.

"Been so indiscreet?" He finally adds cream to his coffee. "Honestly, I didn't know what I knew. Things weren't adding up, but I wasn't in a position to read all the signals. You may not know this, but even though I grew up in Barlow, I was away for much of my adult life before I returned to take over as sheriff. As you might guess, a small department is a tight, close-knit organization."

"I suppose Chief Deputy Duniway thought he should have gotten the job."

He nods.

"Why *didn't* he get it?"

"He's not political." He shrugs. "Neither am I, as far as it goes. But I haven't been around long enough to piss the wrong people off."

"There's still time."

He smiles. "That there is."

"So when you got serious about Nathan Harper, Duniway decided to make me his patsy?"

"He needed someone the minute Quince got cute with the bodies."

"One damn body," Duniway had said. "Quince is an idiot."

"No argument. Quince seems to have thought destroying the bodies would derail our investigation. What he didn't realize was I was prepared to declare the whole thing an accident. We didn't know about Nathan Harper yet, but if the bodies hadn't been taken, I'd have seen no reason for a full forensic exam. He'd be just be another accident victim." He considers his coffee. "Aaron was skittish during the autopsy, but I chalked it up to him being more internist than pathologist."

"So Duniway came after me."

"Yep."

"He picked the right target, didn't he?" Outsider, no real connection to the community, hardly any friends.

"Given how things worked out, I wouldn't say that."

Our breakfast arrives. I've never had a German apple pancake. I tear into it like it's my last meal.

"When did you last eat?"

"Who the fuck knows?"

He chuckles as he chews bacon.

"I told Shelby about her father," I say after I finish.

"So I heard." He nods. "You keep doing my job for me."

I look out the window again. The sun is over the ridge now. I squint against the sudden scintillation of light. "She needed to know."

Our little apprentice mortician is growing up.

He unbuttons his shirt pocket and pulls out a plastic evidence bag containing the locket. "Maybe you can give her this too."

I turn the baggie over in my fingers. If I hadn't tried to take the locket from the gorge wall, Duniway wouldn't have had cause to arrest me, at least not at that moment. No night in jail, no revelation about Pride's livor mortis. Things might have gone very differently.

Even Helene may not have come.

"One thing I don't get is why Mr. Pride didn't tell you he was searching for Shelby from the beginning."

"According to one of his law partners, he'd been having increasingly contentious interactions with the Gresham police almost from the moment he reported her missing."

"When was that?"

"Late October. Why?"

Not long after she left. I ache at the thought of how differently things might have gone for her, and for her father, if only she'd known.

"After one of her friends told him she'd been seen in downtown Portland, he started pestering the Portland cops too. Unfortunately, runaways aren't a high-priority for law enforcement, especially older kids. So he decided to take a leave of absence in order to search for her himself."

The local cops had struck Kendrick Pride as competent, but competent wasn't good enough. Jeremy had said it himself. The Barlow

County Sheriff's Department handled DUIs and bar fights, domestic disputes and drug offenses—not tracing teen girls who didn't want to be found or breaking up baby trafficking operations.

"So how close were Duniway and Lydia to getting away with it?"

"Well, if you hadn't brought that girl out of the forest, and if Paulette hadn't come forward about Quince—" He shrugs. "Omar has lots of friends, people who'll make excuses for him even now."

There's more, but with food in my stomach and a cup of coffee to nurse, I find myself only half-listening. Dr. Aaron Varney had been quietly taken into custody early this morning. So far, he's sticking to the story that he simply provided medical care for the girls. He was unaware of any improprieties. Bullshit, of course. The sheriff thinks he'll open up, especially since Quince has already placed him at the resort home where they grabbed me. The house itself is unoccupied, property of a real estate holding company back east.

It will be a long time before the whole scheme gets unwound, if ever. Who was involved, how many girls passed through the asylum and where they—or their babies—are now. The sheriff believes the actual transactions were laundered through the Hensley School. It may be difficult to prove beyond reasonable doubt the asylum adoptions were illegal.

"Traveling to Barlow County to complete a private adoption through a state-accredited youth facility isn't against the law." He shakes his head. "I expect to spend way too much time with the U.S. Attorney before this settles out, but at least my jurisdictional concern ends at the county line."

Which still leaves him with plenty to deal with.

Quince also gave up Xavier Meyer, and during the ride to the hospital last night, I said he'd fallen to his death while chasing me through the forest. Someone will follow up on that eventually, but I hope to talk to Shelby before she tells her part in it. Best if she's not dragged into that story. She's got enough to deal with.

Turnbull raises the coffee carafe and asks if I want more. I shake my head. The restaurant is starting to fill up, and people can't help but stare. Bandaged, splinted, still in my filthy clothes, I look like a disaster epic extra. I'm sure I'll be a topic of conversation on the Barlow grapevine for a long time. "Can we go?"

He pays the check and then follows me out into the sunlight. It's already starting to get hot. I limp to the corner, in sight of the hospital, then pause.

"I'm sorry about Jeremy."

"You and me both. He was a good kid."

"Last night, you said you knew I hadn't shot him even before Quince told you what happened. How?"

He makes a thoughtful sound in his throat. "I watched the dash cam footage from his car."

I must look confused. "You could tell it wasn't me driving?"

"No, of course not." He chuckles. "The resolution isn't great on those things. Poor lighting on a dark road. No way to tell who was behind the wheel. But Jeremy reacted to something in the back of the van as he walked by. That told me the driver wasn't alone."

"I made noise. Tried to anyway. I was still pretty drugged up, but I knew something was wrong."

"That must have been it. He turned and reached for his weapon. Then the inside of the vehicle lit up with the muzzle flash, and the van pulled away."

"It still could have been me."

"You trying to talk me into something here, Mellie?"

Pride once thought I was trying to talk myself onto his suspects list. "No. Just that doesn't seem like much. Jeremy could have been reacting to anything."

"It *wasn't* much—but when I examined the video more closely, two things stood out. The first was the origin of the muzzle flash. It placed the shooter in the passenger seat. Then, as the van pulled out, a hand pressed against the rear window. A third person was in the back of the van. So I went through the video again, frame by frame. I saw your face, Mellie." He gives me a sad smile. "Just a couple of grainy frames, but it was enough."

He waits until I stop crying, then offers me a tissue. I give him points for not trying to hug me too.

        🙞 🙜

In the hospital, he walks with me to Shelby's room. Deputy Roldán, looking short of sleep, sits on a chair outside her door. "Just a precaution," the sheriff says.

"Lot of that going around."

Shelby is eating breakfast when I enter her room. Not the German apple pancake platter. An English muffin and a small heap of desiccated scrambled eggs. A little plastic cup of orange juice.

"You want me to order you a pizza?"

"God, yes, please."

I sit in the chair beside the bed. "It's possible I saw you the night of the crash." I think about the old rancher squeezing my hand as I caught sight of the pale figure out on the desert. "You'd already made it a long way."

She prods the eggs with her fork. "I just wanted to get away."

It couldn't be her who lured me into the desert the night I found the locket though. She was miles away by then. But if not her, who— or what—did I see?

Uncle Rémy told me the Shatter Hill Spirit appeared to wronged women and girls. Shelby certainly qualifies, as do so many others. Even me. We're all Molly Claire's Girls. But that doesn't mean I saw a ghost. No doubt I imagined the figure I saw. Wove her out of the substance of hearsay and myth.

Yet I keep thinking about how Molly Claire isn't the only young woman who lost her child at the crossroad.

"Fina was in the pickup with Lydia, you know." Shelby's voice shakes me from my reverie.

"Last night?"

She nods. "I never would have gotten near that truck otherwise."

I wonder if she knows Fina is dead. If not, that's one death notification I'll leave to the sheriff. Out the window, past the hospital parking lot and beyond a row of houses, stands the New Mortuary. Wanda, I understand, is arranging the transport of Kendrick Pride back to Portland.

"What happens now? Do you know?"

"The FBI is coming." She shrugs. "My aunt too. I'm going to stay with her."

"What about your baby?"

"It might be Alyssa's. Mine could be thousands of miles away, maybe even in another country." She looks past me, as if she's imagining a vast gulf. "They're doing a DNA test. I'll know in a few weeks." Her eyes glisten, then she starts to cry. "Does it make me a bad person if I hope she isn't mine?"

I take her hand and whisper, "Not at all," over and over again.

The sheriff said he was sorry for what I had to go through. But he has no idea. He'll never have any idea. As decent as he's been today, he's still the man who thought what happened to Paulette was no big deal. As for Kendrick Pride, maybe he left his job to look for his missing daughter, but he's why the search was necessary in the first place. Instead of being there for Shelby when she needed him, he did what my own parents did after Fitz died. Too many of us— Shelby, Paulette, me, even Helene—have been failed by people we should have been able to count on.

"You decide what's best for you, Shelby," I say when her tears stop. "Don't let anyone guilt you into doing something you're not ready for." She nods and wipes her eyes. Then she eats her desiccated eggs. I suggest she make her aunt take her to the Apple Peddler for a proper breakfast before they leave.

Then I tell her about how she should keep her role in Xavier Meyer's death to herself. She argues a bit, saying he deserved it, and I don't disagree. "It's going to be hard enough for you. Let what happened to him stay between us." And then I slip the locket into her hands.

She stares at it for a long time. When she speaks at last, her voice is hoarse. "I thought I'd never see this again. Where did you find it?"

"In the desert near the crossroad." With a ghost as my guide? No, just chance, and a mule deer. "I'm glad it's back where it belongs."

EPILOGUE

Crossroad

Died young, somehow got through it.
—Epitaph of Melisende Dulac

I park the hearse next to the bonfire circle and kill the engine. The Stiff won't be back from the shop for another week, and I miss it. Performing removals in the hearse just seems a little too on the nose. Cooling metal ticks in the desert stillness. Across the road to the north where the tree line begins, I half-expect to see a pale figure. But no, Shelby is gone now.

The scent of sage, sharpened by evening air, drifts in through the open window. I wonder if there will be a party tonight. It's still early, not yet nine o'clock. The sun is just touching the shoulder of Lost Brother. Soon, it'll be gone, and the long shadows will melt into an elusive twilight.

My thoughts drift to Jeremy, whose funeral was this morning in Portland. I thought about attending but had a feeling his family—his mother and two sisters—wouldn't want me. I wouldn't blame them. Sheriff Turnbull was there to represent Barlow County.

Around the time Jeremy would have been lowered into his grave, Aunt Elodie took me aside in the New Mortuary and asked if I was okay.

As Danae said, no secrets in Samuelton. When I tried to apologize, Aunt Elodie shushed me. "Geoffrey has been gone a long time, and Jeremy was a good man."

"Is that how Uncle Rémy felt about it?"

"I don't know how aware of things he was, but I think he'd have understood." With that, she'd squeezed my hand, then let me get back to work. I had a viewing to set up for; just another day at the funeral home on the range.

Uncle Rémy himself had been interred a few days ago in the Pioneer Cemetery. Helene missed it. She's in Seattle, hip deep in law tomes—or the digital equivalent, I suppose. Aunt Elodie decided Uncle Rémy's service would be the Old Mortuary's last. She says the place is too expensive to maintain, though I know it has more to do with how she just can't imagine living there without Rémy. I don't think I can either, even though I'll miss the Weeping Parlor and looking out my bedroom window at the cemetery. Carrie Dell suggested allowing the county historical society to manage it as a museum. Elodie seemed to like that idea. She plans to find a "nice little place" for the two of us between Samuelton and Wilton, maybe on the river. If we're lucky, it'll have a view of the Bluebunch Glen Memory Garden. And a deep bathtub.

My gaze steals to the passenger seat beside me. The box is still there. Sticking out of the open top is an envelope with "Melisende" written in a familiar hand.

Too many people are dead. Jeremy. Kendrick Pride. The boys who drove to the Oregon high desert to rescue a needful girl. The men who tried to stop them. The adopted uncle who was better family than my own flesh and blood. And that may not be all. I could very well be a widow, which sounds exactly like the kind of thing a woman who traveled the modern-day version of the Oregon Trail should be.

"You think Geoffrey died of dysentery?"

"He should be so lucky."

I'm a girl from another time. Maybe I'm the reincarnation of Molly Claire Maguire.

The sun flashes green, then disappears below the ridge. As ichorous shadows flow through the bunchgrass and sage and over the crossroad, I pull the envelope from the box beside me. It arrived with the day's mail at the New Mortuary from a Seattle law firm, the address written in cursive script. Helene once said she taught herself cursive when she was a girl so Geoffrey wouldn't be able to read her journal.

Also in the box is a blown-glass hummingbird, the one I'd bought at an arts fair in Provincetown.

There isn't much light left, but there's enough. I slide my finger under the flap and pull out a sheet of plain white notepaper.

Mel,

Your father sent me this, believing it to be mine. Given what you've told me about your parents, such sentimentality seemed out of character, but perhaps he thought you stole it from me.

I never bothered to tell him you hadn't, that it never belonged to me. Maybe someday it will. In the meantime, I think you should hold onto it.

I know you need time. We both do. And I also know you've been through a lot, more than I can ever understand. But I believe you'll be okay. I wanted to tell you that.

You'll be okay.
Love Always, H

I start to crush the note and drop it out my open window, thinking Landry's friends can use it for kindling at the next bonfire. But then I stop.

"*You'll be okay.*"

She's right. I'm alone, and for perhaps the first time ever I'm okay with it. Fitz may have saved me from Lake Champlain, but I saved myself in Barlow County. I've found a place in the desert and claimed it for my own when others tried to take it from me. "I'm Melisende Aubrey Dulac," I say into the deepening darkness. "Calling me back to myself." The only response is wind through the grass and the distant bark of a coyote.

I smooth the crinkled paper on my thigh and return it to the passenger seat beside me. A moment later, the hearse's engine over-revs as I point it at the spine of Shatter Hill and chase my ghosts home.

Author's Note

Barlow County may be a figment of my imagination, but it's named for a real figure from Oregon history. During his younger days in Indiana, Sam Barlow did indeed kill a man with an ax, as Uncle Rémy told Melisende. Though convicted of manslaughter, Barlow was pardoned after public outcry arose in his defense. The dead man, it seemed, needed killing. Later, Barlow would emigrate to the Oregon Territory and, with the help of Joel Palmer, build the Barlow Road, an immigrant route from The Dalles to the Willamette Valley. Palmer himself provided the name of the river fished by Quince and which nearly claimed Melisende's life. The lake and resort in northern Barlow County are named for the first editor of the *Oregonian* newspaper, Thomas Jefferson Dryer.

Some of the other place names in the story derive from the *Chinuk Wawa*, or Chinook Jargon, a trade dialect arising from a variety of indigenous language sources in the Pacific Northwest (and distinct from, though related to, the language of the Chinook people). For example, Wayette is a variation on the *Chinuk Wawa* word for road, *way'-hut*—making Wayette Highway literally "Road Highway." Similarly, the name for Tsokapo Gorge would translate loosely as Lost Brother Gorge, from *tso'-lo*, meaning loss and *káhp-ho*, meaning brother.

Barlow County itself is a synthesis of several regions in Central Oregon, containing as it does much of the geological, geographical, and historical characteristics of the state east of the Cascades, from roaring trout streams to high desert and rangeland, to the ponderosa

328 | Author's Note

forests of the upper elevations. It is a region both dry and austere, yet fertile and eminently beautiful.

I've had a lot of help and support telling Melisende's story. Huge thanks go out to Janet Reid for her confidence and hard work on my behalf. Thank you also to editor Shannon Jamieson Vasquez for taking such wonderful care of Melisende. And finally, thank you to the lovely folks at Crooked Lane Books for helping make *Crossroad* a reality: Jenny Chen, Ashley Di Dio, Sophie Green, and Melanie Sun.

For their keen insight and kindness I owe an inestimable debt of gratitude to my friends, fellow writers, and critique partners: Andy Fort, Theresa Snyder, Corissa Neufeldt, Candace Clark, Charlie Varani, Suzanne Linquist, Carla Orcutt, Julie Dawn, James Stegall, Heather Petty and Ali Trotta.

And, always, thank you to my wife, Jill, for always being there for me and helping me get out of my own way. I love you.